CARRIED AWAY

"Stop waiting for the storm to pass. Ask yourself—what can I accomplish in the rain?"

-Unknown

Carried Away

ISBN: 978-1-0694567-0-0
First Edition

Cover and interior design by Thomas J. Derry

Printed in Canada by Marquis Book
marquisbook.com

Acknowledgements—

To everyone behind the scenes—family, friends, creative allies—this book exists because of you.

To the cafés that let me sit for hours—thank you for giving these pages a home before they had one.

To the friends who inspired the characters—thank you for your quirks, character, and heart—you're all legends.

To the coastlines, islands, and waves that shaped this story—thank you for your countless lessons.

To those still finding their way—keep going.

And to you, the reader: thank you for being here.

Enjoy.

1

—Am I Dead?—

Chaos erupted as the first wave arrived, detonating the sea around me. My body was tossed backward like tumbleweed, then driven deep below the surface. Paradise had turned violent, alive, and intent on undoing everything.

This is it. I'm not surviving this.

—

It was March 20th—the fourth day of our seemingly idyllic trip. The weather in Indonesia was hot and balmy, with calm winds and clear skies. The water was a creamy cyan blue, its warmth blurring the boundary between ocean and air. Life had been perfect: surfing utopian waves, eating well, and exploring the island with a group of Australians we had befriended. Our plan was simple: venture to a remote outer reef by boat, surf for a few hours, and then return to the resort in time to meet our new friends for dinner. But that hope had vanished as I was pulled deeper into liquid oblivion.

—

When the wave hit, the water temperature dropped sharply, as if it carried a darkness up from the depths. What had moments ago been warm and dreamlike was now frigid and predatory. Pieces of coral and rock debris trapped in the current tore my skin, exposing flesh to the stinging brine. My surf leash yanked at my ankle, tugging harder with each passing second. I prayed it wouldn't let go and leave me stranded without flotation, assuming I was ever able to escape the sea's grip.

I sank deeper.

Sunlight faded to a dim haze behind my eyelids, while crushing pressure clamped down on my ears. I opened my eyes to get my bearings, but debris forced them shut.

Please let this end!

I kicked upward, but the current held me in place. My intentions were meaningless now—the once accommodating and friendly seascape had turned against me.

It was unclear how long I'd been under, but it felt like minutes since I'd last seen Kavi, Fern, or Logan, who'd been paddling next to me when the sea began to swirl beneath our boards.

Were they still alive? If I made it to the surface—what then?

Fighting was futile. The harder I struggled, the worse things got.

Exhausted, I surrendered—

My limbs went slack, chest convulsing in a final, desperate bid for oxygen. I was seconds from inhaling— air or not. The sound of my heart pounding in my ears blurred everything, as a flood of images raced through my mind.

Strangely, I began to accept it.

This is how I die.

I lay still—trapped in black liquid purgatory, spasms working their way through my limbs as I waited for the end.

And then, the sea let go—

Disoriented, I flailed—hoping I was moving toward breathable air. As I rose, the urge took over and I gasped. Saltwater poured down my throat, searing my lungs and twisting my organs into seizure. I vomited repeatedly as I climbed the last few feet, aspirating more water each time. I broke the surface, spewing a bitter mix of salt and stomach acid. All I could hear was the hiss of tiny bubbles bursting around me and the rasp of my own retching. Blinded by the sunlight, I fumbled for my ankle leash and pulled my board beneath my battered torso.

When my eyes adjusted, the scene was otherworldly: brown, frothing water rushed in every direction, forming treacherous whirlpools and a seascape so altered, so violent, it felt like the end of the world. I was nowhere near the reef where we'd been surfing. The island was gone—vanished—replaced by endless horizon.

Faint calls echoed in the distance. My heart jumped as I spun, frantically searching for my friends. Just as I opened my mouth to shout, I caught another wave crashing in my periphery.

I had a split second to inhale and brace before the wall of white water slammed into me, dragging me back into the abyss...

2

—The Beginning—

2 a.m.

We pulled into a decrepit gas bar. Flickering overhead lamps threw stark pools of light and shifting shadows across the cracked concrete and asphalt. The building was surrounded by towering palm trees, their silhouettes merging with the ambient buzz of insects rising from the nearby jungle. Outside the dim storefront, half a dozen fridges hummed, their fluorescent beer logos blinking erratically. Across the lot, a cluster of motorcycles, tuk-tuks, and battered trucks sat parked haphazardly, encircled by a group of shadowy figures. Each held a bottle, the air thick with cigarette smoke. I looked back as one of them took a drag, his face briefly illuminated by the ember's flare.

My taxi driver, whom I'd nicknamed Steve, turned to me with a grin and pointed.

"Beer."

His thick Indonesian accent gave the word an oddly triumphant gravitas. He looked pleased with himself for tracking down a willing peddler at this hour, so I smiled back and thanked him.

"Terima kasih," I replied, unsure if he understood a word I said.

Our earlier attempts at conversation had only confirmed how flimsy my Indonesian really was. I hesitated as I stepped from the vehicle, acutely aware that my passport—and essentially my entire existence—was still in the back seat. There's a peculiarity to the foreign passenger-local driver dynamic—a fragile, unspoken trust. We both knew there was nothing stopping him from simply driving off and leaving me stranded in the middle of nowhere. No one would track him down. I wouldn't be able to explain my situation to the police—or anyone else for that matter. I didn't even know his real name or bother to check whether his taxi license was legit. The thought flashed through my mind:

What would I even do if he sped off?

A thirty-something, white New Yorker with blond hair and blue eyes, stranded in the middle of the Sumatran jungle, explaining to a policeman that a driver named Steve had disappeared with all my belongings at two in the morning. Picturing that scenario sent a chill through me as I cautiously approached the row of humming fridges. Trusting strangers on a trip like this was something I had mostly gotten used to over the years. There are no guarantees, just faith in the basic decency of humanity to see you through.

As I neared the building, a short, skinny man emerged from a doorway between two of the units.

I greeted him.

"Empat bir, silahkan?" I said, rehearsing one of the only phrases I had memorized.

His cold, guarded expression melted into a wide, goofy grin, disarming me immediately. This seemed to be a common trait in Indonesia—a hard shell giving way to surprising warmth. It was puzzling and endearing all at the same time. I briefly wondered what this man's life looked like, selling beer to strangers at 2 a.m. from this remote gas station. But at this stage, those questions needn't be asked.

He cheerfully opened the Bintang-branded fridge and gestured at a few different options like the host of a game show. I pointed to the most generic-looking bottle and handed him a ten-dollar bill, fully aware the price was entirely up to him—and that the fifty-cent beers might be subject to a hefty *Bule* tariff. Whether he decided to overcharge me or honor the exchange with unexpected fairness was irrelevant—at this hour, dazed and vulnerable, I'd already relinquished any illusion of control over these kinds of interactions.

With a smile, I accepted whatever change he handed back, thanked him in my halting Indonesian, and made my way back to the taxi—which, thankfully, was still parked at the pump, now fueled up and ready for the long drive. I climbed into the car, thanked my driver, and we took off at an astounding pace through the jungle. Steve didn't seem the least bit concerned about barreling through rough, forested terrain at night.

Do animals just not venture onto the roads here? Or does Steve know something I don't? I wondered.

Either way, his cavalier approach was something to behold as an uninitiated observer.

———

As we tore through the darkness, I was privy to a collection of local Indonesian music videos playing on his aftermarket LCD screen. The deck was precariously mounted in his vehicle's dash using duct tape and a couple broken Popsicle sticks to jam it in place. The videos were captivating, though mostly in an ironic way. The terrible production value and proud camera mugging somehow put me at ease. I speculated that there's a level of status associated with buying groceries in this foreign land, as many of the videos featured store aisles, fresh produce, and men handing attractive young women bags of food.

"That's all it takes here? I could get used to this," I laughed.

———

The road narrowed and vanished into blackness as we picked up speed, the earthy and floral scents of the Sumatran jungle wafting in through small gaps in the windows. There's something magical about being a North American tourist in a land where wild tigers still live. Limitless adventure, mixed with a little danger, and the unknown seemed a winning equation for a guy from a sterile city, trapped in a nine-to-five, and living in a stuffy, overpriced shoebox apartment.

With nothing but the road ahead, my mind began to wander—imaginative thoughts spiraling in sync with our breakneck speed.

What would happen if we crashed?

At this pace, the chances of surviving a collision with a tree—or being shot off one of these hillsides—would be nil.

Would anyone even find us? What would that do to my family?

Would my friends ever figure out what had happened?

My entire thirty-six years of life, casually rested on this random man's ability to commute safely through the night.

I cracked a beer.

Was he aware of the responsibility resting at his fingertips?

I took a sip... a big one.

Would it be poetry or tragedy if I died here with my life in tatters? Would it even matter? I wondered, recounting all I'd been struggling with lately.

—

Depression had seeped through the cracks of my once impenetrable shell of positivity. That, mixed with the mundanity of fast-paced city life, had left me road-worn and feeling like I was running out of time. I thought about New York—the people—most of them sleepwalking, held aloft by habit, drifting through a life that asks little and answers even less. Mornings in bed staring at my ceiling fan had become routine—each one a battle against the inevitable moment I'd have to get up and face the world.

A few more sips.

I wasn't so sure I was willing to die in search of answers to whatever existential questions had been gnawing at me.

Another big sip.

I had no intention of vanishing into the night—not without experiencing everything the Mentawai Islands promised. I repeated a quote from *Fight Club* that had stuck with me:

"This is your life and it's ending one moment at a time."

At thirty-six, it didn't feel like a punchline anymore. It felt like a warning.

—

Our tires thudded across an uneven section of road, snapping me back to reality and jerking me against the stained gray seatbelt, now locked uncomfortably around my torso.

Are these roads even paved? Or just compacted dirt and gravel? I wondered, tugging at the constricting belt.

Drops of condensation from my sweaty beer bottle dripped onto my chest as I sipped mindlessly, the alcohol had made some inroads, dulling my anxiety. I sat up and looked through the windshield—it was a challenge to see anything beyond the small area lit by the headlights. There hadn't been a single streetlight for miles. It felt like we were piloting a disheveled spaceship through a pitch-black galaxy in an early *Star Wars* film.

—

I turned to the side window, watching trees pass like cracking whips in the night. One last sip and beer number one was a memory.

I popped another—

"This commute's going to require the right mixture of blood and alcohol," I said aloud, taking another big sip.

Steve glanced at me in the rearview mirror, flashing a gap-toothed grin. I smiled back, then turned toward the window as my thoughts drifted back to the flight across the Pacific—another small nightmare in its own right. Twenty-two hours in the air can cause a man to do some serious mental gymnastics, and somehow, I'd only managed an hour of sleep.

—

The real challenge of reaching the Mentawai Islands isn't just the sheer distance—it's the complete lack of major airports within hundreds of kilometers.

First, I flew into Doha, then on to Jakarta. From there I caught a flight to Padang, where I'd arranged a taxi to take me the rest of the way to Sibolga, where my friends were waiting.

Sibolga is a small port city a few hundred kilometers north of Padang, home to about 80,000 people and, the exact epicenter of the 9.0-magnitude earthquake that triggered the devastating Thailand tsunami of 2004.

—

The plan was to meet up with my three friends—Kavi, Logan, and Fern—who had arrived earlier on a different flight, one I had had to miss due to work complications. Once reunited, we'd crash for a few hours in a seedy motel before catching a four-hour speedboat taxi to the island at sunrise. If all went well, we'd be settled in at the resort and surfing by dusk the next day.

But first, I had to survive the drive.

The journey from Padang to Sibolga took an average of three and a half hours—three and a half hours of chaotic roadways, breakneck speeds, and drivers who treat lanes as mere suggestions.

My chances of sleeping before sunrise were slim to none. I was too wired, too anxious, and entirely at the mercy of Steve's questionable reflexes. So here I sat—wide awake, with no hope of rest until I was safely out of the vehicle and united with my mates. I was alone, stressed, and—to top it off—really had to pee.

I took a deep breath—

Best to stay in the moment.

If nothing else, this harrowing commute would make my biography more interesting.

One last sip.

Beer number two, done and dusted.

3

—Planes, Trains & Bintangs—

12 a.m. *(earlier)*

I disembarked the final flight on my itinerary and stepped through the jet-way into what had to be the most interesting terminal I'd ever seen. Vaulted ceilings and intricate artwork gave it the look of a Buddhist temple— more sacred than a hub to process weary travelers. After a long walk down a seemingly endless corridor, I arrived at the luggage carousel. Dazed and disoriented from the journey, I stood silently, praying that my luggage and surfboards had made it.

—

Twenty agonizing minutes later, my bags tumbled down the ramp and onto the conveyor—casual, indifferent, as if there had never been any doubt.

I exhaled hard, slung them onto my cart, and turned toward the oversized baggage area—where, amazingly, my board bag had also arrived.

The thought of losing my gear somewhere along the way had been stressful enough; actually dealing with it would've been unbearable. I looked up at the temple-like ceiling and offered a silent thanks to the travel gods. No delays. No drama. No disasters—for once, everything had gone to plan.

I made my way toward the exit with an added sense of relief knowing I had already cleared immigration and customs in Jakarta. No more lines. No more paperwork. Just one final leg.

—

Stepping through the automatic doors into the humid night, I scanned the crowd for my driver. His service had assured me that someone would be waiting just outside the main taxi pickup zone, holding a sign with my last name.

Nothing—

Dozens of Indonesian men called out, *"Taxi! Taxi!"*— each one hoping I was unprepared and in need of a ride.

I paced back and forth, pushing my overloaded cart— board bag, luggage, speargun, and backpack stacked high—eyeing the crowd of people and cars. Beads of sweat pooled on my forehead and a familiar stress began to creep in. Things were about to get complicated.

—

After half an hour of searching high and low— bumping my overloaded cart into stanchions, clipping corners, and nearly taking out a row of luggage trolleys— it became painfully clear, I'd have to improvise.

There are few things more discouraging than being exhausted in a foreign country and having to negotiate with a local. I'd dealt with these kinds of situations before—it comes with the territory when you travel—but after back-to-back flights, zero sleep, and a complete time zone shift, I felt the overwhelming urge to collapse in a corner for a self-pity party.

Instead, I took a deep breath and forced myself to focus. I searched the crowd for the most docile-looking driver I could find. Eventually, I spotted a short, stocky guy with a friendly smile and decided to approach.

"Do you speak English?" I asked.

"Engish? Leetle beat. Maaf."

He grinned—his attempt at an American accent thick, almost comical.

Before I could respond, he waved over a friend to translate. We worked out a price, but the friend explained that they didn't typically drive as far as Sibolga this late unless it was prearranged.

I sighed, pulled out a couple of twenty-dollar bills, and placed one in each of their hands. Nothing cuts through red tape in the third-world quite like American currency. They each shook my hand and grabbed my bags.

—

We loaded up his beat-up Honda Brio, and I slid into the back seat. My driver's name—at least according to his taxi license—was Syafiq.

"I'll call you Steve," I said, as he settled into the driver's seat.

Close enough.

A sigh of short-lived relief slipped out as the air conditioning cut through the jungle heat—just before the next wave of stress set in.

—

Two hours into the Dakar-esque drive through the Sumatran jungle, unease started to stir. Steve's focus was

15

slipping. His eyes had that faraway glaze, and the car drifted dangerously toward the edge of the road.

He slapped himself across the face—hard.

Shit—he's falling asleep!

My nerves spiked—

In a mild panic, I pulled out my phone to translate a sentence.

"Apakah kamu baik-baik saja?" I asked, which roughly means *Are you okay?*

My driver looked back with a smile.

"Saya baik, saya baik," he said, with a thumbs up.

I checked the translation: *I'm good, I'm good.*

I was not reassured. If anything, he seemed even more drowsy now that I was watching him like a hawk. Stranger still—his commitment to driving at top speed never even wavered.

I exhaled, tightened my seatbelt, and whispered a quick prayer:

"Please get me to Sibolga in one piece… or at least make sure someone finds my passport. Amen."

I glanced at my phone—three bars. Just enough to fire off a message to the group, you know, in case the shit hit the fan:

"Dudes I'm in a cab flying through the Sumatran jungle at 70mph and my driver's falling asleep. Say a prayer and hope I'm there in the morning!"

I stared at the screen for a few minutes, hoping someone would respond and calm my nerves.

Nothing—

It was just me, my narcoleptic driver, and this now tepid, last bottle of beer.

I reached for my journal and scribbled a few lines—just in case I didn't make it—then tried one more time to engage him. With very little confidence in my Indonesian, I interrupted:

"Bisakah kamu memperlambatnya?" I asked, hoping that was the correct way to say *Can you please slow down?*

Steve sat up straight, adjusted his mirror to make eye contact, and flashed a smile—thumbs-up and all.

I felt a flicker of relief as the RPMs dropped noticeably and the engine settling into a steady, almost peaceful hum.

Finally!

But not even ninety seconds later—he hit the gas again. Within moments, we were back to breakneck speed, hurtling forth as if my plea had already been erased from memory. Right on cue, his head began dipping, chin bouncing off his chest as he nodded in and out of consciousness.

What the fuck!?

I decided my best bet to keep him awake, was to keep him talking.

"Apakah anda punya istri dan keluarga?" I asked, hoping I'd translated *Do you have a wife and family?* correctly.

He glanced in the rear-view mirror with a dazed smile.

"Ya, saya menikah dengan putri saya."

I quickly typed his words into my translator:

"Yes, I'm married with my daughter."

He nodded at me with another big smile.

I smiled awkwardly—this conversation was going nowhere.

Door locked, I slouched against it, my bladder now echoing my emotional stress.

—

Another hour of high-speed terror and broken small talk passed, and the engine finally slowed.

We must be getting close to Sibolga.

The road dipped into winding switchbacks as we began a sharp descent, navigating sketchy stretches of pavement into what felt like a different world.

The jungle thinned, and with the clearing came the first slivers of early morning light, peeking through the windshield. The air had changed—now laced with salt, damp earth, and something faintly floral. Despite everything—the exhaustion, the fear, and the bladder full of beer—this was one of the happiest moments I can remember. Knowing my chances of being launched off a cliff or fused to a tree trunk had just dropped significantly lent a sense of lightness to my mood. The adrenaline in my bloodstream quickly began to fade, and exhaustion took its place.

As we descended into the village, soft, straw-coloured sunlight cut through the windows, dappling the car and casting warm beams that danced in the dusty interior. My driver—who looked equally relieved—seemed to catch a second wind. His eyes sharpened and his posture straightened.

Then, without a word, he reached into the glove box and pulled out a can of Red Bull.

He cracked it open, casually.

I stared, speechless—

The idea that he had this container of pure sugar and caffeine the whole time, nearly gave me a stroke. Still in disbelief, I stared silently as he began speaking rapidly in Indonesian, his tone now upbeat, borderline chipper.

"Ini adalah sibolga, sebuah desa nelayan kecil. Nelayan akan segera keluar." he exclaimed cheerfully.

I smiled politely, nodded, and gave the universal thumbs-up.

He smiled back—fully aware I had no idea what the fuck he was talking about.

—

Easing into the core of town, I lifted my arm and did a quick self-assessment—yep. Thirty-plus hours of transit had left me smelling like a dead raccoon in a sauna.

I pulled out my phone and fired off another message to the gang:

"I'm still alive and just about to pull up! Is there coffee here? I'm a mess. My kidneys are on the verge of bursting, and I need moral support asap."

—

Five minutes later, the car slowed to a crawl as we pulled into the driveway of whatever address I'd given Steve. It looked like a motel—or possibly a hostel—built sometime in the 1800s.

The last sunbeam lifted off the windshield and I was ecstatic to find my mates standing around the parking lot, awaiting my arrival. In my highly emotional state, I opened the door and nearly jumped out before the car came to a complete stop.

"YES!" I shouted, stumbling into a giant group hug—careful not to crush my bladder, which now protruded like a second-trimester pregnancy.

All three of them were grinning like it was Christmas morning, hooting and hollering in excitement. Someone handed me a strange, square Styrofoam container stamped with the word *Kopi*—steam curling from the black liquid.

It's strange to travel thirty hours around the globe only to be greeted by three guys from your own neighborhood.

"Dude, welcome to Indonesia!" Kavi yelled.

"Thank you, God!" I shouted back.

"How was the haul? We got your text this morning but there's been no service or wi-fi. We were a little stressed out."

"All good. Luckily, my homie Steve here, held it together in the end. But get this—this guy drove me through the jungle at breakneck speeds overnight, practically falls asleep... then we get within fifteen minutes of Sibolga, and he cracks a fuckin' Red Bull that he had the whole god damn time!? I'm never going to get over that."

The crew burst into laughter—either at the story or at how dumbfounded I was by the Red Bull reveal. Steve laughed too, in solidarity, completely clueless about what I'd said. I introduced everyone to my less-than-faithful driver, then jogged to the corner of the lot and dropped my fly for the most satisfying pee of my entire life. I tilted my head toward the sky and offered a silent thanks to God, Buddha, the universe—whoever was on shift—for getting me through the night and finally letting me drain my bladder.

According to Kavi, the guys hadn't slept much either. They'd stayed up, wired with anticipation for the trip to the islands. For some reason the contents of their board bags were strewn across the front of the motel like a surf piñata had exploded—boards, towels, trunks, wax, fins, and snacks scattered in chaotic disarray. This crew was never known for tidiness, and as the most fastidious among us, I was already wondering how I'd survive two weeks of this charming filth.

Fern—our group's resident dead-weight—had arranged for some transport to the docks to meet our water taxi. His real name was Adam, but he reminded us of Zach Galifianakis, so we started calling him *Two Ferns* several years back, which eventually evolved into the mononym—Fern.

"Fern says the herd of donkeys he booked should be here any minute." Kavi quipped.

Kavi—who tends to lean into the class clown archetype—generally comes armed with an arsenal of wit and quick-fire one-liners. His Jewish mother—a literal genius who designs Manhattan high-rises—fell madly in love with his Indian father, a self-proclaimed comedian. The resulting offspring—a facetious, intellectual, whose perpetual objective is to lighten the mood and otherwise charm those around him.

I chuckled while scanning the map, which showed just a few miles between us and the docks where we'd embark on our journey across Mentawai Bay. Knowing Fern, I wouldn't have been completely surprised if a horse or donkey-drawn cart pulled up—but I kept my hopes high. He'd insisted on playing a role in the trip planning, so we gave him what we considered one of the least critical responsibilities. I remembered an email he sent at 1 a.m., sounding deeply aggrieved, wondering aloud why he felt like a "piece of tumbleweed" in the planning process. He demanded to be included, so—naturally—we gave him the transport gig.

And now, here we were—four months later, sitting in a desolate, sweaty, Sumatran parking lot, checking our watches, and quietly praying that he hadn't dropped the ball.

"Dude, did you even call or email them to confirm?" Logan barked.

Logan—a man of logic and reason—is just as likely to be annoyed as he is to be relaxed, and he has little patience for fools. A surfer caught in a finance bro's body, he doesn't particularly enjoy his job and his whole purpose is to make enough money to escape it.

"Obviously! I'm not a fucking idiot, they said they'd be here at 6am sharp."

"Yeah, but it's 6:15... did you confirm recently, numb nuts? If we miss this taxi across, I'll never forgive you."

Despite being one of his closest friends, Fern has a talent for getting under Logan's skin. Their dynamic—equal parts banter and battlefield—has driven me crazy over the years. Especially in cramped cars or long-haul flights where there's no escape. The ball-busting between the two of them is relentless, like an endless Comedy Central Roast that no one agreed to. Occasionally the bickering escalates into pranks—funny ten years ago, but in our mid-thirties... far less so. I was hoping they'd matured past their verbal sparring by now, but that prayer had already been dashed—and it wasn't even 7 a.m.

—

After about fifteen minutes spent roasting Fern in the sweltering lot, our transportation finally arrived. To our surprise, it was a halfway decent truck—complete with doors and, miraculously, air conditioning. The driver, a cheerful guy named Bakti, hopped out grinning from ear to ear.

"Hey, you guy is Fern?" he asked, in a heavy accent.

We all nodded, then loaded our gear into the awkward-looking Mitsubishi, hoping we'd still make it to the boat on time.

I paid and thanked Steve, who had waited patiently with us, sipping what remained of his energy drink. He took the cash, gave a short bow, and then saluted his countryman Bakti before hopping back into his car. I gave him a final wave before sliding into the passenger seat, while the others packed the rest of their gear.

The inside of the truck smelled like patchouli oil, beer, and stale cigars. The dash was covered in a light brown film of dust, with a game of Tic-Tac-Toe rubbed into it—X's in commanding victory. It reminded me of the truck we'd driven in Nosara, Costa Rica, on our last trip. The roads in the area are mostly unpaved, and in dry season, dust coats everything—the buildings, the plants, and the people. But it's worst inside dark car interiors where it settles in a chalky, off-white layer.

I glanced into the back seat: a few empty beer cans, several banana peels, and some dried-up pineapple rinds decorated the floor. Our driver was clearly an independent contractor Fern had sourced from deep within the bilges of the internet. But honestly, I didn't care. I was just happy to be on our way.

4

—Meet The Aussies—

There was a quiet beauty to this little town—peppered with tall palm trees, surrounded by mountains, waterfalls, and white sand beaches. My assumption that it would be a rundown, industrial fishing village—couldn't have been more wrong. Rather, it revealed itself as a serene paradise, bathed in a gentle onshore breeze from Mentawai Bay and laced with the invigorating scent of the sea.

We pulled into the dock parking lot just as Fern and Logan were wrapping up yet another argument—this time over how many Rupiahs each owed the other for the hostel, cab rides, and several other irrelevant, headache-inducing expenses since leaving home—a sharp reminder to keep my headphones within reach.

After grabbing our bags from the truck, we caught our first glimpse of the bright teal water. I scanned the docks and spotted our resort's boat a couple hundred feet away.

Captain Dani greeted us at the end of the pier. He had an expatriate look to him, weathered and confident, and spoke with a South African lilt. Two young Indonesian crewmen stood beside him and eagerly shook my hand during introductions.

The water taxi was a beast—an oversized motor yacht with four massive outboard engines, clearly built to chew up the long passage to the Ments. We said our goodbyes to Bakti in the lot, hoisted our gear, and made our way toward the boat.

—

It was only 6:45 and the sun was already burning my skin. I couldn't wait to get out into open water, catch a cool breeze, and maybe—finally—sneak in a nap. As we boarded, we met some of the other passengers—all of them Australians. There were two women around my age, seemingly single. I silently prayed that no boyfriends would join at the last minute—and as luck would have it—none did. I took a discreet sniff of my armpit and decided it was best to keep a healthy distance for the moment.

We introduced ourselves to two of the girls—Carissa, and Kendal, who were here from the Gold Coast on holiday. They mentioned that a third girl would be along shortly. According to them, they were here on a girls' trip after a long stretch of work back home had burnt them out. I smiled and nodded but stayed out of the conversation. I know I'm tired when highly attractive and talkative surf girls don't really interest me much. Two couples from New South Wales rounded out the passenger manifesto—their names instantly lost to the haze of exhaustion.

I was cooked—physically, emotionally, existentially.

Kavi and Logan, unsurprisingly, quickly integrated with the Carissa and Kendal, chatting away like they'd known them for years. Fern, meanwhile, was rifling through his bag in a desperate attempt to locate his passport—a scene we'd all become familiar with while traveling with him. I looked for a place to rest my heavy eyes, as I was starting to become delirious. I walked into the boat's salon, found a comfortable vinyl-covered bench seat, and flopped down. The air was hot and sticky, thick with diesel and salt—but I was too tired to care.

Muffled conversations between Captain Dani and the other passengers drifted around me, but they quickly became background blur. The engines roared to life, sending a low hum through the floor and into my bones. It was strangely comforting—just enough white noise to lull me toward dreamland. The boat began to move, slowly making its way out of the harbour and into the open sea as a cool breeze funneled through the cabin, carrying the salty freshness of the Sumatran waters. I sank down into the bench, letting the hum of the engines carry me away.

5

—The Mentawais—

I woke up with a gasp, drenched in sweat—my body fused to the synthetic seat. As I sat up, my torso peeled away from the vinyl with a Velcro-like rip, nearly taking a layer of skin with it. My heart raced as my eyes adjusted to the brightness inside the salon. Fragments of a nightmare still clung to me—something about a storm overtaking the boat. The details were already fading, but one moment remained vivid: Dani tossing me a life jacket and yelling for me to put it on. I shook my head and looked around— nothing but calm water, blue skies, and bright sunshine pouring through the windows. I could hear the conversation and laughter between the girls and my friends—a soothing sound that, along with the boat's smooth glide across the glassy sea, helped ease the lingering tension from the dream. I took a moment to shake off the last of the anxiety before joining the group.

One more sniff of my armpits confirmed it was time to take action. I found a container of lemons in the galley, tore one open, and rubbed it under my arms. A lesser-known life hack: lemons are excellent deodorizers and can neutralize body odor on contact. Lucky for me, and the girls.

According to my watch—and to my bewilderment—we'd been on the water for just over three hours. That meant we were nearing the islands... and somehow, I'd managed to sleep through most of the journey.

I yawned and took a deep breath before slipping on my flip-flops and joining the others outside.

"Look who's up!" Kavi shouted, tossing me a cold can of beer as I stepped outside.

I cracked it open, took a sip, and reintroduced myself to the three girls, who were already a little tipsy.

Carissa, the apparent leader of the group, embodied the archetypal Australian: tall, blonde, fit, with a deep tan, a freckled nose, and a kind of infectious energy that seemed to make people cling to her like static. I guessed she was in her late twenties or early thirties.

Kendal, who'd caught my eye the moment we arrived at the dock, was another surf-or-yoga archetype—deep hazel eyes, sun-kissed skin, and layered brown-and-auburn hair. She wore a silver bracelet above her right elbow and had an OM symbol tattooed on her wrist—definitely a yoga thing. Something about her reminded me of Bambi—those big brown eyes, that wide-open curiosity.

There was an innocence to her that lingered just under the surface.

The last girl—still a mystery—stood beside Fern. She was a lot shorter and seemed younger than the others but looked strikingly similar to Carissa.

———

Part of the dilemma for a single man visiting these more remote places is that there's nothing but surf, sand, and jungle—and according to everything I'd read, one shouldn't expect to meet a woman. The Ments are known explicitly for their waves—raw, remote, and legendary. They attract only the most dedicated surf rats and almost never appeal to the fairer—and perhaps more sensible—sex.

Carissa introduced me. "Cole, this is Hunter."

"What happened to your shirt—did you piss yourself?" Hunter asked, giggling at the considerable wet spot running from my neckline to the bottom hem.

"It's sweat. I had a bad dream… never mind."

"Fern wanted to draw penises on your face while you were asleep. I stopped him. You're welcome."

Fern's maturation had halted sometime during his NYU years, so I wasn't remotely surprised.

"He did, huh? He should be the one thanking you—he'd be swimming the rest of the way."

The girls laughed.

———

The Mentawais—an archipelago about 150 kilometers off Indonesia's western coast—comprise more than seventy islands and atolls. Facing the open Indian Ocean, they generate world-class surf. There's an almost endless supply of reefs, beaches, and points—many offering the chance to surf perfect, nearly empty waves. Our last few trips had been marred by crowds and frustration. But this time would be different. This was the redemption trip—the one that would make up for all the failed missions, packed lineups, and disappointing swells.

Overhead, I spotted seabirds—usually a sign that land is near. Sure enough, when I looked off the bow, our island came into view.

Unlike the Hawaiian Islands, which shoot thousands of feet above sea level into volcanic mountain ranges, the Mentawais have a lower, more subdued profile. They're tough to spot from a distance—often invisible until you're relatively close.

Nias, where our resort is located, sits at the northernmost edge of the chain. It's ringed with beaches and coral reefs, scattered with waterfalls, and wrapped in thick, green jungle.

"I was here last year with some friends," Kendal said, her face glowing with excitement. "It was probably the best time of my life."

"I've never been anywhere like this. Nicaragua or El Salvador are probably the most isolated places I've ever been..."

"That's cute," she teased. "This place is different—like a postcard in every direction. You might want to ditch the phone, though. I don't want to catch you Googling or Instagramming while I'm around."

I raised an eyebrow.

We'd just met, yet she'd already clocked me perfectly. Sure enough, I was mid-scroll on Google Maps when she nudged my hand, pushing the phone back toward my pocket.

There was something about her energy—assertive but light—that charmed me. And she wasn't wrong. I was tired of being tethered to a world I didn't even like anymore—not just because I was halfway around the world, but because even back home, I'd felt detached from everything that used to matter. Being constantly plugged in hadn't made me feel more connected—it had only dulled things. The noise, the scroll, the obligation to be everywhere at once—it all left me with this low, background hum of meaninglessness.

I made a quiet decision then and there: I'd only use my phone to check in with family. No social media. No rabbit holes. Just presence.

"Okay, I get it. Here's the compromise," I said. "I want to shoot photos with my phone, but I'll keep it on airplane mode. Fair?"

"Fair," Kendal agreed, and we shook on it.

—

Nearing the island, the wildlife around us came alive. Pelicans flew past in formation, while sea swallows launched from the still waters as the boat approached, scattering like confetti. Kendal pointed out several dolphins breaching in the distance, setting off a ripple of excitement among the passengers. According to Captain Dani, we'd circle south and dock on the island's southwest side, avoiding a mess of hazards along the final approach.

The water turned from deep green to a bright, almost luminous blue-green as we neared the coral shelf, and Dani began pointing out bits of land and surf breaks dotting the coast.

"That wave's called Toothpicks," he said, nodding to the port side. "Cuz if you fuck up, we'll be using toothpicks to dig you outta the coral." He smiled to himself.

I let out a nervous laugh, a little on edge about surfing here. Stories of dangerous waves and razor-sharp coral lingered in my mind, and airlifts off the island weren't exactly rare. But up close, the serene beauty of it all began to settle my nerves—and maybe even flip them into excitement. Kendal seemed to notice the shift in my energy and returned my smile.

"There you go," she said. "That feels much better."

I smiled, realizing I'd probably been radiating tension since the moment we met—thanks in no small part to my harrowing overnight ride with my narcoleptic cab driver.

She fished around the cooler and pulled out another beer.

"Maybe one or two more of these will get you there."

"Dude, let's hit Toothpicks tomorrow morning!" Kavi shouted from the other side of the boat, a shit-eating grin plastered across his face.

"Yeah, totally. We'd be stupid not to," I said, unable to suppress my sarcasm.

—

We finally rounded a point and caught our first glimpse of the place we'd call home for the next two weeks—a cluster of wooden bungalows nestled into a U-shaped bay. The compound sat protected behind a coastal reef, which made navigation look complicated.

Closer to shore, we were able to make out some of the finer details. Out front was a beautifully built, contemporary boat dock that reached out about a hundred feet from the beach into deeper water. The property was lined with swaying coconut palms and there were several private villas, each with their own front porch, shaded by palms and facing the ocean. The offshore breeze gave way to a warm, earthy current of air wafting toward us. It reminded me of freshly turned soil in spring—rich, alive, and grounding.

We began our final approach into the bay and toward the dock. Dani barked orders at the deckhands, who scrambled to get the lines ready. We pulled up and tied off, without a hiccup. He killed the motors and hopped down from the flybridge. With the boat silent, the isolation of the place became more apparent. A chorus of songbirds and a gentle hum of insects filled the air, joined by the distant crash of waves and the occasional howl of monkeys in the trees.

We were finally here!

"Welcome to paradise," he chuckled. "I'll keep the platitudes comin' all day long, I promise. These two will help you with your gear. Make your way to the main villa to check in with the lovely Maya. She'll give you your keys and towels and explain everything. Don't mess with her; she'll kick your ass all up and down this beach. I'm in the small villa up the hill if you need anything."

Our captain seemed relieved to be back—as though ferrying guests around was the worst part of his job.

"The restaurant, bar, and other resorts are down that path," he said, pointing west. "I usually don't fraternize with the other crowds—bit lacking in class," he laughed.

Ours was the first of several along the winding southeast coast, so there was some community—but it seemed awfully quiet for 11 a.m.

Stepping off the boat, he turned with a sudden sternness in his eyes.

"One more thing—for your safety—so listen carefully. Absolutely no walking alone at night, buddy system, minimum. Always keep a flashlight with you and use it. This is serious—poisonous snakes, spiders, and BIG cats. Sumatran tigers, Bengal tigers, jaguars... even cougars—but those tend to hang out at the fishing resort around the corner."

I laughed—apparently the only one who caught the joke.

"Seriously though, it can be a dangerous place, you name it, we got it. So don't fuck around."

He stared straight at Kavi.

"You lookin' at me?" Kavi asked, tapping his chest with a stupefied grin.

As it turns out, Dani was a good judge of character.

"Another thing—do *not* get drunk and swim after dark. I know it's tempting, but sharks feed late. This bay attracts fishermen, and despite the resort pleading with them, they still dump fish guts in there. That brings in some seriously big fish. I advocate for a good time, but I do not encourage being eaten alive while on vacation. Or ever, really."

He stared each of us down.

"I hate to tell you all this," he added, "but last year we had a guest go missing. Parts of him turned up on shore a couple days later."

"Wait, are you serious?" Kavi asked, skeptically.

"Very. It was no bueno—but it happened. Look, this ain't Kansas. There are a lot of bulls, white and black tips, hammers, and even white pointers swimming around out there. You're free to do as you please, but I'd suggest steering clear. I mean what I say."

His hard look conveyed a message that no words could. It was clear enough that my plan to get drunk and jump off the dock with Kendal that night might need a second thought.

—

The mood shifted slightly as we processed the information. It's never welcome news to hear that someone recently died at the resort you're about to occupy. I looked over the edge of the wooden boat dock, and—as if on cue—there it was: a small Black Tip reef shark chasing something in the shallows.

Kendal looked over at me with a grin.

"There's heaps of them here," she said, with a shrug.

"But they're mostly harmless. He gives that speech every time."

I cracked a smile.

Fern and Logan spotted the shark as well and immediately launched into a debate about whether a shark that size would ever bite a person. The conversation quickly morphed into familiar bickering.

"Dude, why the fuck would a five-foot shark bite into a six-foot human?" Logan said. "It makes no sense, that's like you biting into a full-size cow."

"Yeah, and people eat cows all the time, what's your point?"

"I know people eat cows," Logan snapped, "but sharks don't have freezers to store extra food. I'm saying—a little shark trying to eat you makes no sense. He's chasing bait fish."

Kendal looked at me with a smirk.

"Shall I get used to this?" she asked.

"Maybe... better to just tune it out, though," I shrugged.

Carissa jumped in. "You know what you guys should do? Jump off the dock right now—test both theories. Why speculate?"

She seemed amused by the pair, and who could blame her? Of course, it's not until later that you want to duct tape their mouths shut or slip them a Xanax.

—

Our group had rented two of the villas and planned to bunk up. Kavi and I would take one, Fern and Logan the other—but I wondered whether it was smart to put those two together, as arguments about who got more burnt, or who caught the better wave would no doubt echo across the resort.

Still, better to quarantine them together, I thought, as Maya, our hostess, checked us in one by one.

We were each handed a fresh coconut by another staff member, which was much appreciated.

As I sipped mine, I watched the girls interacting.

Kendal carried herself with an effortless, grounded confidence that made me feel clumsy by comparison. It was like we were different species—she, some kind of earthly angel; me, a mildly buffoonish creature.

I struggled to file her under anything familiar.

"Dude, wake up. We're good."

Kavi handed me my key, snapping me out of my daydream.

"Alright, we'll catch up with you Aussies later," I said, confused by the words that uncontrollably fell from my mouth.

Catch up with you Aussies later? I looked down, briefly wondering if I was losing it, as we exchanged hugs and promises of Piña Coladas.

"Smooth one dude," Fern said as we walked.

"Yep—coming from the same guy that once asked a waitress if she was emotionally available," Logan chimed in, not letting that one slide.

"I told you I was drunk. Why are you bringing that up again?"

"Will you guys shut up; I haven't slept enough for this shit," Kavi replied, hoping to put a full stop to the idiocy.

I looked back and caught Kendal laughing as she watched us walk away.

She grinned at me, and I smiled back.

"Dude, if you already fell in love with a chick on the first half of the first day of the trip, I'm gonna slap your face off," Kavi said, catching the exchange.

"Ha! Chill out. I'm here to surf and relax, not complicate things with a girl. Plus, I'm still not over Natasha," I said—even though we both knew there was a spark with Kendal.

"What? Natasha still? I take it back—go fall in love with Kendal. Anything to get you over that narcissist."

I was still recovering from a relationship with a girl who—to put it gently—treated me like shit and took advantage of my kind nature.

"Let's never mention Natasha again. May she find peace ruining another innocent dude's life. Amen."

"Amen." Kavi echoed.

"I do think Kendal likes me though... it's a curse, I know. I don't wish this level of charm on anyone," I laughed.

"Yeah, you really knocked it out of the park with that 'Aussie' line, Mr. Bond. Listen, man—just stay with me on this trip. There's plenty of time for social shit later. Let's focus on surfing."

I nodded.

"I didn't come all this way to hang out with girls. We've got plenty of those back home where there's no waves or palm trees. And if you end up partying all night and missing sessions again, like in Costa... I swear to God, I'm never letting it go," he continued.

"Oh, come on, that happened... three times. Shit..." I replied, counting my fingers.

I paused.

The man was making a lot of sense. But still—I couldn't help but consider the idea of a vacation fling between day trips.

———

Nearing our quarters, the faint sound of Fern and Logan's bickering began to fade into the distance, leaving a rare moment of quiet.

Our villa was tucked just east of the main resort, about two hundred feet from the beach. The building was a piece of architectural art, with a steeply peaked roof and thatch that looked freshly laid. The wooden structure was covered in a rich bamboo façade, coated in a shiny brown lacquer. There were windows in every direction, allowing daylight to flood the space as well as cool air to flow freely. As we opened the large sliding glass front door and walked in, I was amazed to see the highly detailed interior design.

Two separate bedrooms, each with full en-suite bathrooms, king beds, and vaulted ceilings built from bamboo, with polished tree trunks in place of traditional beams. The kitchen, dining, and living area were open concept and connected, complete with a large sectional couch and a wooden dining table.

"Are you seeing this?" Kavi asked, quietly impressed.

"I am. I can't wait 'til it's covered with all of your stuff and smells like moldy board shorts."

"It's inevitable... inevitable, indeed," he said, stroking his nonexistent beard.

"Make you a deal—I won't stay out all night partying, ruining morning sessions, if you promise to hang your wet shit outside and don't turn this place into a mess."

"That's a deal!"

We shook on it, both fully aware we'd each break the accord in no time.

I walked up to my room, unpacked my bag into the wooden dresser and closet, then checked out the kitchen, which was fully equipped with a water-maker, fridge, and gas stove. Even the building smelled like the tropics—as if someone had burned incense that perfectly captured the place.

"Man, this is a huge step up from my apartment. I don't know how I'm going to be able to go back to my sorry life back home," I said.

Just then Logan and Fern walked in.

"What!? Your spot's bigger than ours—that's bull shit!" Fern said, dropping his bag on the floor.

"Fern. They are literally the exact same. Our kitchen is just on the other side, and the bedrooms are flipped. Chill out."

41

"Well, it looks bigger to me."

"You're five foot six. Everything looks bigger to you."

"Can you guys either shut up or get married or something?"

Kavi had a point. They really did have a certain dysfunctional marriage quality to their relationship.

"Let's go check out the restaurant—I'm starving." Logan said, motioning toward the door.

———

To say the pathway from the villa to the restaurant was incredible would be a massive understatement. Walls of green bamboo and dense plant life encapsulated the trail, creating the sense that we were walking through a living tunnel. To my right, I noticed a day gecko scurrying up one of the bamboo shoots. It was a brilliant emerald green with yellow, blue, and orange spots, and bright turquoise circling its eyes. I paused to admire the little guy before continuing on.

Rounding the corner, the restaurant came into view— our new friends, now in swimwear, were sipping tropical cocktails. The restaurant itself was a massive tiki-style structure, stretching nearly thirty feet high. I'd always been fascinated by this particular aesthetic and wandered around a bit, geeking out at the craftsmanship and architecture.

Around the perimeter were palms, bananas, papayas, sapotes, and even cacao trees. The restaurant sat about a hundred feet from the beach and had a massive saltwater pool with a wet bar built in. Kavi was already ordering drinks by the half-dozen. Logan and Fern made their way to the girls.

I noticed an older couple that I didn't recognize, which made me feel better—like we weren't the only people on the island.

"Hola!" I said, as I walked past them, realizing a second too late that I associate travel with Spanish.

I recalled a scene from *The Tourist*, where Johnny Depp's character does the same thing while in France.

"Hola, todos bien?"

The couple laughed, clearly humoring me.

"Si, todos bien!" I laughed, shaking my head in personal disappointment.

Fuck, I'm awkward! I thought.

—

I took a little solo walk toward the ocean to check out the view from shore—and to my surprise, was joined by Kendal, who seemed a little tipsy already. Her jovial smile was infectious and had already crept its way past my defenses.

"Hey mister, what do you reckon? Isn't this place amazing?"

"I'm honestly speechless. It's perfect. Is this Hunter's first time here? She seems pretty young."

"Yeah, after last year's trip, 'Ris and I decided to drag her here with us."

"They're sisters, yeah?" I asked—with an oddly timed Australian affectation that seemed to come out of nowhere.

Kendal nodded and giggled.

"Nice accent, Crocodile Dundee."

I laughed awkwardly.

This girl made me more nervous than I was entirely comfortable with—

"I had a feeling. She's like a miniature version of Carissa."

"Hey, so what do you guys think? Should we team up for a surf tomorrow?"

"Sure. I think we want to start on something mellow though?"

"Yeah definitely. There's a wave called *Dinosaurs* that breaks heaps of chill waves over sand—just around the corner. It's my favourite spot."

I was just about to pull my phone out to Google it—but stopped myself, remembering my promise.

I'm sure it's awesome, I thought, resisting the urge.

"I'm going to head back to the pool. See you over there. It's nice to see you so calm," she said with a smile, turning back toward the others.

I caught her gaze as she glanced back over her shoulder. Her frame was slender and toned, each step easy and confident, with a wisp of coconut trailing in her wake. I noticed Carissa giggling as she watched me quietly taking inventory of Kendal as she walked away.

I smiled and turned back to face the sea.

"I'm in for it... and so fuckin' awkward," I said, aloud.

—

From the beach, I could see several little islands that looked just big enough to hold three or four palms—a real *Swiss Family Robinson* kind of place—completely untouched by human hands. In the crystal-clear water around me I could see little crabs, darting fish, and various seashells. The sand was as white as paper, and when I stepped into the ocean for the first time, I noticed the water was the same temperature as the air—making it even more inviting. I tossed my shirt, dove below the surface, and swam toward the bottom. The ocean was impossibly clear—details were sharper than I'd ever seen without a mask.

I swam deeper and over the reef, sending fish darting in every direction. There were clownfish, puffers, little crustaceans, even a small octopus that appeared to moonwalk away as I approached. The coral was vibrant and sprawling, stretching as far as I could see along the shoreline. I surfaced with a smile, realizing how lucky I was to finally be here.

—

I returned to the pool just as the group gathered in a loose semicircle around the bar, mid-conversation.

"Okay, so what do they think happened?" Kavi asked.

The bartender—a rotund, bald, Polynesian man named Kai—explained.

"They're not totally sure. It was really sad though... I was working that night right over there at the other bar."

He pointed across the property, toward the bar near the restaurant.

"The guy's name was Robert. He was hanging around the pool, having drinks after sunset with some other guests. They were all drinking a lot... but nothing out of the ordinary. All the staff remember him, because he tipped really well." Kai looked at us for a beat—like he was hinting at something.

I sighed, pulled a wet 50,000 rupiah note from my board shorts, and slapped it on the bar.

He smiled.

"Anyway," he continued, "we shut down that night around midnight, which is pretty late for this place. He was the last one to leave. I remember watching him stumble off alone, thinking I should make sure he got back safely. But I didn't. I stayed to finish cleaning up the bar and that was it. No one ever saw him again."

A long pause followed—

"That's crazy, but what actually happened to him? You think he got dusted by a shark? Dani told us that's what happened," Fern asked.

"We don't really know," Kai sighed. "Like I said, he was here alone, so no one reported anyone missing. We weren't really looking for any evidence. I think maybe he went for a swim—or fell off the dock. Most people think he drowned. But how often does a surfer drown in calm water like that?" he added. "Unless he hit his head on something, but there's nothing but sand around the dock, so it doesn't add up to me."

Another pause—

"So, you figure he got attacked then? Why hasn't anyone heard about this?" I asked.

"The tourism industry here relies on people feeling safe. The *Polisi* are careful with what they report. They don't want to scare off business either, so they kept it quiet. But to be honest, this kind of thing happens around the Ments now and then."

"But you personally think he got attacked by a shark?" Kendal asked.

"You can't tell anyone I told you this, they don't want us talking about it. But if I had to bet, I'd say he was walking past the dock, he had too much booze in him and decided to jump in for a swim—and got into trouble with a shark. I promise you I wouldn't be caught in there at night, not after years of seeing the fish that hang around. A day later one of the staff found a hand on the beach to the east of here—covered in crabs. Whether he drowned, or was attacked, the sharks got him in the end. The resort was full of Polisi for two days."

A somber mood settled over the group.

"So, if he jumped in off the dock or whatever, why didn't anyone find his clothing?" Logan asked.

"He was wearing board shorts and was barefoot—like most guests, including you guys. Anyway, learn from his mistakes. I know this place is magical, but don't forget—the same things that make it magical, make it dangerous too. Shit, he coulda been bitten by a water snake and had massive heart failure, for all we know."

This conversation might have been a mistake, I thought.

Hearing Kai say that he'd never go swimming—at night was sobering—especially since we planned to go surf in these same waters for hours on end.

—

We ordered a quick snack, finished our drinks, and decided to head back for a rest. I was still exhausted, and everyone was feeling jet lagged from the trip. The plan was to meet back for dinner and figure out where we'd surf the next morning.

6

—Just Be Cool—

Shrill marimba notes from my phone alarm pierced the silence, snapping me back to consciousness. For a moment, I couldn't remember where I was—always a good sign I'd fallen into a deep sleep. Overhead, a wooden fan spun lazily against the thatch ceiling. No sirens, no garbage trucks—just the hush of wind and waves. I smiled, grateful to be waking up in a tropical paradise. My mood had improved markedly now that I had a few uninterrupted, nightmare-free hours. I hopped out of bed and into the main part of the villa, where I found Kavi in the kitchen, listening to some reggae. He'd already done a decent job trashing the place: towels draped over chairs, banana peels on the counter, a toothbrush on the table, and surf fins and board shorts scattered everywhere—a quick descent into entropy.

I took a deep breath.

"So, deal's off? I get to party all night and miss surf sessions?"

"I'm just getting organized, relax. Did you get your beauty sleep in? It's almost time for dinner."

Another thing about Kavi—he's got a rare ability to function on very little sleep and doesn't adhere to a traditional circadian clock. There was a decent chance he didn't even stop to lie down. More likely, he spent the past two hours quietly peppering the house with personal sundries.

—

It was almost dark by the time we closed the door behind us on our way to the restaurant. Small, recessed lights lit the pathway with a soft orange glow. The jungle seemed even more alive now that dusk had fallen, a rich harmony of sounds rising around us. Everything from insects to tree frogs pleasantly sang their melodies, while the scent of a nearby campfire wafted through the area— reminding me that I had packed my flint somewhere in my luggage. I keep a piece tucked in my board shorts pocket, in case the opportunity to have a beach fire ever comes along.

"Man, smell that? So psyched for post-surf beach fires," I said.

"Right? Perfect setup for a little fireside romance for you and your girlfriend."

It seemed like Kavi might already be a little irked by Kendal's presence—but I couldn't tell for sure. And even though he was making fun of me—I did like the sound of his suggestion. Still, the insecurity crept in: what if I had enough drinks to make a pass at her, and she shut me down? That would kill the vibe—maybe even throw off the group dynamic.

He stopped suddenly and put his arm across the path to block me.

"You're spiraling already. Cut that shit out—nobody wants side drama while we're here."

As my closest friend, he had seen me crash and burn with girls before, and he was certainly in tune with my energy.

"Shit… how do you do that?"

"I know your weirdo mood shifts. I can feel when you go inward."

He shot me a look—

"Just be cool. Let it be what it wants to be. If she likes you, she'll let you know, so that's the last time you need to think about it for the rest of your goddamn life."

"I mean… fair enough. But come on—she's kind of perfect."

"Como siempre—they're all 'kind of perfect' until they're not. I swear, I'll throw your ass off the dock to join Robert if I catch you moping."

He paused.

"Look around! We're in paradise on the adventure of a lifetime!"

"Jesus, dude. That was dark. Let the man rest in peace, would you?"

"I'm sorry, but you needed to hear it. I just don't want this to turn into some rom-com side plot."

"Okay. I get it, relax already."

"And Cole—don't sit beside her at dinner. Give her space."

"Why are you giving me advice if you don't want us to get involved?"

"Because I know you're going to anyway. This way maybe you won't fuck it up so quick."

"So thoughtful," I muttered.

We continued walking the path toward the restaurant. I left it for a second, but I couldn't resist.

"Are you sure that's the move, not sitting beside her?"

"Trust me, man. It's the only move, steer clear of all the neediness—it'll work."

I shook my head, contemplating how sitting beside someone could be considered needy—but I took his advice, nevertheless.

—

The girls were already seated around a large table when we arrived, laughing among themselves. Kendal was wearing a loose white tank top and tiny, ripped jean shorts. Around her neck was a gold chain with a small palm tree pendant resting next to her collarbone. She looked up and caught my eye. It seemed like she'd picked the outer seat on purpose—but I stuck to the plan. Kavi slid into the spot next to her, diving into the conversation, while I took a detour to the bathroom. After a minute or so I returned and took a seat next to Carissa, across from Kendal.

"Did you leave your phone at home?" Kendal teased.

I laughed—but was interrupted by Fern and Logan arriving in typical form.

"Guys, help settle this! Do mosquitoes here carry malaria?" Fern barked.

"No, they don't carry malaria," Carissa replied. "But I swear I read they can carry syphilis somewhere, probably Instagram," she laughed.

"Have you two been married long?" Hunter asked.

"Whatever. I told you they don't have malaria here, dude," Logan muttered.

The guys sat down on either side of me, completing the group of seven.

I raised my drink—

"To our new friends!"

The positive vibes had returned—Kai's horror story already fading into the background.

"Okay, so we talked to Dani," Carissa said. "He thinks the surf should be good tomorrow, but if we want to hit *Dinosaurs*, we should leave around noon to catch high tide."

She was clearly the most diehard of the three girls, and I had little doubt she'd put on a clinic for the rest of us. Surfing is hard—very hard. It takes an absurd amount of time and effort just to get a handle on. I'd been at it for over a dozen years and still got the jitters anytime there was promise of serious swell.

The last trip we took to Costa Rica got a little hectic toward the end. For two weeks, the swell was small to moderate—but then, about three days before we left, a southern pulse rolled in. We ended up at Playa Marbella with our expat friend Todd, who promised it was the right move—and he was dead right. To call it nerve-wracking would've been an understatement. The ratio of waves surfed to savage beatings was about five to one—in favor of beatings. We came to affectionately refer to that wave as the *Costa Rican Pipeline*. A couple of days in overhead, barreling madness—getting violently tossed, held under, and nearly run over by other surfers—left me with an ironic mix of fear and hunger for more.

—

"Okay, so we were wondering—where's your family from, Kavi?"

"Oh, I see how it is—single out the brown guy. That's racial profiling, you know," he laughed, earning a round of chuckles from the group.

"Yeah, we're profiling you. And what's with the bandana?" Carissa added, teasing.

—

Ever since I've known Kavi, he's worn the same white bandana tied around his neck—even while surfing. I'd never asked him about it, but the girls were a curious bunch, and they liked to prod.

"Cross-examined already. Kavi's a Hindu name... I'm like... maybe a third Indian, but my parents leaned into it. The bandana reminds me to shower... when it goes off-white, I know it's probably time."

"Yeah, you look like a nicely tanned European gang member," Hunter said, with a smirk.

"Yeah, what kind of gang colour is white?" Kendal asked, with a crooked smile.

"We're called the Montauk Minorities, you've never heard of us? We live with our parents in their beach houses... and we're all addicted to Percocet."

The girls giggled.

—

Luckily for Kavi, he was quick on his feet and deflected attention like a pro. From that point on, Carissa's focus seemed to drift toward him—a common phenomenon when it came to Kavi. I shot him a look to make sure he noticed the shift. Of course, he did—not that he cared much for that sort of thing.

Our waiter arrived with menus, and the list of options stretched across several pages—surprisingly pricey by Indonesian standards. They had locally caught fish served cooked, sashimi, or sushi-style, plus incredible fruit dishes and just about everything in between. The drink list was just as extensive. The girls joked that surfing hungover was their specialty—certainly not the case for me. We ordered a solid spread of food and several bottles of wine.

I took in the dining area—about ten tables spread beneath a large, thatched canopy. String lights crisscrossed overhead, casting a warm glow. Tiki torches lined the perimeter—their flames swaying to the salsa music playing from the speakers.

—

The first appetizer arrived: a large, round plate of sashimi, stacked in a spiral and brushed with ponzu. The fish tasted freshly caught—light years from the shipped-in seafood we were used to in New York.

Then came the entrees: various fillets of grilled fish with sides of roasted potatoes, breadfruit, and plantains— each dish incredibly well-prepared.

—

Only after we finished did I realize how much the booze had been flowing. Empty wine, beer and cocktail glasses surrounded me—and without noticing, I'd downed at least eight drinks. After our server cleared the table, the girls insisted we order tequila shots to round off the meal.

"We don't do dessert—we prefer a good tequila. Helps you sleep," Carissa explained.

I shrugged.

Who was I to judge—or break with tradition? So down the hatch it went.

———

By the time we paid the bill, it was nearly 11:30. When I stood, the room tilted—just slightly—and it took a second to find my balance. Kendal appeared beside me, steadying me with one hand.

"Careful, light weight."

"I didn't think we drank that much. Booze must be stronger in Indonesia," I muttered, catching Kendal's grin.

"Nope. You're just a pussy," she teased.

I laughed at her choice of words—brash, but somehow still charming.

Either the alcohol had peeled back some layers, or maybe Australians really were more crass.

We walked toward the exit and said our goodbyes to the staff.

"It's almost midnight... Sumatran time," I said, checking my watch.

I stopped to think.

"So... it's tomorrow, back home. Does that mean we're in the future?"

Kendal laughed and ushered me along the pathway.

"You've got it backwards—it's yesterday where you're from."

I stopped again.

"That's... so confusing."

The rest of the gang was ahead of us—their figures a little more blurry than usual. As we slipped away from the music and lights of the restaurant, the jungle reclaimed the air. The smell, the humidity, the insect chorus—it all came rushing back. I stopped to take it in—but the moment I focused outward, dizziness took over.

"Whoops, no more of that," I slurred, steadying myself.

Kendal giggled as if she knew exactly what I was feeling, then pushed me forward.

"Keep moving, dingus."

I could've sworn I saw Kavi and Carissa holding hands ahead. But it was so out of character for him—had to be my tequila-vision.

—

Kavi was the type of guy who didn't seem to want—or need—anyone's attention or approval. He was always perfectly content to be alone and wouldn't think twice about doing this trip solo. It was a quality I admired—and one not very many people possess. And if the last few years were any indication, that self-assured indifference had become a magnet—particularly for women. I theorized it was his independence, and total lack of self-loathing, that confused the fairer sex—and, as a result, often sent them into quiet pursuit. I'd met a few women over the years who admitted, often with frustration, that they couldn't quite figure him out. He was an anomaly. And people—especially beautiful women—who were used to being chased, flattered, and pursued seemed instinctively drawn to the one guy in the room who didn't try. I kept an eye on Carissa, wondering if that same challenge would interest her. So far… it looked like it might.

—

Kavi and I had met fifteen years earlier, completely by chance, at a bar in the city. He was in a relationship back then—with a girl he thought he'd likely marry someday. But when she suddenly changed her mind and broke it off, something in him fractured. What followed wasn't just heartbreak—it was a full-on transformation. He emerged from it sharp-edged, clear-minded, and fiercely independent. He no longer believed he needed anyone or anything. And if a woman was going to enter his life again, she'd have to pass through a very narrow gate.

"I'll probably end up single for life," he told me once. "And I'm fine with that. If I die alone, who gives a shit, right? I'm going to do what makes me happy in the moment. Fuck it."

I'm paraphrasing, of course, but I found the statement jarring. My own emotional constitution rejected loneliness. I wanted someone to share my life—someone to bear witness to it all. But Kavi had his own goals. And not only did he seem unphased by letting go of the hallmark happy ending... he almost seemed excited by it.

"Listen, I have no issues being with a girl one day," he'd said, "But I'm not donating three more years of my life to something that's probably going nowhere. If the right girl shows up, pins me down, and proves she's got what it takes—then we'll see. Until then, I'm done with the fairytale, heart-on-my-sleeve bullshit. I'm more than happy to wake up alone every day."

A proclamation that so perfectly summed up our differences, Hemingway himself couldn't have phrased it better.

—

Up ahead, the group veered off the main path and headed toward the dock—exactly what I expected.

"Oh my god," Kendal said, squinting toward the water. "Are those crazies going swimming?"

"That would be so stupid and incredible at the same time," I said. "Mainly stupid."

I suddenly realized how much the alcohol had shifted everyone's mood—including mine. Hours earlier, we were spooked enough by Kai's story to avoid the ocean entirely—let alone do the one thing he explicitly warned us not to. Yet here we were—several drinks deep, tempting fate.

Kendal and I reached the dock just in time to hear Fern goading Logan.

"You won't get attacked if you jump in quick. Trust me."

That familiar blend of challenge and manipulation.

"Yeah, that's probably true," Logan replied. "But we're not going to find out. I'd rather not die before we even get to surf here."

I flashed my light off the edge of the dock, but the alcohol made it hard to focus. It was high tide—only about two feet of clearance between the water and the underside of the dock, compared to four or five at low tide.

"Alright, I'm way too drunk for this," I muttered, turning to walk away.

Just then, we heard a splash near the far end of the dock.

Kendal spun around.

"What was that?"

I froze; torch aimed toward the sound.

"Was that a shark?" I said, eyes locked on the dark water.

Another splash—closer this time. We all saw it: a dorsal fin and tail slicing the surface. Then another—this time smacking against a piling and soaking part of the dock. Compelled, I dropped down and leaned over the edge for a better look.

"Whoa, what do you think you're doing, mister?" Kendal said, grabbing the back of my shirt.

"I just want to see what's down there, I'll be fine."

I aimed my light into the water and saw four or five large, silver shapes darting beneath us.

"Shit, there's a bunch of 'em down here!"

Kavi and Kendal dropped beside me, peering over the edge. The sharks zipped around the pilings effortlessly changing direction with impossible precision, as they chased down bait fish. Then, one of the larger ones turned and shot straight toward us—breaching the surface less than a foot away. It slapped its tail as it veered, soaking the three of us and leaving behind a mist of sea spray and adrenaline.

"Shit!" was the only word I could find in my startled state.

It seemed like the shark had charged at us on purpose... but that couldn't have been right.

"Okay, that's enough of that, this isn't safe!" Kendal said sharply, grabbing my arm.

She was right—if it had gotten just a little closer, it could've accidentally wrapped its jaws around one of us. Kai's story crept back into my mind. I couldn't imagine someone willingly jumping into this water, not with that many predators swimming around.

I brushed off my shorts, and we made our way back down the dock toward land—where the chances of being accidentally dismembered were much lower.

"Man, I can't believe we're going to surf here," Logan muttered when we reached the sand. "Fuck…"

No one replied.

We all felt the same, even if no one else said it.

"Right, that was a lot of fun, but I'm going to bed, I'm wiped."

I was so tired and drunk, the words just fell out—more a cake batter of syllables than an actual sentence. I turned to leave, but someone locked arms with me.

"Buddy system, Cole. Captain's orders," Kendal smiled.

I'd already forgotten our stone-faced Captain's warning about walking alone after dark—though I usually chalk those things up as overly cautious and rarely necessary.

—

As we stumbled along, I could feel her energy next to mine—light, unguarded, always grinning. Her eyes sparkled with mischief and ease. I stopped walking for a second and shook off my thoughts. It had been one day, and I could already feel myself getting pulled in.

I cleared my throat and subtly adjusted her arm—loosening the link between us.

She giggled at my awkwardness.

"Too close for ya?"

"No. I don't know… I'm drunk," I slurred, my composure slipping a little as we walked.

"I'll back off. I know linking arms is more of a third-date kind of thing for most men."

I laughed at my own ridiculousness and re-linked arms with her.

"I didn't know this was a date."

"Of course it is! All of my first dates involve two of my friends... and three other random American guys I just met. It's right there on my *Hinge* profile."

We laughed as we drifted further into the dark abyss, surrounded by a galaxy of insect sounds and the heavy warmth of the jungle night. It felt almost psychedelic to walk through such a rich ecosystem in the pitch-black, so far away from anything familiar.

"I can hear waves breaking in the distance," she said, pausing for a second to listen. "When the swell gets bigger, it gets crazy. Last year it was all we could hear—like bombs exploding on the ocean. I kept having nightmares and waking up terrified."

Somehow, I could hear the smile in her voice as she spoke.

"Are you always like this?" I asked.

"Like what?"

"Happy. Smiling. Excited. Full of wonder—and not at all embittered by the world. I guess that's how I'd describe you."

She laughed.

"Not always, sometimes I'm a big suck. I get emotional."

"Shit, I'm so much more jaded and unhappy than you, it's crazy," I lamented.

She giggled and pushed me forward with surprising strength.

"Let's get you to your villa, young man. You've had way too much to think tonight."

She pulled a flashlight from the tiny pocket of her jean-shorts and shone it ahead of us.

"You know, being happy, excited and full of wonder isn't that difficult in this circumstance."

I paused—

She had a point: here I was in the middle of a surf mecca, drunkenly walking with a dream girl, and I couldn't for the life of me turn my anxiety off to enjoy the moment.

"I really need to get out of my head... also, how do you fit a flashlight in that little pocket?"

She laughed, again.

"Yes, you need to shut your mind off. It's impossible to live a fantasy if you keep overthinking it."

She was spot-on. My reflex to overanalyze everything was something I would have to work hard to unlearn.

———

We arrived at her cabin and walked up the steps to the front door. I turned to see whether the rest of the gang was near, but there was no sign of anyone.

"Do you want to come in for a tea?" she playfully inquired.

I paused for a long moment to think it through.

"I'd normally say yes. But I think it might be smart if I went to bed and got some actual rest."

I paused again.

"Plus, that's more of a fifth, or sixth date kind of thing for me," I added, the words spilling uncontrollably from my mouth.

She smiled and paused, as though she was waiting for me to amend my statement with a '*but.*'

"Okay, yeah. No problem. I was just using tea as a guise to lure you in, anyway. I'm a serial killer and herbal tea is how I bait my victims," she laughed, trying to diffuse the awkwardness.

"That's alarming. What's your count?"

"This week? Or all time?"

"This quarter, serial killers use fiscal quarters to keep track... if you were a real one, you'd know that already."

"Busted! I'm just a regular killer—but I'm working on it."

We laughed awkwardly, each of us confused by my refusal to acquiesce.

I smiled and went in for a hug.

"Good night, Australian woman."

When our bodies met, it was pure electricity. Her soft skin against mine had my heart hammering.

Holy shit, I'm screwed.

The hug lingered longer than it probably should have, as we drunkenly swayed back and forth—until I finally pulled away and took a step back.

"Okay, I have to go right now before I change my mind."

"Ah-ha! Another part of my diabolical plan," she teased.

I stumbled backward, catching my foot on a potted plant as I turned to walk away. She seemed amused, giggling at my lack of finesse.

"Get home safe, Dingus. See you tomorrow. Don't talk to strangers."

I kicked clumsily at nothing on the way toward my villa, heart sinking. I'd fucked it up already. I could barely believe the interaction.

Who the hell says no to tea with the dream girl?

I shook my head, sweating from both the heat and the shame as I staggard home.

"Fuck!" I barked, "I should jump in the bay and let the sharks take me."

The distant sounds of laughter broke my spiral. The rest of the gang was walking up the pathway toward the villas. I turned toward them, hoping they'd distract me.

"Yo, we thought you and Kendal were off getting married," Kavi joked.

"No, no. She's gone to bed; I just walked her home."

"I was surprised to see her take to you like that. She gets chased by men heaps, but she never gets involved—and not a vacation fling type," Carissa admitted.

Apparently, they'd been on a handful of surf and yoga trips together over the years and had known each other since childhood—so I knew she was well-researched on the subject.

"Yeah, I don't know, I'm pretty sure she just thinks I'm a dork and it amuses her. I'm off to bed though, I'm the most tired human ever."

I walked past the gang toward the villa and was in bed and asleep within minutes.

7

—Pura Vida, Sumatra—

I jolted awake, momentarily unsure where I was—another nightmare had rocked my slumber, but the details had already vanished. All that remained were sweat-soaked sheets and a racing pulse. The calming sound of tropical birds took over my senses, slowly calibrating me back to reality.

Pots and pans clanked in the kitchen, accompanied by the wafting scent of fried eggs and coffee. I forced myself out of bed. Whatever I dreamt about left me feeling uneasy—but there was adventure ahead.

I stumbled downstairs.

"Morning, lady killer!" Kavi said, with a smirk.

I laughed at the suggestion.

"Don't patronize me this early."

As expected, the villa was in complete disarray: clothing strewn everywhere, dishes left in piles, pineapple and mango peels scattered on the countertop, and coffee spilled over half the kitchen.

"Not patronizing. What even happened? Did you guys get busy?" he laughed, already knowing the answer.

"Nah, nothing happened, we hugged goodnight, and she went to bed."

"You dog. I hope you wore protection—no walk-in clinic for miles."

"No, seriously—she invited me in for tea and I said I'd better go home to bed. She probably thinks I'm on the spectrum now. I bet she'll find another guy that's not a moron and hang with him, and I'll be left replaying our last conversation about serial killers."

"First of all—serial killers? And second—have you not learned anything about anything?" he said, flashing an arrogant smirk. "Let me explain something to you about hot women, since you seem to be clueless. Here's how this works—since probably age sixteen, that girl's had more offers for sex, relationships, and romance than you've had hot dinners. If anything, you just did the one thing that separates you from every dummy she's ever met."

I thought for a second.

"I don't know… it didn't play out so smooth. You could cut the awkwardness with a wooden spoon."

"Be that as it may, if she's interested—you just flipped her from buyer to seller, maybe for the first time in her little hot-girl bubble of a life."

I laughed at the notion.

"I doubt it. She probably thinks I'm some social defect... or gay."

"You're both! But despite that, to her you're probably like a human Rubik's Cube now. I bet she'll chase you to see if she can get you to do what she wants. You might have just lit the ultimate fire under her ass."

"Well, whatever the case, it was awkward, and I hope she was too drunk to remember."

My face heated up, and my palms grew clammy as I replayed the interaction.

Just then, Fern and Logan arrived at the villa and let themselves in.

"Morning, dingers! Hey, where'd you score the eggs and toast?" Fern asked, plopping down at the table.

Kavi had always been a resourceful guy while on trips, so I figured he'd traded a bar of surf wax to a local chicken farmer or something.

"I bought them from the store."

"Ah, very exciting." Fern quipped, "A more important question—what happened with you and Kendal last night?"

I rolled my eyes.

"You guys sound like a bunch of yentas, you know that? I thought we weren't here to hang out with girls, anyway."

"What the fuck is a yenta?"

"It's a Jewish woman who gossips with other Jewish women," Kavi answered.

"That's racist, dude. Their people have been through enough—and we aren't here for girls, but since you seem to be in love, come out with it!" Fern antagonized.

"Nothing happened. She invited me in, and I awkwardly said no. Let's leave it there. It was embarrassing."

I hated thinking about the exchange and really wanted to change the subject to surfing before the anxiety sweats returned.

"So, what's the plan? Eat and then meet the girls over at the dock?" I asked, trying to move things along.

"Yeah, I think Carissa's got the plug—she put everything together," Kavi said, dividing the scrambled eggs and toast.

I don't know whether it was the travel, the hangover, or the tropical air, but breakfast never tasted this good back home.

—

We quickly ate and then packed our boards and day-bags. I threw as many things as I could into my pack, and made sure to bring my speargun, just in case.

"Kavi, I'm bringing my gun. You down?"

"Way ahead of you. It's in my bag."

—

Walking down the path, I spotted Kendal on her front porch, packing up her gear. She was wearing a paper-white bikini, which made her tanned skin look even darker by comparison.

I felt my stomach tighten.

Kavi looked over at me and chuckled.

"Just be cool, dude. Everything's good. Don't act weird."

I straightened my posture as we neared.

"G'day. Stoked to surf, are we?" she asked, noticing my speargun. "And planning to catch us some dinner, as well?"

"We figure we'll hop in on the way back and try to get something... but don't cancel your dinner plans."

"Well let's hope. That restaurant stitched us up good last night."

"Stitched us up?" Kavi asked.

"Means we overpaid."

"Ah, I see. We're still working on our Australian... beautiful language, isn't it, Kavi?"

"So beautiful..." he replied.

Kendal laughed, as she zipped her board bag shut.

I felt awkward talking to her now. Even if Kavi was right, every molecule in me wanted to kiss her and get it over with.

"Just wait a beat, I'll walk with you two," she said, smirking directly at me.

———

In no time the three of us were down at the dock, where the rest of the gang were loading an old fishing boat with their gear. The vessel was shaped like an oversized banana, hand-painted aqua blue and white, with a big red stripe running from bow to stern. It was about 25 feet long, and had a Frankenstein-like outboard motor, mounted to the transom, clearly cobbled together from the remnants of several others.

Carissa and Hunter stood in front of the boat, boards in hand, smiling against a backdrop of teal water and swaying palms. They looked like they'd hopped out of a surf magazine, and into real life. I caught Kavi glancing toward Carissa, who seemed more distracted by the prospect of waves than by him this morning.

Meanwhile, Hunter, Fern, and Logan had formed a strange little trifecta, exchanging inside jokes and some secret handshake they all seemed to know. Barely twenty-four hours after meeting, and we already felt like a happy family of surf-obsessed tourists.

We met our skipper—a man named Carlos, who wore a huge grin as he introduced himself in broken English.

"What's up, guys! I'm Carlos, checkin' out to Dinosaur waves today? Gonna be sick conditions!"

Carlos had a deep voice and looked to be in his mid-thirties. He stood about 6'3", had long hair tied into a bun, a bold looking moustache and a deep tan.

"Carlos, where are you from, homie?" Kavi asked, grinning.

"I'm from here—Sumatra born and raised."

He was a puzzling combination of attributes: a Spanish name, Costa Rican accent, but claimed Sumatran roots.

"That's a sick moustache, dude!" Logan added.

"Ah-ha, sick! Thanks, man. I'm copying to be like Salvador Dali's looks. Pura Vida!" he smiled and stuck his fist out for a bump from Logan.

"Pura Vida?" I quietly repeated, looking at Kavi, who shrugged.

As confusing as it was, we just accepted that our boat captain was a Sumatran man named Carlos who says Pura Vida—and got on with it.

"These your spearguns?" he asked.

"Yeah, is that cool? You know of any good spots we can try?"

"Yeah, lot of good spot—just one rule: I keep the fish after," he laughed, sticking his fist out for another bump, pleased with his dad joke.

We all laughed along with him.

There was no denying the man's charm, and the fact that he was cracking jokes in his second language made him all the more likable. We quickly loaded our gear into the boat and climbed aboard. Kendal specifically waited until I was in position to assist her aboard; her deep hazel eyes glinting in the sun as she stepped down.

Damn! Maybe Kavi was right...

Carlos, Logan, and I strapped board bags to the rack overhead—a canopy made from scrap-metal tubing shaped into an upside-down U. It's surprising how much space seven board bags, two spearguns, and everyone's packs can take up. Of the four rows of seats, only two remained uncluttered. I took my place on the wooden bench just forward of Carlos, moments before Kendal shooed me over to join.

"Hi," she smiled.

"Everyone's ready to go?" Carlos asked, grinning with excitement.

We all nodded, as he pulled on the engine's starter cord. The old four-stroke outboard rattled to life, spewing blueish smoke from the exhaust, and vibrating the hull. We untied and left our little protected bay, toward bigger water.

—

Waves broke across the gap ahead, forming a steep barrier between us and the open ocean. Yesterday, aboard the larger water taxi, I hadn't even noticed the swell—but in this much smaller fishing boat, it was a different story. The waves were only waist-high, but they pitched up sharply, and if we didn't time it right, we'd be drenched before we even got underway. Carlos slowed the vessel, waiting for a set wave to break, and then gunned it—swiftly cutting over the whitewash and avoiding any dramas. He dug around his cooler, and with a big grin, pulled out several ice-cold beers.

"That was the hard part, now we smooth sailing!"

Just looking at the beer made my stomach turn, but I knew if I could hold it down, it might take the edge off. I cracked the can and held it up.

"Salut!" Carlos yelled, as he took a large swig—foamy liquid running from his mustache.

Kavi leaned over and whispered, "That guy's Costa Rican, right?"

I chuckled. "Oh, definitely."

I had to hand it to him—Sumatran or not, he had a pretty sweet gig and was living it up.

"Are you nervous?" Kendal asked, speaking above the rattly engine.

"Nah. I'm a little hung over, but this beer should help. I'm excited to surf—it's been a while."

She grinned.

"I meant nervous to be around me."

"Oh, that... nah. You're not so tough."

"Well good. I did manage to have a good time last night, by the way."

I smiled.

"Me too."

"My favorite part was when I invited you in for tea and you rejected me."

"Very funny, Kendal. I don't know how they do things in the land down under, but where I come from, tea after 10 p.m. with strangers isn't really a thing."

She rolled her eyes at my attempt to defuse the tension and gave me a playful shove.

"You idiot."

"But there's no rush, we have a whole trip ahead of us. Hopefully you'll still want tea later and try again," I teased.

"Try again? I think it's your move, sailor."

I smiled.

—

Several pelicans and seabirds flew alongside as we cruised through turquoise channels and past the most picturesque atolls I'd ever seen—white beaches, palms, and coral reefs scattered everywhere.

Eventually we made it out past the islands and into the open ocean, where we got our first glimpse of Dinosaurs. The wave broke over a shallow sandbar in the middle of nowhere, surrounded by deeper water. Solid, head-high, A-frame shaped waves broke in a gentle, crumbly fashion. They reminded me of some of the waves at County Line, in Los Angeles—which was perfect for me to get my footing back after so many months out of the water. Carlos pointed at the nearest peak where the waves were working best.

"The right is way better—more face and longer rides. Think we should surf it," he said, walking forward to free up the anchor from around our bags.

He tossed the anchor overboard, and we were set... and when I say anchor, I mean a big chunk of metal, with several hook—shaped lengths of rusted steel rebar welded to it. It looked like a grappling hook from a low-budget Indonesian Batman film in a past life.

8

—No Ladder, No Problem—

The midday sun beat down, and my forearms began to tingle. I typically surf at the crack of dawn or at dusk, when the sun is less intense—here, chasing the tides meant occasional UV punishment—so on went the zinc and a long-sleeved shirt. The sweet scent of coconut and pineapple filled the air as Kavi and Carissa rubbed wax into their boards. Before I'd even organized myself, the pair had tossed themselves overboard and were paddling hard toward the peak, their taunting faintly audible from the boat.

"Come on, dig those arms in! That handkerchief slowing you down?" Carissa laughed, splashing Kavi.

"What did you call it?" he shot back.

"Looks like she's found a new surf buddy. This is kind of nice for me," Kendal said, smiling.

I nodded, unable to picture her locked in an intense paddle battle with Carissa.

Kendal was softer and more stable—calm and curious—where Carissa skewed aggressive and fiery.

"You ready? Have you got a bandana you're going to put on as well? Isn't it your gang's thing?"

"No, just Kavi. He's our most violent member, so he wears the bandana." I joked, as I strapped my leash on, preparing to join the others.

"You ought to not make fun of us, we're dangerous." I continued.

She nodded and raised her hand to her forehead, in military salute.

—

My mood changed as soon as I hit the water. The refreshing sea cooled my clammy skin and shook off what was left of the hangover. I casually made my way over to the peak, Kendal paddling next to me, wearing her trademark mischievous grin. She moved with precise, graceful control, as though she and the board were one—too composed to be mistaken for a surf tourist.

—

We arrived at the lineup, and I slid off my board to have a look below. I could see various details, including a few needle fish hanging out, gently swaying in the current. The bottom was mostly sandy with the odd section of rocky reef—perfect for my first session back on the board.

I surfaced just as Kendal was setting up to paddle. She took two strokes and began to glide, snapping to her feet effortlessly and into a sweeping bottom turn before disappearing behind the wall of water. Spray burst over the backside of the wave as she sped along, eventually popping over the shoulder to head back to the peak.

Watching her in her element reminded me of how different our worlds really were. According to our drunken dinner conversation, she had grown up near the beach on the Gold Coast of Australia—a dreamland for anyone who loves the sea. Most of her life had been centered around exploring and playing in the ocean, surfing each day.

I, on the other hand, grew up in a hostile, northern climate, surrounded by concrete and commerce. A place where you're taught to chase the American dream. A vapid, manmade ecosystem of nine—to—fives, taxes, oppressive rent, and eight-dollar coffees. Yet somehow, the two of us had much in common. Everything from our taste in music, to our philosophies on life, sense of humor and basic interests—all of which supported Plato's nature vs. nurture argument.

———

"Nice wave, little mermaid. You're way better than me," I laughed.

"It's not a contest. The best surfer is the one having the most fun," she smirked, "I read that on a bumper sticker."

I smiled and turned, intent on finding the perfect wave—which wasn't going to be difficult in this consistent swell.

After a minute or so, I found the right peak and started to paddle. I felt a little under the gun: Carissa, Kendal and Kavi had all nailed their rides, and I'd hate to be the outlier. Luckily for me, the wave generously scooped me up and sent me sliding down the face into an easy bottom turn. I set my rail in the buttery surface, spraying loads of water before swinging into a top turn and on down the line.

—

I was alive again—

All the monotony of city life, gone in a millisecond. It was like I was weightless—floating my way along the wall of perfectly formed water, casually linking turns. I could even see a faint outline of the sand bar below me through the crystal-clear wave as I neared the end of the ride. I popped over the shoulder and onto my chest—mission complete, inner peace acquired.

"All it takes is thirty hours of flights, four hours in a water taxi, and a fishing boat ride," I mused, as I paddled my way back to the peak.

Next, Logan dropped in and carved hard off the top, spraying me as he flew past—grinning like a lunatic.

"Locals only, haoli!" he yelled.

"Fuckin' dork," I chuckled, as I arrived back in the lineup.

I felt at ease. Suddenly, how many waves I caught or how well I surfed didn't matter. The simplicity of it all— the waves, the sun, the people—offered a rare kind of peace for me, lending meaning to a life that so often felt like it had none. I just wanted to soak it in fully before it slipped away.

Logan and Fern, on the other hand, were fully engaged in their usual competitive upstaging—oblivious to everything but the next wave and the scoreboard in their heads. Each paddled for every wave that came through their part of the lineup, heckling one another to no end.

Carissa and Kavi had a friendly rivalry going as well, though theirs was much more civil—and flirtatious.

Hunter simply surfed at her own pace, laughing at Fern and Logan's antics, and occasionally joining in the stream of challenges and harassment.

Oh boy. She's becoming one of them. I thought.

—

I caught Carlos in my periphery, frantically shifting positions, pointing at the water. A dorsal fin surfaced about a hundred feet past the breakers.

"Huge pods of Dolphin!" he yelled, holding his arms wide.

I breathed a sigh of relief after a brief jolt of panic—evidently, Kai's shark story was still freshly etched in my mind.

Another hide glistened in the sun as one dolphin breached—and then another, and another. The closer they got, the more dolphins I could see, and the louder the bursts of air rushing from their blowholes became. In no time the pod had surrounded me, moving toward Kendal and the rest of the gang. Some passed so close that the turbulence from their fast-moving bodies almost knocked me off my board.

"Oh my god, there's so many!" Kendal shrieked, paddling up beside me.

There had to be fifty of them, each around six feet long. Kendal reached her hand out and touched one as it surfaced next to her.

"Holy shit, did you just touch that thing!?"

She turned to me with a smile and nodded.

"What'd it feel like?"

I stuck my arm out and just about touched another as it passed by.

"Kind of like a wet rubber boot," she said, wide eyed. "I've never seen them this bold!"

The younger dolphins seemed especially curious. They zipped around playfully, sometimes launching into the air and spinning, almost like they were showing off. The sounds they made—high-pitched squeals and rapid clicks—filled the air around us, above and below the surface.

"They sound so cool!" Kendal said, reaching out to touch another one. "It's like they're talking to each other about us!"

"We need to get below to see this!" I said.

Kendal nodded, and we undid our leashes and dove under. Below, I was hit with a symphony of sound. It was like listening to an intricate tapestry—pulses and vibration woven into something that felt like conversation. I smiled as I dropped through a shimmering nebula of bubbles that partly clouded my vision. Once I got low enough for the water to clear, I was floored—dozens of dolphins criss-crossed in every direction—some as deep as twenty feet. Behind me, perfect rings of air drifted upward like transparent hula-hoops. The younger dolphins chased them, darting through and bursting them like kids chasing bubbles across a lawn.

Running low on air, I kicked for the surface.

"Holy shit! There's dozens of them!" I gasped.

"I know! I've never seen anything like this before," Kendal said, just as awestruck.

We barely caught our breath before diving again. This time I swam hard for the bottom, clearing my ears with quick bursts as I dropped. Several dolphins shot past me like torpedoes, barely acknowledging my presence.

Near the sandy floor, I grabbed a small boulder and used it as ballast to stay down. As I settled, a soft tap landed on my shoulder. I turned to find Kendal, smiling at me. For a moment, we stood beneath the waves, watching the chaos and grace of the pod. Then, lungs burning, we swam toward the light above and broke through.

"What do you reckon is going on?" Carissa asked, paddling next to us.

"I have no idea," Kendal said. "We were just on the bottom—there were dozens of them all. It was madness!"

I dipped my face under again, but just like that, the pod had thinned out, leaving just a few stragglers.

"Looks like they're moving on."

"That was absolutely magical!" Kendal laughed. "Maybe they're going to surf the wave with us—let's go!"

"That might have been the coolest experience of my life," I admitted, as we paddled back to the peak.

"When I was little, I used to dream about being a mermaid and swimming with dolphins," she said. "That was as close as I'll probably ever get."

———

A new set approached. I paddled into the first wave and carved a few mellow turns, scanning the water beside me—sadly, no dolphin party wave erupted—just me. I popped over the shoulder and back onto my board.

"Any dolphins?!" Kendal yelled, paddling into the next wave.

"Nada," I called back, just as she zipped past, playfully spraying a sheet of water in my face.

———

We surfed for another two hours, trading waves and teasing each other under the tropical sun. After my finest ride of the day, I paddled back out to find Kendal lying face down on her board, her wet hair fanned out across the deck like delicate seaweed. According to my watch, we'd been out for over three hours.

"I'm puffed," she said, with a playful pout.

"It's almost 3:30—I'm going to be so damn sunburnt," I said, examining my hands and arms.

"Shall we head back to the tinny for some water?"

"We absolutely shall!" I smiled.

We returned to the boat, paddling noticeably slower than we had earlier. I figured we'd be waiting awhile—Fern and Logan were still battling it out, and Carissa looked like she was just getting started, dominating the lineup while Kavi struggled to keep up.

We arrived at the boat, which gently bobbed in the swell. I lifted my board over the gunnel and hoisted myself aboard, then turned to pull Kendal's board up. Captain Carlos was napping—beer in hand, straw hat over his face, a newspaper spread across his chest. He was a vision straight out of a postcard, or maybe a caricature of a Latin American, mid-siesta.

As he stirred awake, he grinned sleepily and helped us to stow the boards.

"How was it, guys? Craziest dolphins pod I've seen in a long time."

He casually stuck his fist out for a bump.

"That was incredible. Do they show up like that often?" I asked.

"Sometimes pods rolls by, but not crazy like this. How you did, Kendal? Got some waves?"

"Great! Lots of waves, lots of dolphins... I'm knackered."

"It's okay, you get a water and a pineapple, relax. Pura Vida!"

I got the sense that Carlos was something of a local legend—and the type who forged lifelong friendships every time a new group came through the resort.

Kendal and I sat down on the bench seat, the wood warm beneath us. The low-hanging sun sparkled across the surface, casting sharp orange patterns that painted Carlos as he organized gear. I took a deep, relaxed breath and turned back to watch the gang surf, but to my surprise, Carissa and Kavi were already headed back to the boat.

"Wow, I can't believe she's had it, I figured they'd be out until one of us went and collected them," Kendal said.

Carlos helped the pair with their boards, stowing them overhead on the board racks.

"How'd you guys go?" Kendal asked.

"I had a blast—this guy can't cut-back for shit, though!" Carissa laughed, pointing at Kavi, who shook his head and smiled.

"Dude, how crazy was that!?" I said, grabbing his hand to help him aboard.

"Yeah, that was all time. I can't even believe that was real!" he replied, flopping down to relax.

I passed them both a bottle of water and looked back over at the break to see Fern, Logan, and Hunter heading toward us. As they neared, Logan and Hunter dismounted their boards and passed them up to Kavi, then hoisted themselves aboard.

"Hey, amigo! Got a ladder here, or what?" Fern called out to Carlos.

Carlos looked around the boat.

"No ladder. Sorry man."

"Seriously? How are we supposed to get back into the boat?"

"You do how your friends did—grab the side and pull up. We help you," Carlos replied, miming a pull up as he continued to stow and secure the boards in preparation for the trek home.

Still sprawled on his board, Fern squinted at Carlos's "easy" demonstration and shook his head in quiet objection.

"This is amateur hour. Who doesn't have a ladder on their boat?"

"Dude, just fuckin' hoist yourself up, numb-nuts! What's the problem?" Logan barked.

"Well, I'm tired. I don't want to climb right now."

"Climb? What are you talking about—just get in the boat, weirdo," Kavi interjected.

Fern cursed to himself, slapped the water, and awkwardly dismounted his board.

"This is amateur hour," he repeated under his breath.

He reluctantly passed his board up to Carlos, who politely stowed it overhead.

Then—suddenly he latched on to the imposing vessel like a tree frog to begin his mission. It was tricky to tell whether it was sheer exhaustion or his terrible technique that kept him flailing against the hull—but one could speculate.

Each attempt produced a new, uniquely agonizing variation of failure, and after half a dozen tries, he gave up—clinging to the side of the boat, his face flushed, breath ragged.

"Fuck! This is so stupid. Why wouldn't you just have a ladder?" he repeated, frustrated and short of breath as his body bobbed with the gentle swell.

"Dude, just pull your foot up over the rail, then use your leg to hoist your body up," Kavi suggested, shaking his head in disbelief that this was becoming an issue.

Fern began the arduous—and frankly, hilarious task of trying Kavi's suggestion, manically flailing his legs upward, muttering and lamenting to himself. Part of the problem was that he was built like a linebacker, with shorter-than-average legs that lacked the reach—or dexterity—to hook his foot over the boat's railing.

After a few minutes spent observing the spectacle, Logan had had enough. He reached over the side of the boat, grabbed Fern by the ankle, and lifted his foot up and over the gunnel, while Fern let out an uncomfortable grunt.

"Fucker!" he cried out.

"Oh my god, you can't be this out of shape, dude."

"Time to dust off the yoga mat," I said, quietly laughing to myself.

"I can't do the fuckin' splits, if that's what you mean, dickhead!"

"Dude, come on! Just pull yourself up. You make a scene everywhere we go, I swear."

"Fuck you, Logan!"

"Fern, what are you even doing?" I asked, with a grin. "Just get in the boat so we can go. Quit horsin' around."

Fern, who had somehow managed to wrap himself around one of the metal canopy stanchions like a taco, looked up at me.

"I'm fuckin' stuck dude!" he yelled, equal parts panic and defeat in his voice.

The crew burst into laughter as Fern hung in physical purgatory—trapped between the ocean and the boat, helplessly bent around the metal pole.

After a solid minute of uncontrolled laughter—cut with Fern's groaning—Logan and Hunter finally stepped in. They grabbed his arms and hauled him into the boat.

His body spilled onto the floor, landing in a dark brown pool of bilge water that had accumulated between the seats. He lay sprawled in the stagnant slop, too exhausted to move.

"Fucker, who doesn't have a ladder?"

"Nice job, dude. Ladies, he's single—tell your friends," Logan said, shaking his head.

After a few moments, he mustered the strength to sit up, now dripping with bilge waste.

"Can someone pass me a towel and a beer, please?" he asked quietly, unamused by the experience.

Carlos, sufficiently entertained by now, smiled at the group and passed Fern a beer, then pulled on the starter cord of the old outboard motor. The engine fired up, belching dirty exhaust into the air. He walked forward and began pulling up anchor.

"Ready to go?" he asked, with a facetious grin on his face.

"Yo, can we hurry? That exhaust is making me nauseous," Fern muttered, slouched over the port side, towel draped over his head.

Carlos took his time, fiddling with ropes and double-checking the board racks.

"Does anyone else feel sick from that gas smell?" he asked again.

Suddenly—and to everyone's bewilderment—he heaved and convulsed several times before throwing up over the side of the boat. We all stared in stunned silence as he projectile vomited for the next minute straight.

I shrugged—

At this point, nothing Fern did really surprised me anymore.

"Bro, you okay? Need me to get you something?" Carlos asked, having paused his organization of the anchor chain to observe the scene—his eyes wide in disbelief.

Fern said nothing as he hung over the side of the boat, spitting occasionally.

"Seriously dude—we can't take you anywhere," Logan said, breaking the silence.

"That's really messed up," Hunter added.

Fern heaved one last time, evacuating whatever was left in his stomach, then collapsed against the rail of the boat.

There was a long pause.

"So… are you alright?" I asked.

"Can we please go? This exhaust is making me sick." he said, quietly.

I shrugged again and sipped my water.

"The exhaust is making the man sick… what can you do?" I said, quietly laughing to myself.

9

—Hunter; Gatherer—

Carlos gripped the throttle, and the boat peeled away from the sandbar. Fern, finally away from the fumes, tilted his head back like a freed hostage, drawing in the clean breeze.

"I still can't believe how close those dolphins came; I've never seen them act so playfully before!" Hunter said, her face glowing.

"Carlos said he almost never sees them like that," Carissa added.

"Right? I still can't believe how embarrassing Fern is," Logan laughed.

I smiled and reached for my speargun.

"Hey Carlos, think we could stop at one of your spots to try to get some dinner? Fern, you cool with that?"

Fern shrugged, stoic as ever; Carlos nodded and winked, hinting that he had something special up his sleeve.

"Are you girls cool with us stopping for a quick one?" I asked, not wanting to take any liberties with the sunburnt crew.

"I'm cool with it, catch us some dinner, Aqua Man!" Kendal joked.

"Yeah, I'm all for it. Go nuts," Hunter agreed.

I suddenly felt a little under pressure to deliver. I looked over to Logan and Fern, hoping for some backup.

"You guys coming?"

"Fuck that. I'm not going back in there..." Fern grumbled. "... guy doesn't even have a ladder."

"The bigger issue is your skin," Kavi laughed, as he pointed out Fern's deep-red burn.

"Yeah, you alright dude? You're lookin' lobstered out," I laughed.

"I'm fine, just hurry up."

Fern had run out of patience, which amused the girls, who had quickly acclimated to his capricious ways.

"Don't worry man, that burn'll turn a nice maple syrup brown by tomorrow," Logan joked.

Fern had never been much for tanning, historically. He would burn, peel, and then go right back to pale white—like clockwork.

—

We sped along for about twenty minutes until we reached a stretch of crystal clear, shallow water, dappled with coral heads. Farther out, a lone wave broke in the distance—unexpected, powerful, and seemingly detached from the rest of the sea.

"Carlos, what's that wave out there? Can you surf it?" I asked, staring into the open ocean.

Carlos looked up.

"That's called Glaciers... when it's good swell directions, it's sick. It should work with the new swell coming, but it's heavy."

"Looks sick, we should come back," I said.

I watched as a set approached. The sea bulged, jackknifing up before toppling heavily and bursting against the reef. I stared, locked in a quiet trance, only pulled back by the sudden drop in RPMs as the boat slowed.

Carlos cut the motor and walked to the bow of the vessel to anchor.

"That wave gets so fun; we can come check it out in couple of days to see," he suggested. "You can jump in here—tons of fish on these reefs."

"How deep are they?" I asked, trying to trying to snap out of the post-surf fog.

"About forty foot to the bottom. Sometimes the fish are hanging by the rocks around twenty—depends."

I stood up and shook off my fatigue.

"Fuck it!"

I tossed on my thin neoprene vest and clipped my weight belt around my waist—*no point in stalling now.* Moments later, I was in the water—gun in hand, nerves and excitement buzzing through me. Once the bubbles cleared, the world revealed itself—layered in shifting shades of cyan, azure, and neon blue. The rocky spires Carlos had mentioned rose from the seafloor, each one teeming with life. Colourful reef fish darted back and forth, and a few small sharks hovered near the bottom. I reached the nearest formation and began my breathe-up routine.

I dove down, feeling the weight of my friends' expectations. Far from an expert, I had only done this a dozen or so times—but what I lacked in skill, I made up for in naivety.

I made my way down and took a moment to rest. My thoughts snagged briefly on the sharks nearby, but I tried to relax. The urge to breathe came sooner than expected, so I surfaced to calm myself before trying again.

"How is it?" Logan shouted.

"Crazy! It's like an aquarium in here!"

Kendal leaned over the edge of the boat, smiling at me.

"Have fun mister," she said with a grin. "Fetch us some dinner."

I nodded.

I gathered myself with a few calm breaths, reset my focus, and dove—this time for the bottom. Once there, I took in the scene—parrotfish and butterflyfish darted past, while shafts of yellow sunlight wrapped around the hull of the boat above. This dive felt calmer. My heart rate had slowed, my mind settled, extending my time below and sharpening my focus on the hunt.

Searching the rocks, I spotted a set of lobster antennae jutting from a ledge. Something to circle back for, later. A few distant coral trout hovered ahead, moving slowly in my direction. I churned up sand with my free hand, drawing their attention—pulling them closer. The urge to breathe grew, but I waited, hoping for an opportunity. One of the trout drifted within ten feet, then turned, giving me the perfect shot.

I squeezed the trigger. The spear cut through the water and struck true, punching cleanly through the fish's midsection. It jerked once, then went limp—dangling lifeless at the end of the shaft.

Holy shit!

I hauled the fish in, kicking for the surface, heart thumping. My grin broke the seal of my mask, letting water seep in right as I breached.

"Got one!" I shouted.

The crew turned—and to my chagrin, everyone but Kendal looked genuinely shocked.

"Holy shit! You actually shot something? What'd you get?" Carissa shouted.

"Coral trout. But I also found some lobster down there. Pass me the dive bag, Logan."

I offered a quiet thanks for its sacrifice, then handed the fish up to Kendal, who dropped it into the cooler.

"No shit, lobster for dinner? So sick!" Logan said, passing me the mesh bag.

"Wait up! This is too good to miss," Kendal said, grabbing Logan's dive gear.

She launched herself in with such excited energy, she nearly landed on top of me.

"I'm going to follow you down," she smiled.

"Stay behind me, maniac—my speargun's loaded, and I don't trust the safety."

We took a moment to breathe deeply, preparing for the dive.

"You ready?"

She nodded, and after a final breath, we slipped under.

——

I felt even calmer this time but kept an eye out for sharks now that there was fish blood in the water.

Reaching the seabed, I spotted the same lobster antennae poking out from the rock ledge. We inched forward, careful not to spook it into hiding. Spiny lobsters don't have claws like their cousins, but do come equipped with razor-tipped, bacteria-laced spines—more than enough to ruin your day. I pulled my vest sleeves down over my gloves, set down the gun, and grabbed the lobster. It flailed wildly as I yanked it from the crevice and jammed it into the bag. I turned to celebrate with Kendal, but she was already waving me over—locked on two more lobsters hiding under the next ledge. I swam over and passed her my speargun. Then, with a slow approach and a quick grab, I yanked both lobsters from the crevice by their antennae. Kendal opened the bag, and I stuffed them in as we kicked skyward.

We broke through, elated by the successful mission.

"We got three lobsters!" she announced.

"Egg salad! Well done. Kavi got a fish too!" Carissa yelled, holding up a snapper.

"Yes Kavi! You legend! Beach fire cook up tonight," I yelled back, as we swam to the boat and passed the bag up to Carlos.

"Nice bro, you got it!" Carlos said, flashing the *shocka* with his right hand.

It had only been about twenty minutes since we anchored, but we decided to quit while we were ahead—and boarded the boat, free of incident.

"See that, Fern? That's how normal people get into a boat," Logan laughed.

Fern said nothing, he simply shook his head.

"You gringos did good, I didn't think you would get anything. Fern, you good? Can I start the motor?" Carlos joked.

Fern moved to the front of the boat.

"…just to be safe."

Carlos chuckled as he stowed the anchor and fired up the motor.

———

When we pulled up to the dock, dusk had settled—and so had Dani, cigar in one hand, scotch in the other, looking like the king of the island. He helped us tie-off and unload our gear.

"How'd you guys do? Good turns out there?"

"We did well!" Carissa replied, popping the cooler open to show off our haul.

"You guys shot those things?" Dani asked, noticing the spearguns up near the bow.

"Yeah, out at that spot by the Glacier reef," Carlos said, grinning.

"We had the craziest encounter with a huge pod of dolphins!" Kendal added, excitedly.

"No shit, where?"

"Dinosaurs—like the time last Summer. That's the only time I saw them like that before," Carlos replied.

"Damn, you guys are the chosen ones, I guess," Dani said—an omniscient smile on his face.

"We're gonna cook them up on a beach fire in a bit, if you wanna join," I offered.

"Nah, you kiddies have fun. There's a spot around the corner to the eastside—just walk down that trail about five hundred feet," he said, pointing past the dock. "It'll drop you onto a beach. You can have a fire there, no one will bug ya. Stay out of the water and play safe."

He turned with a wink, pausing a few steps later.

"Oh, and hey—I'm taking a small boat out tomorrow to dive with some sharks. If anyone's interested in checking out some big fish, now's your chance. Once in a lifetime. We leave at 11. Twenty-five bucks and I'll feed ya lunch, too," he said, as he turned back toward the villas.

The mention of lunch made my stomach growl; we hadn't eaten since breakfast, and I was starving. We unloaded, thanked and tipped Carlos, and gathered our gear off the dock. The girls volunteered to collect plates, cups, and utensils from their villa, as well as track down a few bottles of wine. It was my job to prep the fish, while Kavi would gather some spices, and the other guys would search for a grill.

10

—The Good Life—

It was 7:30 when I arrived back at the villa. The sun had dropped below the horizon a good half hour earlier, but the sky was glowing pink and purple above the jungle canopy, casting a warm magenta glow across the porch. After rinsing our catch in the outdoor shower, I got to work in the kitchen—scaling and filleting the fish, then butterflying each lobster tail before tossing everything into a plastic bag.

The guys returned—lugging a rusted old grill nearly four feet long. It wasn't pretty, but it'd do the trick. Kavi, ever the diplomat, had bartered some seasoning, butter, and garlic from the restaurant in exchange for a few crumpled rupiah.

—

We arrived at the girls' villa. Kendal and Carissa were outside packing up, while Hunter was inside changing. They had rounded up plates, forks, glasses, and—most importantly—three bottles of wine, a perfect antidote to sore muscles after the long day.

Flashlights lit the narrow path as we made our way through the dark, the sound of crashing waves growing louder with every step—evidence of the rising swell.

"Man, sounds like it's building! Tomorrow's going to be sick," Kavi said.

"You're crazy, I can't even think about more surfing right now. I'm cactus," Hunter said—another one for my growing Australian lexicon.

A few minutes later, we arrived at the beach. It was was a couple hundred feet long and shaped like a horseshoe, flanked by jungle and rocks on either end. In the moonlight, the water glowed a soft turquoise, lapping gently on the shore. The bay felt more like a secluded lake than the open ocean. We funneled onto the sand, kicking off our sandals to go barefoot. The girls danced around, buzzing with excitement, while I picked a spot for the fire. Kavi arranged driftwood benches, and Logan used a flat rock to dig a shallow pit. Kendal and Hunter gathered kindling, and Fern built a teepee with the tinder, occasionally muttering about his sunburn. I shredded some cotton batting I had brought, and struck the flint.

"Who have you come as? Davy Crockett?" Carissa laughed. "Have you no lighters in North America?"

I looked up at her and smirked, continuing my efforts.

"Don't get me started," Fern, chimed in. "He won't let anyone start a fire with a lighter. It's a whole thing."

"I like the pageantry. What's the problem?" I laughed.

After a half-dozen strikes, the cotton smoked, then ignited. The fire spread to the kindling quickly, roaring in no time. Carissa popped open a bottle of red and passed the cups around.

We settled on the sand to take in the moment, finally resting our tired bodies. The beach was still and serene, with barely a breath of wind in the air. The fire's heat aggravated my burnt skin—I'd underestimated the Sumatran sun and was already paying the price.

"Damn… I'm burnt to shit." I said, examining my arm.

"You North Americans are a whiny bunch," Hunter joked.

I rolled my eyes and laughed.

This group of girls didn't hold back—ball-busting their specialty.

———

After a quiet moment with our wine, I took the grill down to the water to scrub it in the sand—while Kavi and Fern propped a couple logs on either side of the fire pit. I returned and placed the grill across, creating a bridge. I stepped away and wandered to the shore, digging my feet into the wet sand as I took a sip of wine. The full moon hung low on the horizon, casting silver-blue light across the bay—like I was standing inside a painting. The day had left me feeling deeply grateful for this place. The anxiety and desperation I'd brought from home had faded, replaced by a rare sense of peace. The trip had barely begun, yet I already felt like a different person.

———

Kendal appeared at the water's edge—hesitating for a moment before linking her arm through mine.

"It's our second date, I figure it's okay to link arms now, right?" she teased.

"Well, your two friends are here—so are three American men—so I guess this is a date."

"Yep. You know the rules," she laughed.

I took another sip of my wine—now gritty with sand. I held it up, inspecting the grains settled at the bottom.

"Typical..."

"Did you just call me typical?" she asked, un-linking arms and shoving me back playfully.

"No. Not you. Somehow, I have sand in my cup and just drank a bunch of it," I laughed, spitting discreetly.

Kendal laughed and relinked arms.

"Good! I'd have to punish you for being rude," she said, grinning.

There was a long, quiet pause.

"So… this isn't moving too fast for you then?" she asked, softly.

I started to respond, then remembered Kavi's advice—and kept it simple.

"You know, I don't think I've ever met a girl like you before."

"In a good or bad way?"

I paused, genuinely surprised by her query.

"Are you being serious?"

Another beat passed as I resisted the urge to over-explain.

"I've met guys like you," she said. "Physically, your type's everywhere in Australia. But there's something else. I'm never interested in anyone as more than a friend—it's honestly so rare. I was starting to wonder if I was asexual."

I smiled at her.

"I'm not special, Kendal. Just a regular guy," I replied. "And asexual? That'd be a real shame for me."

"I think I know what your problem is."

"My problem?"

"Yep. You've got... personality dysmorphia."

"I don't know what that means."

"It means you don't see yourself objectively."

"Fair, but who does? There are just so many people more interesting and more talented than me. I could throw a rock and hit one."

"Well, we've established that you're definitely an idiot. Maybe it's not dysmorphia—more like the Dunning-Kruger effect," she laughed.

"What's the Dunning-Kruger effect?"

"It's when someone has way too much confidence because they're too dumb to realize they're not as savvy as they think. But you're the opposite—smart enough to have confidence problems," she replied, laughing at her own deduction.

I took a sip of my gritty wine, crunching on grains of sand as I stared up at the moon.

"Hmm, that's confusing stuff. I don't know how true it is, though. Maybe you just don't know enough yet. Your data set's low-resolution."

"Maybe... or maybe I'm just damaged."

"Damaged? How so?"

"Well, the first guy I'm actually drawn to romantically isn't interested," she said, a faint pout in her voice. "Maybe I just want what I can't have."

My jaw nearly hit the floor.

Kavi had called it. But the truth was—I wasn't disinterested—I'd just been too nervous to show it.

"What you can't have?" I said, laughing.

And with that, I pulled her in for a kiss. She hesitated—just for a beat—then kissed me back, arms sliding around my sunburnt neck. She kissed with the same wild spirit she brought to everything, her energy magnetic, sparking against my skin. We got lost in the moment, only to be interrupted by clapping and hooting from the campfire.

"Yeah, Cole! Finally!" Logan yelled.

I looked over just as several camera flashes went off.

"Thank you, thank you... let's be adults though," I said, sticking up my middle finger to the group.

Kendal, still with her arms around my neck, pulled me back for another kiss as more teasing cheers rang out.

—

Back at the fire, it felt different—like we had crossed some invisible line. She stuck close, her hand tightly wrapped in mine, her eyes stealing little glances at me when she thought I wasn't looking. She was like a different person.

Is it possible for a girl this hot to be clingy?

I'd had experience with needy women before, but none of them looked like Kendal. And honestly—after years of aloofness from the fairer sex—it was refreshing to see someone so unapologetically open.

"Should we get this show on the road?" Carissa asked, noticing the fire was about ready.

"Let's do it." Kavi agreed.

We placed the fish fillets on the grill first, then added the butterflied lobster tails, shells down, filling them with melted garlic butter. After about ten minutes, everything was ready, and we loaded our plates. The group went quiet, save for the occasional murmur about how good the food was.

———

By the time we finished eating, it was close to 9 p.m., and everyone was spent. The sun, surf, and physical exertion had taken their toll. We rinsed our plates in the ocean, then packed everything up.

"What do you guys reckon we do tomorrow?" Hunter asked.

The group, now on bottle number three, exchanged looks.

"I think I'll check out some sharks with Dani. My chest needs a break after today," Logan replied.

I felt the same. Surfing after months off had left my ribs and chest tender—and I'd developed some nipple chafe, which didn't help.

"Yeah, I might join you," Fern said. "Could use a chill day."

"I'm in," Hunter added.

I thought for a second.

"I might pack a bag and explore the west point for waves—maybe find some lunch along the way," I said, stifling a yawn, mid-sentence.

"That sounds fun, I'm into that... if I'm invited?" Kendal said, half kidding.

"Yeah, you can join. Kavi and Carissa, are you in?"

"We're into that," Carissa answered with a smirk. "Right Kavi?"

Kavi nodded in approval.

"Sick, this'll be fun. I just hope I recover overnight—I'm wrecked," I said, holding back more yawns. "Anyway, hate to be this guy, but I'm cactus, as they say. Gotta pass out if I want to do it all again tomorrow."

"Egg salad slang," Hunter laughed.

"I keep hearing you say that—what the fuck does 'egg salad' mean?" Fern barked.

All three girls laughed.

"It means excellent," Carissa explained. "But it's more our little group's slang—not really an Australian thing. And no objection from me, I'm ready for bed."

I half-expected someone to rally for a late night, but everyone seemed just as ready to call it. We covered the fire with sand and cleaned up, making sure to leave the beach as we'd found it.

Heading back toward the trail, I noticed a layer of clouds had crept in, blocking the moonlight.

"Shit, I think it might rain," I said.

Just then Hunter pointed toward the far end of the beach.

"You guys! Check it out!" she yelled.

We all stopped and turned around to see the far end of the beach glowing an indigo-blue colour.

"Bio-luminescent plankton!" Kendal said excitedly, grabbing my hand and pulling me toward it.

Raindrops began falling, stirring the sand and creating electric-blue reactions, right as we reached the spot.

"Crazy—it's the rain causing it," I said, studying the effect.

About fifty feet of shoreline glowed in a surreal, alien-like light show. Each raindrop created a tiny glowing circle on the sand that dissipated a second later. With the moon now hidden behind clouds, the effect was bright enough to light up our faces. I knelt for a closer look, and as I brushed my hand through the shallow water, a trail of light followed. Next to me, Kendal was writing in the sand, watching the letters appear and vanish.

"Man, what I would give for a bag of mushrooms right now," I laughed.

"I've never done mushrooms—what's it like?" Kendal asked.

I took a moment to think.

"Tough question… it makes you feel like a tiny being in a vast universe. Like your problems don't matter. It's quite freeing."

"Oh, I like that!" she replied.

"It lets you talk to the trees and the stars and shit," Kavi laughed.

"Maybe you think the trees are talking," Carissa interrupted, "but really, you're just high, acting like a crazy person."

"Could be," I said, grinning, "But I definitely lose my humanly concerns—including worrying whether or not I'm crazy."

"Okay, well that sounds wonderful, actually. We should find some and go strand ourselves on one of those islands and have a spiritual awakening," Kendal said, excitedly.

"An awakening's a good way to describe it. And I'm down. I'll ask Dani and Carlos—those guys definitely have a plug."

I stepped back, watching as Kendal, Hunter, and Carissa danced in the rain, their movements creating a hypnotic light show. Blue circles glowed around their feet and legs as they splashed through the shallow water, laughing and spinning. The diffused moon dimly backlit them, while pulses of bioluminescence chased up their bodies and across their faces.

After a few minutes of frolicking and hysterical laughter, the rain picked up, and we decided to head back. Kendal, now soaked, grabbed my hand, her arm glistening in the pale moonlight.

"Can you lead me back home, I'm all wet," she smirked.

"Allow me," I replied. "That was so cool. I wish you could have seen it from my perspective."

She laughed and squeezed my hand.

"I'm definitely awake, again."

"I bet," I said, "I'm still knackered, but if you want to hang out at my place for a bit, you're welcome to... though I can't promise I'll be entertaining."

"Sure, I'd love to. Will there be tea?"

"Oh yeah, bag, loose leaf, ceremonial matcha... whatever you want."

She laughed, then fell in step beside me as we headed back toward the resort.

11

—Tea for Two—

We paused in front of my villa as the tropical downpour thickened around us. The palm canopy above offered some shelter, but a fine mist still clung to the air. Rain drummed on the leaves and the jungle floor in a steady, deafening rhythm.

"This is like a scene from a cheesy American rom-com," she joked.

"Exactly, that's why it's always raining in movies, it's romantic. Filmmaking 101."

"Well, it's making me cold, we should go in," she said, teeth chattering.

"You're ninety pounds—everything makes you cold. Come on, soak this in for a second, how many times is this going to happen in your life?"

I grabbed her by the belt loops of her shorts and pulled her close. Our wet skin touched as we made eye contact.

The chemistry between us was undeniable, and although we had barely kissed up to this point, there was little doubt this would escalate quickly. She moved closer, wrapping her arms around my neck to pull me in. Rainwater ran into my mouth as our lips met. I kept opening my eyes—half expecting to wake up.

As things intensified, she hopped up onto my waist, straddling me and pulling me closer. The rain had cooled the air, but heat surged between us.

"Okay, time for tea," she said, pulling her head back to smile.

She slid down and grabbed my hand, leading me up the steps to the front door. Our wet feet squeaked against the floor as we made our way across the common area toward my room. I hadn't even closed the bedroom door before she jumped back on top of me, pushing me sideways into the wall.

I pulled away and smirked at the awkwardness—expecting we'd share a quick laugh—but she was focused, grabbing the scruff of my neck and kissing me hard.

—

Her intensity took me by surprise—like she'd been holding it in forever, even though we barely knew each other. I let her take over for a moment before gently tossing her featherweight body onto the bed.

She giggled as she lay there, T-shirt and shorts clinging to her wet skin.

"You're really strong," she said, eyes scanning me.

I smiled.

"Or you're really light."

The bedside lamp cast a soft glow over her glistening skin. Her dark, wet hair spilled messily across the white sheets. Our eyes locked—an invisible connection stretching between us. She bit her lip in anticipation as I held back a little longer, taking time to simply appreciate her beauty. She was impossibly gorgeous—and suddenly, her posture wasn't so casual. The way she lay there gazing up at me—back slightly arched, arms above her head—it was desire, plain and simple. How a woman this fit and athletic could also be so soft and elegant was a paradox to me. She was the kind of girl who could make anyone, male or female, feel insecure by her mere presence—including me. I pulled off my wet shirt, still holding contact with her big brown eyes, and crawled forward to meet her. She lifted her head to pull me closer as I got within range, then grabbed me by the neck, pausing only to pull her clingy white tank top over her head and toss it aside.

"Finally." I blurted out.

"Finally, what?"

"I can die with a smile on my face," I joked, as I tugged at her tiny jean shorts, while she lifted her hips from the mattress.

Now, completely bare, with a soft smile on her lips, she urged me toward her.

"I forgot to wear underwear."

I smirked.

"Don't be hard on yourself—there's so many things to remember every day."

She laughed as I knelt over her, pausing again just before we made contact.

"Why did you stop?"

I grinned, stretching the moment.

"I'm just taking mental photos for tomorrow—or, you know, the rest of my life. Like whole rolls of photos, just give me a second."

"You perv. Get down here!"

She reached up and grabbed my neck again, pulling me toward her.

—

The next half-hour dissolved into colour and sensation. The room thickened with energy, my vision warping at the edges. Nothing remained but motion, heat, and the sense that two souls were merging. Whatever happened wasn't just sex—it felt like a closed circuit between bodies, electricity flowing back and forth. I could feel her heartbeat in sync with mine, pulsing in unison, as if we'd slipped free of the physical world, fused together somewhere beyond it. The sensation built layer by layer, until we reached something like euphoria—visceral, sacred, and disorienting—a feeling I could never fully describe. At the edge of it, I lost control of my limbs and collapsed shaking with some strange cocktail of exhaustion and ecstasy.

—

After a long pause and a few scattered laughs, she tapped me on the shoulder. I opened my eyes—somehow, we were both lying on the floor now. I had no memory of getting there.

"What just happened?" she asked, still a little dazed.

I took a breath.

"I don't know. Are you a witch or something?"

"No… are you?"

"Maybe. Can men be witches? Are you pregnant now?"

She laughed, then paused—

"I hope not. I don't feel like I was in my body for most of that. Or maybe I was completely in it?"

"What do you mean?"

"Like… an out-of-body experience. It felt like I was floating above us, watching from another dimension."

"No shit! You felt that too? Did you girls put strange Australian drugs in our wine?"

"I don't think so. I'll double check with 'Ris."

"If she did—please have her do it again tomorrow."

She laughed and attempted to stand.

"Oh boy, my legs are NOT working!" she groaned, bracing herself as she shuffled toward the bathroom.

I lay there for a moment longer, then clumsily crawled over to the mattress and collapsed. I wanted to ask her more, to make sense of whatever that was—but my eyelids were already beginning to close.

12

— Natural Medicine —

My alarm cut through my slumber like a razor blade. Dust hung in shafts of bright sunlight that raked across the room, nearly blinding me as I opened my eyes. It was 10 a.m.—and the first time I'd slept soundly since leaving home. Kendal's shorts and tank top were draped precariously on the dresser next to the bed. She was curled up beside me like a puppy, unfazed by the screeching alarm or the garish sunlight. I hit snooze and kissed the top of her head.

She stirred, glancing up at me with half-lidded eyes.

"Good morning," she mumbled, quickly burrowing back into the sheets to escape the light.

"What time is it?"

"It's just after 10."

She rolled onto her stomach and pulled the sheets back, peeking at me with her signature grin.

"I don't even want to get out of bed, let's just lay here all day."

"I'd love to, but we're in paradise, and there's too much to see and do," I said, gently patting her on the bum to get her moving. "Let's get you up so you can get your stuff together for our day trip."

She sighed, pulling the sheets back over her head and hugging me tighter in protest.

"Oh god, are you a morning person? I hate your kind."

"Well, it's 10, not sure that counts."

"It counts when you were up all night making passionate, explosive love."

"Fair enough. And sorry about the explosive part," I laughed. "But passionate love is meant to energize you, not tire you out... you've got your facts backwards."

She shook her head.

"Not true—only in the northern hemisphere. For Australians, it's the opposite. We need more sleep."

"Like toilet bowl flow direction?"

"Exactly like toilet bowl flow direction! And if I'm being honest, you're the one who's wrong here, just like your weirdo toilets."

My alarm blared again, interrupting my laughter. Her clever wit had earned her one more snooze button.

"Okay. Five more minutes. Then we're up and packing our day bags."

She sighed again.

"You're frustrating, I don't wanna move right now. I'm tired and sore."

"Yeah, I know, but there's plenty of time to be lazy together when we're not on an island in the middle of the Indian Ocean."

"Ten more minutes!"

"Nope—seven minutes!"

"Fine. And was that a Freudian slip? Did you just imply we'll be hanging out beyond this trip?"

"Semantic hiccup, more than Freudian. You're my vacation wife at most."

"Ass hole! That was absolutely Freudian, admit it," she laughed, swatting me playfully.

"Glad to hear my vacation wife knows the difference. Very smart, indeed."

—

We lay quietly until the buzzer sounded again.

I sat up and tugged the covers away. She curled into a ball to escape the chill of the air-con, her bare form catching the morning glow, somehow even more staggering in daylight—like she should be on the cover of a magazine.

"Time's up, young lady." I said, scooping her up and onto her feet.

"God, you suck. Just one quick thing first!" she turned to me and pushed me back on the bed with surprising force.

"You're not getting rid of me that easily... don't worry, this is medicinal."

I looked up at her and smiled as she climbed back on top of me.

"Well, I'm a big believer in natural medicine."

She hushed me with her hand.

—

A few wildly compelling minutes later, we collapsed in a tangle of sweat, limbs, and sheets.

"I do feel much healthier after that," I said, catching my breath and wiping beads of sweat from my brow.

She giggled, attempting to stretch her legs out.

"You okay?"

"Yeah, I'm fine," she replied, still breathing heavily, just a little leg cramp.

I stood up to fetch her shorts and tank top.

"Okay, Little Mermaid, swim yourself home so we can get this adventure going."

She sighed for a third time and rolled her eyes. My urgency was clearly irritating to her—something I'd been accused of by others. After a bit more prodding, she finally got to her feet, tugged on her tight jean shorts and tank top, kissed me, and headed for the door.

"I can't believe you're still kicking me out after that performance," she pouted. "Tomorrow we're sleeping in and lying in bed all day," she said, with authority, closing the door behind her.

"Yeah, we'll see about that."

I smiled to myself, replaying the night. It all felt like a euphoric blur—some parts dreamlike, others scattered like snapshots. I took a deep breath, stretched, and jumped into the shower.

—

When I emerged, laughter echoed from the kitchen. To my surprise, I found Carissa, Kendal, and Kavi seated around the table, drinking coffee.

"Good morning, babe," Kavi said, with a smirk.

"I've been overruled, have I?" I laughed.

"Yes—decidedly, we're in no rush. Have a seat," Kendal replied, patting the chair beside her.

I quickly concluded that Carissa had also stayed over. Odd since she and Kavi didn't seem interested last night. Then again, Kavi's hard to predict where women are concerned.

"Did you crash here too, Carissa?" I asked, hoping to stir the pot.

"Ha! You think I'm that kind of girl, do you? I'm offended!" she replied, throwing an accusatory look at Kendal.

Kendal shoved her.

"Hey! Don't be rude. I *never* do this."

"I'm kidding, I did," Carissa grinned. "I drugged the poor bloke and had my way with him... luckily he didn't pee himself—heard that can happen."

I chuckled, shaking my head. I still hadn't quite adjusted to Carissa's brash tongue.

"I didn't pee myself, but I quietly got up in the middle of the night and peed all over you—so now who's funny?" Kavi replied.

"Okay, enough pee jokes!" Kendal said, rolling her eyes. "'Ris, let's head back and get ready. Cole's *dying* to get going."

She shot me a playful look.

"I wanted to lie in bed all day, but here we are."

"Fine, I'm not so sure I like being kicked out of here, but I concede—just this once."

The girls finished their coffees and exited the villa. Once the door shut behind them, Kavi peeked through the blinds to make sure they were gone.

"Dude! What a *crazy* night!"

I looked back at him with a smirk, very much on the same page.

"Yeah, that was pretty much the best day and night of my life."

"Did you score?" he asked.

I laughed, recalling the events again.

"As if I even had a choice. I barely got a word in before I was boosted and sold for parts."

"Damn, she's in deep, huh?"

I shrugged.

"You mad?"

"Nah, it's too late now, I'm just fired up for you. We were all betting whether or not you'd be leaving this trip together."

"I can't believe how fast it's all happening. I'm just going with it. I'll go to Australia, or she can follow me home, move in, take half my shit, rename my dog—I don't care," I laughed. "What about you? Has your mysterious indifference charmed Carissa? Seems like she's pretty into you, too."

"I guess so, but I don't think she takes me seriously. Listen to this—I was super beat and just wanted to sleep, so I walked her home, we kissed, and said goodnight," he laughed. "I came back here, brushed my teeth… and she was standing in my room… nothing on but a smile and a tan."

"Get the fuck outta here!"

"No lie. That chick is confident. I'm completely out of testosterone, though. She kept waking me up for more. Friggin' Australian chicks."

I shook my head, amazed at the turn of events.

"Let's pack up and go. I'm itching to get back in the water—spearfishing is addictive."

We grabbed our bags, slung on our gear, and headed for the girls' villa where they joined us. I checked my wrist—it was already 11:30, and the heat and humidity, plus my alcohol-induced dehydration were hitting hard.

"Any sign of Hunter and the guys?" Kavi asked as we walked.

"I didn't see her this morning, but her bag is gone, so probably off on the boat with the lads." Carissa replied.

"True. I haven't heard any arguing yet today, so you're probably right."

13

—DiCaprio's Beach—

We continued down the path toward the boat dock. The plan was to head southwest, past the restaurant and along the coast, eventually reaching some deserted beaches and decent waves—far from any sign of humanity. The sound of waves pounding the reef grew louder as we passed the dock. The swell had picked up since last night—water now exploding into the air just outside the bay.

We stopped to watch.

"Damn, I guess it gets a little sketchy boating out in big swell."

"Yep. But looks like we're going to score a bunch this week," Carissa replied.

"Please, no more scoring," Kavi muttered, with a smirk.

___

We continued along the coast, navigating through shifting terrain—giant rocks, coral-lined tide pools, and the odd fishing and surf resort. The farther we hiked, the rougher it got, forcing us to forge our own trail through the jungle underbrush and occasionally scaling rocky outcrops.

At one point, Carissa spotted a pod of humpback whales a kilometer out, swimming in the same direction we were headed. We stumbled along, unable to look away as they breached and slapped the surface with their tails, playful and unhurried, until they finally slipped beyond the horizon.

—

Some beach stretches were blindingly white, others a volcanic brown that scorched our feet. The water was a surreal blend of sapphire and pale jade, the kind of blue that looked edited—like pictures I'd seen of the Maldives: luminous sand and neon sea.

—

After ninety minutes, we reached a beach that looked perfect for setting up a base camp. A thick row of coconut palms gave way to lush jungle rising up a small hill. Offshore, a right-hand point break peeled across the reef, shallow but potentially surfable as the tide rose. A belt of outer reef tamed the waves, keeping the inner bay calm and ideal for snorkeling while the tide was low. We dropped our gear in the shade of the palms and spread a blanket. Carissa and Kavi took off for a swim, while Kendal and I searched for the best coconut tree to climb. My friend Lester from Costa Rica, once spent the day laughing at me as he tried to teach me how to scale a palm using a figure-eight rope loop around the feet. He zipped up the trunk with casual grace; I, on the other hand, never quite figured it out—and mostly felt like the rope was strangling my ankles as I flailed clumsily.

"How's that one?" Kendal asked, pointing at a tree crowded with green coconuts.

I eyed it—about twenty-five feet tall and narrow. Not ideal, but doable. I tied the machete to my shorts, wrapped my feet and took a deep breath. Hopefully, my brain had banked enough from last time—motor imagery and all—to keep me from making an ass of myself.

"Up you go, Cap'n Jack Sparrow. And please be careful!"

I laughed.

"If I'm Jack Sparrow does that make you Davy Jones?"

"I think so—I'm slowly hunting you down because you stole my heart."

"Impressive inference," I said. "And the heart is on lease, I'll return it, good as new."

Kendal pouted at the suggestion.

Climbing up was easier than I remembered, and although I was dripping in slippery sweat, I was in position in no time. I unsheathed the machete and looked down.

"Can you move back a little?" I called.

She stepped away, and I hacked at a few vines, sending dozens of coconuts to the ground. I slid down the trunk carefully, until I was back on the sand.

—

Kavi and Carissa returned from their swim, holding a couple of ripe mangoes from a nearby tree. It was around 1 p.m., and we were all hungry after the hike. We sat down on the blanket.

"Man, I've had dreams that don't even compare to this," I said, taking in the view.

"That's a lot of coconuts! Think we'll drink all those?" Carissa asked, eyeing the pile.

She stood up and got to work opening a couple with the machete and passing them around. I rinsed my dive knife and sliced into a mango, so ripe it nearly collapsed in my hand.

I took a bite.

"Dang, is this how mango is supposed to taste?"

"What do you mean?" Kendal laughed.

"Whatever we have in North America, is not the same as whatever this is."

"Seriously," Kavi added. "I'm never buying a five-dollar mango again."

Carissa shook her head. "Five bucks for a mango? That's robbery. I don't believe you."

I nodded.

"Believe it. And hard as a rock."

———

After our snack, Kavi and I suited up for a dive. Unless we wanted coconuts and mangos for lunch, it was on us to bring in some fish. I gave him a salute before slipping on my fins and pushing off toward a cluster of coral heads two hundred feet out—classic fish territory.

"I'll start here," Kavi said, pointing to the closest one.

"I'm with you."

"Good luck. If you see anything sketchy, holler."

———

The coral here was much more vibrant than anywhere else I'd seen—a panoply of life and colour in every direction. The ecosystem teemed with fish and anemones—healthy, wild, untouched.

I did my breathe-up and then dropped about fifteen feet. There were so many fish, it would've taken more talent to miss a shot than to land one. A bright red-and-yellow trout came within range. I checked to make sure Kavi was safely behind me, then took my shot. Bullseye. The fish bolted downward, but I hauled the line steadily, surfacing with the catch before it got caught on the rocks below.

Thirty feet down, Kavi hovered mid-water, lining up a shot. That's when I saw it—a medium sized reef shark, gliding in fast from behind him. He took his shot, nailing the fish dead-on—the shark veered toward him, drawn to the sudden struggle. I flailed to get his attention, then dove hard, angling my gun between the shark and my friend.

As I closed the distance, Kavi finally noticed me barreling toward him and turned—just in time to catch the shark in his periphery. He spun around, startled but quick, locking eyes with the threat. It wasn't exactly funny, but the whole scene had that absurd rookie energy—two amateurs with fish on their lines, now fending off a six-foot predator.

He kicked hard for the surface, fish in hand, probably desperate for air. We both knew that one shark probably meant five others nearby. Time to bail.

"That was insane! We should probably get out of here... like now."

Kavi removed the fish from his spear and reloaded the gun as a precaution. We swam backward to keep an eye on the shark, which slowed our progress. I adjusted my mask and dipped below—two more sharks had joined.

The smallest one darted closest, flicking side to side in short, twitchy bursts. Giving up a fish wasn't a good option—it'd serve more as an amuse-bouche than a real distraction. Instead, we held them above the surface, hoping the blood scent would fade. But the sharks stayed in pursuit.

The smallest one surged toward me like a silver torpedo. I jerked backward, trying to keep my distance. It veered off momentarily—but circled back, tailing us closely.

What if one of us got bitten? We were miles from help. No way to treat a wound.

Kavi, visibly rattled, gave me a nervous look.

We were about a hundred feet from shore, but the sharks grew bolder as the water shallowed. The smallest took another run at us, cutting in dangerously close. Kavi lunged forward, spear first, driving it back.

"Fuck! This is sketchy!" I yelled, glancing toward shore where the girls stood frozen, watching.

I dipped my face below the surface—two sharks were closing in—only a few feet away now. Kavi and I kicked, shouted, and jabbed our spears—barely holding them off. I considered prodding one in the snout, but worried it'd escalate things now that they were in a frenzy. I could hear Kendal and Carissa's panicked voices, as they watched us helplessly from the beach. Each time I checked below, the sharks were closer, chasing with purpose, unwilling to give up a free meal.

"Shit, what's the play? Do we spear 'em?" Kavi asked, nervously.

I raised my head to answer—

Then something tore into my heel.

"Shit!" I shouted, twisting around.

Did I just get bitten?

"What? What happened?!"

I reached down, heart pounding, half-expecting to feel teeth still clamped around my foot. Instead, my fingers struck something hard.

"I hit a rock!" I yelled. "It's shallow here!"

We kicked a few final strokes until our feet touched bottom. Finally free of the sharks, we waded backward, fish and limbs miraculously intact.

"Holy fuck!" Kavi shouted, collapsing on the sand.

"You guys are bloody idiots!" Kendal yelled. "Don't ever do that again!"

"That was so gnarly!" Kavi hollered at the sky, breaking into a shaky laugh.

"How did you know what was happening?" I asked the girls.

"We could see dorsal fins and tails slapping all around you idiots!" Carissa said, visibly shaken.

"We thought for sure you'd been bitten," Kendal added.

"Sorry to stress you out. That escalated quickly!" I said, walking toward her with my arms wide for a hug.

"Brick killed a guy," Kavi laughed.

"Look at what we got you though!"

I held up the large, colourful fish while we hugged.

Kendal shook her head in mock disappointment, then broke into a slight laugh.

"You're an ass. I'm going vegan after that."

I animated the fish's mouth like a puppet, mouthing "Sorry Kendal." from behind.

She leaned back and pushed me away.

"You're a jack ass. Never letting you touch me again!"

I checked my left foot—a little bloody and swollen.

"Pretty sure I brushed against some fire coral. Anyway, who's up for surfing?" I joked.

"Forgive me if I don't feel too sympathetic," she muttered, inspecting the small cut on my heel.

I waved it off—small price to pay for not getting eaten.

—

We regrouped and got to work lighting a fire for lunch. The girls had dug a pit, stacked kindling, and even had a pineapple cut and ready.

"Damn, you girls were proactive. I appreciate your confidence in us bringing back some fish."

"We almost didn't. But pity makes a great motivator," Carissa teased.

"You're such a smartass!" Kavi said, wrapping his arm around her.

Without a grill, we improvised—rigging up driftwood spits for the fish. Kavi found some thin, bullrush-like reeds, sharpened the ends, and skewered chunks of pineapple. Carissa sourced Y-shaped branches to prop the spits over the fire. I was genuinely impressed by their teamwork.

"Damn, with skills like that, you really should be able to find gainful employment, Kavi," I joked.

"Employment? You know I can't be controlled like that."

"Pretty sure 'pineapple skewering man-child' is trending in the freelance market," Carissa teased.

"Hey, everyone's building their own brand these days. Watch for the book deal next year, like and subscribe to the channel," he laughed, easily batting back her shit test.

—

We relaxed to the sound of the crackling fire.

"So can you tell me why you're rarely attracted or available to guys, Kendal?" I asked, intentionally prodding, mostly for my own amusement.

"Yeah, good luck extracting that info," Carissa laughed.

Kendal rolled her eyes, then shrugged.

"I don't know… I'm just really specific about who I'm into. It's more about how they carry themselves. Guys who push too hard make me uncomfortable."

I thought back on how things had unfolded with her—

"So, not about looks, it's more about level of restraint?" I asked, teasingly.

"Sort of. I definitely have a type, but lots of Australian men look similar. They're hot, but just so… thirsty. It's gross."

"So basically," Kavi said, grinning, "Cole wins by being the least annoying option. Impressive."

The girls laughed.

I shook my head, trying not to smile.

"Hey, I'll take 'quietly tolerable' as a win," I said, shrugging.

"She gets hit on constantly... anyone would get annoyed if they got harassed that much," Carissa added.

"Yeah, I got that same thing," Kavi said, deadpan.

Carissa smirked.

"Kendal's adorable, but so naive," Carrisa went on. "For a long time, she genuinely thought every man was just the nicest person ever."

"Hey, take it easy," Kendal said with a crooked smile. "I can be a little naïve–but you get hit on just as much as I do."

131

Carissa raised an eyebrow.

"I just want to be in a love story—not involved in the sleazy hookup culture," Kendal finished.

Turns out what she saw was ease—I'd call it paralysis—but hey—whatever works.

"I didn't mean to put you on the spot, just curious," I said, shifting the conversation to something lighter.

"Now you know," she replied, "and don't worry, we'll psychoanalyze you soon enough."

"Oh good, I love a deep evaluation."

Kavi, still smirking while tending to the fish, caught my eye. I knew exactly what he was thinking.

I smirked back, scratching my nose with my middle finger as he chuckled.

—

The gentle crackle of the fire released a savory, citrusy aroma into the air—and within twenty minutes, nothing was left but fish bones and smiles.

"I don't think I'm going to surf here."

I looked over at Kavi, who shook his head in agreement.

"I might jump in for a quick snorkel to see if any sharks are still around. I want to surf," Carissa replied.

"I'll join you," Kendal said.

I was surprised by Kendal's willingness, considering how shaken she'd been by the earlier encounter.

"If you're going out, take a speargun—both of you," Kavi said, suddenly serious as he handed them over. "Okay?" he added, clipping into a Tony Montana accent as he pointed to each of them.

"Si, papi," Carissa replied in her best Spanish accent.

—

The girls suited up and we walked down toward the water.

"I'm sure the sharks are gone by now," I said. "but still... be careful. We don't need any dramas."

Kendal looked me straight in the eyes.

"Of course. If I see a shark, I shall shoot him and bring him back for dinner."

"Smartass."

With a smile, she pulled on her mask and pushed off, into the bay. I watched from the shade as they paddled, diving under occasionally.

—

Twenty minutes later, they returned to the shallows, walking up the last stretch of sand. Suddenly, Kendal shrieked—a sharp, startled scream—leapt straight into the air, and after a few frantic steps, collapsed backward into a few inches of water.

"Whoa, what was that?" Kavi asked, leaping to his feet.

I jumped up and ran toward her.

"Stingray?" I shouted, closing the distance.

"Yes! Bloody stingray! Fucker!" she cried out, whimpering. "Oh my god, he got me bad!"

I knelt, examining her foot. Her big toe was bleeding heavily, like she'd stepped on a razor blade.

"Oh my god, what is with this bay? Everything is trying to kill us," she groaned.

"We need to get your foot into hot water," I said, glancing at the smoldering fire pit. "It'll help neutralize the sting."

"I've heard that—does it actually work? " she asked, wincing.

"Clearly you've never surfed in Nicaragua," I replied, slipping into mock authority

"Well, yelling 'fucker!' at full volume seems to help," she muttered through clenched teeth.

"Kavi, can you grab a coconut shell? We'll heat some water in it."

"On it!" Kavi called, sprinting to grab the biggest shell he could find.

He split it in half, filled one side with seawater and set it over the hot coals.

I carried Kendal to the blanket while Carissa tried to calm her.

"How bad is the pain, one to ten?" I asked.

"Eight—or nine!" she panted, like she was in labor.

"Hang in there. Hot water's coming soon."

Carissa stroked her hair while I checked on the coconut shell, which was miraculously holding up.

"I think the water keeps the fire from burning through," Kavi said.

I nodded and dropped a few hot rocks into the shell to speed things up. As they hissed in the water, a thin black film spread across the surface. That sparked a memory—activated charcoal. I'd used it once to treat a bee sting. I grabbed a couple charred chunks from the fire and dropped them into the shell, stirring gently until the water darkened into a murky black solution.

When the water was hot enough, I brought the shell over and gently set Kendal's foot inside.

"Ow—that's really hot!"

"I know. But try to hold it. It'll help."

She clenched her jaw, but after a few seconds, her breathing started to slow.

"It actually feels a little better."

We'd done what we could—but we still had miles to cover, and she could barely stand.

14

— Return to Sender —

Kendal winced as she stood. Four surfboards, four packs, two spearguns—and a long, unforgiving coastline between us and home.

This'll be fun, I thought.

I considered piggybacking her, while Kavi and Carissa each took a bag and two boards. But with Kendal clinging to me, I couldn't wear my own pack, which left us with an extra bag and the two spearguns to carry. And the coastline wasn't just long—it was jagged, uneven, broken up by rocky ledges and soft sand, none of it friendly to a crew hauling gear.

It was about 4 p.m., and we'd need several hours to reach the resort—leaving soon would be essential if we wanted to beat sundown.

"How's the foot?" I asked.

"It feels a little better, but it's still bloody painful. The pains pulsing up my calf."

I brought over a bowl of unheated water to rinse the wound. Her toe was swollen and slightly blue—painful to the touch. Kavi arrived with a freshly heated coconut shell, and we swapped her foot into the new solution.

I motioned for Kavi to join me for a quick sidebar.

"I don't like the look of that toe. It's blue and swollen. We need to get back."

"Okay, I'm ready any time."

"I was thinking I'd piggyback her, you guys take a couple boards, and I'll manage with the spears… just gotta figure out my pack."

"We'll sort it out," he said, reassuringly.

———

Carissa buried the fire and tidied up camp while Kavi and I organized the gear. Kendal stood and tried to walk, but as expected, she couldn't put much weight on her foot. Carissa slipped her pack on and helped hoist Kendal onto my back.

"You barely weigh a thing," I laughed, though I knew that assessment was fleeting.

I looked up at the sun. It had to be pushing 34°C, and with the breeze gone, the beach felt like a sauna. Add in our shared body heat, and things were only going to get worse. I looked to Kavi—he had a board under each arm and wore both backpacks, one on his back, one on his chest.

"You're an absolute legend, homie," I said, beads of sweat already forming on his forehead.

Kavi winked.

"Thank you for carrying me," Kendal said softly. "And thank you guys for being so nice."

Carissa squeezed her shoulder in silent support.

"We should all drink a couple coconuts before we get going, no?" Kavi offered.

"Yeah, good idea."

Carissa grabbed the machete from my pack and skillfully cut the last eight coconuts open. We each drank two of them as fast as we could.

"Alright, shall we?" Carissa said cheerfully, passing me and Kendal the two spearguns.

"Nothing to it!" I said. "You can hold onto the machete."

She grinned.

"I am the captain now!" she said in her best pirate voice, and leaned in to kiss Kendal on the cheek.

"You'll be fine, love. Think back to Cooly, you're tough as nails!"

Kendal nodded.

—

We began the long trek back to the resort.

"Did something crazy happen in Coolangatta?" I asked.

"I got jellied bad there one day. Had to limp all the way back to the car. It was brutal."

"Ah shit, what kind was it?"

"Bluebottle. It was a horrible experience. I had welts on my skin for weeks."

"Man—you are tough."

She laughed as we moved swiftly toward home—

As expected, she went from light as a feather to heavy as a bag of concrete in no time. I pushed hard, trying to cover as much distance as possible while my energy was still high.

—

Crossing the third beach, I glanced at her foot. It was badly swollen, with purplish bruising creeping around her toe and along the top.

"Are you worried about the colour?" she asked quietly.

"I wouldn't say worried, but I've seen better," I replied.

"It's tingling quite a lot."

Her foot looked like a severely sprained ankle—swollen and pale. I wondered if this was typical for a bad sting.

"I have a very obvious question to ask—you're not allergic to venom, right?"

"Well, not that I know of, but I'm beginning to wonder."

"You'll be okay. If I have to sprint with you on my back, I will. Just tell me if it gets any worse."

—

After an hour of walking through the sweltering heat, our bodies were practically fused together with a layer of sticky, salty sweat. Despite keeping to the shade as much as possible, there were long stretches of blazing, unavoidable direct sun. Kendal dabbed my face with a towel as beads of sweat dripped from my forehead. Kavi, noticing my condition, walked up beside us.

"Dude, you don't look good. I can take over for a bit if you need a break."

"I think I'm okay. I don't really want to touch those sweat-drenched bags you've been wearing, either. Maybe we just take five?"

"Good call," Carissa suggested. "We should cool off in the water."

"You want a dip, kiddo?" I asked Kendal, who was looking rather morose.

"Please, yes."

Still clinging to me like a baby koala, she stayed latched on as we ditched our gear and waded into the sea, carefully shuffling my feet to avoid any more stingray encounters. Eventually, she separated and swam around, relishing her moment of freedom.

I paused, treading water and mentally preparing for the final stretch.

"All right, let's keep moving," I said after a few minutes. Prolonging our break wouldn't help our cause.

"I'm fuckin' psyched! Let's do it," Kavi said, boosting morale.

Kendal swam back and resumed her spot on my back as we set off again. I looked down at her freshly rinsed foot. It didn't seem any worse, but it wasn't better either. I handed her one of the spearguns, then wrapped my free hand gently around the arch of her foot, offering a reassuring smile.

"Does that feel better?" I asked, hoping the pressure would give some relief.

"It actually does. Keep doing that."

She was surprisingly composed, despite the distressing scenario.

—

We passed more jungle and a few more small sections of beach, pushing forward with whatever vigor remained.

"I don't recognize any of these beaches," I said, quietly.

"They all sort of blend together," she replied.

The farther we walked, the softer the sand became, sinking beneath each step and draining what little strength

THOMAS J DERRY

I had left. The added weight of carrying someone on my back was starting to break me down. A few times, I nearly lost my footing, and Kendal slid down my sweaty back, forcing us to reset and stabilize before moving on. I laughed it off each time, but my patience and energy were thinning by the minute.

—

Around the two-hour mark, my vision began to blur. The sun was lower in the sky, but still unrelenting, wringing out the last of my hydration. I pushed forward with whatever auxiliary power I had, praying we'd find signs of the finish line before I lost control of my motor skills.

15

—The Longest Beach—

Kavi pointed ahead at the first sign of civilization we'd seen in hours. Running on autopilot, I barely registered the sight of the small resort we had passed earlier—it felt strangely unfamiliar.

"We made it," Kendal whispered, kissing my sweaty cheek.

"That was nothing. I could keep going," I joked, though I was edging dangerously close to collapse.

"Should we stop to see if they have a doctor or first aid?" Carissa asked.

"It's up to Kendal. What do you think?" I asked, trying to catch my breath. "I'll go ask them for help if you want,"

"I'm okay to keep going if you are—I don't think it'll make a difference," she replied.

Everyone agreed, and we trudged on toward our resort.

—

After a grueling final stretch—and just as I began to see stars—we reached the entrance, where Maya sat at the check-in desk

"Maya! Can you help us? She got stung by a ray," Carissa called out urgently.

She rushed over to examine Kendal's foot.

"Wait here," she said, scurrying off.

I carefully crouched down to let Kendal off my back onto the lobby couch. As I stood back up, a wave of dizziness hit—I sank down again, feeling faint. Noticing my instability, Carissa quickly ran for a pitcher of ice water.

Moments later, Maya returned with an older Indonesian man with white hair and a first aid kit. Introducing himself as Dr. Amat, he assessed Kendal's eyes, cleaned the wound, and injected a local anesthetic.

"I make a couple stitches, close this. You can carry her my office?" he asked in broken English.

"Sure," I replied, downing another mouthful of water, which had already steadied me considerably.

———

I laid Kendal down on a medical cot. Dr. Amat stitched her toe without fuss, calm and practiced. He handed Kendal a couple of painkillers, then turned his attention back to the hot water treatment.

"We put it the hot water for the venom. Should help the swelling," he said, snipping the final thread.

On cue, a kitchen staff member arrived with a large pot of hot water.

"Please put the foot," he instructed.

Kendal winced at the hot water, while Dr. Amat inserted several acupuncture needles into her palms above her thumbs. He poured the steaming water over her calf and thigh, pausing to massage the muscles.

"The venom, he gets trap the muscle, we need to loose up you muscle," he explained.

"Oh wow, the acupuncture is actually helping a lot," Kendal said, even managing a smile.

After about a minute, he instructed her to remove her foot.

"Okay, that's it, you can go now, drink lot of water," he instructed, applying a small bandage around the cut.

We thanked him for his help and walked Kendal back toward her villa.

—

We entered her cool room. I collapsed onto her bed, finally surrendering to the exhaustion and dehydration.

"Oh man, I'm cactus," she said.

"I'm puffed as well."

She smirked—amused by my continued uptake of her language.

"Thank you so much for everything today. You were a hero," she said, her eyes warm with gratitude.

I looked over and smiled.

"I just did what any living legend would do," I shrugged.

"And humble too," she said, smiling.

"Okay—you should rest. I'll grab some coconuts and send Carissa to keep you company."

She smiled back and closed her eyes.

"Please don't leave me alone for too long."

"Of course."

I chuckled, as I walked out—realizing this surf trip had produced a full-blown relationship in 24 hours—the very thing Kavi had warned about.

I stepped out into the fading light, the heat still clinging to the air as I made my way toward the restaurant. As I turned onto the path, I spotted Hunter walking toward me, sunburned and noticeably tipsy.

"Hey, how'd you guys go?"

"Great at first. Then not so good. Kendal caught a stingray on the toe."

"Oh shit, is she okay?"

"She's been better, but I think she'll be alright by tomorrow. She's just trying to nap in her room. Do you mind keeping her company? I'm off to grab some coconuts."

"Yeah of course, you two are so cute!"

"Oh boy..." I muttered, feeling a little awkward as I walked on.

—

Back at my villa, I found Fern and Logan, also burnt to a crisp.

"Lads! How'd it go?"

"Burnt to shit! Logan forgot the sunscreen."

"For the last time, I'm not your dada. Bring your own shit!"

I sighed—

"Okay. Good chat. I'll catch up with you dudes later, I'm after some coconuts," I said, moving beyond earshot of their bickering.

—

I found a few shorter trees by the beach and quickly chopped down three nuts. On the way back, I ran into Carlos.

"Yo, Cole!"

"Carlos. How's it goin', brother?"

"It's good, everything Pura Vida. Just got back from a sick shark dive, you missed it!"

"Oh man, I had an accidental shark dive of my own today while fishing. Super scary."

"No way, you shore dive?"

"Yeah, it was intense, but we made it out okay."

"Nice! Got to be super careful, better to have a boat," he replied, sticking his fist out for a bump.

"You guys feel like checking it out Glaciers tomorrow afternoon? Swell and tide is perfect."

I paused and thought about it.

"Maybe. Kendal got stung by a ray today, so she'll be on ice for a bit, but I'll see if the guys are down."

"Oh no way, she's okay?"

"Yeah, all good, just needs a little rest."

"Let's do a boys' day then," he replied, handing me his card.

"I'll ask the guys and hit you."

"Hopefully see you tomorrow, brother. Yew!" he said, excitedly.

—

I made my way to Kendal's villa, where Carissa and Hunter were chatting and laughing.

"Is she awake?" I asked.

"Should be, she was a few minutes ago," Carissa replied.

I entered her room and found her half-asleep. Insisting she have a drink before drifting off completely, I handed her the coconut.

"Up you get, little one. How do you feel now?" I asked, helping her up.

"Better, the pain killers have kicked in."

"Drink this coconut and let me check you out."

She pulled her foot from under the blanket to show me. It was in better shape than before—the swelling reduced.

"Lookin' much better."

"Thank god, that was horrible. Thank you for making me feel safe," she murmured, a bit drowsy now.

"What do you think about tomorrow? I figure you need a day of nothing, yeah?" I asked.

"I think I might want to just hang around and relax. Will you stay with me?"

I laughed, partly knowing it was coming.

"Well, Carlos asked me if I wanted to check out Glaciers tomorrow afternoon, so why don't I hang out 'til then, and I'll surf for the afternoon, then come back and hang after."

"Okay, yeah. You should have a boys' day."

"I'll ask the gents if they're into it. Be back in a bit. Try to get some sleep."

Out in the common area, Carissa and Hunter were chatting.

"Her foot's looking a lot better, I'm headed to discuss options for tomorrow with the lads, we're thinking about a boys' trip to Glaciers, since Kendal's out of commission."

"Sounds perfect," Carissa said. "We're probably just going to stay here with her, take it easy, read, yoga… girl stuff."

"Let's grab dinner later," I suggested, heading out the door.

—

Back at the villa, the guys were relaxing, drinking beer, and listening to some local music.

"How's Kendal? Any better?" Kavi asked.

"She's okay," I said, "Did you give these two the rundown yet?"

"He did, you must be wiped out," Logan laughed.

"A little sore, I'll live."

Logan passed me a beer.

"I've never seen anyone sweat so much," Kavi said, smirking. "Careful with that beer."

"Yeah, you got played. I'm glad I wasn't there for that," Fern chirped.

"Yeah thanks. How was the shark dive? You guys see anything sick?"

"Man, there are monster sharks here," Logan replied, pulling out his GoPro. "We saw some Bulls and Tigers big enough to bite you in half—no joke."

He showed me the footage. Even through the tiny camera, the sharks looked massive—clearly a different category than the ones we'd seen at the dock.

"So, you guys didn't go in and snorkel?" I asked.

"We did at the start when there was a bunch of Black Tips, but Dani tripped out and made us get back in the boat when those things showed up," Logan explained.

"Damn, that's really unsettling. Glad I asked."

"Dani said that in all the years he's surfed, fished, and lived here, he's never seen them anywhere near the breaks, though. He says they stick around the calm reef areas or just stay where it's super deep."

"Right, because he'd never lie to make us feel more comfortable," Kavi joked.

"To be fair, Dani's not much for sugar-coating. The dude's told us to stay out of the water three times since we got here," I laughed.

"Right? Best guide ever!" Fern added, grinning.

"I ran into Carlos on the beach. He wants to check out Glaciers tomorrow afternoon around two. Says it's going to be firing. The girls are hanging back, so we could do a boys' trip if you're in."

"Definitely," Kavi said, leaning forward. "I'm burnt out from today, I need a real strike mission to recharge."

Fern and Logan both agreed.

I pulled out Carlos' card and sent him a message to confirm.

"All right, we're on. Plan for 1:00 at the dock."

———

With my beer in hand, I took a walk to the bay to clear my head. The day's dramas had worn me down, and I needed a moment to decompress. As I neared the main building, I ran into Maya, sweeping up the concierge area.

"Hey, how's your friend?"

"She's a little better... she'll be good by tomorrow."

"Good! Where were you guys surfing when it happened?"

"We walked about an hour and a half southwest past the resorts to an isolated beach," I said, pointing in the direction of the incident. "The ray was in like six inches of water."

"Yeah, you have to shuffle your feet around here. So many things are hiding in the sand."

"No kidding—hard-won lesson for Kendal."

"If you guys don't have plans, there's a full moon party happening tonight on Pulau Ular just down the coast. There's going to be a giant bonfire."

"Pulau Ular?" I asked.

"It just means Snake Island... but don't worry, there's no snakes."

I laughed at the irony of a snake-less island called Snake Island.

"That all sounds good to me—not sure Kendal is going to be up for it. How would we get there?"

"We're all heading over at 10:30. Big boat; we can make room."

"Sweet. I'll ask the gang, and hopefully, we'll see you there. Thanks for the invite, Maya. And thanks again for earlier—Dr. Amat is a king."

"You're welcome, hopefully see you tonight!"

I continued on my way.

Despite the exhaustion, I was excited about the prospect of another adventure. I paused at the end of the wooden dock, gazing out at the bay. The water was perfectly calm—a liquid mirror reflecting an incredible palette of colours in the sky: deep purples, pinks, oranges, and teals all blending at the edges. The sunsets here seemed otherworldly, a daily reminder of this place's magic. I took a deep breath, stretched my sore muscles and enjoyed a rare moment of quiet.

—

After a few minutes, I turned back toward the resort, feeling recharged. I half expected the quiet to follow me back—but the villa was a madhouse. All three were up and drinking in the common area, dancing and singing loudly to some terrible K-Pop.

"It's alive!" I said, smirking.

"Yeah, I feel much better. Thanks for all your care— you're the best nurse ever."

"Nothing wrong with male nurses, don't be sexist," I laughed. "Anyway, I ran into Maya, and she suggested we join her and the staff for some full moon shindig they've got going tonight."

The girls perked up.

"Full moon party, huh? Where?" Carissa asked.

"We all hop in a boat at 10:30 at the dock, and we shoot over to some island about fifteen minutes down the coast. She says there'll be hundreds of people and a huge bonfire."

Hunter stood up in excitement. "No way! Let's go, obviously! Kendal, think you're up for it?"

"I think so," Kendal replied, "I just don't want to mess up my foot again."

"We could wrap it in gauze, then duct tape it— practical and stylish," I said, grinning.

"I love it when the fashion-to-function ratio hits exactly even, that's peak sexy," she teased.

"I'm going to get the guys on board. Back in a bit."

I arrived to find Fern and Logan passed out on the couch, and Kavi sprawled on his bed.

"Shit, I leave you all alone for an hour and you defect, huh?" I said. "Wake up, Dingers! The party gods have blessed us."

"You score some blow?" Fern asked.

"Some blow? No—I found us a party. A full moon party on Snake Island, actually."

"Snake Island? Where's that?" Kavi asked.

"I don't quite know, Maya said we hop in a boat with the staff at 10:30. It's about fifteen minutes by water."

Logan perked up. "Maya's goin'? I'm in."

"Me too! That power blackout was all I needed," Fern added.

"Power blackout?"

"Yeah, power blackout. How don't you know that?"

"Wait, why are you blackout-level drunk, this early?" I asked.

"Because last time I checked—we're on vacation."

"That's good enough for me," I smirked.

"Speaking of blow, did you figure out where we can get some? Can I ask Maya or Dani?" he asked.

Fern was many things, but discreet was not one of them, and while I was confused about needing cocaine in a place as beautiful as this, I was simultaneously impressed by his newfound discretion.

"Do whatever you want, man. It probably won't be hard to find at this party. Anyway, let's get our stuff together and grab some dinner. We'll need full stomachs for tonight."

—

We arrived the dining area, where we found our three friends, already tipsy and loud, drawing glances from nearby tables.

"Look Kendal, there's your husband!" Hunter said.

"Shut up Hunter," Kendal replied, rolling her eyes.

"You all look ready to party. What have you been drinking? And can I have some?" Kavi asked.

"We had some Mezcal, but it's all gone," Carissa replied.

"Figures." he muttered.

I took a seat next to Kendal, her foot now wrapped in tape.

"Your foot seems better. Didn't think you'd be up for joining after all the drama."

"Yeah, maybe it's the alcohol, but it does feel better."

"Ah, the classic painkiller-Mezcal cocktail—doctor recommended," I said, smirking. "Whatever works. You can give it some real TLC tomorrow."

16

—The Full Moon People—

After a quick meal and a couple more drinks, we paid and hurried toward the dock.

"10:23 on the dot—we should walk faster. They're probably waiting on us," I suggested.

"Anyone check how we're getting back?" Logan asked.

I hesitated.

"I didn't check, but I doubt they'll leave us stranded— bad optics."

As we approached, we saw a group of about eight people already gathered by the boat, music playing from a small speaker. There was an air of excitement—some of the girls were dancing, big smiles all around. I recognized a few of the kitchen staff and other guests. The boat— similar to Carlos's—had seven rows of seats and twinkle lights that ran bow to stern. Its engine hummed, filling the air with the rich smell of raw exhaust.

"You gonna be okay, big guy?" Kavi asked, nudging Fern.

"Just keep me off that thing until we're moving," Fern grumbled.

A few snickers broke out—Fern's last encounter still freshly imprinted.

I spotted Maya in the crowd wearing a flower lei around her neck, a white tank top and a jean skirt—much more casual than her work attire.

"Hey, we made it," I greeted her as Kendal and I joined the group.

"Glad you could come! You're the last ones, so we're ready to head out," she smiled, accepting the small pocket of rupiah I offered.

"This is for gas or whatever. Also, how do we get back?"

She handed the money to a colleague.

"The boat returns at 3, we light a firework at 2:45 to warn everyone."

"Good enough for me."

"Try not to miss it, I'd hate to leave you," she added with a wink.

I nodded and turned back to the group, relaying the plan.

"Boat comes back at 3, they'll warn us with a firework, cool?"

The group nodded, and everyone but Fern boarded.

"Want me to carry you, sweetheart?" Logan teased.

"I'll wait until we're untied," he muttered.

"It's short," I added. "Fifteen minutes, tops."

Fern exhaled like he was about to be waterboarded.

Our skipper, a short Indonesian staff member with a thick accent, urged him. "Come on, man! We waiting for you!"

With a reluctant sigh, Fern climbed in and took a seat beside Hunter, who couldn't stop laughing at his antics.

"You're a special bloke, Fern. Hope you know that."

"Can we go, please?" he replied, his tone desperate yet comical.

We pushed off, carving through the moonlit stillness—Snake Island waiting in the dark ahead.

17

— Snake Island —

Now underway, cold beers were passed forward from one of the employees. We cracked the cans open and shared a big group cheer. It was clear that the workers were excited—a sign of the epic experience ahead.

"Do these parties happen every full moon?" Kendal asked Maya.

"No, they only happen sometimes. I don't think I could handle going every month, it's too much."

"Too much what?" I asked.

Maya giggled and lifted her can. "Just too much partying, too much crazy... you'll see. It's a lot!"

The boat sped parallel to the coast, rather than through the usual reef gap—a relief, as navigating the larger swell with a boat full of partygoers could certainly stir up some drama.

"Where's the island?" Kavi asked.

"It's ten minutes down the coast, then out to sea for about a kilometer," Maya replied.

I took a deep breath of cool sea air and let go of logistics, easing into the ride. The sky was clear, and the full moon hung low, casting us in a soft blue light, while shadows raked through the boat. It felt like perpetual dusk as we glided through perfectly still water. The wake played off the moonlight, casting reflective patterns on the hull and some of the guests' faces. I nudged Kendal, and we sat watching it in a kind of quiet trance.

—

At last, we arrived at the reef gap. The water had shifted from still to kinetic; foamy waves lapped at the boat. I watched as our captain expertly navigated the balmies and rock outcroppings, barely slowing to make the pass, threading through with perfect precision.

"He's done this a thousand times," Maya said, noticing my expression.

"Clearly."

"I see the fire!" Kendal said, pointing forward and slightly starboard.

I turned to see a massive orange inferno in the distance.

"How big is this thing normally?" I asked.

"It's usually huge, at least twenty-foot flames."

"This is going to be so sick!" Fern yelled from behind us, stomping his feet excitedly.

—

Nearing land, the sand below us began to glow white, illuminating the water a deep turquoise shade. The smell of campfire filled the air as our captain cut the motor and lifted the prop, letting the boat glide gently onto the sand.

The roaring bonfire sent waves of warmth toward us, its orange glow illuminating the entire beach. With the engine off, we could hear distant drumming and laughter. Some staff members leapt off the boat, pulling the vessel fully onto the sand. One crew member dug the anchor deep into the sand and cracked a glow stick, placing it on top of the metal hook to mark its position.

"Yep, these guys are pros," I said to the gang, who were amused by the procedure.

Everyone gathered near the boat for a quick safety rundown before joining the party.

"Okay everyone, coming back to here at 2:45. Don't be late, we leaving at 3 exact!" our captain said. "Have fun and be safety, if you need me, I'll be close the fire."

The group shared in a quick drink before walking toward the party. Kendal, still visibly tipsy, wore her trademark smile, looking around with wide-eyed wonder.

"What's got you smiling, young lady?" I asked.

"I just can't believe today... it's been the biggest roller coaster of emotions. The hike to that beach was amazing; it was paradise, and then the sharks freaked me out," she paused thoughtfully. "Then I was relieved you didn't get bitten, then we had that perfect lunch, and then I got stung by a stingray. The hike back, the doctor, dinner. And now I'm at the most amazing party with my favourite people. It's like a miracle, and I'm just so grateful for everything."

She made a good point—several, actually.

It had been a whirlwind day, and somehow all the chaos made this celebration feel even more special. My shoulders were toast from carrying her, but I couldn't complain.

"I'm glad you're happy—and that I'm not carrying you anymore. Good-on-ya for staying calm through that whole ordeal—amazing."

"Good-on-ya!? You're becoming the Aussie slang king!" she laughed.

"Yeah, your group's collective weirdness is wearing off on me."

We walked toward the bonfire, with Kavi and Carissa ahead of us, wrapped up in their playful back-and-forth, shoving each other and laughing at inside jokes. Behind us, Fern and Logan were locked in an animated debate over whether whales had more in common with sharks or elephants, of all things, while Hunter was doubled over laughing.

The closer we got, the louder the fire crackled and the drums thumped, heat radiating in waves around us. Beads of sweat rolled down my forehead, reminding me how much I'd already endured—and how dehydrated I'd gotten. I took a sip of my beer, eyeing it like the traitor it was—only deepening the hole I was already in. Kendal, also glistening with sweat, did a little dance-walk toward the outer ring of the fire—only to stop short as the heat hit us like a wall. We could barely get within forty feet of the flames.

She turned and wiped my forehead with her hand.

"Woo! This is amazing, let's dance!" she yelled, as she began to bounce around jovially.

"Yeah, I don't really dance—more of a sarcastic comment maker, while I judge everyone's dance moves."

"Sorry. Not gonna work for me!"

She grabbed my hand and pulled me in, twirling herself around with a big grin.

I laughed, stumbling forward and linking fingers with her. Just then, loud EDM music began thumping from across the fire. We looked over to see a cheesy-looking LED-lit DJ table with massive speakers, already gathering a crowd.

"Oh shit! Where did that dude come from?" I asked as Kendal dragged me toward the new centre of the party.

After a few clumsy but joyful moments of stumbling through a dance routine, someone tapped me on the shoulder. I turned to see Fern drenched in sweat, sporting a huge, proud smile—one I knew well. It was the same look he had every weekend since knowing him.

"Dude! I scored us some party favors!"

"Oh my god, yes! Do tell!" Kendal interrupted.

I glanced at her, surprised by her openness for illicit substances.

"You? Ridin' dirty? I can't picture it."

"For sure, how often are we going to be here in this situation, living in this moment?"

"That's fair!"

She was right, and as much as I supported the use of mind-expanding drugs, I never would've pegged her as the type.

"Yeah, I mean, I'm not one to say no to a good time. What did you get?"

Fern leaned in, still grinning—

"I got us a bunch of Molly. Apparently, the guy who gets this shit has a Norwegian DJ connection who only brings him the top-grade stuff. He comes up here in a private jet every few months to surf and always brings a ton of it with him," he answered proudly, pulling a small plastic bag out of his pocket

—

I've always joked that Fern is basically a human drug-sniffing dog—magnetized to anyone with something he could pop, smoke, or snort. I remember one trip to Mexico, while I was still unpacking, he'd already found cocaine and was breaking it up on the kitchen counter—legendary stuff.

—

He stealthily handed us a small black pill each, glancing over his shoulder.

"How much do we owe you?" I asked.

"Don't worry about it. Just make sure you take the whole thing at once. The guy said it's the best of the best, and we'll be flying all night."

I looked over at Kendal, who had already swallowed hers with a smile, and so Fern and I followed suit.

"Jesus, woman, you're a maniac," I smirked.

Fern lifted his beer, and we shared a quick cheer before he danced off toward the DJ, hooting in typical Fern fashion.

"We're all in now, no turning back."

"Does commitment scare you?" she asked, grabbing my hand again and twirling herself with the beat.

"Of course, it does!"

She shoved me playfully, and kept dancing.

18

—Sensory Overload—

About thirty minutes after taking the pill, it started. First, a small wave of euphoria washed over my body, followed by an odd staccato visual effect. It reminded me of my grandparents' old film reels, flickering and full of texture. Motion warped—sometimes sped up, other times slowed down—and my brain made a game of trying to keep pace with the changes. I looked over at Kendal, who was evidently in the same frame of mind. She beamed at me, dancing around and fully immersed in the kineticism of the drug.

"Do you feel that!?" she asked, laughing as she twirled.

"I might," I slurred.

"It feels amazing!"

I paused.

"Yep, I'm floating now."

"This is the best night ever!" she exclaimed.

"Ha! I love how happy you get," I replied. "And... guess what?"

"We're going on an adventure?"

"Yep! How'd you know? Should we let the group know? Don't want them to worry."

"Let's just go. They'll either try to talk us out of it... or want to come along. Plus, they're heaps high."

"Egg salad. Follow me," I said.

I grabbed her hand and led her past the fire, toward the far end of the beach. Behind us, Fern and the gang danced their hearts out next to the DJ. None of them seemed to notice us walking away, and I hoped they wouldn't realize we were gone.

"I'm soaked!" Kendal laughed.

"Already? I haven't even touched you yet!"

"From sweat, you idiot!"

I looked down at my own shirt, which had gone from bright white to semi-translucent. This country was a lot of things, but cool—even at night—was not one of them.

—

A few hundred feet from the blazing fire, the cooler air finally started to take effect, chilling the sweat on my skin. We passed by several beached boats, winding our way toward some semblance of privacy.

"There are so many people here. I love this place!" Kendal said, her cartoon-like smile lit by the moonlight and the distant fire. "I'm going to rip your clothes off as soon as we're alone."

"Fair warning, I'm about as sweaty as anyone's ever been, so I'd temper your urge to lick or kiss any portion of my body... unless you're into sweaty, salty dudes."

"I am, if the dude is you... after what you did for me today, nothing could stop me."

"That's possibly the hottest thing you've ever said to me."

———

After what felt like an hour—but was probably closer to five minutes—we reached a secluded spot on the beach. We settled beneath a canopy of palm fronds, shaded at last from the oppressively bright moonlight—giving my eyes a long overdue break. The bass and drums from the DJ pulsed faintly in the distance, rising and falling in a strange, inconsistent rhythm.

I stood still, caught by the strange rhythm of the sound—bright and full one second, then thudding and distant, as if the club door kept opening and closing somewhere in the distance. My drug-saturated brain fixated on the effect, trying to make sense of it.

"What the fuck is that?" I blurted.

"What's what?" Kendal asked, hardly pausing as she danced on the spot.

"The music. Why is it quiet and muffled and then crisp and loud for a second, then muffled again? I feel like I'm losing it."

"What? I don't know, just enjoy yourself, weirdo," she said, spinning again like nothing was wrong.

I stood in silence for a few more seconds, focusing on the strange sonic fluctuation—mildly distressed. Kendal took my hand, urging me to join her in her uninhibited, drug-inspired dance, but my mind was stubbornly stuck on the strange pulsing of the sound waves.

"What's wrong?" she asked, noticing my distraction.

"Nothing, I think I'm tripping!"

"Yeah, you are. Just relax!"

I tried dancing for a few beats, but the sound kept pulling me back. With every change, my vision followed—the more crisp the music got, the more vivid the colours and details appeared, and when it softened, everything dulled and desaturated.

"Maybe there's a breeze that's carrying the sound waves with it, and that's what's causing the difference," I muttered.

"What the hell are you talking about?" she laughed.

"That can't be it," I said, looking up at the perfectly still palm fronds, grasping for an explanation.

And then, suddenly, it clicked—

"I got it! It's the people moving in front of the speakers. When someone stands in front of the speaker, the sound dulls, and when they move, it comes through clear!" I blurted out, feeling an immediate release as my brain finally let go of its obsession.

Kendal gave me a bemused look. "What the hell are you talking about? What difference?"

"Never mind. That was driving me crazy! I can relax now."

I took her hand, twirling her on the sand as she danced, entirely present and lost in the moment. She was an absolute natural at letting go. As I watched her, the realization hit me—I was her opposite. Always analyzing, dissecting every detail in sight. The thought stole my focus, yanking me away from the now, again.

"Fuck, why do I do this?" I muttered, frustration building.

"What do you mean?" she asked, still smiling.

"I do this all the time. I get caught up overthinking things, and I miss the moment. You don't get caught up in any of it—you just enjoy yourself."

Kendal looked at me quizzically.

"Just relax, you're actually ruminating about how you ruminate too much. Just let go, it's fun!"

She was right, and now I felt guilty for not being fully here with her. This pill was definitely messing with my psyche.

"Okay, I'm done. I'm back. Just me and you, here. Nothing else," I said.

"Yes! I love it. Focus on that!"

She leaned in, kissing my neck and tugging my sweat-soaked shirt off, then wrapped her arms around me, trailing kisses across my chest and stomach.

"Yep, you taste sweaty. I love it."

I pulled her tank top over her head, and for a second, I just stared, frozen by how perfectly sculpted she seemed—statuesque and surreal in the moonlight.

"You've officially ruined every other girl—past, future, parallel dimension—for me. I hope you realize that."

"Future? You'd better not be thinking about the future right now. Or the past," she teased, leaning in close.

"That's fair. I'm here! Totally here."

"You have a lot of trait neuroticism for a man," she laughed.

Before I knew it, she had slipped my shorts off and was working her way down my sticky torso. A tingling sensation shot up my spine as my vision sparked with shimmering patterns and bursts of light. I closed my eyes, fully immersed in a wave of euphoria—as her touch and the MDMA collided in my nervous system.

The drug had shifted gears—less like floating, more like dissolving. My body buzzed with sensation, like static in my bones, but my awareness felt scattered, slipping through the edges of the moment. I couldn't tell where I ended, and the night began.

Ater a few minutes of pure euphoria, she pushed me past a tipping point. Fireworks and tracer trails bloomed behind my eyes, and something in me just... let go. For the second time in two days, she'd short-circuited me. My body collapsed into the sand, all systems offline—too much all at once.

All I could hear was her laughter above me.

"Wow. Uh, I need to cool off. Back in a sec," she said, giggling as she scampered off.

I lay there, scarcely able to move, feeling like a human jellyfish left on the beach. It was like my entire body had just completed a marathon, and all I could do was trust I'd regain motor control eventually.

A moment later, she returned from the water and knelt beside me.

"That was fun... I've never seen anything like that in my life. It was like you were gently electrocuting me. That was so weird!"

I tried to reply, but all I could manage was a slight turn of my head.

"Are you alive?" she asked, grinning.

I attempted to answer but my mouth still wouldn't cooperate.

Finally, I managed a few words. "I can't... need a minute."

She laughed. "Take all the time you need."

Another thirty seconds passed and I finally caught my breath. "How did you do that?"

"I didn't do anything unusual. Come swim with me, the water feels amazing!"

"Okay… just let me wait for my legs to come back to to life," I grinned.

She leaned in to kiss me, maybe hoping it'd speed up my recovery. With her help, I slowly stood up, a bit unsteady.

She smirked. "Hey, you're totally naked."

"Yeah, well, so are you," I said, watching as she took off excitedly toward the water.

In the moonlight, her tan lines stood in stark contrast to her deep bronze skin—like she was wearing an invisible, white bikini.

I looked down, assessing my own patchy tan.

"Man, my tan lines suck!" I called after her.

"Come on, swim with me!" she yelled, splashing into the waves.

I chased after her, barreling into the shallows. The warm water lapped at my legs with a surreal smoothness, almost like stepping through liquid silk.

"Holy shit, this feels insane!" I said, finally catching up and wrapping my arms around her.

"It's perfect. I could just float here in these waves forever. I'm so content."

"You're so high, is probably more accurate."

"Yeah, but I feel like this is where I'm supposed to be right now."

"You are absolutely where you're supposed be right now... you can't be anywhere you're not supposed to be. It's impossible."

"That's not what I mean, dummy. I mean this is where my heart wants me to be."

"Good. I'm pretty relaxed too... it's nice."

"I'd probably feel that relaxed if I were you, too!" she replied. "Seriously, what was that?"

"Not sure. And is that an invitation?"

"Maybe it is…" she teased, splashing me with a mischievous grin.

We floated in the shallow water, barely speaking, swaying gently with the movement of the sea. The MDMA had done enough that words felt unnecessary. There was a quiet connection between us, and we simply basked in the comfort of the moment.

In the distance, the massive fire still burned—a flickering nucleus surrounded by dancers who looked like swirling, orange apparitions.

———

"I can't tell, but I think I'm getting cold. Should we go hang out on the beach to warm up?" she eventually interrupted.

"Yeah, I think you might be right, but I can't tell either."

"Do you know where my clothes went?" I asked. "It'll be embarrassing if we've lost everything and have to show up back at the boat in banana leaves."

"I actually can't remember either—it's all a big blur to me," she replied. "But if we can't find our stuff, we're staying here and setting up camp on Snake Island from now on."

"I'm in. Mostly because I'm not ready for everyone to stare at my naked ass—especially while I'm high."

—

As we got to dry land, something caught my eye that stopped me cold—a giant object running perpendicularly to the shoreline.

"What is that!?" I asked.

Kendal paused next to me, staring straight ahead.

"I've no idea. Was that there the whole time?"

We stood studying whatever-it-was. It sat about forty feet ahead, long and narrow—maybe thirty feet in length and just a few feet wide.

"I don't get it… is that, like, a beached whale??"

We both paused, squinting in the moonlight.

"I don't think so. It's too flat—and we would've noticed a whale."

"Yeah but... it's shaped like a long fish and there's no fish that big."

"Let's go check it out."

She agreed, and we walked forward with trepidation, unsure of what lay ahead.

"Are we just tripping out? It almost looks like a giant silver feather."

"Oh, we're absolutely tripping," I said, "but there's also a giant feather-shaped, silver thing on our perfect private beach, and I'm pretty sure it wasn't there before."

The closer we got, the less sense it made.

"Is it… like a giant squid or something?"

"It can't be, it's too thin to be an animal. It has to be an alien," I laughed.

She shoved me, unimpressed by the alien theory clogging her drug-addled brain. As we closed the gap—now just ten feet away—it became clear: whatever it was, it had no depth. No height. Just a perfectly flat shimmer against the sand.

"Is it really an alien, though?" Kendal asked, whispering. "Or did some creature leave a giant, silver slime print on the beach?"

"I'm far too high to be trying to sort this out," I whispered back.

"I don't want you to get any closer to it though, it's scaring me."

I knelt, bringing my face level with the sand, thinking a change in perspective might offer some insight.

"What if it's dangerous?" she whispered.

"It's totally flat! I have to figure this out—it's way too strange," I said, shuffling closer, with determination.

"This is probably dumb, but… should you be wearing pants for this?" she said suddenly. "Like, is it more dangerous if you're naked?"

Her comment flipped the mood instantly from tense to hilarious, and I collapsed onto my back, laughing.

"Wait—you think I need to be clothed to investigate the alien?" I gasped between fits of laughter.

"It made sense when I said it!" she said, cracking up as she dropped down beside me.

"It still makes so much sense to me, somehow," I replied.

"We certainly shouldn't greet extra-terrestrial life naked—that's just bad manners," she gasped.

Once our laughter subsided, I resumed my slow crawl toward the mysterious object.

"I don't get it—why hasn't it moved or done something?"

"I have no idea!"

Kendal circled around toward the edge of the shape, crouching slightly to get a better look.

"Be careful," I warned, watching her inch closer.

She leaned forward, squinting at the silvery shape.

Then it jumped—

I jolted up, heart hammering as I frantically scrambled backward.

Kendal was already twenty feet away, doubled over in the dark, laughing so hard she could barely stay upright.

"Oh my god, were such idiots!"

"What? Why? What's so funny?" I asked, my heart still racing. "It's back to the original shape."

With a newfound confidence, she strutted back to the object and leaned over it, extending her hands. As she did, the shape changed once again.

"...it's a moonbeam!"

"A moonbeam?" I repeated in disbelief.

I stepped forward and placed my hand above the object, and sure enough, the pool of light illuminated my arm, casting a perfect hand-shaped shadow below. She was right—a single moonbeam had pierced through a gap in the palm fronds above.

"Well, that's embarrassing."

"It's because we're so high! Look—there are a few more down there."

She pointed down the beach, where a handful of similar patches of silvery light were scattered along the shore.

"How did we miss those?" she asked, squinting.

"In our defense, these are extremely dramatic moonbeams. I've never seen anything like this in my life."

"We actually walked out of the water, stared at a patch of light for five minutes, and then realized it was just… light," she said, shaking her head.

"Yeah, not our best moment. Let's hope no sober people saw that. There'd be no explaining it," I laughed. "Let's find our stuff and look for a darker spot. This light is burning my eyes."

"Definitely," she agreed, "but let's keep this nocturnal nudist vibe going. I'm kind of loving it."

—

We wandered the beach until we finally found our belongings, scattered a solid fifty feet from where I remembered hanging out—which also felt vaguely extra-terrestrial.

"What did you do, throw my shorts like a Frisbee?" I asked.

"A boomerang! And at least you found them, I can't find anything," she replied, less amused.

We made a few more circles around the area until we finally stumbled on her tank top and the rest of our scattered gear.

"Shall we head back to the fire to see what everyone's doing? Or find a tree to climb and possibly live in forever?" she asked.

"I mean, I want to find a tree to live in with you, but it's getting pretty late. Plus, I think we'll get eaten alive by bugs," I laughed, checking my watch and noting it was almost 2. "We have an hour before our ride leaves."

"Well, I vote we live in a tree and abandon civilization together and start a little family of Molly dependent children," she said, slightly slurring her words.

"Why would they be Molly dependent?"

"I don't know, I guess because it's so fuckin' fun!" she said, giggling.

"That's very, very true. Though I don't quite know how to provide them with the Molly out here. There must be a way to create it using coconuts and pineapples... there must be."

I thought about this for a moment, briefly spiraling over how every creation in the modern world originates from the earth. The thought tripped me out.

"It's insane that everything in the world—cars, planes, phones, TVs—all of it comes from like... minerals and nature. It's completely incomprehensible."

"That is weird. Like how is my phone made of the planet? It seems crazy."

She paused. "This M is amazing—I can't stress that point enough."

"Let's get you back to the fire, I bet the gang's wondering what's happened to us by now."

"Don't remind me, I just want to keep the humans away tonight."

"I get it, and honestly, I'm not eager to see you put your clothes back on. That just feels wrong,"

We quickly hopped back into the ocean to wash the sand off and then tossed our gear on. It was time to rejoin our friends and cross the inevitable, nerve-racking threshold back into reality. The MDMA had me feeling weirdly reclusive, like it had shattered my usual social compass.

———

I focused on Kendal's hand in mine, trying to ignore the creeping anxiety of interacting with others. She squeezed, seeking the same comfort as we moved toward the fire's warm glow, back into the frayed edges of civilization.

"What's it going to be like... talking to the humans?" she asked, her voice low.

"No idea. Are they going to ask us things? What are we supposed to say? I've never had MDMA make me feel this socially anxious," she said. "Isn't it supposed to make you feel open and connected?"

"Yeah, this is a new one. Just don't let go of my hand."

———

As we neared the fire, Fern spotted us and immediately ran in our direction, yelling over his shoulder,

"Yo! I found them!"

"Uh-oh," Kendal said, leaning in. "Look how fast his legs are moving!"

"Fern gets intense sometimes, this ought to be entertaining."

He slowed to a walk, breathless and coated in sweat, then grabbed both our wrists like we might vanish again.

"Dude, where did you two go? We've been freaking out looking for you!"

"We went on a magical journey," I replied, trying to keep a straight face.

"Yes, a physical and spiritual one," Kendal added, her eyes dancing with amusement.

"A metaphysical one. To be precise," I said, mock-serious.

"Well fuck, that's not cool, you should have told us! We've been looking for you, asking around everywhere."

"Fern, you can't predict a spiritual journey—everyone knows that," I replied. "These pills don't care for etiquette… plus, you're covered in face-paint and have a glow stick around your neck—how stressed could you have been?"

Kendal dropped to her knees, laughing uncontrollably.

"Sorry, Fern," she managed between giggles, "I know you're pissed, but you gotta see how ridiculous you look right now."

"This isn't funny!" he protested.

Just then, Kavi and Carissa showed up, both painted in obnoxious neon orange and green swirls.

"'Sup, homie," Kavi said, grinning. "Where'd you two lovebirds run off to? We missed you guys."

"Dude, we went to a strange, dark void. There were giant sea creatures and fireworks and shit," I answered.

Kavi laughed and shook his head, unconvinced but entertained.

"That sounds like one hell of a trip. We've just been here drinking, dancing, and getting painted up. It's intense—a bunch of wild Australian dudes running around high on coke."

"That checks out," I replied, as I scanned the crowd, spotting about a dozen culprits.

"Where are the other two?" Kendal asked.

"They're around somewhere. Hunter's way up in the clouds." Carissa said, "Let's head back to the fire. Fern's been a champ and scored us a bunch of drinks. Guy's super resourceful," she added, patting his back with a smirk. "...And really sweaty."

———

We joined Hunter and Logan by the fire, dancing to the relentless, bass-heavy beats of EDM as the night blurred on. Eventually, a firecracker burst into the sky, signaling that it was time to go.

———

"I don't know if I'm ready to leave—I'm still so high!" Hunter said, looking up. "And the moon is just absolutely beautiful!"

I was still flying high myself, but I had reached a new level of dehydration and would need to procure a lot of water if I stood a chance of fending off this hangover. The beach was more crowded now—twice as many boats, twice as many anchors to dodge. Eventually, we reached ours, where our trusty crew was reassembling—now a little more technicolour than when we'd arrived."

Our captain gathered up the anchor, signaling his crew to help push the vessel out into the water. Once we were far enough out, everyone climbed aboard, and the engine sputtered to life.

"Everyone is here?" our captain asked, quickly counting heads as we idled in the shallows.

"I think that's everyone," Maya confirmed.

The engine rattled up, and we sped off back to the resort. The air felt much cooler this time—a mix of damp clothes and wind creating an intense chill across my skin.

By the time we docked at the resort around 3:30 a.m., I was freezing and more than ready to crash.

19

—Quiet Sea—

My alarm pierced the air, vibrating the mattress and drilling into my skull for the third morning in a row. I picked up the phone, struggling to focus on the dusty screen. To my amazement, it was already noon.

"Fuck... why is the AC off?" I muttered, taking in the muggy heat and the thin layer of sweat that clung to my skin.

I pushed the blinds aside, blinking against the harsh daylight that confirmed the hour. Kendal rolled over to face me, sweeping the hair away from her eyes.

"My head hurts... and my toe hurts again."

I moved the blanket away from her foot to check.

The duct tape and gauze were now tattered and gritty, embedded with sand and small pebbles, leaving a pale, gritty smear across my once-white bed sheets.

"It looks a little irritated, but there's no blood or swelling—you're probably good," I said, patting her calf.

"I knew this would happen, dancing and stingrays don't mix," she sighed. "They should post a warning at check-in."

"Definitely. Right next to the WiFi password," I grinned. "Maybe we should soak it in salt water later, just in case."

She sat up, stretching her arms and torso, looking unfairly athletic despite the hangover.

"You snored, by the way."

"I told you, it happens sometimes when the mix of substances is just right." I said with a shrug.

"And a few times, your phone chimed, and you tried to imitate the sound in your sleep," she laughed. "It was like... you were trying to harmonize with it?"

"I did?"

"Yeah, it happened a few times, I almost woke you up— I couldn't stop giggling."

"I learn new things about myself every day."

"You were dead asleep, but your mouth kept moving like you were trying to sing along. It was weirdly cute."

"Oh god. Well—good to know I can entertain in my sleep," I replied. "Surfing might be the last thing I want to do right now. I feel like a bag of wet cement."

"Maybe a little breakfast will put you back on course."

"I need water. Immediately. I can't even blink," I groaned.

I sat up and shouted toward the wall, "Kavi, you up?"

Kendal smirked, "Did he even stay here last night?"

"I have no idea. I feel like we're all playing musical chairs with the villas at this point."

We stumbled over to Kavi's room. The door was wide open but the bed was still made.

"He must've crashed at your place—or in a ditch somewhere," I joked.

"Do ditches even exist here?"

"An estuary, then. Let's check your place. I have a feeling today's surf plans might fall through."

As we walked toward her villa, I fantasized about diving into the ocean on loop—a classic sign of dehydration.

—

We arrived at their villa, front door ajar. Hunter and Logan lay spooning on the couch; both covered in smeared body paint. The counter and table were lined with empty wine, tequila, and beer bottles—evidence that the party had continued.

Kendal stifled a laugh, "Looks like the rave never ended for these two."

"No bailing on the surf today, Logan," I said eyeing the carnage.

"We're surfing one hundred percent," his voice cracked from the couch.

"Nice, you're in? I wasn't sure if you were even breathing," I laughed.

"Yep, just give me an hour. I need to purge and reset," he muttered.

"Gross, dude," Hunter groaned, pushing him back as she rolled forward off the couch.

"Where are the rest of you crazies?"

"I don't know, I think at breakfast or the beach... they left twenty minutes ago."

"Cool, we're going to eat. We'll be back in an hour," I said. "Nice face paint, by the way."

———

We found the rest of the gang finishing breakfast at the restaurant. Everyone looked gray, save for the bright neon patches of paint that remained on their faces and arms.

"Whoa, aren't you all a sight for sore eyes! I thought you'd be face down still."

"Nah man, I'm all fired up," Kavi replied. "I puked a couple times this morning, but I'm good to go."

We sat down to join them.

"What a night!" I laughed. "Did you guys keep partying when we got back? Hunter and Logan looked pretty rough."

"Yeah, we kept going. Fern had one more pill, so we split it," Kavi confessed. "Super dumb choice, in hindsight."

"You guys are maniacs, this wave's the real deal—you gonna manage?"

"Oh, I'll manage. Plus, if it kills me, I'll be too hung over to care."

"Bogan logic, at best," Carissa said, sarcastically. "What do you want to do today, K?"

"I'm not doing anything, my foot's killing me again. I'm happy not to join."

"Ditto! You guys are nuts. I need darkness and air con."

"We'll be fine, it's going to be epic. Plus, we'll be back before you know it," Kavi reassured them, glancing out at the water. "Hopefully Carlos shows. I saw him dancing at the party and he was not sober."

I chuckled, having no memory of Carlos's antics.

"I didn't catch that. I guess we'll let the Ment gods decide for us."

From our seats, we could see the swell had picked up—foam balls now erupting along the horizon.

"Damn, swell's definitely up, huh?" I said, quietly.

"It's a perfect day, too. No wind at all," Carissa added. "You're going to score for sure. Maybe I should come."

"No, please hang out with me today. I need company," Kendal said, nudging her.

"Yeah, stay with Kendal. Boys only," Kavi smirked.

"Fine. We'll just stay here, paint our nails, and have a pillow fight," Carissa replied, laying on the sarcasm.

Kavi grinned, pushing his chair back and standing up.

"Maybe we should stay here and watch them instead. Sounds hot." I mused.

"Not a chance!" Kavi said, throwing his napkin on the table. "Let's get a move on, Cole."

"Have fun, you two!" Kendal called, waving cheerfully.

I smiled back at her, catching her gaze one more time.

"Man, I'm so cooked! How did this even happen?" I muttered.

Kavi shoved me again. "Yeah, big shocker—you fell for the first girl you met. Keep it movin', Don Juan."

—

Back at the villa, we packed up our gear. As the lingering booze started to metabolize, a slow, nauseating sweat took over. Anxiety crept in while I packed, but I stuffed it down with my gear—I didn't want to ruin the vibe on our first real strike mission or give Kavi any more ammo.

We zipped up our packs and headed for the door. As we stepped outside, the anxiety returned—stronger this time. My legs felt heavy, my breath shallow. Something was definitely off.

"Dude, I hate to say it, but I feel weird about today. Maybe it's the hangover, but something doesn't feel right."

"You'll be fine, man. As soon as we get there and jump in, you'll relax."

"Yeah. Maybe I'm psyching myself out about that slab we're charging."

"Just chill. There's channels on both sides. Hang out in there all day if the vibe's wrong. And I already think you're a bitch, so you have nothing to lose," he grinned.

"Fuck you," I said, flipping him off.

"You're just worried you'll have separation anxiety from your wife."

"Right? I actually do need a minute to clear my head."

—

We headed out to find Fern and Logan. I hadn't heard them bickering for a while, and part of me expected them to be dead-asleep in bed.

"It's suspiciously quiet today, do you think they killed each other?" Kavi asked.

"Killed? No. Maybe they lost their voices last night. One can dream."

—

Their place looked like it had partied too, but oddly, they were sitting quietly—packed and ready to go.

"What happened? You dudes finally run out of things to argue about?"

"I'm too hungover to talk. Please don't talk," Fern muttered.

"Nothing kills a hangover like overhead barrels," Kavi laughed.

"Just shut up, let's go," he answered again, while Logan quietly sipped from a coconut, looking ghost-white for someone who'd been sunbaked all week.

"So, who here is never drinking again?" Kavi asked as we started the short walk to the dock.

All four of us raised our hands in unison.

—

At the dock, Carlos was waiting, grinning at us as we approached.

"Damn, you guys not looking good today. You had fun at the party last night?" he teased.

"I feel like shit," Fern replied, deadpan.

Carlos laughed. "Sure, you want to check it out to Glaciers?" he asked. "Can be a dangerous wave, and the swell's up."

"Yeah, we're all good, if we're not feelin' it, we'll come back," I answered.

"So let's go, then!" he said, climbing aboard.

Just as we were about to push off, Kendal appeared with a take-away container.

"The girls and I got domestic and packed you boys some fruit."

"Thank you, that's super thoughtful of you."

She hugged me tight.

"Wow you're such a great vacation wife!" Kavi teased.

"I know that was a dig, but I am a nice wife!" she shot back.

"Yes, you are," I agreed.

"Okay, well just wanted to say goodbye. Have the best time ever, and maybe we can grab dinner tonight?" she said, turning back to the resort.

"Sure, we should be back by, what, 6:30?" I looked to Carlos for confirmation.

"Yeah, three or four hours," Carlos nodded.

She blew a kiss over her shoulder and made her way back toward the resort, all five of us watching her go.

"Damn Cole, you guys meet on this trip?" Carlos asked, not breaking his gaze.

"Yeah, we did. Crazy right? Sometimes stuff just aligns I guess?"

"It's vacation love. That shit ain't real," Fern muttered.

"Right, because you're such an expert, Fern," Logan retorted. "When's the last time you loved anyone but yourself?"

"Okay, I don't care what you think—can we please go surfing before I puke?" I interrupted, climbing aboard.

"Yes please!" Kavi agreed.

Fern paused mid-step, staring down at the neatly coiled rope ladder on the deck.

Carlos caught his eye and gave him a sly wink.

"Small victories, Fern," Logan muttered, smirking as he stepped past.

Fern smiled back at Carlos and stepped aboard, quietly relieved that he wouldn't have to reenact the harrowing experience from a couple days prior. With one pull of the starter cord, we were off—finally chasing our first real wave of the trip.

20
—This One Goes to Eleven—

Our small boat cut swiftly through the glassy bay, the only source of waves in the otherwise motionless sea. The water was so clear I could make out every rock and piece of coral beneath us as we glided past. My earlier butterflies and lingering hangover had been temporarily replaced by calm excitement—after all, I was in paradise, and no amount of nausea was going to dampen that.

"It's the best day, no wind. Hot and perfect swell direction for Glaciers. You guys are going to score!" Carlos shouted over the scream of the four stroke engine.

We nodded in agreement—our collective stoke rising, despite how green we all felt.

"You guys gonna be okay?" he laughed. "It's okay if you puke. Sometimes it's better."

We turned to Fern, who was slumped with a towel over his head, clearly entertaining the idea. I gave his shoulder a reassuring shake.

"Hear that pal, you can puke if you want," I shouted.

"Yeah Fern, let 'er rip." Logan added, as the group burst into laughter.

The mood was beginning to lift, just in time for us to near the reef channel and get our first real glimpse of the swell.

"Holy shit, it's big today!" Kavi yelled, standing for a better view.

I joined him, my eyes locking onto a head-high wave bursting on the surface below. Carlos eased the boat to an idle, his expression turning serious.

"We going to have to time this one," he said, his eyes focused on the white-water ahead.

We waited, watching a set roll through and crash over the shallow reef. As the last wave thundered down, Carlos gunned the motor, charging at the gap. The boat pounded through walls of white water, soaking us and jostling the board bags. Before long, we were out of the impact zone and into deeper, open water.

—

The sea beyond the breakers lay perfectly still—like a teal oil-slick, unbroken and eerily calm. It mirrored the faint clouds above so perfectly it looked painted in place— too calm to be real

Carlos slowed the boat, taking it all in—

"Man, total glass! I never remember seeing it this calm before. Not even any birds anywhere. It's like Chernobyl." he said, his tone half-joking, half-unsettled.

I scanned the horizon curiously.

He was right. There wasn't a single bird in sight. No gulls, no pelicans—just empty skies over an abandoned sea.

"Weird. Where are all the birds? That doesn't make any sense," I said.

"No idea. Normally there's a tons of bird, especially at these little islands," he said, pointing ahead.

I squinted, remembering how alive it had been just days ago with birds circling and calling. I craned my neck to scan the sky in a full 360, but it was empty.

"Am I the only one that's a little weirded out by this?" I asked.

"Uh, definitely not," Kavi said, his own gaze fixed on the lifeless horizon.

"Maybe they were all at that party last," Logan laughed.

Carlos burst into laughter. "Ah-ha, you got it."

"Whatever," Fern muttered, his voice muffled by the towel. "We don't need birds for waves. Let's just go."

Carlos smiled and gunned the motor, pushing us through the unnerving silence toward Glaciers.

—

The ocean stayed bizarrely smooth, even our spearfishing spot, where birds and fish had teemed just days ago, was completely void of life. Ahead, Glaciers loomed—like a dark, liquid monolith, breaking with mechanical precision in the ghostly calm sea.

"Shit. That thing's huge today!" Fern yelled, voicing exactly what we were all thinking.

Up close, it looked even more massive, tearing at the reef with a deep, concussive thud that rippled through the air and water, followed by a chaotic plume of white foam.

"Fuck..." Logan muttered, shaking his head. "We're going to die."

I nodded, equal parts nervous and excited.

———

We stopped in the northeast channel, just beyond the impact zone. Carlos moved to the bow and tossed the anchor, letting out about fifty feet of chain until it caught. The boat steadied. With the motor off, the thunderous sound of the wave took over. From here, we could see the wave was five or six feet overhead—thick-lipped, surging, and merciless.

"Can you guys feel that?" I asked, noticing the boat trembling.

No one replied—

Everyone was transfixed; their eyes locked on the massive surf ahead.

"It's heavy today. Be careful out there," Carlos said, pointing toward the center of the impact zone. "It's shallow, and those reefs are sharp."

"Oh great, that's good news. I woke up half-dead— might as well finish the job," Fern quipped, his sarcasm doing little to mask his nerves.

"Yeah, same," Logan added. "I really didn't want to sit through that long flight home anyway."

I smirked to myself.

You know it's serious when Fern and Logan start agreeing.

"Yo, I brought presents," Kai said, tapping me on the shoulder.

"Presents?"

"Yeah, I figured this might come up, so I snagged some proper leg ropes. Those little comp leashes we've got will snap in no time," he said, rummaging through his day pack.

He handed me a leash twice as thick as mine, with a red, helix-shaped core woven through it.

"Dude this is going to strangle me," Fern said, holding the leash up to his neck like a noose.

"You mean it's going to save you. Trust me—last trip, my leash snapped, and I almost drowned. You don't want that," Kavi shot back.

Carlos nodded in agreement, eyeing the leash. "Yeah, smart. If your leash breaks here, it's sketchy."

"I'm sold," I said, swapping out my flimsy rope for the industrial-strength one.

I strapped the thick Velcro cuff around my ankle and turned my attention back to the wave. It was mesmerizing—a fast and hollow A-frame with a clean, smooth right-hand section, and a channel on either side. The rides were short, maybe a couple hundred feet at best, but explosive and perilous.

"I'm going to hug the channel to start," I said aloud, more to calm myself than anything

"Yeah, if you bail or miss one, go to the channel," Carlos confirmed. "I'll pray for you from here," he smiled.

"Yeah, thanks man. You're not coming for a surf?"

"Hell no, man. I got a wife and new baby at home."

"That's super comforting," Kavi laughed.

Carlos smirked, "Don't worry. If you hit the reefs, I got lemons here," he said, nodding to the cooler.

I knew exactly what he meant. Just thinking about lemon juice on fresh reef rash made my skin crawl. Coral's filthy—full of bacteria that burrow and fester. The stinging citrus might save you, but charged full price for the privilege.

"Put my name on half a dozen of those," I replied dryly.

Despite the light banter, my anxiety was building. The size and speed of the wave—paired with its unforgiving reef and Carlos's reluctance to join—painted a picture far from comforting. I was hungover, underprepared, and hadn't surfed much since we'd arrived. But backing out wasn't an option—for any of us. Show weakness and the gang would be on you like hyenas.

Kavi pulled his board out and started waxing, breaking the silence. The rest of us followed, the mood somber—a slow march toward the edge of a cliff. I rubbed the coconut-scented wax along my board, my eyes locked on the wave, trying to absorb every detail of the sets bursting on the reef. I kept waxing until my board looked like a snowdrift—stalling like a kid refusing to get out of the car at the dentist.

"I think you got it, homie," Logan interrupted.

"Yep, just delaying my death for a few more minutes."

"As one does."

I stood up and took a deep breath before nervously diving overboard.

21

—Glaciers—

I resurfaced—the sea's warmth soothing me like medicine, peeling the hangover off like a second skin. The creamy, teal-blue water glowed; its hue intensified by fine white sand particles suspended below the surface. I took another deep breath and paddled away from the boat, following Kavi, with Fern and Logan close behind.

As we approached the peak, the air grew dense with a briny smell. The deafening sound of the waves erupting on the reef made my heart pound faster.

"This is fucked!" Kavi yelled, grinning nervously as a giant wave exploded ahead, sending mist and spray skyward like confetti from a cannon.

"Yeah, this is either going to be the best day of my life or the worst," I shouted back.

—

Before long, we were sitting on our boards in the channel, just within range of the peak.

"Who's first?" Fern asked, excitement mixed with dread.

"Rock, paper, scissors?" Kavi suggested.

"Yep, sudden death RPS is the only fair way to decide who'll actually die suddenly."

The four of us formed a circle and began the game of games to decide who would be the canary.

My scissors were crushed by Kavi's rock, while Logan's rock was smothered by Fern's paper.

"Shit! Looks like it's you and me, pal. Loser's up," I said, locking eyes with my opponent.

I threw rock, but Logan's paper sealed my fate.

"FUCK YOU!" I yelled, leaning my head back in mock despair as Logan celebrated his victory.

I turned and paddled for the peak before hesitation could take hold.

"Good luck, dude! Don't kook it!" Logan shouted after me, his voice dripping with smug amusement.

I flipped him off without looking back, blood buzzing with a sudden spike of adrenaline.

—

I arrived in the takeoff zone and began my search. The goal was simple—find a forgiving wave and avoid becoming a permanent part of the reef. Each approaching set jacked the water beneath me, lifting me with coiled power—a visceral warning of what a botched takeoff might cost. I steadied myself and looked down. Through the crystalline water, the reef's jagged outline came into view, sharp and unforgiving. When the moment came, hesitation would be fatal. I'd need to pop up fast and either carve right immediately or free-fall down the face, then sweep a bottom-turn into position. It would all depend on where I stood up and how close I was to the peak.

"You got this," I told myself.

"Let's go, Cole! This one's yours!" Kavi's voice rang out from the channel.

A medium-sized set rolled in—

"This is the one," I muttered to myself.

I spun my board and paddled hard as the wave approached. The energy of the swell surged beneath me, and within moments, it picked me up and shot me forward. I snapped to my feet, dropping down the nearly vertical wave—a rush of wind and spray engulfing me— the ocean roaring like thunder. Heart pounding, I dug my fins deep and carved hard toward the channel, setting a line across the buttery face. The water was smooth as silk—slipping beneath me with that familiar floating sensation as I drove down the line. Before I knew it, I was deep inside the barrel, charging forward as the wave curled overhead, forming a shimmering glass tunnel. Seconds felt like an eternity as I raced through the hollow tunnel. Then, like a torpedo, I was shot out of the barrel, the wave spitting me into the open sea.

"Holy shit!" I breathed, half-laughing, half-shaking, as I flew back into the channel—barely able to believe I'd made it through.

Hand to heart and shivers running down my spine, I let myself collapse backward into the water. I swam down a few feet to savor the moment, then broke the surface to find Carlos and my friends cheering like mad.

"Yeah, dude! Fully barreled! What the hell?!" Kavi shouted, his voice cutting through the sound of the waves.

Carlos was clapping and yelling something incoherent, but the enthusiasm was clear.

—

The guys took my success as a green light and paddled excitedly toward the peak.

"Any tips?" Fern called back.

"Just don't hesitate!" I shouted, paddling furiously to position myself for another wave.

By the time I reached the peak, Logan was already sizing up the next set.

"Pray for me!" he yelled, flashing a nervous grin before turning to paddle.

His strokes were strong and committed, and within seconds he disappeared behind a towering wall of water.

We waited; eyes locked on the channel—no sign of him. I glanced at Carlos, who finally gave a small wave from the boat—a signal that he was okay.

"Confidence killer!" Kavi muttered, lining up for the next set wave.

"I mean, someone's going to get smashed today—might as well accept it now," I said, laughing despite myself. "Don't worry. Carlos brought lemons—we're fine."

Kavi smirked, then paddled hard into what looked like a monster of a wave, easily the biggest of the day. He popped up cleanly and disappeared as the slab thundered down behind him.

"Holy shit, that's loud!" Fern shouted, grimacing at the impact's deafening roar.

Seconds passed, but Kavi didn't reappear.

Carlos, now visibly concerned, shouted something toward the impact zone, clutching his head.

"This might not be the smartest call, surfing this beast so early in the trip," Fern said nervously, though a chuckle escaped his lips.

"Yeah, probably not," I admitted. "You up next?"

Fern hesitated, glancing at the lineup like a man eyeing his own open casket.

"Uh. Maybe I'll wait for a smaller set. Not risking my trip for one wave."

Logan paddled into view, coughing intermittently.

"Dude, how'd you go?" I called out.

"Not good. That was heavy. I swallowed, like, a gallon of water and got held down forever."

"But no reef?"

"No reef," he confirmed, taking a deep breath. "Just my confidence."

"What about Kavi? Did you see him?"

"Yeah, same deal. Nose full of water, but he's fine."

I turned back toward the horizon and spotted a smaller set rolling in.

"Fern, this might be your shot, this one looks chill."

"Shit!" Fern yelped, as if his body decided to paddle before his mind was ready.

He slapped at the water, launching himself toward the first wave in the set—a more forgiving swell compared to Kavi's monster.

"Get it, Fern!" I yelled, catching Logan's concerned gaze.

Neither of us said it, but we were both thinking the same thing. I crossed my fingers as he popped up, disappearing behind the wall of water. I turned to Carlos to gauge whether he'd succeeded or been swallowed by the wave. To my relief, Carlos was clapping and cheering, jumping up and down on the boat, and eventually bowing theatrically.

"Yo! He must have smoked it!" Logan yelled over the booming surf.

Moments later, Fern shot over the shoulder into the channel, pumping his fist and screaming blissful obscenities into the air.

"Unreal!"

"Nailed it! He can't climb a boat for shit, but never count that guy out." Logan laughed.

Kavi paddled back to the lineup, looking less enthusiastic than before.

"How'd you go, bruv? Kiss any reef?" I asked.

"Dude, I got pinned. No makeouts."

"For how long?"

"Probably fifteen seconds... felt like fifteen minutes."

"Shit! It's my turn again." I said nervously, as I turned to face the open sea.

The next set approached—medium-sized but still intimidating.

"This one's me," I said, as I turned to paddle for the first wave in the set.

The swell picked me up like a freight train, launching me forward. As I popped up, water sprayed into my eyes, blinding me momentarily. My lead foot landed just ahead of the waxed section and slid forward, grinding my inner heel into the nose of the board—setting off a violent chain of events.

I was forced into an awkward partial split and toppled backward, sliding down the face of the wave and into the trough, my board tumbling beside me. Water blasted into my sinuses as the wave collapsed on top of me with a deafening explosion. I braced for impact, but after a short chaotic pause, felt myself propelled toward the surface. I tumbled through the turbulence until I finally broke free. Struggling against the drag of the thick leash, I managed to pull my board toward me. Thankfully, I was mostly out of the impact zone and only had to paddle a short distance to reach safety. I flopped onto my board, coughing and gasping—relieved and utterly violated. The worst part? My nose had siphoned seawater like Fern with a rolled-up bill in a dive bar bathroom.

—

I reached the channel, water draining from my sinuses as inexplicable laughter overtook me. Maybe it was the lack of sleep, the adrenaline, or the absurdity of the near miss. Whatever it was—it broke me. I looked toward Carlos, who clutched the plastic produce bag, a serious expression on his face—his enthusiasm for the lemons, somehow funnier now.

"You okay, amigo?!"

"Yeah, I'm all good. Put the lemons back, you weirdo" I laughed.

Carlos gave the guys a thumbs-up to signal to the guys.

The next set rolled in and Logan paddled. I tensed as he dropped in, silently willing him to succeed. Moments later, he exploded out of the barrel at high speed, his board slicing the air as he shot over the shoulder and dove in, grinning ear to ear.

"Holy shit, Lo'! That was insane! Wish Carlos had a camera—would've been a framer!" I shouted.

"God damn!! What a feeling!" he yelled, paddling past me, eager for more.

———

From that point on, the session clicked. We traded waves, took our slams, and somehow came away unscathed. It felt surreal—perfect surf, flawless weather, and the knowledge that three gorgeous women waited for us back at the resort. Watching my friends ride some of the best waves I'd ever seen filled me with psyche I hadn't anticipated.

———

By 4 p.m., we gathered in the channel. The swell was still pumping, the wind hadn't changed, and the sea remained glassy.

"Should we take a break on the boat and come back out? I feel like this is too good to head back," I said, looking at my watch. "It's just after 4:00, we probably have another hour before it's time to jam."

"I don't know, I'm pretty burnt. And pretty beat." Logan replied, looking at his arms and hands.

"My eyes are fried. I need shade," Fern added.

"Let's head back to the boat, catch our breath, and decide from there," Kavi suggested.

We agreed, paddling back toward Carlos and the boat—sunburnt, exhausted, and full from an unforgettable session.

22

—A Sudden Problem—

About a minute into the paddle, a noticeable rip current began pulling me sideways. Assuming it was just part of the usual hydrodynamics from the wave, I ignored it and kept going. But the water beneath me quickly shifted from smooth and glassy to choppy and erratic.

"Do you guys feel that?" I called out, more intrigued than worried.

"Yeah. What the hell—is the tide going out or something?" Fern asked from behind me.

I glanced around, trying to make sense of the sudden outflow. Everything looked deceptively normal, but the pull was getting stronger. We pressed on, but halfway back to the boat, things escalated. The sea began to swirl—churning with bubbles, crosscurrents and whirlpools that appeared and vanished in every direction. Something was off.

"What the hell is this?!" I shouted, spinning to see my friends now scattered, each of them battling the surging water to stay close.

"This can't be the tide, right?" Kavi yelled, struggling against a rogue current that had dragged him twenty feet away.

In the distance, Carlos was shouting something, but his voice was lost in the rising chaos.

"Is he coming to get us?" I yelled back to the guys.

No one answered.

Pockets of warm water began surging past me—first intermittently, then constantly—until the ocean was no longer refreshing, but disconcertingly warm.

What the hell is causing this?!

My confusion turned to creeping panic. The current was no longer amusing—it was turning savage. The ocean had become a river, flowing hard and fast out to sea.

"Carlos is coming to get us!" Logan called, his voice fraying as he pointed toward the boat.

Carlos was trying to pull the anchor, but the vessel bucked and rocked with each surge. I watched, helpless, as he was knocked over repeatedly, barely able to stay upright in the chaos.

"Carlos! Carlos!" we all shouted, our voices blending with the roar around us.

Is this some kind of super tide!?

The thought of the full moon flashed through my mind—could it really cause a tide this extreme?

Carlos became smaller with each passing second, his figure rocking violently in the distance.

"Cole!" The guys yelled.

I turned to see Fern, Kavi, and Logan now linked together, holding onto each other trying to stay connected as the sea threatened to tear them apart.

"Link up!" Fern yelled.

I stopped paddling and let the current drag me backward and laterally—counterintuitive, but necessary to stay with my friends. After a struggle against the ceaseless flow, I managed to latch onto Logan's board, completing the chain.

"I don't understand. What the fuck's causing this? Are we in trouble?" Logan asked, a note of fear in his voice.

"Where's Carlos?!" Kavi shouted.

I spun in place, searching the water where Carlos had been anchored moments before. The boat was gone.

"What the hell?! He was right there, wasn't he?" I yelled, pointing to the empty stretch of water.

"Did he leave us?"

I spun in a circle, but he was nowhere.

"No way. Carlos wouldn't do that," Fern shook his head. "No chance!"

The pull of the current grew stronger still, dragging us toward the open ocean with alarming speed. The water around us churned—chaotic and merciless.

"There's no way this is just the tide! It can't be!" Fern yelled, panic breaking through.

I paused.

There was no rational explanation for such a sudden and violent outflow. It felt like a plug had been pulled, sucking the ocean toward the horizon.

A chilling realization began to dawn on me. I stopped paddling and glanced back toward the open sea.

"I felt shaking earlier… on the boat, and while we were surfing," I said, the pieces starting to come together.

"What do you mean?" Kavi asked.

I hesitated, my breath catching in my throat—

"I don't know," I started, my voice uneven. "This isn't normal. This much water moving like this." My words trailed off as I searched the sea around us.

Kavi stared at me, waiting for more, but I couldn't bring myself to say it outright—not yet. The thought had burrowed its way into my mind but saying it aloud would make it real. I clenched my jaw, forcing myself to focus on the chaotic water beneath us.

"Spit it out, man!" Logan shouted, more panic than patience in his voice.

My stomach churned.

"What if it's a tsunami?" I said, my voice barely audible.

The word hung in the air like a death knell, heavier than I'd expected.

Everyone stopped paddling to think. Maybe an earthquake had struck unnoticed—easy to miss, given we were offshore and engulfed by the sound and motion of breaking waves. My mind jumped to everything I'd learned about tsunamis. It was textbook. I remembered the footage from the Boxing Day disaster in Thailand— the ocean receding rapidly, tourists standing in the shallows, confused, moments before the ocean came roaring back. I panicked at the thought of what might be coming and glued my eyes to the horizon.

Kavi broke the silence, pointing inland.

"Look at the island!"

I turned—

A few kilometers inland, the island's beach had expanded dramatically, exposing coral reefs that had been submerged just minutes ago. Around us, rocks and jagged reef now jutted from the water like skeletal remains—stark against the sunlit sea. The towering waves that had battered Glacier Reef were gone—only bare rock remained, glistening where the water once crashed.

"This is fucking insane," Fern muttered, panic cracking his voice. "What if a wave comes? What do we do?"

I wanted to reassure him, but every sign pointed to the inevitable: the exposed reef, the vanishing shoreline, the sudden pull of the ocean—it was all prodrome—every sign pointing toward catastrophe.

"I knew it. I fucking knew something was off today," I muttered bitterly.

—

The current dragged us further from the reef, pulling us toward the unknown. We were several thousand feet from where we'd been surfing. I caught Fern's eyes—his expression locked in pure terror, a look I'd never seen before.

"What do we do?!" he stammered, over and over.

"I don't know. Don't panic," I said, fighting to keep my voice steady, though panic clawed at me too.

I watched the horizon, searching for the wave I dreaded.

"If it's a tsunami, maybe we're far enough out that it won't hit us as hard?" Logan called, grasping for hope.

We'd been surfing an outer reef and had drifted even farther out—maybe far enough to miss the brunt of it, if it really was a tsunami.

"Maybe," I said. "Should we paddle out to try to get to deeper water to miss the impact?"

The four of us stared at each other, each weighing the impossible options against the unknown.

"Well, what else can we do? Let's try!" Kavi finally said.

—

We quickly formed a line, paddling hard toward the empty horizon—away from land, and away from the illusion of safety. Each stroke felt heavier than the last, my arms burning as fear fueled me forward.

I thought about Kendal, Carissa, and Hunter.

Were they safe? Could the bay or the island's low peaks shield them if a tsunami hit?

I prayed they'd stayed near the restaurant—close enough to hear a warning, far enough to escape. The island's highest point couldn't be more than a few hundred feet above sea level, but with enough time, they could make it to higher ground. They had to.

Regret gnawed at me—

I replayed every sign I had ignored—my gut knew something was wrong, and I'd silenced it.

Why the fuck didn't I say anything!? Why didn't I stay at the resort?

The questions spiraled, echoing with the kind of clarity that only comes too late. Each thought was a confession, compounding the weight of what now felt inevitable. The uncertainty wasn't whether something would happen—it was how bad it might get.

—

My eyes stayed locked on the horizon, mind racing through a million panicked thoughts.

Any second now, I expected to see it—water rising from the depths, hurtling toward us.

Why the hell did I come here? Why didn't I just stay in bed with Kendal?

Paddling harder, I forced myself to focus. If the wave came, I couldn't stop it. But I wouldn't stop fighting.

23

—Water on the Horizon—

Then, we saw it—

A few kilometers out to sea, a dark wall of water rose, spanning endlessly across the horizon. I froze mid-stroke and sat up on my board. I squinted—unsure if what I was seeing was real. But as the wall swelled, denial buckled. My pulse pounded, phasing out the wet slosh of the sea draining beneath us. The shape didn't vanish. It grew. Rising, stretching, solidifying.

The wave was real. And it was coming.

"Is that it?" Fern's voice cracked, barely above a whisper.

No one answered.

We all just stared.

The silence broken only by ragged breaths and the rush of water.

The horizon bulged grotesquely, warping into an uneven swell that defied comprehension.

"I can't fucking believe this is happening," I finally said.

"What do we do? Do we keep paddling?!" Logan cried out.

"Yeah! We have to paddle!" Kavi shouted, arms already digging frantically into the water.

He was right—it was the only thing we could do.

I forced myself to move, even as my brain screamed to stop, to turn back, to do anything but paddle toward the thing that had come to unmake us. Every stroke disobeyed instinct, but we kept going—driven by the faint hope that deeper water might spare us.

—

Each second brought it closer—steeper, heavier, more monstrous. Its surface had turned an almost metallic blue, rippling with the same deep force that tugged at our boards and churned beneath us. As it reached shallower depths, sections sheared off and folded forward, sending chandeliers of white water tumbling down its face—only to be absorbed back into the mass, as if it refused to let anything escape.

"Look at that fuckin' thing! We're dead. We're fucking dead!" Fern's voice cracked as he paddled frantically.

"Just keep paddling!" Kavi barked.

—

My arms and shoulders burned with every stroke, the lactic acid building into an unbearable, anxious ache. Still, I paddled, driven by fear and the need to survive. My breath came in short, shallow gasps as I choked back the rising panic.

This has to be a fucking nightmare!

I shut my eyes tight, hoping that when I opened them, I'd be back in bed, next to Kendal.

But this was real.

I glanced back again. The water had drained away from the island—the distant beaches—barely visible from where we were—scraped raw. It looked more like a set from a disaster movie than the paradise we had left behind.

My thoughts fractured—

What happened to Carlos? Were the girls safe? Why the fuck did I ignore my gut?

—

The wave gained on us, its form beginning to unravel. Sections of the towering wall peeled and collapsed, exploding in jagged bursts of whitewater as it met the shallows. It didn't lose force—it multiplied it, churning violently, dismantling the sea itself as it surged forward. My mind faltered, slipping into a surreal haze as the moment closed in. I saw flashes of us from above—four small bodies, paddling helplessly into oblivion. The sounds around me morphed into a sharp, high-pitched ringing that choked out my friends' voices. It was like a scene in a war movie—Fern's twisted expression, Kavi shouting something lost to the noise, Logan frozen, wide-eyed and pale.

The wave was closing on us. and with it, the unbearable truth: we might drown—scared, alone, erased—in the middle of the Indian Ocean.

"We're so fucked!" Fern shouted, breaking my daze. "It's gonna break!"

I ducked my head below the surface, desperate to gauge our depth. Though the swirling sediment clouded my view,

I could make out the tops of coral and jagged rock, just below.

My heart sank—

We'd lost the race.

I stopped paddling and let my arms fall limp, surrendering.

"Stop!" I yelled.

"What? Why?!" Logan shouted back.

"We're not going to make it!" I gasped. "It's too shallow—we're wasting energy!"

"What? How do you know?" Fern called out, his voice quivering.

"I can see coral below us," I managed, my voice cracking under the weight of my fear.

One by one, we stopped paddling and collapsed onto our boards, our breathing ragged. Defeated, we floated, utterly spent, as the wave continued its relentless approach.

Thirty seconds, maybe less—that was all we had. And we were already exhausted.

"What do we do?" Fern muttered, his voice barely above a whisper. "We're going to die."

"If we grab on to each other—stay together—" Logan started.

"Stay together?! Are you insane?!" Fern cut him off. "We're fucked! We're about to drown!"

"Do you have a better idea?" Logan shot back. "Grab my wrist—now!"

With no other options, the four of us linked wrists, holding on as tightly as we could. The wave was only a few hundred yards away now, towering at least thirty feet above sea level. Its face had gone almost vertical, nearly blocking out the sun. I inhaled deeply, trying to fill my lungs, even as my chest constricted with panic.

—

Then, it happened—

The wave tipped forward and began to collapse. In an instant, the colossal mountain of water turned into a cascading waterfall, freefalling onto the ocean's surface with unthinkable force. The explosion of white water ripped outward—releasing megatons of energy, hurling coral, water, and fragments of reef airborne in a savage blast.

The sound followed—an overwhelming, bone-shaking roar that vibrated through my sternum. The horizon disintegrated into frothing chaos. It wasn't just a wave—it was hell, summoned from the deep. It had come to erase the world—and take us with it. I gasped in shallow bursts, trying to top up my lungs with whatever air I could before it hit—but deep down, I knew we were cooked.

—

I looked to Logan, Fern, and Kavi—possibly for the last time. Their faces mirrored my own—a silent blend of disbelief and pure terror. Logan's eyes locked onto mine, wide and glassy, pleading without words. Fern and Kavi barely moved, their grip white-knuckled, as if holding might save us. I had so much to live for—I'd met the girl of my dreams just days ago. For the first time in years, I felt happy and fulfilled. If this was how it ended, it was a cruel joke.

I grew angry.

Why hadn't I trusted my gut? Why hadn't I spoken up? *Please. Please, God. Just get me through this. I don't want to die.*

The words repeated in a loop—a last-ditch prayer screaming inside my skull.

The wave was here—

I inhaled one last desperate breath and braced myself.

24

—Impact—

A shockwave of air blew me backward just before the wall of water struck. I was ripped from my board in an instant, tumbling violently in the whitewash before being yanked beneath the surface. I held onto Logan's wrist with everything I had, but the surging water wrenched us apart in a heartbeat. The roar of water was deafening as I was flipped and spun like particles in a centrifuge. The wave had devoured everything in its path, and now debris— rocks, coral, and sand—lashed against my skin, slicing me open as I fought to shield my head with my arms.

The water was shockingly cold, a brutal contrast to the warmth of the outflow just minutes ago. The chill cut straight through, stripping away the last vestige of comfort. I kicked and clawed, trying to fight the vortex pulling me deeper, but it held me fast, my limbs ensnared like a fish in a gillnet.

Pain shot up my leg as my leash yanked violently, straining against the pull of my tangled board. Each tug cinched the strap tighter—a noose threatening to snap. Even this stronger leash wouldn't last. If it broke, I'd be left to fend for myself—no flotation, no chance.

I was dragged deeper still, the pressure building in my ears as my body plunged into the murky abyss. My eyes stayed clamped shut against the sting of sediment and coral shards, but I could sense the darkness growing around me. The light was fading—it wouldn't be long before my lungs gave out.

A searing shock tore through me as my back collided with jagged reef, slicing deep. My body was dragged mercilessly along the underwater terrain, raking a wound from my shoulder to my tailbone before being flung once more into the torrent, the entire cut now stinging with salt.

Only thirty seconds had passed since impact, but my lungs were already convulsing, aching for a breath I couldn't take. I fought with everything I had, but the current fought back, dragging me down deeper and slamming my body against anything in its path.

—

For a moment, my mind cracked open.

Kavi. Fern. Logan.

Were they alive? Were they fighting as I was, or already gone?

I thought of Kendal and the girls. I prayed they'd made it to higher ground. I wanted to yell in anger at the world for ripping my life to pieces in one instant, turning me into a cautionary tale. The regret gutted me: I had finally found something good. And now it was slipping away.

—

The harder I struggled, the weaker I became. My body was on the verge of rebellion, the need for air overtaking everything else.

Desperation collapsed into surrender.

I let go—

Please let me go, Please let me go. I begged silently.

I opened my eyes one last time to see a galaxy of bubbles against endless darkness. My body trembled as my lungs screamed in protest. I closed my eyes and waited for the end.

—

Then—release.

The leash went slack, and the current let go.

For a second, I was free.

I scrambled forward, no longer pinned by the current, following my leash blindly, praying the board it was tethered to still floated above. My lungs burned for air, my chest convulsing with desperation. I caught a faint glimmer of light above and paddled frantically, kicking with everything I had.

I'm going to make it! I thought, even as my body screamed.

Barely ten feet from the surface, I finally gave out, involuntarily gasping and inhaling a lungful of seawater just as my head broke through into open air. I gasped and coughed, vomiting and heaving as I struggled to draw breath, re-aspirating ocean water and stomach acid with each gasp.

My body shook—every sense overloaded.

Blinding white light filled my vision, and the roar of swirling water and retching drowned out every other sound. My eyes slowly adjusted, revealing the chaotic scene around me. The ocean churned with milky-brown foam, swirling with silt, fragments of wood, torn leaves—anything the wave had consumed. Bubbles hissed and popped across the surface. Violent whirlpools spiraled unpredictably, clutching at my limbs and threatening to drag me under.

Nearby, I spotted the fractured remains of my board—jagged, dented and barely buoyant—its Styrofoam core chewed through with cracks and punctures.

I clawed my way to it, hoisting myself onto the splintered plank, clinging desperately for stability as my breathing began to steady.

—

Disoriented, I spun—searching for anything familiar. The nearest island was gone—its beaches erased, its outline swallowed. It was as if I'd been dropped in the middle of the Indian Ocean with no sign of land.

Then I heard it—a faint voice, muffled by the chaos.

"Help! Help!"

Was that real?

My ears were still clogged with water, but I caught the sound again—clearer this time. I turned frantically, scanning the frothy mess, desperate to find its source.

"Help!"

There it was again!

I whipped around, ready to shout in return—but froze.

Something was behind me.

25

—Wave Number Two—

I had less than a second to brace before the next wave overtook me. I snatched a quick, futile breath, before being hurled backward, tumbling violently back into the depths. My board ripped from my grasp instantly, its tether resuming its pull against my ankle in a cruel game of tug-of-war. This one hit harder—piledriving me straight into the ocean floor. My body skidded along more jagged reef, raking through already torn skin. Pressure mounted in my skull, threatening to rupture my eardrums as I was plunged once again into the churning abyss. My muscles were weak, my chest already begging for air—but I was trapped in the jaws of a monster.

I cracked my eyes open, searching desperately for a sense of direction, but there was nothing—just a kaleidoscope of bubbling chaos. The first wave had already drained me, leaving my limbs heavy and useless—my stamina a shadow of what it had been moments ago. The thought of reliving the sensation of drowning made me panic. I couldn't take much more of this. I forced myself to go limp, conserving what little oxygen I had left.

My prayers turned feral as my chest convulsed, muscles tightening to stave off the inhale that would re-flood my lungs with saltwater.

Please—just let this end!

—

Then the current shifted, grabbing my body and wrenching me upward. Water flooded my sinuses as I shot through the tumultuous flow. I braced for another collision, but instead, I broke the surface—gasping, choking, vomiting seawater. My lungs seized and clawed for air, desperate to refill.

The ocean churned around me, a maelstrom of froth and debris—too aerated to keep me afloat. My head dipped again, and I inhaled another breathful of water. The remnants of my board bobbed nearby, barely recognizable as the lifeline it once was. I yanked on my leash, each movement labored, my arms trembling as the battered chunk of foam came within reach.

"Hey!" I croaked, my voice barely audible over the roar of the sea. "Hey!" I yelled again, desperate for any sign of life.

I tried once more—but no sound came out.

—

I lay my head down on what was left of my board, gasping for air, every muscle in my body trembling with exhaustion. I scanned the churning water around me, desperate for any sign of my friends, but the foamy chaos gave no answers.

If they had surfaced, they weren't near me. The thought gnawed at the edges of my mind: the odds of anyone else surviving were microscopic. I shoved it aside, forcing myself to focus on the undeniable truth—I was alive. Somehow, against all logic, I was here—and if I could just hang on a little longer, maybe there was a chance to survive and find my way back. I clung to that fragile thread of hope, even as the undertow dragged me further out to sea, pulling me deeper into the unknown. My chest tightened as I searched the horizon for movement, for a voice—anything to prove I wasn't alone. The silence pressed in, heavy and absolute. The crushing realization began to sink in: I might be facing this hell alone.

"Fern! Logan! ... Kavi!"

"Fern! ... Logan!"

"Fern!..." my voice tapering into defeat.

I rolled over and stared up at the sky, my back stinging from the dozens of fresh scrapes, my ears dull with trapped water.

"HELP!" I screamed to the sky.

I rolled again, pressing my cheek to the board.

"Help! ... Help!" I wailed, voice cracking with emotion.

—

The sun beat down, unmoved and indifferent. It felt wrong—cruel even—that it could continue shining as though nothing had happened. It just hung there, untouched by catastrophe, shining over the chaos below, oblivious to the suffering it illuminated.

"Fuck you!" I spat, rage overtaking despair.

I looked down at my watch: 4:47.

Twenty minutes ago, we were laughing. Twenty fucking minutes!

I can't believe it. I can't fucking believe it! I repeated, pounding at my fractured board.

Sobs overtook me—uncontrollable, primal, tearing out of me as I floated, just one more piece of wreckage in the vastness of the Indian Ocean. I pictured grieving families back home—faces twisted in sorrow, loved ones left without answers. If I died, they'd never know what had happened. And if I lived, I'd bear the impossible weight of surviving alone.

I reached behind, fingers trembling, and felt along my spine and shoulders.

Divots. Gashes. Raw, stinging flesh.

My hand came back slick with blood.

I'm fucked. No one's coming.

The reality settled in like a sickness. I began to shake—the salty water creeping deeper into my wounds.

I closed my eyes.

The pain dulled. Time warped. I slipped into something like a dream.

I'm going to die, this is it. I won't get out of here.

The thought didn't come with panic, but softly—like it had already been decided.

26

—Alone—

"Cole... Cole!"

I snapped back, eyes open, heart pounding—as my vision adjusted slowly to the glaring light.

Shit—I'm hallucinating.

Frothy, hissing foam surrounded me—my muffled ears blurring the line between reality and delusion.

"Hey!" I croaked, my voice a brittle rasp.

I shook my head violently, trying to dislodge the water clogging my ears.

"COLE!"

This time it was unmistakable. I spun around, battling the chaotic current, and finally spotted a figure about thirty feet away.

"Kavi?!" I yelled, my senses snapping into focus.

I tried to paddle toward him, but a sharp pain lit up my torso as I shifted on the broken board. I looked down—a long scrape ran from my navel to my right hip, bleeding sluggishly. Fresh streaks of crimson smeared my left forearm and right shoulder, each revealing raw, torn flesh.

I'm in trouble, I realized, forcing myself forward through the stinging pain, awkwardly paddling the shattered remains of my board.

—

Eventually, I reached him—clinging to his board, which was in rough shape: creased at the midpoint, nose snapped clean off, jagged fiberglass protruding. His face was a mess of scrapes, and blood trickled steadily from a deep gash near his left ear, staining his forearm and the churning water below.

I pulled him closer, placing his free hand on my board to keep us from drifting apart.

"You're alive," I gasped, relief crackling my voice, my teeth chattering. "Are you okay? What else is wrong?"

He lifted his hand from the side of his head, revealing a deep, raw wound—easily a dozen stitches under normal circumstances.

I tried to get a better look, but the current tore us apart.

"I think I'm okay," he said uncertainly, his eyes darting to my injuries. "How bad is it?"

"It's not great," I admitted, squinting through the chop. "But if we can stop the bleeding, I think you'll be alright."

"I've got scrapes and cuts everywhere," he added, eyes scanning me. "You?"

"My back's the worst, but I can't tell how bad it is."

I leaned forward, letting him see.

"Shit."

"What? Is it bad?"

"You've got a lot of gashes, and you're bleeding pretty bad... but I think you'll be okay".

A heavy pause—

"... and Fern? Logan?" I asked, though I could sense the answer.

He looked away, silent.

"We need to wrap your head," I said, changing the subject.

"You're going to need both hands."

I reached for the bandana around his neck as he gripped my board to keep us steady. After a few tries, the knot came free. I folded the cloth as best I could and wrapped it around his head, my hands trembling—clumsy from cold and exhaustion—but I managed to tie it off.

"How is it?"

"You look like Tupac," I said, almost managing a grin.

He gave a weak smirk, pressing his hand over the bandana.

I turned my attention back to our worsening situation. This wasn't normal undertow. It was stronger. Ceaseless. A sick thought took hold—what if—

"Wait! Is that them!?" Kavi shouted, pointing past me.

I spun around and squinted. Two heads bobbed in the distance, surrounded by broken boards and debris.

"Fern! Logan!" I yelled.

"Guys!" Kavi added. "Guys!"

I waved weakly, trying to signal them—no response.

"Fern! Logan!" Kavi called again.

"They're not responding," I muttered, more dread setting in.

"We have to slow down," Kavi said.

We slid off our boards and angled our bodies against the current, dragging ourselves backward, to intercept them. Cold and warm patches of water stung my skin—each shift a new punishment. Wreckage floated between us—tree limbs, flip-flops, broken Styrofoam, splintered wood, coconut husks. The wave had stripped the land clean and pulled it into the sea.

They drifted closer, but still no response.

"What if they're—" Kavi started but didn't finish.

I clenched my jaw and forced myself to breathe, refusing to let the thought take shape.

—

The current finally delivered them into reach.

"Guys! Fern, Logan!" I yelled.

Still no answer.

Then—movement.

A flicker from Fern, the subtle lift of his head. We reached out and grabbed them. Both boards were snapped clean in the middle—Fern's was barely held together by jagged strands of fiberglass.

"Are you okay?" I asked, my voice raw, barely able to push out the words.

Fern looked up at me and moaned something.

"Logan are you okay?"

"I'm alive," he croaked, coughing into his hand.

Both looked dazed.

"Logan, talk to me," Kavi pressed.

"Another wave's going to come," he whispered.

I paused, studying his pale face and dilated eyes.

"I don't think so," I said, gently. "I think that was it."

"It's not over," he muttered. "Another wave's going to come."

I hesitated—

He might be right. But panic wasn't going to help anyone.

"It's been a while. I think it's done."

He didn't answer.

"Tell us what's wrong," I continued, my teeth chattering as I spoke.

"My stomach... his leg," Logan mumbled, gesturing to Fern.

I looked to Kavi.

Logan lifted his arm, revealing a gash across his abdomen—deep, but not gushing—its edges jagged with loose skin and flesh.

"You'll be okay," I told him. "It's not that bad."

"There's nothing you can do," Fern mumbled. "We're dead."

I shook my head. "Maybe, maybe not."

Kavi leaned toward Fern, inspecting his leg against the swirling current. His face darkened.

"It's broken. And gashed up bad."

"How bad?"

He hesitated.

"We need to—"

He stopped mid-sentence, eyes darting around.

"Need to what?" I asked.

"Nothing. We're probably fucked," he said. "Fern's right."

I met his gaze—he was scared.

"Maybe," I admitted. "But I'm not giving up."

There was a long pause.

"Okay. Fern's bleeding out—so what the hell do we do about that?"

I shuffled past Logan and carefully sank below the surface to check the wound. It was gushing from below his knee. I surfaced and detached Fern's leg rope from his board.

"We'll use this as a tourniquet," I said, firmly. "Kavi, stay focused."

I turned to Fern.

"This is going to hurt, but it'll help. Hold on."

I wrapped the cord tightly above the wound, looping it and tying a firm knot.

Fern groaned, in agony.

I dunked under to check—the bleeding had slowed.

"We need to get your leg out of the water. Can you lift yourself onto your board?"

He groaned again, but managed. We propped him up, one leg dangling in the water, the other elevated on the chewed surfboard.

—

We were adrift—kilometers out, no land in sight—a disorienting and deeply unsettling reality. I moved closer to Kavi. My body was wrecked, every muscle trembling with exhaustion. The surf session alone had pushed me to my limits; the struggle since had drained what little strength I had left.

"We should lash our boards together," Kavi said, reaching down to undo his leg rope.

I nodded.

We worked steadily, tying the boards into a makeshift raft.

"If another wave comes…" Logan started.

"If another wave comes, nothing will matter," Kavi cut in, voice sharp.

He removed Logan's leg rope and tied it to the others. We worked in grim silence, securing the boards together to ensure we wouldn't be separated. But I kept my eyes fixed on the horizon. I couldn't help it. If another wave came, it was over.

———

Acrid salt and the taste of blood coated my tongue. My throat was raw. I'd been dehydrated before the wave hit—but now I was far worse.

And Fern… he was slipping. Fast.

More debris floated past—

"Look—coconut shells," I rasped. "Maybe some full ones will float by. We need water."

"And how are we gonna open a fuckin' coconut?" Kavi snapped. "We're in the middle of the ocean."

I ignored him.

"How deep are we?" Logan asked.

I slid off my board into the water to check, but the sediment made it impossible to see.

"Can't tell," I said, pulling myself back onto the board, my skin stinging where it had met the saltwater.

"No one knows we're out here," Fern muttered.

I froze.

The thought hadn't fully formed until then: no one was coming.

27

—The Choice—

"Look!" Logan yelled, his voice trembling as he pointed at the horizon. I turned to see another blue wall far out at sea, creeping closer. This one looked different—rounder, less steep—deceptively calm.

"I knew it—I fuckin' knew there'd be more!" he shouted, panic sharpening his voice.

We stared out to sea in silence, sizing up the third wave.

"Think it'll pass under us?" Kavi asked.

My heart thudded.

I imagined the wave cresting and dragging us under again. We'd barely survived the last set—one more hit like that, and there'd be nothing left to save.

"I told you more waves were coming!" Logan barked, fumbling to untie the web of leg ropes.

"Okay, dude, we get it!" I snapped. "Just focus!"

We scrambled to untangle the makeshift raft, preparing ourselves for whatever came next.

Kavi's voice cut through the chaos: "Stop! If we untie Fern's leash, he'll bleed out."

"He's going to die if he loses his board anyway," Logan shot back. "So, what's the difference?"

A tense silence hung in the air. I turned to Fern.

"It's your call. What do you want?"

"Untie it," he said, his voice shaking. "I don't want to drown."

Within seconds, the tourniquet was off, and Fern was reconnected to his board. A thin plume of blood spread through the foam, staining it pale pink.

"I think it's going to pass under us," Kavi muttered, studying the wave. "The current's not as strong this time."

He was right—the pull had eased. Nothing like the violent suction that came before the earlier waves. I sat up to get a better look at the approaching swell. It was different. Slower, heavier—like it had patience. The last ones had come to kill. This one was here to finish the job. But out here, in deeper water, we might be spared its teeth.

—

I held my breath as the swell picked us up and swept us forward, my board humming beneath me from the force. The surge knocked me off balance, spinning me briefly in a vortex of icy, debris-filled water.

To feel something that massive pass beneath us—so mechanical, so indifferent—was deeply unsettling. We meant nothing to it. Its path was already written: to destroy homes, uproot trees, erase lives. We were just collateral.

I sat stunned as the swell passed, dropping us nearly twenty feet and leaving only a churn of cold, murky water in its wake. A hollow frustration took hold. There was nothing we could do—no way to stop the destruction, no way to warn anyone. The scale of it made me dizzy.

—

The current shifted, now pulling us gently inland, drawn forward by the wave's lingering inertia.

"We need to get Fern's tourniquet back on," Kavi reminded, breaking the stunned silence.

We watched as the distant swell finally toppled and crashed. A white plume exploded skyward, easily four stories tall. Moments later, the deafening crack of the reef echoed toward us, vibrating through the air and water.

"… right," I said, snapping out of my trance.

—

We were tying the tourniquet again when a flicker of motion pulled my eyes to the horizon—another dark swell rolling toward us.

We froze—

"I think we're still fine." Logan said, cautiously.

"When the hell is this going to end?" Kavi shouted, his voice raw.

Fern winced as we tied the rope off. His skin had blanched, his breathing shallow. A chill passed through me. He looked drained—lips tinged purple, eyes bloodshot. I couldn't tell if he had minutes or hours. But I kept tying. We didn't have time for doubt.

"Fern, try to get back on your board," Logan urged.

Fern groaned but managed to hoist himself up, his movements strained. I leaned in to check—the bleeding was under control. For now. With Fern stable, we moved quickly—lashing our boards together again before the current could scatter us.

———

Then came the fourth wave. Just as tall. Just as ominous. It surged, once again lifting us high into the air. But this time, something was different. When it passed, we didn't settle back down. The ocean stayed elevated—like the sheer volume of water had permanently reset sea-level. The scale of the destruction became sickeningly clear. Death hung in the air—not just near us, but everywhere. Islands around the Mentawais would be wiped clean— some never seen again. Entire communities lost to the sea, and if something didn't change soon—we'd join them.

28

—Marooned—

The sun dipped lower in the sky, casting long shadows over the chaotic sea. We had about an hour before it set, and the coming night would present all new challenges. The full moon might offer us some light, but not enough to spot predators lurking below. The hope of spotting a boat, plane, or helicopter before nightfall felt increasingly slim. If the coast had been hit like we had, rescue efforts wouldn't be coming soon.

My thoughts turned to Carlos. Had he managed to pull anchor and flee behind one of the nearby islands? Was he waiting for the waves to subside to return for us? Deep down, I knew the truth: he'd never have abandoned us willingly. Mourning his loss would be another burden we'd have to bear.

I forced myself to focus, searching the horizon for any sign of land, but all I could see was the endless froth of turbulent, swirling water. The only indication of land's direction was the trajectory of the last two waves. The usual ground swell was gone—groomed flat by the tsunami. I clung to the hope that as night fell, the sea would settle, and we might spot a distant tree line or hill. But with every passing moment, that hope dimmed.

How far had we drifted already? The question gnawed at me as I gazed up at the darkening sky.

My body felt like it had been through a shredder, every cut and scrape stinging independently. My lips and face burned from hours of saltwater. My hands were so pruned they ached.

—

A patch of debris about thirty feet away caught my eye—a tangle of twigs, driftwood, palm fronds, and bits of plastic packaging.

"Debris," I said, pointing it out. "Maybe there's a coconut in there."

"I still don't know how we're supposed to get into a coconut, even if we find one," Kavi muttered.

"There might be other useful stuff over there."

Logan and Kavi's faces were marked with exhaustion and defeat, and Fern was barely conscious. Still, they followed my lead and searched the water for anything salvageable. Once we focused, we noticed similar patches of rubble floating in the current—tree branches, plastic trash, clumps of vegetation.

"What's that?" Kavi blurted, spotting something white about a hundred feet from us.

I slid off my board, cringing at the discomfort, and paddled toward it. Each movement was agonizing, but I finally reached the object—an old construction bucket with a lid still intact.

"It's a bucket!" I called back, grabbing it and paddling toward the raft careful to conserve what little strength I had left.

"Why do we need a bucket?" Fern asked, his voice tinged with frustration.

"We can use it for a lot of things now that we're stuck out here," I replied, looping my leash through the handle and securing it. "Plus, it floats."

I crawled back onto my board and checked my watch. Over five hours had passed since we'd jumped into the ocean to surf. Despite my efforts to keep parts of my body out of the water, I was constantly half-submerged, the discomfort building with every passing minute.

Pain from my back, abdomen, and arms had merged into a single, pulsing ache. I didn't need a doctor to know what was in store for me if I didn't get some medical attention. Carefully, I reached behind me, fingers grazing the raw terrain of torn flesh and deep pits along my lower back. I winced—every contact like sparks between open wires. Thankfully, the bleeding seemed to have slowed, a viscous layer of fluid now coating the wounds. Fern wasn't as lucky. His leg remained our most immediate concern.

"I think we might need to cycle the tourniquet," I said.

"What do you mean?" Logan asked, his voice hoarse.

"If we leave it tied off too long, his leg won't get any blood," I explained. "We'll need to release the pressure now and then."

"So... untie it for a minute, then re-tie it?"

"Not sure, but yeah, I don't think we can leave it on full time."

"How often?" Kavi asked. "Every thirty minutes?"

"Maybe less," Logan muttered.

"Alright. Every twenty minutes for sixty seconds," I proposed. "We'll take turns."

Everyone nodded.

I shifted my focus back to the horizon, searching for anything—a landmark, a vessel, some form of hope.

"Maybe a shipping boat will pass and see us," Logan said.

It wasn't impossible. A large ship far enough from shore might've missed the tsunami entirely—and could still be on course.

"It could happen," I replied, though I didn't believe it.

———

We floated in silence, the ocean a blank page stretching in every direction. Nothing broke the stillness—not land, not life, not even birds. Eventually, I reasoned, we'd see land again. Once the sea dropped and the mist from the pounding waves settled, the islands would return to view. The smaller ones might still be submerged, but the larger island of Nias had to be just beyond our line of sight.

"It's weird that we can't even see the main island," Kavi muttered.

"I know. We should at least be able to see the hills," Logan added, a frustrated edge creeping into his voice.

"We will," I said firmly. "The surge just needs to drop."

Logan hesitated.

"What if the island got completely crushed?"

"It's hundreds of feet high—it'd take something apocalyptic to wipe it out," I said, trying to convince us both.

If we could spot even a sliver of land, we could paddle toward it, regroup, and make a plan. Provisions, shelter, and tending to our wounds—all would be possible if we could just find dry ground.

"What do you think? Can we all paddle once we see land?" I asked, trying to inject some hope into the group.

"If I paddle, my head wound's going to reopen," Kavi said flatly.

"Okay, then we'll work on the bandana if that happens. But we're going to have to try something. If we stay out here—" I trailed off, letting the obvious hang in the air.

The group fell silent again—too wrecked to argue. Rest was all we could manage for now, waiting for the tide—or our luck—to turn.

—

"Look," Fern said suddenly, his voice faint as he pointed over my shoulder.

I twisted around to see what he had spotted. A pair of large logs bobbed about fifty feet away, floating aimlessly in the foam-streaked water. Without a word, Logan flopped off his board and began swimming toward them.

"Wait," I called, but the urgency in his movements pulled me with him.

I slid into the stinging salt water, gritting my teeth as it seared the open wounds on my back and abdomen. I hesitated—afraid that if I let go of my board, I might not make it back. But the logs might prove invaluable. Pushing past the pain, I struck out after Logan, hoping the gamble would be worth it.

After a few minutes of sluggish paddling, we reached the logs. Up close, they looked more like utility poles than driftwood—each about ten feet long and roughly twenty inches in diameter, tapering slightly toward one end.

Tangled among some palm fronds at the far end of the poles was a coil of bright orange cord—thin, tough, the kind used to bundle construction materials.

"This'll help!" Logan said, grabbing the line and testing its strength. "It's pretty tough," he added, giving it another yank without breaking it.

"Perfect. We can lash these logs together," I nodded.

We got to work, untangling the poles from the mess of palm fronds, trash, and nylon. Nails and staples jutted from the wood in random spots, forcing us to work carefully to avoid tearing our hands. The task was slow, leaving my already raw fingertips burning, but after a few minutes, we managed to free the logs and secure the string. We pushed the poles sideways through the current, swimming back toward the others with slow, deliberate strokes.

—

Back at the surfboard float, we got to work. The nylon string was about fifty feet long—just enough to lash the two poles together at both ends and create a rudimentary raft. Stable. Buoyant. It might keep Fern out of the water long enough to allow his leg to clot.

We aligned the logs so that the narrower end of one met the thicker end of the other, hoping to balance the shape and distribute weight evenly. Using the orange cord, we lashed them tight with a figure-eight pattern, cinching the ends until the poles held firm. We looped one of the leashes through, anchoring the array of boards.

"Fern, we need to get you onto the raft," Logan instructed. "You'll have to help pull yourself up."

Fern gave a faint nod.

Kavi and Logan positioned themselves to assist.

"Okay," Logan said, "On three. One... two... three."

Fern's face contorted in agony as he slid off his board and moved toward the raft. I pushed down on the logs to sink them lower as he carefully climbed aboard. He finally settled onto the float—his uninjured leg still dangling off the edge.

With his leg finally above water, I could properly assess the damage—and it was bad. The lacerations ranged from shallow scrapes to gaping wounds, but the worst of it was the tibia. It jutted through the skin just below his knee, framed by raw, torn flesh. Blood seeped steadily from the wound, painting the water a faint, cloudy pink.

"Oh, shit." I muttered to Kavi, who had spotted it too.

"I thought it was just cut," he whispered. "We have to tell him."

He leaned closer—

"Fern, listen. Your shin is broken pretty bad. The bone's out. We've got to keep you as still as we can. Once we get to shore, we'll deal with it."

Fern groaned, barely lifting his head. "Get to shore? What shore?"

"We'll figure it out," I interjected, trying to steady my voice. "Once the water levels drop, we'll head for land."

Fern let out a bitter laugh. "We're in the middle of the fucking ocean, man."

I hesitated, weighing my response. He wasn't wrong—but giving up wasn't on the table.

"Well, we either try, or we give up now. Your call."

He turned his head away and said nothing.

I exhaled slowly, scanning the endless sea. He was right—it felt hopeless. But I couldn't accept that we'd been carried so far away that even the bigger islands were out of view.

It wasn't possible. It couldn't be.

———

I checked my watch—5:29.

We had less than an hour before total nightfall. Once the sun was gone, the risks would multiply. Sharks hunted at dusk—that thought circled the edge of my mind. And we were bleeding in open water. The idea of fending off predators atop everything else triggered a fresh ripple of dread through me. But I kept it to myself. Our morale was fragile enough.

"We need to find some fresh water," I said, trying to redirect my thoughts and theirs.

"Do any of the boards still have fins?" Kavi asked.

We reached under our boards to check. Several remained intact, however damaged, cracked or splintered. Some were jagged and sharp, which was something.

"I've got a fin key," Fern mumbled weakly, motioning toward the zippered pocket on his board shorts.

"Nice!" Logan said, carefully unzipping the pocket and retrieving the tiny hex tool.

I took it between numb fingers.

"Flip my board over," I told Kavi, sliding into the water and bracing myself on the raft

Kavi rolled the board over, and I got to work. One fin stood out, serrated and sharp—almost like a blade. I began loosening the set screw, my fingers fumbling against the resistance. After a few painstaking seconds, I freed the fin and passed the key to Logan for safekeeping.

The task reminded me of something else stashed in my own pocket. I patted the outside of my board shorts, feeling the familiar bump.

"My flint!" I said, pulling it out with trembling hands, holding it up for the others.

Logan and Kavi both grinned.

"Thank god you're a nut job," Kavi muttered.

I nodded with a faint grin.

"This fin's pretty sharp, almost like a knife," Logan said, running a finger gingerly along its edge. "Now we just need some coconuts to magically appear."

I pictured trying to rip through a husk with my gnarled hands—it felt hopeless—but I stowed the fin in the bucket, just in case.

"Look," Logan said, pointing behind me.

I turned—

Low, heavy clouds hovered over the water—ominous and slow-moving. It was tough to say, but they did appear to be moving slowly in our direction.

"Maybe it'll rain," I said. "We could catch water in the bucket."

"What else can we use?" Kavi asked, searching the area.

"Shake the saltwater out of the bucket, just in case," Fern offered, a rare flicker of presence.

I tipped the bucket and shook it, banging the edges to release the brine, while Logan slid off his board and paddled toward more floating debris. He returned with a tattered black garbage bag and a cloudy plastic bottle.

He handed me the bottle, which had a few drops of yellow liquid inside. I wrinkled my nose and rinsed it thoroughly while Kavi cleaned the garbage bag as best he could and we stowed both in the bucket.

"We can use the bag for surface area to catch more rain," Kavi said. "Let's keep looking. More stuff might float by."

———

Every muscle in my body had seized up, the soreness stiffening me like rigging drawn tight. My lips burned, already cracked and raw—as if we'd been stranded for days, not hours. I glanced at my friends—none of them faring much better. Kavi's cheeks were hollow, his eyes dark and sunken. Fern looked worse—his breath shallow, his colour bleached out. Maybe it was the blood loss. Maybe the stress. Or maybe five hours in the sun, salt, and panic did more damage than we realized.

The dark clouds loomed in the distance, stalled in place. There was still a sliver of hope for rain, but it was thinning by the minute. Without water, we'd have to rely on coconuts or some other freak miracle to keep Fern alive. He was bleeding out and needed hydration more than any of us. The thought of losing him during the night—pushing his body off the raft, watching it vanish into the black—haunted my thoughts.

I clenched my fists, forcing myself back to the present. That nightmare wasn't an option—not for him. Not for any of us.

"Guys, I don't know if that cloud's coming our way, but we need to find water for Fern soon," I said, leaning in to check his condition.

Fern groaned softly, barely lifting his head.

"Big guy, how do you feel?" I asked.

"My leg hurts... hurts to breathe... thirsty," he replied weakly, the words slurring together. "Don't... don't move my leg again."

"We're doing everything we can," I said gently. "There's some dark clouds—maybe it'll rain."

He didn't respond but stayed conscious, his eyes fluttering open and shut. The bleeding had slowed considerably, but the wound had ballooned into a grotesque blend of purple, blue, and raw crimson—clotted and slick with fluid.

There was nothing more we could do beyond cycling the tourniquet and keeping him as comfortable as possible. His leg would need surgery—if we ever got out of here. If we even made it through the night.

29

—Still Alive—

The sun had dropped just above the horizon. Only a few scattered currents disrupted the stillness, swirling lazily around our makeshift raft. I craned my neck, sweeping my gaze in a full circle, when something caught my eye—a faint outline—hazy and distant.

My breath hitched.

It was diffused by sea mist, barely visible, but I thought I could make out the tops of trees.

"I think I see land!" I said suddenly, pointing.

Kavi and Logan perked up, lifting themselves partly out of the water to get a better look.

"Where? I don't see anything," Kavi said, squinting in the direction of my finger.

"Far out, over there," I replied, still pointing.

The shape was faint, almost illusory, and its position didn't align with where I thought land should be.

"I swear, I can see the tops of trees. Maybe hills behind them."

Logan shook his head. "I don't see it either."

I blinked rapidly, trying to steady my vision. The harder I focused, the more the formation seemed to dissolve into misty clouds.

"Where did it go?" I muttered, frustration mounting. "It was right there a second ago."

Kavi slapped the water, exhaling sharply. "You're seeing things, man."

I slumped back onto my battered board.

Am I losing it?

Maybe the blood loss and dehydration were starting to play tricks. I closed my eyes, just for a second, trying to reset my focus. —then looked again. Still nothing. Just haze and cloud. Whatever I'd seen, if it was real at all, had vanished.

———

A cool breeze brushed against my face, startling me against the day's oppressive stillness.

"Look!" Kavi shouted, pointing skyward.

Above us, a thick cluster of dark gray clouds had rolled in, spreading ominously across the sky. Small ripples broke the glassy surface of the sea beneath them, mirroring the sky's unrest.

"We should get the bucket ready," Logan said.

I had heard him say this exact sentence plenty of times in the past, usually it was because Fern had had too much to drink. Sadly, this wasn't one of those times. Fern was in real trouble, the kind that didn't pass with sleep.

———

We began organizing. The plastic bag—tattered and sun-bleached—might not hold up long, but it gave us extra surface area to channel water.

"Okay," I rasped. "When it starts, one of us keeps the bucket steady, the other two hold the bag in place."

Everyone nodded.

A few raindrops fell, rippling across the sea in soft, concentric rings. Instinctively, we all tilted our heads back, tongues out like children, but it sputtered out just as quickly as it started.

"Fuck, come on!" Kavi shouted, voice shredded with desperation.

"It'll start again," I croaked. "It has to."

Moments later, another light drizzle began, too faint to mean much. I stared at the sky, silently willing the storm to unleash what we so desperately needed.

Then the rain came—

A strong breeze signaled its arrival—then a sudden torrential downpour. The intensity escalated in seconds, pounding us with intense force, accompanied by gusts that whipped around us.

"Grab the garbage bag!" I yelled.

The bucket wobbled precariously in the turbulent air, inches from tipping. Kavi scrambled to steady it while I tore off the lid. The rain blasted us like a giant shower head, each droplet striking like a needle. Blood and water streamed down Kavi's cheek as the downpour reopened his lesion, soaking his bandana until it sagged uselessly. He pressed his hand against his head, holding the wound closed as best he could. Logan and I, on opposite sides of the raft, wrestled with the plastic sheet as it flapped violently in the wind, threatening to tear free with every tug.

"Shit—hold on Fern!" Logan shouted as Fern slid toward the edge of the unbalanced float.

We lunged to stop him, but it was too late—he splashed into the water, his broken leg submerged again.

"Fuck!" he griped.

His face twisted in pain, but he never let go.

"Hold on, dude! We'll get you up when the rain stops," Kavi yelled.

"Open your mouth! Try to get some water!" Logan yelled.

Fern hesitated, then tilted his head back, sticking out his tongue. I pulled myself higher onto the raft to check our improvised rain catcher, praying it was working. To my relief, a thin layer of water had already collected at the bottom.

"It's working!" I shouted.

—

The cool rain hitting my face was medicine—a fleeting gift from the same force that had so recently taken everything. Kavi and Logan felt it too—their voices cutting through the storm in bursts of joy. The downpour gradually intensified, becoming an overwhelming sensory barrage. The roar of droplets hitting the sea drowned out everything. Communication was impossible, and visibility shrank to almost nothing. The raindrops struck my face, blinding me with a mix of fresh and seawater. Still, I couldn't shake the feeling that this was a fragile truce. Mother Nature had unleashed her fury, but this gift felt like a small, solemn acknowledgment of our will to endure.

—

A few minutes later, it stopped, and the punishing stillness returned. The bucket had collected two or three centimeters of water—a considerable success.

"It worked. We've got enough for Fern," I said, my voice hoarse.

The sea was inert again—no ripples or waves in sight, as though the tsunami had drained every last ounce of her energy. Logan and Kavi began positioning themselves to hoist Fern back onto the raft—a process that promised to be grueling.

"Let's get you up here, buddy. We've got water to drink," Kavi said, gently, knowing Fern wasn't in a state to share in our small victory.

He nodded weakly, waiting as I snapped the lid shut and threaded my leash through the handle. I tested its buoyancy, hoping the seal would hold. The thought of losing our precious water to the ocean made me nervous. I pulled lightly at the lid, popping it loose, barely attached.

"Shit! I can't let go of the bucket. The seal's too weak," I said. "You'll have to get him up without me."

I tossed the fins back into the bucket to free one hand and steadied it atop the float.

"Okay, count it down from three," Logan said. "Fern, pull yourself on, we'll sink the logs. The sooner you're up here, the sooner you'll get water."

"Three, two, one—" Kavi commanded.

Fern groaned, his face clenching in pain as his leg shifted.

"Ah, fuck! Stop!" he shouted.

"What's wrong?" Logan asked.

Fern buried his face against the raft, groaning. "The log's crushing my balls," he muttered.

The tension cracked. We exchanged brief, silent smirks—just for a second, it felt like Fern was back.

"Okay, I'm ready," he mumbled after adjusting his position.

Fern finally slid onto the raft—face-down, motionless. We shared a glance—a flicker of who we'd been just hours before the disaster—before the weight of reality settled back in.

—

Kavi was retying his bandana when I noticed Fern's whole leg had taken on a light purple hue.

"We need to redo his tourniquet," I said.

I untied the cord, releasing the blood flow to his lower leg. He jerked slightly, groaning as fresh blood seeped from the wound into the water around us.

"It feels like pins and needles," he muttered.

After a couple of minutes, I re-lashed the rope, and the bleeding stopped.

Fern whimpered, his body trembling.

"Sorry, man. It has to be done," I said, guilt heavy in my throat.

Logan examined the bucket, holding it steady. Just a few cups had been collected.

"How do we do this?" he asked. "We can't drink straight from the bucket; it'll spill everywhere."

Kavi and I joined in, scouring the debris-littered sea for anything that could serve as a ladle. Using our hands would be inefficient and risk contaminating the precious water with salt. Carefully pouring it would likely waste even more.

"We have the plastic bottle," Logan said, holding it up.

I shook my head. "The water's not deep enough to fill it without tipping the bucket, too risky."

"Right," he muttered. "Then we need something else. There has to be something, an old cup—anything."

"I think I saw straws tangled in that palm branch earlier," Kavi said, gesturing toward the logs we'd retrieved. "Maybe there's more out there."

About fifty feet ahead was a larger patch of debris. It was promising but far enough that getting to it would take effort.

"Probably something useful in there," I said. "But it's going to be a slog. Only one of us should go to save our energy."

"Agreed," Logan replied, slipping off his board.

A few minutes later, he returned with a handful of items: a badly cracked red plastic cup, a halved coconut still partially covered in husk, and a battered, cracked straw.

"We can make this work," I said, grabbing the coconut shell.

The husk was stubborn, clinging tightly to the bowl-shaped interior. I wrestled with it, my trembling hands barely able to apply pressure. We took turns tearing away the remaining husk, each pull sapping our limited strength. What should have taken seconds dragged on for minutes, but eventually, the shell came free—a crude but functional cup.

I handed the shell to Logan—

He flicked it dry, shaking off as much saltwater as he could before dipping it into the bucket—his movements deliberate, careful not to waste a single drop.

"All right, Fern," Logan said, steadying himself. "This is important. Tilt your head back, open your mouth wide, and try not to spill."

Fern groaned, his body protesting as he shifted on the raft. Logan leaned forward and poured the rainwater into his mouth with painstaking precision. Fern swallowed slowly, his parched lips trembling as he took it in.

"I can't drink anymore," he said hoarsely after four small shells of water.

"How much is left?" I asked.

Logan peered into the bucket. "About half."

"What's the move? Do we keep it for Fern, or do we share and hope for more rain later?"

"I need some too," Kavi said.

"Same," Logan added, his teeth chattering.

He refilled the shell again, carefully passing it to Kavi. Then it was my turn. I brought the shell to my lips, fighting the urge to gulp it down. The water hit my tongue, and I swallowed slowly. My throat ached with relief, each sip dulling the burn of dehydration.

Finally, Logan took a scoop for himself, then put everything—the fin, the plastic bag, bottle, and the coconut shell—back into the bucket and snapped it shut.

30

—No One's Coming—

I looked up at the sky again, searching for more clouds. That brief taste of water had awakened a new, gnawing thirst. Unfortunately, there was nothing promising on offer. Still, I held on to the hope that another break might come before too long.

"I feel a little better," Kavi said quietly, breaking the silence.

I, too, felt less like a corpse. That small drink of water had restored some internal function and coherence.

"I need more," I admitted.

The sun hovered at the horizon, its glow bleeding into the sea. Darkness was creeping in, and with it, the dread of spending the night adrift in the open Indian Ocean, vulnerable to whatever came next.

"We don't have much time left," Kavi murmured.

"Yeah. If we can find more logs or something to add to the raft, we'd have a better chance. I'd rather not stay in the water all night," I said, trying to sound more optimistic than I felt.

"Light's fading." Logan started. "I don't need to say what we're all thinking—"

"Don't," I cut him off. "Let's not talk about that. Plus, maybe the tsunami threw the ecosystem into chaos. I bet there won't be anything for days."

He nodded but didn't look convinced.

The idea that predators could arrive any minute hung heavily in the air, unspoken but shared.

I thought about the scene in *Jaws*, where Quint talks about his harrowing experience aboard the *USS Indianapolis*. I could hear his voice describing the sharks picking off survivors one by one in the night. That memory—once a piece of movie-night fiction—was suddenly my reality. The idea of fending off sharks from our splintered raft in the dark made my stomach twist.

I strained my eyes, desperate to spot anything useful, but the water around us was barren.

"Anyone see anything?" I asked, my voice raspy, barely above a whisper. "If you see anything we can use, I'll swim for it."

"There hasn't been any new debris for a while," Logan said after a long pause. "I think the current's stopped."

He was right. The water had settled. Still, I couldn't let go of the idea that we might have missed something. Just as I was about to surrender, Logan pointed.

"There—branches."

I nodded.

—

We paddled slowly, staying close. The ocean was glass—eerily still—but I no longer trusted that kind of calm. Not after what it had done. My body wasn't working right. Each stroke was weaker than the last. Even breathing hurt.

"I don't know if this is worth it," he said faintly.

I glanced over.

His expression mirrored my own doubt, but I kept paddling.

"What else can we do?" I asked.

He shook his head. "What are we going to do? Fight sharks back with sticks?"

"Do you want to turn back?"

"I don't know. This whole situation is ridiculous."

With fifty feet to go, we stopped paddling, letting the silence settle.

"Let's just keep going," he said, at last. "It'll be better than nothing."

"They're just poking sticks, dude." I said, cracking a weak smile to lighten the mood. "It's always good to have a stick or two on hand."

He returned the faintest smirk before his expression darkened again.

—

We reached the clump of debris—palm fronds, wrappers, a couple insoles, and two larger sticks—each about an arm's length—about as thick as a baseball bat. They might not be weapons in the traditional sense, but at least they could put some distance between us and a predator, if needed.

Something glinted in the mess of detritus.

"Hang on," I said, squinting my eyes.

Bundled around one of the branches was a length of old fishing line, knotted and coated in green slime. My heart quickened as I pulled at it.

"If there's a hook, we might actually catch something."

Finally, the line snapped loose.

"Anything?"

"No lure, but..." I held up the messy coil. "There might still be a hook in here. Let's deal with it back at the raft."

I stuffed the line into my pocket, careful not to dislodge the piece of flint. With sticks in hand, we began the slow paddle back.

—

The raft rocked gently in the same spot, untouched since we left.

"What did you get?" Kavi asked.

"A couple of sticks," I said, setting mine down. "And this mess of fishing line. Might have a hook."

"How you doing, buddy?" I continued, laying my hand on Fern's shoulder.

"I'm great," he replied, flatly.

It was tough to tell whether he was being serious or sarcastic—but I took it as a good sign.

"Excellent. Hopefully there's a hook in this thing, that'd come in real handy."

Fern gave a faint thumbs-up.

I pulled the line from my pocket and set it down next to Fern. The bundle was roughly eight inches in diameter, a chaotic tangle of loops and knots. I tried to work at it for a minute, but my fingers were too shot.

"Can one of you take over? My hands are cooked."

Kavi nodded and took the ball.

He began picking it apart while Logan held one end steady.

"This is bad," he muttered. "It's really knotted."

"Just do what you can," I said. "Even twenty feet of line could work—if there's even a hook."

Minutes crawled by as Kavi sorted through the gnarled mess, cursing under his breath until he let out a triumphant shout.

"I got it!"

He pulled the end loose, revealing a rusted hook, embedded in a piece of Styrofoam. The hook was small— maybe a half inch long—fragile-looking and thick with rust. The barb was barely intact and the metal looked like it might snap under the slightest tension. Kavi tested it, gently bending it back and forth.

"That thing's gotta be ten years old," Logan muttered.

"Probably," Kavi said, holding it up against the glowing sky. "But it's still sharp enough to hook something. I just don't know if it'll hold."

"If we free up more of the line, maybe we can try it," I said, hunting the sea for potential bait.

"I saw a tiny dead fish float by earlier," Logan added. "Maybe there'll be more."

Under normal circumstances, food wouldn't have been urgent. But nothing about this was normal. There was no knowing how long we'd be out here to fend for ourselves. We were on fumes, and even a few calories might keep one of us going. Kavi straightened as much of the line as he could and tied the end securely to the raft.

"Let's just toss it out for now," he said, kissing the rusted hook. "Maybe something'll bite it."

I smirked.

He flung it far—the line arcing then disappearing into the silty deep.

31

—Nightfall—

The last sliver of sun dipped below the horizon, dragging what little hope we had with it. No sign of land, no more water collected. The day had failed us, and now, night was here—dark, cold, merciless. I felt betrayed by the sun for retreating and leaving us to face this new phase, with no regard for whether we lived or died. Somewhere back on land, Kendal and the girls were probably beside themselves—imagining the worst. And I hated that I couldn't reach them—couldn't stop the panic I knew was setting in, or let them know we were still alive, still fighting.

I punched at my board as frustration boiled over.

"FUCK YOU!" I shouted at the sky.

I considered letting go entirely—just falling backward into the water and thrashing like a toddler throwing a tantrum—but I didn't. Instead, I gritted my teeth and tensed every muscle, breathing heavily, forcing myself to hold it together.

—

For all it represented—deprivation, cold, predators—the sunset was breathtaking. Pinks, purples, greens, and yellows swirled in the sky, like watercolour bleeding on wet paper. But instead of awe—I felt rage bubbling up again.

"Bullshit!"

"What?" Kavi asked, his voice weary.

I pointed to the sky, unable to contain my bitterness.

"It's just going on like nothing happened, like nothing's wrong. We're fucked, and the planet's just giving us this postcard-perfect sunset. Here—enjoy the view, suckers!"

Kavi stared at me in silence—

I knew my anger was irrational. Hating the sky made no sense and wasn't going to change our situation. But I hated it anyway. I hated that it chose this day of all days to flaunt its beauty. And I hated how powerless I felt.

I choked back tears. News of the tsunami had certainly reached my family back home by now. They'd be calling, texting, trying anything to reach me. The thought of their panic clawed at my heart. What would be worse—dying out here or leaving them behind with no answers?

I'd give anything to be back home. To be bored on my couch, staring at my apartment's blank walls—lonely, but safe. This trip had been the best thing that had ever happened to me—and now, it felt like the cruelest joke. But as much as my own despair pulled me under, I thought of everyone else it would affect. My family. My friends. Kendal. The weight of their grief, should we not make it, hardened my resolve. I still couldn't believe any of this was even real. No land in sight. Just water in every direction, like the world had been erased.

I slammed my fist against my board again. "I'm not doing it!" I shouted into the night. "I'm not gonna let it happen!"

The silence that followed my outburst was suffocating. Logan, Kavi, and Fern said nothing; there was nothing to say. My chest heaved as I stared out at the endless waterscape, scouring the darkness for any sign of hope. The small flashes of defiance I managed to summon felt hollow—but they were all I had.

—

The last fleck of light vanished, leaving us under a vast, glowing firmament. In the sun's absence, the temperature plummeted, and the blood loss we'd all suffered left us shivering—defenseless against the cold.

"Are we fucked now?" Fern asked, his voice barely more than a whisper.

"I don't know," Kavi replied quickly. "Someone has to come for us at some point. Tomorrow, someone will see us," he shivered as he spoke.

"Tomorrow, someone will come for us..." Fern repeated to himself, the words trailing off into the black silence of the sea.

32

— Estrellas —

One by one, the stars revealed themselves in the descending night, as if the gods were carefully puncturing tiny holes in the fabric of the heavens. Soon, the entire expanse above us was freckled with their light. I'd never known a silence like this—total and unbroken. It made the stars feel impossibly loud. With nothing to distract me—adrift in the eerie stillness—I found myself utterly captivated by the world above.

———

The stars brightened as the ambient glow faded away, swallowed by the deepening void. With the moon still hidden below the horizon, nothing softened the darkness or interrupted the sparkling texture overhead. The difference between up and down blurred entirely, leaving a seamless black chasm peppered with trillions of white points. It was as though the universe itself was reflected below us, the surface of the water mirroring the cosmos in perfect clarity. Kavi, Logan, and I stared in quiet awe, soaking in the unsettling beauty surrounding us. The reflections of the stars seemed to stretch endlessly into the liquid abyss, as though they were suspended millions of miles below.

Occasionally, shooting stars tore through the atmosphere, painting fiery orange trails across both the sky above and its twin below. Afloat in what felt like the center of the Milky Way was breathtaking—but also profoundly disorienting. At times, I lost track of whether I was looking up at the stars or down into the reflection. Again, it seemed the universe was indifferent to our peril, carrying on blissfully unaware, while we fought to hold on.

—

A faint, blurry indigo light caught my attention below the raft. I froze, unsure if it was real or a trick of the eyes. Squinting, I tried to focus on the source of the light deep below.

My voice cracked as I broke the silence. "Do you guys see that blue glow down there?"

There was a pause—

"I see it… looks like a jellyfish," Logan said, finally.

More glowing figures emerged gradually, scattering dim blue, orange, and red light around us. The sight reminded me of the phosphorescent algae from the girls' beach dance a few nights ago. One of the glowing shapes drifted within feet of the raft, its pulsating, amorphous body spreading light outward in waves—like an underwater firework.

Jellyfish after jellyfish rose toward the surface, surrounding us in a kaleidoscope of colour. As they passed, their glow lit Logan and Kavi's faces, painting the scene in shifting hues. I almost forgot our predicament—briefly lost in nature's theatre.

But the awe didn't last.

I wondered if we'd see or hear whales during the night. That thought led, inevitably to sharks. If the jellyfish had returned to their usual patterns, it stood to reason that predators might be doing the same. I tried to bury the thought.

Of course, that's right when it happened—a sudden slap on the surface, thirty feet away, followed by splashing that faded into the distance. We all snapped our heads toward the noise but saw nothing—just ripples disturbing the otherwise still water.

"Fuck, what was that?" Kavi whispered.

"You have to be kidding me," I muttered, my heart sinking.

Deep down, we all knew. It was the same sound we'd heard that drunken night from the dock—the haunting splash of something large moving aggressively through the water. I gripped my stick tightly, willing myself to believe it was something else.

Minutes passed as I lay there, breath tight and shallow, too afraid to move. Just as I began to ease, another splash—farther off this time. I turned to see ripples distort the water's mirrored surface.

"Could it be a dolphin? Or a big fish?" Logan asked, his voice thin with desperation.

None of us answered.

269

THOMAS J DERRY

The odds were slim. Dolphins usually hunt during the day, which left one likely conclusion. My muscles tensed as I tried to pull myself further onto my board.

"If it's a shark, it's probably staking us out, right? Why else would it be this close?" Kavi said, cutting through the silence.

He was right. A shark wouldn't be this close unless it was drawn here—for us.

"Do sharks eat jellyfish?" Logan asked. "Maybe it's here for them?"

"I don't know," I muttered. "Maybe."

I tried to think of another explanation, but panic overpowered reason. My skin prickled as I realized the jellyfish were gone. They'd vanished—slipped away while we weren't paying attention.

"It must have scared them off," I said, my voice trembling.

—

I didn't know what I had left—what any of us did. My limbs were shot, my mind frayed, hope shrinking by the minute. I thought of that story from *Catch Me If You Can,* where Christopher Walken's character described two mice falling into a bucket of cream. One gave up and drowned, while the other kicked and flailed until the cream turned to butter, and escaped. I had no idea which mouse I was—but if I stopped kicking now, I knew how it would end.

"We can't lose it now," Logan said softly, gripping his poking stick with white-knuckled hands. "There has to be something we can do."

The three of us huddled closer on the raft, trying to keep ourselves as far out of the water as possible without tipping it. Not being able to see below made it worse—how do you defend against something you can't even see? I trembled, stunned by how quickly everything had turned.

"What do we do?" Logan asked, his voice cracking. "There has to be something."

"I don't fucking know!" I said sharply.

"What about banging the bucket? Would that scare it off or just make things worse?" Kavi asked.

"I don't know!" I said, sharply. "Just shut up for a second and listen."

I pressed my forehead against the damp wooden raft, breathing in shallow, laboured bursts, staying perfectly still.

Something was out there.

Circling.

33

—Voices in the Fog—

Something lit up my eyelids, startling me awake. As I came to, I could see a beam of sharp light scanning across Fern's body, then the raft and onto Kavi's face, highlighting his blood-stained bandanna.

I must've fallen asleep.

I sat up quickly, searching for the source of the beam.

"What is that?" Fern mumbled, quietly.

A few hundred yards ahead, the point of light swung erratically—left and right, up and down. I tried to shout, but my throat was so dry that only a cracked rasp escaped. The light cut through a thin mist hovering above the sea, lighting up patches of water and splitting off the glossy surface like a mirror.

The beam settled on my face, this time accompanied by a voice.

"Hey! Is anyone alive out there?" A deep, American voice called through the dark.

I waved my arm, groaning incoherently, trying to get their attention.

"I see movement—they're moving!" a voice shouted, locking the beam back onto our raft.

I snapped up.

"O... Over here!" I finally croaked, my voice scratchy but audible.

"U.S. Coast Guard, this is rescue vessel Delta Echo Two—we've located four stranded. I repeat, we have eyes on four, over," the man radioed, his voice echoing into the stillness.

The radio crackled back.

"Copy that, DE2. Awaiting status report, over."

"Copy, stand by, over," the man replied.

"Who is that?" Kavi asked, barely lifting his head.

"I don't know." Logan said, sitting upright on his board, eyes wide.

Two uniformed men appeared out from the fog, flashlights in hand, one stood at the bow of a black-and-grey Zodiac, one at the helm. The motors hummed quietly as the boat approached. Spotlights, antennas, and glowing monitors crowned the radar arch—every element brimming with modernity.

My eyes filled with tears.

It was over.

We'd been found.

"Jesus. Are you guys, okay? How badly are you hurt?" One of the men asked.

"We're... we're pretty bad," I answered, barely holding it together.

"You're safe now, just sit tight—we'll get you out of here," one said, sweeping his flashlight across.

"U.S. Coast Guard dispatch, this is Delta Echo Two, requesting EMS on standby. We've got a head wound, compound leg fracture, multiple lacerations, and blood loss. All four are alive, over."

The beam settled on Fern's face, stirring him.

"What's happening?" he asked, in a daze.

"The Coastguard's here. We're getting rescued," I said, tears pooling under my eyes.

"We'll move you aboard one at a time. Anyone with spine or neck injuries?"

"No, I don't think so." Kavi said.

"Copy that. Sit tight."

One of the officers extended a long aluminum pole.

"Grab hold," he instructed.

A moment later a hook ladder splashed into the water next to Logan. As we got closer to the boat, I could smell the fumes and feel the heated water from the engines.

"We'll bring you aboard. Use the ladder. We'll lift your friend with the fracture once you've boarded. Understood?"

We nodded.

They started with Logan, then Kavi, then me—finally splinting Fern's leg before hoisting him aboard. As I crested the pontoon, my feet hit the ribbed aluminum floor. It was cold, synthetic and jarring against my waterlogged feet—something I might have scoffed at back home—another sterile layer of modern life. But here it was an emblem of salvation. Engineered, man-made, unmistakably artificial—and the most beautiful surface I'd ever felt. It meant we'd made it back to the world.

—

We leaned against the pontoons, wrapped in emergency blankets, sipping bottled water. Fern lay flat, one officer checking his vitals and asking him a battery of questions. I turned and watched our crude raft drift away—back into the black, shark-infested night. In my overwhelmed state, I felt a pang of guilt. It had saved our lives, and we had left it to face the dark, alone. In my overwhelmed state, a strange sorrow manifested—as though we'd abandoned a friend.

I snapped back as one of the officers leaned in. He held his flashlight up to my eyes.

"Are you awake?" the man asked.

"Am I awake?"

"Yes, are you awake?" he repeated.

"Yeah, I'm awake."

He shook me.

"Wake up!"

"What? I am awake."

He shook me again.

"Wake up, Cole. You need to wake up," he repeated.

"What? Need to wake up? I am awake," I replied.

"Wake up Cole—come on. Wake up!"

34

—Wake Up Cole—

"Cole, wake up!" Logan's voice pierced through the haze of sleep as he shook my shoulder. I opened my eyes in a panic, heart racing. It was pitch black—the cold ocean stretching endlessly in every direction. My mind reeled, searching for something—anything—that made sense.

"Where did they go?" I gasped, my voice breaking.

"Who?" Logan asked.

"The Coast Guard! Where did they go?" I stammered, whipping my head around for any trace of their boat. But there was nothing—just the dark, lifeless sea. The moon had risen while I was out, now casting a soft sheen over the water, and the faint shimmer of stars reflected through a thin layer of mist hovering above the surface.

"What? What Coast Guard? You were asleep."

The air left my lungs—

It hadn't happened.

The Zodiac, the spotlights, the officers' voices—all of it, gone.

"No!" I yelled, slapping the water in frustration. "I can't fucking believe this! They were right here! Two officers on a pontoon boat. They found us!"

"Dude, calm down," Kavi said sharply from the raft. "The sharks are back."

My breath hitched as tears welled in my eyes, blurring the already dark world around me. I spun in frantic circles, desperate to find the boat, the lights—anything.

"It was so real," I whispered, my voice trembling. "They were right there!"

I slumped against the raft, trembling with a mix of rage and despair. The safety I'd felt only moments ago was gone—ripped away, replaced by a brutal emptiness.

—

A sharp splash cut through the silence—less than twenty feet away.

"Shit," Logan whispered, clutching his stick as he peered into the darkness.

I stared into the black void, my shoulders sagging. The sound confirmed what Kavi had said—but I hardly cared anymore. If something wanted to end this, let it.

I was ready.

"Come fucking get me, you prick," I muttered under my breath.

Without thinking, I grabbed the bucket and began slapping it against the water, the hollow sound echoing across the still sea.

"Come on, come get me!"

"Cole! Stop!" Logan shouted, grabbing my arm and trying to wrench the bucket from my hands.

"What difference does it make?" I shouted, shaking him off. "What's the fucking point?"

Logan's voice cut through the chaos, sharp and unflinching.

"The point is that acting like a child won't help. If you want see your family—or Kendal—again, then fucking stop."

I froze—

My breathing came in short, ragged bursts. I stared at the raft, at the water, trying to ground myself. He was right. I'd lost it.

"Morning's going to come," Logan continued, voice lower now, more steady. "If we don't get eaten or bleed out, we'll spot land. Do you want to be around for that?"

I set the bucket down slowly, hands trembling. I leaned forward, pressing my forehead to the damp wood of the raft, eyes shut tight. I focused on the rhythm of the waves. On the faint glimmer of moonlight rippling across the water.

The shark slapped the surface again, this time behind me—circling. Was it interested in us—or something else? Maybe the raft had attracted sea life, and the shark was chasing bait fish nearby. Or maybe it was investigating us. Another splash interrupted my thoughts, this time just feet away.

"Don't move!" Logan commanded, his voice sharp and low.

"Is it messing with us?" Kavi whispered.

We clung to the raft, pressing ourselves as close as possible without tipping it over. The only sound was the steady, maddening rhythm of the bucket tapping against the wood.

Then it happened—

"Shit!" Logan shouted.

He splashed his hand into the water and slipped from his board, vanishing beneath the surface before I could react.

"Logan!"

I dove in, swimming to where he had vanished. The black water swallowed everything, offering no clue of his whereabouts.

My heart pounded.

"Logan! Where are you?!"

I dove under, searching, but there was nothing—just a deep, dark, effervescent void where he once lay.

"Logan! Where the hell did he go?!" Kavi's frantic voice cut through the dark.

Seconds later, a gasp came from behind me—it was Logan!

"What happened?!" I called, rushing to meet him.

Kavi swam beside me. "Are you okay? What happened?"

He splashed desperately toward the raft, just a few feet away, his breath ragged and panicked.

"Something… something pulled me under!" he stammered, voice breaking.

"Did it bite you? Are you hurt?" I asked, placing a hand on his shoulder to steady him.

"I… I don't know!" he managed, his wide eyes darting between us as he hoisted against the wooden logs.

"Dude, you're going to flip the raft! Stay in the water!" I yelled, pulling him back to stop him.

Then another splash—closer this time.

"What the fuck is it?!" Logan snapped, spinning toward the sound.

Before I could respond, something brushed against my calf and foot—rough, deliberate, unmistakably alive.

"Oh shit!" I yelled, kicking away and swimming frantically to the other side of the raft.

"What? What happened?!" Kavi shouted in a panic.

"I felt something—something big touched me!"

The three of us froze, treading water as terror gripped us. Whatever was out there, it wasn't done.

"Did it bite you?!" Kavi shouted.

"I don't know!" I stammered, reaching down to feel my leg and foot.

My fingers brushed against a small, stinging cut on the back of my calf.

"There's a cut on my leg—"

Before I could finish, Logan scrambled higher, tipping the makeshift raft and dumping Fern into the sea. The entire structure flipped, sending the array of boards and leashes into a tangled web.

"Fern!" Kavi yelled, swimming around the capsized raft.

I followed close behind as Fern surfaced, spluttering and thrashing. His frustration flared immediately.

"What the hell are you doing?!" he shouted, his arms floundering as he struggled to stay afloat.

"Hold on!" I yelled, swimming toward him with Kavi.

As I reached him, he latched on, arms locking around my neck in desperation, pulling me beneath the surface. His forearm drove into my injured back and shoulder, igniting a sharp, blinding pain as saltwater rushed into my mouth and nose. I kicked hard, but his weight was too much.

Thankfully, Kavi acted quickly, pulling him backward and breaking his grip. I surfaced, coughing violently and gasping for air. He dragged Fern toward the raft as I swam over to steady it.

"Logan, you have to move! We need the raft for Fern!" I shouted, my voice hoarse.

"I don't want to go back in there," he replied, eyes darting around the surface.

"Fern can't stay in the water. He'll bleed out."

Logan hesitated, his hands gripping the raft tightly.

"Something big pulled me under," he whispered, shivering uncontrollably.

I locked eyes with him, the pale moonlight casting sharp shadows across his sunburnt face. Aside from a few cuts on his ankle, he didn't look hurt. Whatever had grabbed him hadn't done real damage.

"Logan, if you don't get back in, Fern won't make it. You don't want that."

—

It was wild how fast things had flipped—Logan had been pulling me back from the edge of insanity one minute, and now I was the one talking him down. Maybe desperation made leaders out of whoever was still upright.

—

Though the threat still lingered. Whatever had pulled Logan under hadn't yet returned—it seemed, for now, to have relented.

He stared at me, his breathing ragged. Slowly, he reached out. I grabbed his hand firmly and helped him to slide off the raft and back into the sea.

"Good. Let's get Fern up."

Kavi and I worked together, hoisting Fern onto the raft as carefully as possible. He groaned in pain as his injured leg shifted, his body trembling.

"Sorry, man. We'll try not to let that happen again," I said softly.

I swam back to my piece of board and lay still, straining to listen for any sound of the shark—or whatever had been circling us. Kavi and Logan were quietly untangling the mess of leashes and boards, reassembling what little order we could manage. My adrenaline was still surging, keeping my core temperature up for the moment, but my wet body and hair were already starting to feel the chill of the night air. I pressed my forehead against the wooden raft and forced myself to take slow, steady breaths, trying to calm my frayed nerves.

"What if it comes back?" Logan asked softly from beside me.

A long pause stretched between us.

"I don't know." I finally replied, my voice low and resigned.

"Maybe all the commotion scared it off?" he offered, his tone tinged with hope.

"Maybe."

———

The silence returned, broken only by the faint sound of water lapping against the raft. My thoughts were scattered, my body trembling as I fought to stay grounded. I remembered the fishing line still tied to the orange nylon strapping.

"I'm going to pull the fishing line in," I said, more to myself than anyone else. "No point in leaving it out."

No one responded—they didn't care one way or the other. I reeled the line in slowly, coiled it into a ball and stuffing it between the two logs of the raft. The task gave me something to focus on, however small and insignificant.

—

I closed my eyes and let my mind drift. I found myself longing for the life I used to resent—the one I'd tried so hard to escape. My shoebox apartment, the hum of distant traffic, the flicker of streetlights bleeding through the blinds. Boring, safe, predictable. I'd traded it all in for adventure—and now I was floating in the dark, praying to live through the night.

Somehow, that old life and this new one folded into each other—two versions of myself colliding in the cold. I thought about the girls.

Were they alive?

I pictured us sitting around a warm campfire back on Nias, the soft glow of flames lighting up our faces. I could almost taste the wine, hear the laughter as Kendal, Carissa, and Hunter joked and teased one another. That memory felt distant and fragile, but for a moment, I clung to it. I needed something to carry me somewhere far from the cold, the hunger, and whatever waited in the depths below.

35

Morning

The subtle glow of first light warmed my shivering body. I slowly opened my salt-crusted eyes to see the ocean stretching out ahead, the sun's soft orange reflections rippling through the faint marine fog, diffusing gently across the raft and my friends. A light breeze tousled my hair as I lifted my head, marveling that despite the odds, all four of us were still together. Not a single breath of swell had materialized—the ocean surface remained unnervingly lifeless. I ached in ways I didn't know I could, as though my muscles and bones had fused together during the night.

The cold air clung to my wet skin, numbing it almost entirely. My hands seemed alien—white and blue, chapped and wrinkled so severely I could trace the bones below. I tried to flex my fingers, but they were stiff, barely responsive.

Logan was still asleep, his face angled awkwardly toward the water, slack-jawed against the side of his board. His breath came shallow, teeth faintly chattering. Kavi sat upright, backlit by the sun, staring at the horizon. His bandana was caked in crimson blood that ran down onto his face and neck—it looked like a scene pulled from *Apocalypse Now*.

"Hey, Cole," he said in a shaky, quiet voice.

"Hey, Kavi," I replied, almost smiling despite myself.

"We made it."

Logan stirred, slowly lifting his head from the raft. He turned toward us, expression blank, a mask of exhaustion. Trembling, he reached over to Fern and gently rocked him.

"Fern... wake up."

No response—

He tried again, shaking him a little harder.

"Fern, wake up. It's morning."

Still nothing.

My heart sank as I reached out with my weathered, shaky hand, placing my fingertips against his neck to check for a pulse. A faint warmth met my icy fingers, and Fern shifted slightly, letting out a groan as he pulled away from the chill.

Logan exhaled, relief softening his expression. "Thank God."

—

Off in the distance, a handful of pelicans appeared, swooping low from the sky before landing gracefully on the water, several dozen feet from our raft.

"Birds," I croaked, my voice crackling awkwardly.

"They're not out here for us," Logan smiled

I nodded.

And then, I saw it—the distant apparition of land I'd imagined the day before. This time, it was real. I pointed behind Logan, smiling for the first time in what felt like an eternity.

"Look!"

All three of us turned, staring at what might finally end this nightmare. I stretched upward, trying to confirm it wasn't a trick of the light.

Palm trees. A beach. Rocks. It was faint, but it was real. The land was several miles away, but it was there.

"There's actually land," I said, stunned.

Kavi turned to me, his face set with determination.

"I think we can paddle for it," he said.

—

We had a little water left in the bucket. It wasn't much, but it might be enough to give us the energy to move. Fern wouldn't be able to paddle what remained of his board, so we'd need to organize a way to tow him and the raft. It wasn't ideal, but it was the only move left.

"Let's split what's left of the water and get to it," I suggested.

Logan winced as he struggled with the bucket lid, his hand stiff and claw-like, unable to fully bend his fingers. Finally, with a soft pop, the lid came off. He ladled water with the broken coconut shell, carefully offering it to Fern.

"Fern, open your mouth."

Fern didn't answer, but his lips parted slightly.

Logan poured a small stream into the gap, careful not to spill. He then took a sip himself, struggling to swallow the liquid, before passing the bucket to Kavi and finally to me. I carefully ladled what remained and tipped it into my mouth. The cool water soothed my parched, burning throat, a brief reprieve from the constant discomfort. I coughed slightly as the last drops slid down, then set the bucket back on the raft. Logan carefully re-secured the lid.

"It's pretty still. I think if we paddle our boards, we can drag Fern and the raft to land," Logan suggested, eyes fixed on the island.

"It's worth a try," Kavi agreed.

—

After some discussion, we lashed the boards into a crude, makeshift dog-sled rig, with the raft trailing behind. The good news was that the sun was high enough to start warming my body... the bad news was that this sweet spot wouldn't last. In no time, it would be back to its usual routine—roasting us alive.

—

"You guys ready?" I asked, voice still shaky from the cold.

Logan and Kavi nodded, and we mounted our boards.

I took my first stroke and immediately felt pins and needles radiating up my arm.

"Hold on," I said, stopping abruptly. "My arms are asleep."

The sensation subsided slowly.

"Okay, I think I'm good," I said finally, more determined than confident. "Let's go."

—

At first, it felt like we were dragging an anchor. Each stroke was a battle, our progress painfully slow. But gradually, the raft began to move. The sight of land glowing in the morning sun drove us forward—a faint, distant promise of safety. I imagined myself lying on the sand, free from the relentless stress of the ocean, away from predators and the punishing sun. I could barely remember what it felt like to be dry, to feel at ease—as if safety itself had become a myth.

I focused on my breath, forcing a rhythm and pushing my body through the lactic burn. Each stroke ground my battered chest against the board, a raw reminder of my injuries. I glanced at Kavi beside me. His face was set in tense determination; his eyes locked on the horizon as he adjusted his blood-soaked bandana every few strokes. Behind him, Logan paddled steadily, his gaze also fixed firmly on the distant target.

—

A small breeze swirled around us, tickling my spine and blowing strands of hair into my eyes. Its direction was hard to pinpoint as it circled us in brief vortexes, but I prayed it would push us toward our goal.

"Let's hope this turns into a tailwind." I said, pausing for a beat.

Kavi and Logan nodded.

After a few minutes of aimless swirling, the wind settled at our backs and began creating small ripples in the water, nudging us forward.

"That's definitely a tail wind," Kavi said, glancing up as he paused to assess.

Logan just kept pushing, only pausing briefly every seven or eight strokes. He didn't look up—just paddled, like he'd made a deal with himself. We were running a tight operation, all things considered, but with the tailwind, we might make better progress than expected—so long as it stayed gentle and didn't stir up too much chop.

—

A flock of pelicans soared past from behind, heading straight for the island. Their presence felt comforting—like they were guiding us to safety. The morning fog had burned off, leaving the sky and ocean a brilliant, vivid blue. The land ahead came into sharper focus, coconut palms peppered the shoreline, their fronds shifting lightly in the breeze.

I glanced at Kavi. "Can you see them?" I asked.

"I can. Are we getting closer? I can't tell," he replied.

"We must be."

As we inched closer, pelicans became more frequent, their swooping dives and gliding wings filling the air with a low hum. One landed directly on Fern's back. It stood there grooming its feathers like we were just part of the scenery. The sight made the three of us laugh softly, a moment of levity in our ordeal.

But Fern didn't react—not even a twitch.

I called his name, but he remained still.

Concern flickered in Logan's and Kavi's eyes.

I splashed water at the raft and the pelican flapped off with a squawk.

Fern let out a low groan.

The truth was unspoken but clear: the longer it took to get him to land and provisions, the slimmer his chances became.

—

By 11, the island was finally within clear view, its features sharpening with every stroke. Palms that had once been a smudge of green now stood distinct, their shapes swaying gently in the breeze. I counted twenty or so trees spanning the landscape, with more clustered further back. It didn't look like much, just a scrap of earth in the middle of nowhere—but it was real, and that was enough.

36
—Landfall—

Four hours of nonstop paddling had left our shoulders throbbing, our arms shot, and muscles nearly seized—but the shoreline was finally within reach. The water had turned a minty-blue as we approached, revealing glimpses of the sea floor. Dark fingers of rock and coral reef stretched out toward the ocean, broken up by patches of pale sand that shimmered with shifting light patterns cast from the ripples above. Below, I could see the shadow of our makeshift rig creeping across the bottom, inching ever closer to more forgiving terrain. I stopped paddling and rested my face against my board, letting my battered muscles relax for a moment. Every part of me—from my arms and back to my shoulders—had grown numb from the constant exertion.

"I can see the bottom," I croaked, struggling to catch my breath. "We're so close. Let's rest."

The three of us collapsed, trying to collect ourselves and ease the agony in our overworked bodies. Outside of the brief pauses to cycle Fern's tourniquet, this was our first real moment of reprieve.

—

Kavi broke the silence.

"Alright, who's ready?"

Logan and I both groaned but got back into position. We resumed paddling, inching forward into shallower water. A small ground swell began to rise, breaking about fifty or sixty feet from the shore. As we drew closer, the coral became more dense—one last hazard before reaching safety.

"How are we going to do this?" Kavi asked, lifting his head to survey the scene ahead.

"I don't know. This is going to be sketchy," Logan admitted.

—

The shoreline looked like a warzone. The sand was uneven and peppered with gravel, tree limbs, and trash, while waves broke over jagged coral and rock. The tsunami had stripped the beach of most of its sand, leaving a harsh, eroded coastline. I glanced back at the raft, analyzing how it might behave in the chaotic surf. Fern, lying motionless, was our biggest concern. If it flipped, his leg could be wrenched or torn further, risking more blood loss.

We watched the shore in silence, searching for the deepest channel or the least aggressive section of waves to minimize the risk. But it didn't really matter—the bay was ringed by jagged reef and a long shelf of shallow water stretching hundreds of feet—so casually strolling in was off the table.

"I think the only option is to time it," Logan said. "We wait for a lull and get the raft inside the break before the next set of waves. From there, we let the whitewater push us the rest of the way."

Kavi and I nodded silently.

———

The plan was simple in theory but daunting in practice. We'd dismount our boards and wait for the right moment. When the waves subsided, we'd push the raft through the break zone and into calmer water near shore. From there, we'd keep Fern steady and let the surf do the rest—hoping the whitewater would carry us in without flipping us or dragging us over the coral. With no better options, we steeled ourselves for the task ahead.

I paddled to the aft portion of the raft and checked the lashings. The calm seas had been a blessing—the knots held firm, and the wooden poles remained securely bound. At the front of the raft, the scrap fishing line was still wrapped tightly and jammed between the orange nylon and logs. Behind us, Fern's board and the bucket dragged, tied off and ready.

"Fern are you all set? We need you to hang on tight— this might get rough," I said, as Logan and I took the aft and Kavi held the bow.

He nodded faintly.

Before long, the swell lulled—

"Go!" I shouted.

We kicked with whatever strength we had left, holding the raft with one hand and paddling with the other. Slowly, we began to move, creeping toward shore. As we entered the impact zone, I glanced back to see a set wave forming, lifting and growing as it crept toward us. If it hit the raft on the wrong angle, it could flip.

"Hold on, Fern!" I yelled.

As the wave overtook us, Logan and I pushed down on the wooden logs in unison, sinking the aft deeper into the water and raising the bow. The swell lifted the raft a few feet and pushed us forward in a controlled surf. The ride was brief but nerve-wracking. When the wave finally passed, my shin grazed something solid.

"I hit something!" I yelled, the excitement in my voice unmistakable.

"Paddle!" Logan shouted.

The undertow from the first wave tugged us backward, undoing some of our progress. But the next wave quickly rolled in, lifting the raft and propelling us forward again. Logan and I repeated the process, pressing down on the raft's rear to keep it stable. When the wave passed, my foot struck solid ground—a mix of coral and sand. I planted down firmly, my head and neck just above the surface as the undertow pulled me back.

Ahead, Kavi was in chest-deep water, struggling to support himself on the uneven ground, as he guided the raft. Gravity felt alien after so many hours afloat—every step was a battle. Logan and I exchanged a glance and paddled the final stretch until a rock clipped my knee, sending a jolt up my leg. I stood again, my body more than halfway free of the sea's grip. The undertow clawed at us as we trudged forward, coral and shells biting into our feet with every step.

None of it mattered anymore.

We were safe.

One last surge of whitewater pushed us the final fifteen feet until the logs rested on solid ground. Fern and the raft bobbed gently in the shallow surf, no longer at the mercy of the sea—this part of the nightmare was finally over.

37

—This Will Do—

I let go of the raft and took my first steps onto the island, finally able to take in my surroundings. Up close, the devastation was more brutal than it had looked from the water. The sand was coarse and uneven, torn open in places to expose rock and rubble. Tree trunks lay snapped like toothpicks, their splintered ends jutting out at strange angles. The air stank of wet vegetation and stagnant seawater. Flies hovered around matted seaweed and half-buried debris scattered across the high-tide line. Plant life looked scorched and skeletal, stripped of colour. I stood still, taking in the wreckage and silence—despite the totality of the disaster, somehow, we were still here.

I fell to my knees in an emotional tailspin. My abdomen tightened, and my body convulsed. Stomach acid and bile spilled onto the sand, a brutal purge of everything I'd held in: the fear, the grief, the sheer weight of the event.

I collapsed, breathing hard, my face inches from the gritty shore. A million points of pain shot from my battered torso as I touched earth, each one searing into focus. I lay there for what felt like an eternity, my clenched jaw finally loosening as my body gave in to exhaustion.

—

I started to laugh—

Nothing was funny, it was a laugh born of exhaustion, shock, and sheer absurdity. It bubbled up uncontrollably, defying logic. Quietly, Logan joined in from his place on the other side of the raft, chuckling intermittently. Then, finally, Kavi joined us.

For a few moments, we laughed together—illogical, nonsensical laughter that slowly tapered into giggles and then faded into silence.

I sat up, adjusting to the harsh reality of our new surroundings. Kavi clutched his bloodstained bandana against his head, Fern was motionless on the raft, and Logan lay face down, letting out the odd residual chuckle, as though the absurdity still hadn't fully worn off. I moved my attention to Fern, making sure he was still with us. I untied his leg cinch, unsure of how long it had stayed tight.

"Fern, we made it. We're on shore."

He didn't respond, only wincing as I re-tied the cord. Every part of me sagged with exhaustion. I lay back again, feeling the coarse sand grind into the raw, torn skin on my back. The sting was intense, like I was lying on a nest of fire ants.

I checked my watch: 1:21.

We needed to rest, all of us, but time wasn't on our side. Shelter, water, and fire had to be sorted before sundown. My fingers brushed the zippered pocket on my shorts, confirming the flint was still there. Fire was non-negotiable—it would mean warmth, protection, and a signal for rescue.

I resolved to give myself half an hour. Just thirty minutes to let my body recover before tackling the long list of tasks ahead. I glanced at Kavi, Fern, and Logan. None of us spoke, but the silence carried a shared understanding. Within seconds, I slipped into a restless slumber.

—

I woke abruptly, gasping for air as a coughing fit rattled my chest. My eyes adjusted to the brightness—I was on solid ground, no longer trapped in the open sea.

I checked my watch—2:03 p.m.

"Guys, we need to get moving," I said, firmly.

I staggered upright, every step sharply uncomfortable as the soggy, raw skin on the soles of my feet pinched under my weight. I walked toward the water, letting the cool tide wash over my back, rinsing away the sand and pus that clung to my wounds. The tide had receded slightly, and the swell seemed to be shrinking along with it.

"Kavi, Logan... we need to get a move on. We're running out of time," I called back at them.

Slowly, they stirred, sitting up in the sand, their faces drawn with exhaustion and confusion. Both hobbled toward the water to rinse the clinging sand from their battered bodies.

—

I moved inland, sizing up the island for anything that might help. The tide was still dropping, so Fern was safe for now, but we had to get him out of the sun and hydrated as soon as possible.

Moving him wouldn't be easy—the raft was far too heavy to carry, and the broken boards wouldn't support his weight. Without something rigid beneath him, any attempt would likely do more harm than good to his leg.

The island, no bigger than a few football fields, offered little hope. A patch of banana trees stood ahead—stripped bare like everything else.

"Anything?" Logan asked from behind me.

"Nothing," I replied.

—

Ahead, at the island's center, stood two towering palm trees surrounded by small green coconuts scattered on the sand below. I picked up two of the largest nuts and shook them, confirming they were full. Kavi and Logan joined me, each grabbing a coconut and assessing it. Logan began futilely smashing his against a nearby rock.

"Stop," I said, cutting him off before frustration could take over. "Save your energy—we need to work smart."

My mouth watered at the thought of coconut water, but we needed to find a way to break into them without wasting time and strength.

"Let's make a pile and figure out how to crack these later," Kavi suggested.

He nodded.

Kavi and I began stockpiling the nuts while Logan set off in search of anything useful. We quickly gathered about a dozen—each one heavy with liquid. A few minutes later Logan returned holding a weathered plastic ice cream container—something we could use to collect the water once we figured out how to get inside.

—

Venturing further inland, we spotted the remains of an old structure—a jumble of wood, bamboo, and palm thatch strewn around its foundation. The waves had devastated the area, leaving sharp lava rock formations exposed where layers of sand had been stripped away. Walking barefoot was hazardous, each step a challenge on the uneven, eroded ground.

We reached the wreckage and began taking inventory: dozens of tangled bamboo lengths, each about three inches in diameter—some stretching eight feet long, others shorter—lay scattered among the debris. There were small slabs of thatch, scraps of plywood, and even a broken white window frame—its cracked glass still clinging to the edges.

"We can build a stretcher with this," Kavi said, pawing through the bamboo.

The find was a stroke of luck. The bamboo and thatch would allow us to build both a stretcher and some form of shelter for the night.

—

We got to work—

Logan and I began freeing pieces of bamboo, tossing them into a pile. Each bend and lift made my arms ache— it wasn't the pain that got to me, but the steady drain of strength with every repetition.

After collecting what we could, we carried our materials a short distance from the wreckage and began laying out the stretcher's framework: four long pieces of bamboo in parallel, with three shorter cross braces. We salvaged some bark strapping from the original structure to lash it together. Logan and I worked on binding the pieces, the material proving stubborn and requiring significant strength to cinch. Several painstaking minutes later, the rectangular frame was assembled.

"This isn't great," I said, noting its flimsiness.

"The cross brace will help," Logan replied, placing the shortest piece of bamboo across the center.

Kavi brought over several large, woven palm thatch pieces to line the stretcher, adding rigidity and creating a surface for Fern to lie on. Each joint needed to be strapped diagonally to ensure stability. My hands trembled, protesting with every pull of the bark, but eventually, it was complete.

I bent down to lift one end of the stretcher—surprised by how light yet solid it was. Kavi draped the thatch over the top and lay down to test it. Logan and I lifted him, and the stretcher held.

"This'll work," Logan said, with a nod. "Fern can sleep on it until we get out of here."

"Ready?" I asked.

"Ready."

We lifted the stretcher and began the slow, careful walk back to the raft to fetch Fern.

———

Gathering water was our next priority, as dehydration had reached critical levels.

"How do we get into those coconuts? Any ideas?" I asked as we walked past the pile.

The thought of smashing one open using my battered hands was far from appealing, but we might not have a choice. As we crested the island's highest point, I spotted Fern lying just as we'd left him. The fear lingered that we'd return to find him lifeless, but I pushed the thought aside.

—

"Fern, you ready to move?" I asked, arriving next to him.

"Wake up, buddy. We gotta move you," Logan added, crouching beside him.

He lay unresponsive.

I knelt, gently patting his cheeks to rouse him.

Nothing—

I pulled back one of his eyelids—bloodshot and vacant.

I sighed, checking his pulse beneath his jawline, I found a faint heartbeat.

"Yep," I said, exhaling sharply, "but I don't think he's going to cooperate."

"What if we drag the raft into the water and float him onto the stretcher?" Kavi suggested.

I gave the raft a shove, but it didn't budge.

"This thing weighs a ton," I said. "We're not moving it without help from the ocean."

"Then what?" Logan asked. "Flip him over—like an omelet onto a plate?"

I shrugged.

"Sure, that works."

We positioned the stretcher beside the raft and began. Kavi and I eased Fern's body inch by inch while Logan supported his injured leg. He moaned weakly, face contorted in pain as we rolled him from his stomach onto his back, settling him onto the stretcher.

Little by little, we moved him onto the stretcher until he was secure, ready for transport. The three of us took positions—Logan at the front, Kavi in the middle to steady the load, and me at the back. We lifted slowly, careful not to strain the rig, and began the awkward march away from shore.

A small flat patch sat a few hundred feet from the shore, flanked by the two tall palm trees—far away from the shoreline. Kavi cleared debris—rocks, fronds, and old coconut husks—while Logan and I carefully lowered Fern into position.

"What do you guys think? Are we safe here?" I asked, glancing up at the heavy coconuts hanging just above the clearing, swaying slightly as I stood.

Logan walked a few feet away, eyeing the overhanging branches. "Looks like it."

I fought to steady myself. The effort had left me lightheaded. My hands tingled and my head throbbed—the sound of my heartbeat pounding in my ears.

"Let's get at those coconuts," Logan said, returning with four of them.

Nearby, a sharp volcanic rock, unearthed by the tsunami, stood out like nature's machete.

"Who wants to give it a shot?" Kavi asked.

"There's no way I'm stopping now," Logan said confidently.

He sat behind the volcanic outshoot and slammed the nut several times. Its husk dented and began to tear. Gripping the broken fibers, he pulled hard, the husk peeling away in slow, painful strips. After a few savage minutes of smashing the rock, the shell was exposed.

"Got you!" he grumbled.

I handed him the ice cream container, brushing off any sand.

"Fingers crossed," I said.

He grabbed a small rock and struck the inner shell—after a few hits, it split open, spraying liquid into the air. About two cups of liquid spilled into the container—a precious, electrolyte-rich lifeline.

"Nicely done," Kavi said, smiling faintly. "I think you've got a future on this island."

Logan grinned as he prepared the next one. I resisted the urge to gulp the liquid as I picked up the container and brought it to Fern.

"Coconut water time, buddy," I said, leaning in.

Kavi and I worked to maneuver him into drinking position.

He groaned weakly as Kavi pried his mouth open gently. I began to pour the liquid, drop by precious drop. After a few seconds, he started to react, his throat working to swallow the water.

"There you go, buddy. Drink it up. You're going to be okay," I said quietly, keeping my focus steady.

Before long, the container was empty. Fern, who had been teetering on the edge, now had a renewed chance. Kavi and I exchanged a look of cautious optimism—a flicker of hope that we might not have to spend the evening burying our friend.

—

We returned to Logan, who had broken into two more coconuts, the exposed shells already leaking their contents into the makeshift container. Together, they yielded at least four more cups. Kavi drank slowly, stopping after a few gulps.

"You next," he said softly, his chin glistened with coconut water as he wiped it with the back of his hand.

I looked to Logan who gave a nod of approval as I took the container in my trembling hands. The liquid spilled into my mouth, soothing the cracks and blisters around my lips. I could feel it cooling me from the inside as it moved down into my stomach—an almost electric sensation of life returning. It took every ounce of self-control to stop drinking and pass the remaining water to Logan.

"Cheers," Logan said with a weak smile before finishing the container.

"I can keep opening the coconuts. My hands are fucked anyway," he said, breaking the silence.

His fingers were raw, bloody, and battered, evidence of his relentless efforts.

"Jesus, dude! Maybe you should stop," Kavi said, grimacing at the sight.

Logan shook his head with a humourless chuckle.

"What does it even matter? We need water, and I'm already wrecked," he said, heading back to the coconut pile.

"I can help," I offered, standing up. "We'll alternate."

He nodded and got back to work, his technique now honed. Bash until the husk split, tear it, bash some more, tear more, then crack the shell.

He finished another, pouring the liquid into the container.

"Your turn," he said, passing me the next coconut.

I braced myself.

"Here goes," I muttered, slamming it against the rock.

The force reverberated through my hands and arms, igniting sharp pain in every injured joint and muscle. Gritting my teeth, I mimicked Logan's technique—

ripping the husk away, splitting the shell and pouring the water into the container.

"I appreciate the help," Logan said, picking up another, "but you and Kavi should start on the fire and shelter."

He handed me the container—

"Here—split this between you. I'll drink the next one."

Kavi and I shared the water, each sip bringing us closer to hydration.

38

— Build the Fort—

Kavi gathered the remains of our broken surfboards, palm fronds, and bark stripped from the lower trunks of nearby trees. His mission was to build a floor—something to keep us off the damp, uneven ground. My task was to light a fire—possible in theory, but far from easy. Most of the island's debris had been soaked by the tsunami and even after a full day of baking in the sun, everything was still damp. I scoured the area for anything dry enough to light. Some old coconut husks and dead palm leaves seemed like a start. I shredded them into tiny bits, creating a softball-sized collection of tinder before spreading it out in the sunlight to dry.

With that set, I walked to the water's edge to explore the shoreline. The coast near our raft was sandy, but jagged rocks dominated both directions beyond it. I headed to the right, searching for anything useful.

About a hundred feet in, I froze—

THOMAS J DERRY

A smooth, wide drag mark cut through one of the remaining patches of soft sand—unmistakably left by a crocodile. I crouched to examine it more closely. The trail started about twenty feet up from the waterline and continued inland for another thirty feet before ending in a circular sweep pattern where the croc must have turned back toward the sea. Deep impressions marked where its clawed feet had pushed against the ground, leaving piles of displaced rock and sand. Judging by the size and depth of the tracks, this wasn't a small reptile.

I exhaled sharply.

I had no real experience with crocs, but I knew enough. I considered warning the others, then let it go. No sense adding crocodile anxiety to the pile—not yet. I turned back toward the spot where we had originally landed. I passed the raft and continued onto the more rugged, rocky shoreline.

——

There had to be something useful here—twine, fishing nets, anything to help us catch food, light a fire, or defend ourselves from reptiles. A hundred or so feet in, I stumbled on a grouping of larger rocks covered in black oysters. Common in Indonesia, these could be a game-changer— if they weren't dead or rotting. I picked up a smaller rock and smashed one of the shells. Inside, the meat was pale pink, dripping with fresh brine. I scooped it up, gave it a cautious sniff, and tossed it in my mouth—maybe it was the extreme hunger, but it was the best oyster I'd ever tasted.

"Holy shit! Guys!" I called up the beach. "Oysters— tons of them!"

Kavi and Logan hurried over, their exhaustion momentarily replaced by curiosity.

"Check this out," I said, smashing another shell and handing it to Logan.

He didn't hesitate, eating it in one bite while I prepared one for Kavi.

"Wait—should we even be eating these raw?" Kavi asked, holding the slimy meat like it might bite him.

"Good question," I said, pausing.

Eating them raw might be fine, but the last thing we needed was to risk adding vomiting and diarrhea to our list of problems.

"I've got a plan—we need fire."

I started back toward the pile of tinder I'd made earlier, Logan close behind.

"So… is the plan cooking them?" he asked, falling in step beside me.

"Yep. If we put burning brush on top of the oyster rocks, the water in the shells should boil and they'll open," I explained. "In theory, anyway."

"That's kinda brilliant," he said, nodding.

—

We began digging the fire pit about halfway between our base camp and the rock. In my absence, Logan had managed to rip into several more coconuts, filling the ice cream container nearly halfway. Kavi had done an excellent job gathering driftwood in various sizes and stacking it neatly nearby. The tinder shavings were just about dry. I shaped them into a loose ball at the center of the pit, then pulled out my flint.

"Ready?" I asked, glancing at Kavi and Logan.

They nodded; each poised with more kindling in hand. I crouched onto my hands and knees, wincing as my back wounds stretched and cracked. I began rapidly scraping the flint, sending small sparks into shredded husks. I kept at it until a faint wisp of smoke began to rise from the tinder. Gently, I lifted the pile, cupping my hands around it, and breathing life into the small incendiary. Smoke thickened, and a small flame licked upward. I set the tinder back down and began stacking thin twigs and dried palm leaves on top. The flames grew quickly, and in no time, they were half a foot tall, their warmth washing over my face. I jumped up and grabbed more substantial pieces of wood to keep it fed while Kavi and Logan set out for larger brush. A few moments later they returned, each carrying an armful of dead palm fronds.

The flames consumed the branches and my energy rose. The coconut water had dulled my headache, and the thought of food spurred me forward. The fronds burned quickly, generating a fierce, brief heat. We carried the flaming branches toward the oyster-covered rocks and dropped them onto the densest patch. The flames crackled over the shells for about a minute before starting to fade.

"I'll get more," I said, darting back toward the campfire.

I gathered up an assortment of smaller branches, and ran back to Logan and Kavi, who piled them on. The fire grew again, blasting the shells with another wave of intense heat.

"This won't be enough—I'll get some coals." Kavi said as he headed toward the fire, with Logan close behind.

While they fetched embers, I walked over to the abandoned raft and pulled the fishing hook from the wood.

Soon, we'd have bait from the oysters—but whether the line and hook would hold a fish was another question. I gathered it into a bundle and headed back to join the others.

—

Kavi and Logan returned with several coconut shells filled with glowing red coals. We spread them across the rocks and layered more fronds and twigs on top. As the last flames faded, we circled the rocks, waiting to see if any shells had opened.

"Alright, let's check this out," I said, using a charred branch to push the remains of the fire aside, exposing the shells beneath.

It had worked—

Dozens of oyster shells had popped open, wisps of steam curling up into the air.

"No fucking way!" Kavi exclaimed, grinning. "I thought that was a long shot."

I smiled back, sharing his disbelief.

Using small, jagged rocks, we carefully dug them out of their shells. In no time, we had devoured several. The flavor was almost indescribable—briny, savory, and just a little fishy. It was pure heaven. I must have eaten a dozen or more before finally stopping.

"Let's bring some to Fern!" Logan said, grabbing a larger, flat rock.

He rinsed it off in the water, loaded it with several oysters, and started back toward camp.

"I'll catch up," I said, threading one of the smaller, overcooked oysters securely onto the hook as bait.

—

I made my way across the rocks, looking for an area that was sheltered from the waves and—hopefully— crocodiles. A large, barnacle-covered boulder caught my eye, blocking the brunt of the wave energy and creating a tide pool with rock walls on either side.

"Perfect."

I kissed the rusty, baited hook for luck and cast it into the pool. The ecosystem had been violently disrupted just a day earlier, but things were shifting, and there was a chance we'd get lucky. I pulled the line in a jigging motion, imagining the tug of a fish on the other end. A single catch could change everything. A full belly and a decent night's sleep were exactly what we needed to keep moving.

After a few casts, I coiled the line around my hand and made my way back to the beach. Helping Logan build the shelter and assigning Kavi to continue fishing seemed like the most logical use of our strengths.

—

Back at camp, I found Logan and Kavi huddled around Fern, who looked to have eaten some oysters.

"He ate two," Kavi said, smiling faintly.

"Nice job," I said, patting him gently on the shoulder.

"Alright—we've got maybe a couple more hours of light. Logan, you and I can work on a shelter. Kavi, let's get you set up for fishing, yeah?"

"Yep, let's do it," Logan replied, getting to his feet.

—

I found a flat piece of driftwood near the shoreline. Wrapping the line around the wood, I fashioned a makeshift hand reel—a sort of maritime cod jig— something Kavi could hold onto while fishing. If he managed to catch something, it would be sturdier than bare mono in the hands.

We crawled across the rocks toward the tide pool.

"This is the best spot I found. Just jig it and hope for the best, I guess," I said, tossing the hook into the water.

He took the rig and gently yanked at the paddle to test the line.

"I got it. Prepare for a feast."

"I believe it. I'll be back in a bit... and hey, watch for crocs. You never know," I added, feeling a pang of guilt for not mentioning the prints I'd found earlier.

"Watch for crocs, catch fish. Copy that," he replied with a grin.

I climbed the rocky terrain back toward base camp, still turning over whether I should tell them what I saw. I decided to wait until the shelter was done. At least then, we'd have some semblance of security before dealing with the added threat.

—

Back at camp, Logan handed me a fresh coconut.

"Let's split this," he offered.

I nodded, sipping from the shell. Compared to that morning, I felt hydrated—enough to notice something strange.

"I just realized—I haven't peed in over twenty-four hours, but I think I'm finally getting there," I said.

Logan smirked.

"That's funny. I forgot people pee."

He stretched his arms with a groan. "Alright. Coconut break's over. Let's get this thing built."

With that, we set out to work—no plans, no blueprint— just whatever we could do, with what little we had.

39

— Shelter, Not Safety —

Construction would begin with a bamboo frame salvaged from the remains of the decrepit shack. The two palm trees at either end of our camp served as natural supports to anchor the bones of our shelter. The trees leaned outward, creating a natural taper—ideal for wedging in a cross brace.

"This one looks about right," Logan said, hoisting a ten-foot length of bamboo, the biggest in the pile.

We wedged it between the trunks, jamming it downward until it rested about four feet off the ground— a good height for the peak. Using rocks, we hammered the bamboo down into place, jamming it tightly.

"We can use the orange cord to strap this down," I said, over my shoulder, as I headed toward the shoreline.

—

When I reached the raft, I began unraveling the line, but the weight of the last twenty-four hours unexpectedly hit me. I squatted down next to the raft and sobbed quietly. It felt like we'd been living inside a nightmare—pages torn from a horror script. My role had been to hold everything together, to meet every impossible scenario with calm resolve. But stillness gave way to sorrow, and the bottled emotions spilled out. We weren't out of the woods yet, but releasing the pressure left me lighter.

Eventually, I collected the twine, composed myself, and trudged back to camp.

—

Logan was hard at work collecting materials and tending the fire. He glanced up as I approached.

"You good, dude?" he asked.

"Yeah," I replied. "I just needed a minute."

"I don't blame you. This shit's already added years of therapy to my life," he said, cracking a wry grin. "And possibly physio."

"I hear challenges make you stronger, at least that's what the podcast people say," I laughed.

He smirked.

"A podcast and a coffee sound nice right about now, something light and apolitical."

"Plenty of time for that soon. Let's get this shelter up."

"Done deal."

Logan held the bamboo cross-brace steady while I lashed it tightly to the tree trunks, crisscrossing the orange twine.

"Solid," I said, giving it a test.

Then we grabbed four uniform bamboo lengths, and brought them to the cross-brace, leaning them in place to form the shelter's back wall. Using coconut shells, we scooped sand and rocks, burying the base of each piece of bamboo and tied them to the cross-brace using the remaining twine and strips of bark.

"You know what? That's not bad," Logan said, testing the stability of the bamboo joints.

"For sure, it'll only get sturdier once it's covered," I added.

The shelter's interior was about six feet deep and just under ten feet wide—enough space to cover all four of us comfortably.

The next step was collecting fresh palm fronds to layer atop the bones. Without a machete, we resorted to pulling them free by hand, occasionally breaking the stubborn ones loose with a rock. In no time, we had twelve harvested.

We carried the stack of fronds back to the shelter and began splitting each one down the middle, doubling our coverage and giving us two symmetrical halves. By aligning the thick bases at the high point of the frame and letting the leaf tips angle downward, we created a surface designed to shed rain and block wind. Once everything was in place, we stepped back to admire our work.

The shelter looked solid—sturdy enough to keep us dry, shaded, and maybe even a little warm overnight. We spread a thin layer of thatch along the base—just enough to lift us off the sand and blunt the worst of the uneven ground. Feeling accomplished, we returned to Fern and moved him under the structure, finally out of the relentless sun.

The shelter complete, we decided to head back for the bucket to pack the bedding with sand. Nearing the raft, I stopped. The bucket was gone.

I paused, glancing around—that's when I realized I hadn't seen Kavi in a while. My stomach dropped as worst-case scenarios flashed through my mind. I broke into a jog, heading toward the oyster rocks. A few tense strides later, I spotted him just beyond the boulders—crouched at the tide pool, grinning beside a bucket full of fish.

"There you are," I said, breath catching slightly.

"Howdy," he replied proudly. "Caught some."

"No shit! This is amazing!"

I lifted the bucket to inspect his haul: three small sea bass and a couple pink reef fish.

Logan arrived and peered into the bucket.

"You legend! Doesn't even bother to tell us he's got dinner sorted—just keeps going."

Kavi shrugged, still smiling. "Got on a roll. It's pretty soothing, honestly."

As if on cue, the line tightened—

He yanked the paddle with quick, practiced motions until out came another fish. He removed the hook and tossed it into the bucket.

"That's six, bitch! I'm done," he said, standing triumphantly.

We laughed.

"What a mic drop," I said, grinning.

———

Back at camp, Kavi caught sight of the shelter and nodded in approval.

"This is pretty solid," he said, examining the structure.

"Now that we've got fish in camp, we should think about making weapons for the night," I said, the thought nagging at me.

"Why? What do we need protection from?" Logan asked.

It was now or never—

"Okay, here goes."

I sighed.

"I found croc prints earlier—before I found the oysters."

There was a pause.

"Seriously? Where?" Kavi demanded, his voice rising.

I pointed toward the far side of the beach. "Over there."

"Why didn't you tell us?" Logan snapped.

"I almost did, but I didn't think you needed the extra stress. Telling you we have a giant predator nearby didn't feel helpful at the time."

"Yeah, but you sent me to fish in that cove," Kavi barked. "That's *need-to-know* information."

"You're right. I wasn't thinking," I admitted. "I figured that fishing hole was too rocky and tight for a croc that big to navigate. Plus, I *did* say, keep an eye out for a croc."

Logan and Kavi exchanged a look.

"What? *Keep an eye out for a croc?* Dude, I thought you were kidding," Kavi shot back.

"Wait, hold on—a croc that big? How big are we talking?" Logan interrupted, his brow furrowing. "Have you seen it?"

I hesitated.

"No, but it doesn't look like the slide of a small animal."

"Show us."

40
—The Island Has Eyes—

"Here," I said, pointing at the sunken footprints.

Kavi stared in awe.

"Are you serious? That's a fucking monster!" he said, pacing back and forth nervously. "This croc—or whatever it is—probably lives here. We're on its land!"

Logan knelt, holding his hand next to one of the imprints for scale.

"Yeah, that's great… it's bigger than my hand. This thing's a bull!"

He stood, pacing now.

"You should've told us, man."

"Well, what exactly do you guys think we could've done if I had?" I shot back. "Would you have gone on a crocodile hunt?"

I paused, softening my tone.

"Look, we can't change the fact that it's here," I said, steadying my voice. "But here's what we can do—we cook well away from the shelter, burn the bones, bury whatever's left, and clean up in the ocean. No scraps, nothing left behind. We stay alert, and we don't give it a reason to come looking."

Kavi threw his hands up. "Dude, the croc doesn't care about fish—to him, we are the fish," he shot back. "What if it ambushes us at night? How do we defend ourselves from a fucking dinosaur?"

"I'll take that over being circled by sharks in the middle of the pitch-black ocean," I muttered.

We stood in silence for a moment, staring at the prints.

"What if we just turn the fire into a wide wall of flames between us and the croc?" Logan offered. "We can find some big rocks and bamboo for weapons?"

"It might help," I said. "But we're cutting it close—it'll be dark in forty-five minutes—we need to move."

—

The three of us split up, each searching for materials—not just to keep the fire alive through the night, but also to arm ourselves. A small surplus of driftwood was drying next to the flames, but it wouldn't last the night.

We returned to the ruined shack; its scattered wreckage sprawled across the sand like the remnants of a forgotten war. Pools of stagnant water from the tsunami still clung to the area, soaking the ground and turning the wreckage into a minefield. Broken glass, exposed nails, and half-submerged debris forced us to tread carefully.

Kavi, undeterred, pressed into the chaos, shoving aside logs and cautiously wading through brackish puddles as he unearthed pieces of bamboo and tossed them our way. Logan and I worked along the edges, scooping up rogue pieces of driftwood and tattered thatch, adding to the growing pile. The salty air mingled with the musty scent of wet wood as we picked through the ruins, sidestepping splintered boards and rusted debris, scattered like traps. Kavi ventured closer to the foundation—his movements deliberate as he shuffled his feet through the knee-deep water.

A faint clink broke the silence as his foot tapped something metallic.

He stopped cold—then crouched low like a hunter locking onto prey.

"What is it?" I asked, stepping closer.

He grinned, plunging his hand into the murky water. When he stood, a rusted blade glinted in his hands.

Logan and I stared, wide-eyed.

"No fucking way," I whispered. "A machete? We have a fucking machete?"

Kavi shuffled back toward us, cradling the blade like treasure.

"It's dull as shit," he said, turning it over, "but we can sharpen it—open coconuts, clean fish, hell... even make a spear!"

I inspected the blade. Despite its wear, it was sturdy—and brimming with potential.

"This is going to change everything," Logan murmured.

—

We returned to the shelter and laid everything out. Kavi knelt beside Fern, checking his pulse. After a tense moment, he gave a tenuous nod. He was still alive.

"I'll cycle the tourniquet—that should wake him up. Logan, grab some coconut water."

As they worked, forcing him to drink and cycling the rope, I grabbed the bucket of fish and started toward the shore—intent on setting it far from camp. The croc prints still nagged at me, but I shoved the thought aside. Between the cooking setup and the much larger main fire, we were going to run short on fuel.

"We need more wood," I called. "I don't think we have enough to get through the night."

Both nodded.

"I'll sharpen the machete and prep the fish," Logan replied, already scouring the ground for a grinding stone.

Kavi joined me to gather anything remotely burnable—driftwood, dried fronds, even damp debris that might throw smoke.

Nearing the croc tracks, I couldn't shake the feeling we were being watched. I found myself scanning the tree line, half-expecting something to emerge.

"It's almost dark. Crocs are nocturnal, I think. Keep your eyes open," Kavi said, voice tight.

I nodded—

This area near the slide was strewn with driftwood and bordered by low-lying brush and grassy shrubs near the forest's edge. The sun had finally dipped below the horizon, leaving everything soaked in bluish twilight—just enough light to see, but not enough to feel safe. As the shadows deepened, the noise floor of insects began to rise—a cautious symphony gaining confidence with each passing minute.

We worked quickly, gathering half a dozen logs each and dropping them next to the fire before heading back for another round.

"Think we should sleep in shifts?" Kavi asked, quietly.

"Yeah, we need someone to keep the fire going," I replied.

We finished collecting what we could and made our way back to camp, arms full. The fire had burned low but was still alive, crackling gently as we returned. We arranged the logs to dry. Logan sat nearby, grinding the machete against a flat rock. The once-rusted blade now gleamed faintly in the firelight.

"Nice wood haul," he said, handing it over. "That should keep us going most of the night."

I inspected it. The edge wasn't razor-sharp, but it was functional.

———

I walked toward the water's edge to finish setting up the cooking fire, while Kavi and Logan reshaped the main pit. I scraped a shallow divot into the sand about thirty feet from camp and gathered wet driftwood to use as makeshift spits. By the time I returned, the main fire had transformed into a roaring, trough-shaped blaze, ten feet across.

"This is great," I said, admiring their handiwork. "We just need to keep it burning."

We loaded three coconut shells with glowing embers and carried them to the new pit. Once the flames took hold, we mounted two fish at a time on the driftwood spits, propping them securely above the heat. Kavi returned with freshly plucked banana leaves to use as plates.

———

The fish hissed over the flames, each drop of fat crackled like a twig snapping in the woods. Smoke drifted upward, thick with the scent of char. The aroma was mouthwatering—but it also felt like bait. A dinner bell for the crocodile. I stayed on edge, my eyes flicking toward the shadows beyond the firelight.

After ten minutes, the first four fish were cooked. We placed them on banana leaves to cool while the remaining two finished. The beach was shrouded in darkness, lit only by the flicker of our fire and the faint afterglow of the vanished sun. I kept my gaze locked on the stretch of beach between us and the water, scanning for movement. Being in a predator's territory left no room for ease. Every shadow seemed to shift, every rustle of the breeze through the palms sounded like a warning.

My mind began to spiral—conjuring the image of a crocodile sliding out from the surf, its body low and deliberate. Vanishing into the night as it stalked closer.

"Hey."

"Cole," Logan interrupted, breaking my trance. "These are ready. Let's eat so we can get back to Fern."

He handed me a banana-leaf-wrapped fish, snapping me out of my anxious reverie. It felt miraculous to hold a hot, fresh meal after everything we'd endured. Kavi's fishing, the oysters, the janky line—even the flint— somehow, all of it had worked. This island—far from perfect—felt like a gift compared to where we were twenty-four hours ago.

We each took a steaming fish and carefully picked its bones clean. The rich, salty flavor was nearly indescribable—pure heaven in that moment. As I ate, everything went quiet. For years, I'd eaten at high-end restaurants, indulging in meals that came with distractions—work deadlines, buzzing phones, or endless conversation. It had taken a brush with death to finally arrive in the present. Still, some part of me remained on edge—eyes flicking toward the tree line, aware that peace out here was provisional.

———

We tossed the remaining bones into the fire, one by one, watching them smolder to ash—reducing the meal to memory.

"Okay, Fern's turn?" I asked, breaking the silence.

Both nodded.

We worked methodically sliding the meat off the bones and onto the banana leaf. The flakes of white flesh were soft and fatty, perfect for Fern to swallow. Carrying the fish back to camp, that creeping uncertainty returned.

Was he still alive?

I knelt beside him with the tray of food.

"Buddy, we cooked you a feast," I said, nudging him gently.

"Come on, man. Wake up," Logan added.

I shook his shoulder until a faint grunt escaped him.

"There he is," Logan said, relief in his voice. "Fresh fish. Open up."

He placed a small piece of fish on Fern's lips, but he didn't react.

"Let me try," I said, carefully prying his jaw open. "C'mon, buddy... just a bite."

Finally, the fish made its way into his mouth, and his eyes fluttered open briefly. Slowly, his jaw began to work, chewing the food. Logan raced back to the coconut pile and returned with a container of water. Fern ate in tiny bits until he was done.

"Enough," he whispered, his voice barely audible.

The three of us exchanged looks of relief—he was still with us.

"Water," he added, faintly.

I poured the last of the coconut water into his mouth, tilting the container carefully. He raised his face just enough to drink before sinking back into the stretcher.

"That's it for now. Rest up, pal," I said softly.

———

We returned to the fire and sat in the sand. We'd barely slept in two days, and it showed.

"How are we going to do this?" Logan asked.

"One on duty while two sleep?" Kavi suggested.

"Makes sense," I said, checking my watch. "We each get about six hours total before sunrise."

We agreed: Logan and Kavi would sleep first while I kept watch. The machete and bamboo staffs were left within reach—just in case.

"Alright, let's make this work," Logan said, settling below the lean-to shelter next to Fern.

"Wake me in two hours."

I nodded.

———

I stoked the fire and kept the machete within reach. The croc was out there—I could feel it—but unlike last night, I could feel hope creeping in.

41

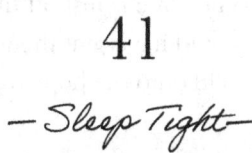

— Sleep Tight —

The dark felt even heavier now. For the first time since the accident, there were no tasks to distract—no chaos to smother my thoughts. The breeze, the insect hum, the crackle of the fire, and the hush of distant waves became the soundtrack to my spiraling mind. I replayed the last twenty-four hours on a loop. Most of it still felt surreal. Like grief delayed—I hadn't fully accepted it yet. And even with the small wins, our survival was far from guaranteed. A slow death from infection remained a nagging possibility.

"This is going to be a long two hours," I muttered, trying to slow the hamster wheel spinning in my head.

My thoughts drifted to Kendal. She probably thought I was dead—assuming she had even survived. I didn't know what had become of the Nias coast—only that it couldn't have been spared.

We'd left land four hours before the tsunami struck—surely someone had sounded the alarm. Maybe they'd had enough time to get to higher ground.

—

The *Sunda* tectonic plate is just off the Sumatran coast, and a quake there could have sent the wave racing toward Nias in minutes. I held onto the hope that she and the girls had made it.

Two hours of sitting in the dark, stewing in anxiety, wasn't going to help. I looked around the camp for something—anything—to occupy my mind and keep me busy. Bits of plastic, driftwood, coconut husks, and palm leaves were scattered across the beach. It was a mess, and while tidying wouldn't aid our situation, it might quiet my thoughts.

I stood and got to work.

—

The fire's glow faded behind me and the air cooled as I worked. Overhead, the sky unfurled—so vast and startling it stopped me in my tracks. In any other circumstance, this place would be heaven. The stars dappled the sky by the trillion—a celestial haze stretching across the endless black canvas, like powdered sugar. The moon hadn't yet risen above the horizon, leaving the island steeped in a soft, unbroken darkness. Dozens of meteors streaked through the heavens, their fiery trails glowing for long seconds before fading into the void.

I lay back on the sand, my mind stilled for the first time in hours. The constellations I'd grown up recognizing shone brightly—Orion's Belt cut across the sky its line pointing straight toward Sirius, blazing low over the horizon. Around the edges of my vision, shooting stars flickered in and out, brief streaks of light that felt almost rhythmic, like the sky was breathing

I imagined Kendal somewhere out there, looking up at the same sky. I closed my eyes and pictured her surrounded by the girls, safe and sound, waiting for me to find a way home.

—

I snapped awake—

"Shit!" I blurted, scrambling upright.

12:13—I'd slept for over two hours!

I shot to my feet and searched the camp behind me. Logan, Kavi, and Fern still lay, fast asleep—no crocodiles in sight.

"Dumb ass," I cursed to myself, shivering in the cool night air.

The fire had reduced to embers during my unintended nap. I rushed to stoke it, grabbing anything nearby that could catch quickly. Driftwood, husks, scraps of thatch—it all went in as I shook off the failure.

Then I heard it—

A deep, guttural bellow echoed through the quiet, freezing me in place. I dropped the coconut husk in my hand and held my breath, straining to listen. It came again—a low, prehistoric sounding rumble that vibrated through the sand beneath me. My worst fear was confirmed—the crocodile was here.

I stood frozen, listening over the crackle of the fire, my eyes sweeping for any sign of movement. I stepped back quickly, grabbing the machete and bamboo lance on my way to the shelter. I considered waking the others, but they needed rest. Once the cat was out of the bag—sleep would be off the table. I piled more logs and husks onto the fire, stoking the flames until they roared bright. The light flickered around me, shadows jumping with each shift of the breeze.

Machete in one hand, bamboo lance in the other, I edged toward the shore. Each step felt heavier than the last as I approached the waterline, heart hammering in my chest. The firelight barely reached the shallows, but the moon had finally risen, casting a soft bluish glow across the beach. My eyes darted across the shore, searching for movement, irregular shapes—anything out of place.

Only the hush of the waves filled the air, rhythmic and steady. Somewhere beyond the reach of firelight, the croc was watching. I stayed a moment longer, straining to make out its shape—every shadow a possible outline. But it didn't reveal itself.

Turning to head back to camp, something caught my eye on the horizon—a distant pinprick of light.

"Holy shit!" I yelled. "A ship! That's a fucking ship!"

I locked onto the tiny orange dot, barely visible against the inky backdrop of the ocean. It was distant—dozens kilometers out—but not beyond reach.

I bolted toward the camp and grabbed the largest burning log I could find. Flames roared above me as I sprinted back to the shoreline, waving the makeshift torch in wide arcs.

"Hey! HEY!" I shouted, jumping up and down.

The log's heat seared my hands through the bark as I waved it, the firelight spilling across the sand. I poured every ounce of hope into the gesture, willing the distant ship to see me, to notice the signal and call for help. For five minutes, I flailed and shouted, the flames dying down to smoldering coals, smoke trailing into the dark. But the light on the horizon grew smaller, the ship drifting further out of reach.

"Dammit!"

My shoulders slumped in defeat. The odds had been slim, but the fleeting hope stung, nevertheless. I trudged back to the camp, the log now a smoldering stump in my hand. I tossed the remains into the fire, then stood still for a moment, watching the flames consume it. The ship was gone, but maybe there'd be another. Maybe morning would bring someone closer.

"This is good—ships are out," I muttered to myself.

Hunched over the sand, I realized I'd completely forgotten about the croc during my frantic attempt to signal the boat. The insane spectacle I'd just put on might have scared it off—or worse, intrigued it.

—

We were well past due for a shift change, and Logan was next in the queue.

I gently shook his shoulder—

"Logan. Wake up, pal."

He stirred, sitting up with a yawn.

"Oh, sick. We're still here?" he muttered, his voice dry with sarcasm.

"We are."

"Awesome. I love this place. Is it my turn?"

"Yeah, something like that," I said, helping him to his feet.

"Man, I actually feel halfway decent. I slept way better than I thought I would."

We moved toward the fire.

I sighed.

"I fell asleep, dude. I kind of fucked up. It's already 12:30."

Logan paused, then shrugged.

"Well, you can't win 'em all."

"That's fair. I've been winning so much lately, I guess I was due for a flop."

"Exactly. Let someone else take a *W* for once, would ya?"

We moved to Fern, whose tourniquet needed attention. I untied the knot carefully, bracing for the inevitable groan of pain. Fern stirred weakly as the pressure released, but this time, only a faint trickle of blood seeped from the wound—far less than before.

"That's gotta be a good sign, right? His leg's clotting?" I pontificated.

Logan examined the leg, his expression unreadable. "Maybe.

Or it could just mean the leg's too far gone."

"So… just so you know, I've been hearing the croc. It's definitely close by."

"Yeah? Where from?"

"It was bellowing and growling from near the shoreline—right out front."

Logan raised an eyebrow. "You know, I watched a documentary about the making of *Jurassic Park*—they used crocodiles for some of the T.rex sound effects."

"Oh, good. That's comforting," I smirked. "What if it had crawled up here while I was asleep and attacked me? Or worse, grabbed one of you guys?"

"Well, it didn't, so maybe cut yourself some slack. Thirty-plus hours of hell. No one signed up for this.

Besides..." he cracked his neck. "If it came near us, I'd have kicked its scaly ass, skinned it on the spot, and we'd be eating croc steaks wearing hand-stitched sneakers by breakfast."

Logan's mood was noticeably lighter—sleep had clearly helped. I, on the other hand, was a wreck.

—

We sat by the fire for a while, chatting quietly.

"My hands are covered in Fern's blood, and I'm 100% not rinsing them in croc territory," Logan said, holding them up.

"Yeah, dude—dry clean only."

He laughed and mixed them with the sand, trying to work the red stains away.

His eyes drifted across the beach, landing on the piles of plastic and driftwood I'd sorted earlier.

"So... you cleaned the beach a little, did ya?"

"I did. I cleaned up the beach."

"Okay, totally normal. Any reason?"

"Sitting still wasn't working. I couldn't turn my brain off... my family, Kendal and the girls."

"Yeah, I get it. I mean, it'll be in my novel, but I understand," he said with a laugh. "I've been thinking a lot about home too... about everyone. I feel helpless. By now, they definitely think we're dead."

"At least our families have each other," I said. "And the silver lining is that they'll all get to experience a miracle tomorrow."

"That's true. I like the confidence. You figure we're out of here tomorrow?"

"Yeah," I replied, gazing at the fire. "I saw a ship way out at sea earlier."

"No way. What kind of ship? How far out?"

"Hard to say—looked like a freighter. Too far to signal, but I waved a flaming log for a while. Probably pissed the croc off, but I don't think they saw me."

"Well, tomorrow might be it, then. We can make a mess of smoke. Maybe someone will come check it out."

"Yeah. We can't be far from Nias. It's just a matter of time."

A long pause settled between us, the fire crackling softly.

"I feel kind of like Job right now," I said, breaking the silence.

"Job? As in Old Testament Job—the biblical one?"

"Yeah. I mean, I make it to paradise, meet this perfect girl, we fall for each other, and it's the best few days of my life. I had it all. Things were really shaping up for a second there."

Logan raised an eyebrow. "Since when do you cite the Bible?"

I shrugged. "I saw it on a *South Park* episode."

"Of course you did," he laughed. "Right, so you have it made, then disaster wipes it all out?"

"Exactly."

He paused.

"In that story wasn't god testing the guy's faith?"

"I think so."

"Okay… then have faith, dude. Wasn't that the message?"

I stared at the dark shoreline.

"I get that this sucks, but comparing yourself to a biblical figure? A little much, don't you think? Plus didn't that dude have a perfect life? A family, crops, some goats and shit?"

I chuckled.

"Maybe it's a stretch."

"The ego on this guy," he teased. "Hate to break it to you, but you're not that special."

I laughed harder.

"Narcissists these days, " he laughed. "Do me a favour, turn this coconut water into wine, I could use a drink."

"Malbec or Riesling?" I laughed.

"Malbec? In this heat? You must be outta your mind. You definitely need some rest."

We both cracked up—once again, stress and sleep deprivation twisted everything into comedy. For a few minutes we laughed uncontrollably, the sound echoing into the night.

Finally, I sat up, trying to catch my breath. My face ached from smiling and my chapped lips had cracked open again, stinging sharply. I wiped my mouth and slowly got to my feet, feeling lighter than I had in hours.

"Okay, those weren't even good jokes, I need sleep," I laughed, as I handed Logan the machete.

"Vaya con Dios," I said with a grin, turning back to the shelter to try for some much-needed rest.

42

—Smoke Signals—

The scent of smoke nudged me awake. I opened my eyes just as first light was tickling the tops of the coconut trees a warm orange hue.

I checked my watch: 5:52 a.m.

The near-full moon lingered faintly above the powder-blue horizon, fading into the backdrop of the morning sky. Waves lapped gently at the shore, and a faint breeze carried the refreshing tang of the sea. I stretched, wincing, as overnight scabs pulled tight and cracked with each movement. To my left, Fern lay atop the bamboo stretcher, motionless save for the faint rise and fall of his chest. Kavi lay next to him, bandana still stained a deep, scarlet red.

"Shit." I mumbled.

Kavi should have been on watch.

I sat up and turned—Logan was sprawled by the smoldering fire, machete clutched loosely in his hand. Our security detail had failed again. God only knew how long we'd been left vulnerable.

I sighed.

At least I wasn't the only one to slip up. I got to my feet and walked over to Logan—stiff but more clear-headed than I'd been in days. My cuts and bruises throbbed with a dull, deep ache, the sharp sting having faded overnight.

"Logan, wake up," I said, shaking his shoulder lightly.

He stirred quickly, yawning as he sat up and rubbed his eyes.

"Hey, man."

"You fell asleep, too."

He glanced around, taking stock of our surroundings. He looked sheepishly at Kavi and Fern, still asleep in the shelter, before offering a lopsided grin.

"Would you look at that... oops. Well, at least you all got to sleep through the night," he joked. "And hey—no one got eaten by a croc, so I'd call that a win."

I smirked, shaking my head.

"Yeah, everything's fine. But it's time to get moving. Boats and planes will be out soon, and we're getting off this rock today."

He nodded and stood, tossing some loose driftwood into the fire.

I turned to rouse Kavi, crouching by Fern's side as flies buzzed around his stretcher. The smell of smoke and seawater clung heavily to the air. Fern's leg was a swollen, discoloured mess—angry purple with deep blue veins spidering out from the gash, an infection was spreading visibly beneath his skin.

"Kavi, up you get, bud. Time to go home."

He blinked groggily, rubbing his eyes.

"Aw. I was having the best dream."

"Yeah? Was it us not being stranded in the middle of nowhere?"

"Yup. We were having an airplane race," he said with a sleepy grin. "I won."

I chuckled, shaking my head. "You wish, pal. I never lose airplane races."

Fern stirred faintly, his eyes fluttering open, glazed and distant. His chest rose and fell unevenly as I wiped the sweat from his face. Though his leg remained a mottled mess, it seemed the tourniquet was no longer necessary.

"This is getting infected," I muttered.

Suddenly an idea took shape.

"I've got a plan," I said, grabbing a halved coconut from the pile and heading toward the shore.

—

A few steps past the fire, I froze—A fresh trail of crocodile slide marks and prints cut across the beach—not from the water's edge, but from farther inland, near where we'd been sleeping.

"Holy shit. Look at this!" I called out.

Logan and Kavi joined me.

"Jesus. I guess we got lucky," Logan said, crouching to inspect the massive tracks.

"Yeah. Truly the chosen ones," Kavi deadpanned.

It was unnerving, but I pushed the *what-ifs* aside and got to work.

First priority: rinse Fern's leg. Seawater might've kept the worst at bay, flushing things clean—but now, out of the ocean and baking in the sun, infection was setting.

Charcoal might slow it—maybe just enough to buy him time.

I filled the coconut shells with seawater, keeping a wary eye on the shoreline for the lurking croc, then walked back to the shelter and began to slowly pour the seawater over the wound. Flies scattered, and a faint stench rose as the grime loosened—like something was beginning to rot. Fern whimpered, his body tensing as the briny liquid washed away the oozing mess of blood and grit, exposing raw bone and shredded tissue. It was brutal, but we had to act.

"Sorry, man," I murmured as I poured the last of the seawater over the wound. "We can't let this get worse."

I took the second coconut half to the fire and sprinkled in as much clean charcoal as I could find, mixing it into a dark solution.

"Maybe this will help too," I said to Logan and Kavi, who had just returned from examining the crocodile tracks.

They nodded silently.

—

I poured the black liquid over the wound. The mixture trickled down in thin black streams, staining the exposed bone and flesh. Fern wrenched in agony, his groan slicing through the quiet morning air. The sight of the charcoal coating his wound sparked a thought. I crushed more charcoal into a fine powder and gently packed it around the gash—forming a crude barrier to contain the spread and keep the flies away. It wasn't pretty, but better than nothing.

—

I joined Logan and Kavi, who were breaking into more coconuts with the machete. We drank quickly, then hacked down a couple dozen palm fronds and several broad banana leaves—fuel for the smoke signal—stacking them beside the fire, ready for ignition. We'd have to time it right—late morning, when eyes were more likely to be on the horizon.

"Kavi," Logan said, gesturing to the stained and tattered bandana around his head, "we should clean that cut. Maybe pack a little charcoal on it—see if it helps. If we don't do something, it's gonna get infected., too."

Kavi nodded and sighed.

—

We stood by the decrepit raft, scanning the small waves for any sign of the crocodile.

"What do you think? I don't see that fucker, do you?" I muttered.

Kavi shrugged and carefully removed the bandana and handed it to me, quickly meeting my eyes. He took a nervous breath and dunked his head into the salty shallows while Logan and I kept watch. He tensed as the saltwater flushed the lesion, rinsing away layers of dried blood, sand, and pus. He repeated the process half a dozen times, swishing his head back and forth, before collapsing to his knees in the surf.

"AH! Fuck, I can't do that again," he gasped, shaking from the pain.

"No worries. It looks better now," I said, rinsing the bandana in the water until it was clean.

I wrung it out and folded it back into shape. Kavi tied it around his head with a grimace, jaw clenched against the sting.

We dusted more clean charcoal into the gash, wiping the excess black solution from his brow and—with a smirk—smeared a streak on each cheek.

"You're a warrior," I said, locking eyes with him.

He managed a weak smile, still trembling.

"You're a fuckin' nerd."

"Whatever John Rambo," I shot back. "Just don't kill anyone while I replace your bandana, okay?"

I folded the freshly cleaned cloth and tied it around his head. He stiffened, but didn't flinch.

"You'd make a killer John Rainbow," Logan teased.

Kavi laughed as I patted his shoulder.

"You're both idiots."

"If you do go full Rambo, just promise to direct the rampage at the croc, okay?"

"No promises," he replied.

—

We settled near the fire to regroup and relax before tackling the next step.

Logan broke the silence. "Is there a solid reason we're waiting? Now seems as good a time as any to start signaling."

I checked my watch—7:23.

"You're right. Let's do it. We can smoke this beach up all day."

We quickly stacked fresh driftwood to build up the flames, then piled on the palm and banana leaves. The greens hissed as they hit the heat, smothering the fire beneath. Within seconds, the leaves were smoldering. Wisps of smoke curled upward, growing steadily denser until we were forced back ten feet by the thick, acrid plume.

—

The smoke billowed aggressively, spreading through our small camp and rising into the clear morning sky— thick, white, and impossible to miss. I walked to the shore and climbed onto the beached raft, squinting into the distance. Above me, the plume stretched higher, stark against the powder-blue horizon.

"This might work!" I called back to the others.

If anyone was out there—on a boat, in a plane, even on a nearby island—they'd see us.

THOMAS J DERRY

350

43

—Hello, Jack—

I was about to turn back to camp when something dark caught my eye. Swaying gently in the small waves, twenty feet from shore.

There you are, you bastard!

The animal was even bigger than I had imagined—easily over a dozen feet long, its thick, muscular body like an overstuffed sausage. It lay perfectly still, its glassy eyes locked on me. Something in that absolute stillness made it worse—like I'd wandered into a standoff by accident.

"Kavi! Logan! Get down here! Bring the machete!" I shouted over my shoulder, careful not to take my eyes off the croc.

I stood frozen, pulse thumping in my ears.

It just drifted there—huge, deliberate, watching. I wasn't sure what the next move was. My gut told me to assemble reinforcements—a wall of opponents, something that might intimidate it into retreat. But another part of me wondered if we'd only be advertising ourselves as an all-you-can-eat buffet for the beach's top predator.

Logan and Kavi arrived moments later, Logan clutching the machete.

"What's going on?"

"There he is," I said, pointing at the massive shape in the water. "Jack."

"Jack?" Logan asked.

"Yeah. Been calling him that. It suits him," I said, shrugging.

"Oh, shit," Kavi muttered, "Look at the size of that thing."

"It's been staring at me for a while now," I said, not breaking eye contact. "I'm not sure what to do."

"Should we throw something? You know—scare it off?" Logan asked, quietly.

"I don't know. If we piss it off, it might just come after us. Maybe we leave it alone and hope to keep the peace," I replied.

"Votes?"

"I'm in the 'don't piss it off' camp," Kavi said.

It was unanimous—out of our depth, and smart enough to know it. The last thing any of us wanted was to trigger a death match with a Cretaceous lizard.

"Let's just keep working on the smoke," I said. "Somebody will see it eventually, and then this croc will be someone else's problem."

I took one last look over my shoulder as we turned to leave. The crocodile hadn't moved, still bobbing ominously in the surf like some ancient sentinel. I forced myself to tune it out and focused on the task ahead— getting off this godforsaken island before we became part of the food chain. We kept at it, doing what we could to keep the smoke going. At some point, I sat down to rest—just for a moment.

—

Blazing heat dragged me back to consciousness. I'd passed out in the full glare of the sun—my body now sleeping when and where it pleased.

11:05—

The air bore down like a stifling blanket. Kavi and Logan were by the lean-to: Kavi silently staring at the horizon, Logan methodically working the machete against a stone. I shuffled toward the shade near the shelter and looked out across the beach for any sign of Jack. The sand shimmered under the sun's assault, heat rippling the view like a paved road in the desert. Then something caught my eye at the seam of the horizon.

My heart skipped—

I blinked repeatedly, unsure whether what I was seeing was real or a rogue eye floater. But the dot remained—a human-made object zipping along at a fast clip, its faint rooster-tail of white water trailing behind.

"Kavi! Logan! There's a boat!" I yelled, my voice cracking with excitement.

They bolted upright and ran to my side.

"Where?" Logan asked, scanning frantically.

I pointed.

"Right there, 10 o'clock... maybe 10:30."

"I don't see anything," Kavi replied, squinting.

"It's right there!" I insisted, my finger jabbing toward the horizon.

Was I seeing things again?

I squinted harder, my pulse pounding in my ears. But no—there it was, unmistakably cutting through the water.

"Oh shit, that little thing?" Kavi finally said.

"Yes—it's moving fast!"

The three of us stood frozen, watching the small vessel carve its path across the sea. It was far—too far to guarantee we'd be seen—but we had time.

"If someone's out fishing, the main island couldn't have been totally wiped, right? Maybe the girls are okay?" Kavi said.

I nodded.

"We need to beef up this smoke signal—now!" Logan said, snapping into action.

He snatched the machete and darted toward the tree line, hacking at the trunk of a smaller banana tree with furious determination. Kavi ran to help him, while I turned to the fire, tossing on anything burnable I could find.

"Fern!" I called. "There's a boat, man! We might be getting out of here! This could be it!"

Kavi and Logan returned, dragging an entire banana tree between them. We stripped the leaves from the trunk, piling them onto the fire. The greens hissed and crackled, thickening the column of thick white smoke already rising. We threw the remaining trunk into the fire, embers glowing as it caught.

Logan didn't stop—

He charged back toward the palms, cutting down more fronds and returning with armfuls, his sweaty, sunburned face streaked with determination. I grabbed the last of the coconut husks and hurled them into the fire, eyes locked on the distant blur at sea.

"What I'd give for a mirror right now," I muttered, searching for anything reflective.

"The surfboards!"

I grabbed one and planted myself in front of the fire. Holding it like a beacon, I angled and tilted it side-to-side, catching sunlight and bouncing flashes toward the horizon. If the captain was paying attention, there'd be no mistaking our presence. I kept flashing the board in rhythmic patterns while Logan and Kavi grabbed two more and joined me, amplifying our efforts.

The smoke now spiraled high into the sky; a dense white plume visible for miles.

"This is going to work!" I shouted, as I ran toward the shoreline, frantically waving the board above my head and jumping to make myself visible.

"Hey! Over here!" I yelled, knowing the futility of my voice against the ocean's expanse.

"I think it's getting closer," Logan called out, his voice cracking with excitement. "It's turning toward us."

My heart pounded in my chest, the possibility of rescue suddenly real.

—

Colours began to glint off its hull—clearly a fishing vessel, like the one we'd taken surfing.

"No chance that's Carlos, right?" I wondered aloud, daring to hope. "Maybe he survived and came looking for us?"

"That would be fucking insane!" Kavi yelled.

The horror of the past forty-eight hours faded into a distant haze as we stood knee-deep in the surf, yelling and waving like maniacs at the speeding boat. The joy was palpable.

Then the crocodile struck—

A dark mass burst from the shallows, brown scales gleaming in the sun. The monster lunged forward with violent force, its massive jaws snapping shut on the bottom inch of my board with a sharp, bone-rattling crack. I staggered back and wrenched the board from its grip, hurling it behind me as I scrambled for balance.

The predator recoiled, ready to strike again.

"Shit!" I screamed, turning to run—but I tripped over Logan and crashed into the wet sand.

The crocodile shot forward again, jaws wide and snapping furiously. Kavi and Logan yanked me back just as its teeth slammed shut inches from my foot.

"Fucker!" I spat, scrambling back while the three of us stumbled clear of its range.

Jack looked even more menacing on land—easily the length of a canoe, and nearly as wide. He let out a deep, guttural bellow, fixing us with an unblinking stare that wasn't a warning. It was a threat.

"Jesus Christ, look at the size of that fuckin' thing!" Kavi gasped.

"We're going to have to do something," I said, picking up the largest rock I could find.

We launched a desperate counterattack, hurling rocks, driftwood—and anything within reach. The impacts bounced harmlessly off its thick, armored hide. Logan swung a stick at the reptile's head, but the leviathan remained unmoved.

"It's not even flinching!" Kavi shouted, throwing another rock that ricocheted uselessly off its scales.

Jack stood his ground, snapping and bellowing—a savage roar that rattled the air. We weren't scaring it off. At best, we were buying seconds.

"Why isn't it falling back?" Logan grunted, retreating as the croc advanced another step.

I stole a glance toward the horizon. The boat had closed the distance—no hallucination, no false hope. It was real.

"The boat's coming—look!" I shouted, barely cutting through the chaos.

Kavi and Logan paused mid-retreat, eyes snapping to the water. It was close now—maybe a few hundred feet out—but the reef and low tide would stop it from reaching the beach.

Between moving Fern and dealing with this prehistoric nightmare, things were about to get complicated.

"What do you think? How the hell do we get from here to the boat?" I asked, hoping someone had a plan.

"I don't know," Logan said, his voice tense. "We can't swim for it—not with Fern."

"That'd be super dangerous, even without Fern to worry about," Kavi added, his eyes locked on the croc, which had dug its heels into the sand—an immovable obstacle.

The boat was close enough now to make out the green and yellow paint striping its hull. It wasn't Carlos's boat. But with the bow riding high, the driver stayed hidden, and I clung to a shred of hope.

"No way this is Carlos, right?" I asked, barely breathing.

"I doubt it," Logan said. "He would've been back sooner."

We stared in tense silence, the engine now close enough to hear, its low churn rising above the sound of the surf.

Then—I saw it.

A flicker of movement at the bow.

"Did you see that?" I asked, squinting into the glare.

"What?" Kavi asked.

A burst of blonde hair lit up in the sun. A moment later, a second figure stepped into view—this one dark-haired.

I froze—

"There's no way," Kavi muttered.

Logan shook his head.

The figures at the bow grew clearer, their hair whipping in the wind, rendering me speechless.

"How the hell did they do this?" Logan yelled, his voice choked with emotion.

Kendal and Hunter stood at the bow, arms slicing through the air in wild arcs, their voices faint but unmistakable.

My knees buckled—

"This is insane," Kavi breathed, transfixed by the girls we thought we'd lost.

The boat slowed, its bow dipping to reveal a third figure at the helm.

"Carissa!" Kavi choked. "It's Carissa driving!"

Kendal and Hunter were still waving wildly and jumping up and down, while Carissa navigated the vessel.

The engine throttled down, sputtered, and fell silent. The boat coasted to a stop maybe a hundred feet offshore.

44

—Heroes—

"Oh my god! Are you guys okay!?" Kendal yelled from the bow of the boat, her voice carrying over the sound of the waves.

"We're okay! Thank you! Thank you for coming! Are you okay? Did you get hurt?" I shouted back, my voice cracking like an awkward teenager.

The three girls erupted into a flurry of overlapping questions, their voices a chaotic mix of relief and urgency. It took a moment before any clear English cut through the commotion.

"We're fine! We got to safety! Where's Fern?" Kendal shouted.

"He's back there in the shelter!" Logan yelled, pointing toward the lean-to. "But he's in rough shape."

"We can't get any closer, there's huge coral heads everywhere!" Carissa yelled.

I glanced up at the sky and exhaled deeply, releasing a reservoir of stress I was holding. Not only were we finally on the cusp of rescue, but I was also floored by what the girls had pulled off.

"How the hell did you guys even find us? And where'd you get the boat?" I called out.

"It's a long story!" Carissa shouted from the helm. "We'll explain later!"

Logan gestured toward Captain Jack, still lingering between us and the water's edge.

"We've got a bit of a croc situation over here!" he yelled, resuming his futile attempts to shoo the beast backward, swatting it with a long stick.

"We're going to figure something out," I shouted. "Just anchor there for now—don't jump in!"

"Okay, we'll wait!" Kendal replied.

The girls stayed aboard, organizing themselves as we huddled together.

"Alright, what's the play here?" Logan asked, sweat dripping from his brow.

"Well," I began, "we could try luring Jack somewhere else on the island, but that could take ages and might just piss him off. Or we back him into the water and hope he pisses off... or we move the girls to another anchor spot. None sound easy."

"Right," Logan said. "If he gets back in the water, it's game over. That thing would pick us off like fish on a line."

"Exactly," Kavi added. "Plus, moving Fern is a nightmare. Even if we get him to the water, we'd have to hoist him over the hull, and that's gonna take time."

"And moving the boat's risky," I said. "I'd rather deal with the devil we know."

Kavi nodded.

"Same. So, what's left? Chase it up the beach away from the boat and Fern, then make a run for it? What about the stretcher? Will it float?"

We all stared at the makeshift mess of bamboo as if it might answer the question itself. It looked flimsy and barely functional on dry land, let alone in the ocean.

"It definitely won't float," Logan said. "Even if it did, Fern would roll off the second we hit any chop."

"Do you think the girls have rope?" Kavi asked.

I stood and called. "Did you bring any rope?"

"We have some!" Kendal called back, lifting a bundle from the stern.

It wasn't much—maybe fifty feet.

"There's a lot more tied to the anchor chain," Carissa added, lifting a thick coil from the deck.

"Okay, hang on!"

I huddled back in—

"We could tie the rope to the stretcher and one of us could swim it out to the boat." Kavi suggested.

"Yeah, but rope'll pull the stretcher apart, that thing's so janky," I replied.

—

It was unexpectedly complicated—every option fraught with risk. The boat was so close—rescue within reach, but the pathway was anything but simple. We stood in tense silence, the croc aggressively holding its ground, a hulking reminder of just how precarious our situation was.

"We'll figure it out," I said finally. "We've come this far. We're not quitting now."

I couldn't stop replaying the memory of Fern trying to climb into Carlos's boat just days ago—back when all his limbs were intact, when he wasn't ravaged by injury. Now, with his leg shattered and a massive bull croc ten yards away, the idea of floating him out and hoisting him aboard felt close to impossible.

———

The alternative was waiting. High tide would arrive in six hours, maybe allowing the boat to beach near us. That would make lifting Fern aboard much less complicated. But the thought of staying on this island a second longer, with Jack lurking nearby, made that option just as unbearable.

Frustrated, I stepped away, leaving Logan and Kavi to brainstorm.

"Things are complicated. Fern's got a bone sticking out of his leg, and he's lying on a bamboo stretcher," I called to the girls.

"Would this help?" Hunter bent down and hoisted up a foam longboard—easily nine feet long.

"Yes! That'll help a ton!" I said. "What else do you have on board?"

Carissa took inventory. "Water bottles, fruit, a speargun, a knife, towels, a flare gun, some whistles, and life jackets."

"Amazing!" I shouted back. "Okay, can you cut whatever rope from the anchor chain you don't need and tie it to the other rope? Then…" I trailed off, realizing the distance between us.

There was no way to throw the rope across.

"Has anyone shot a speargun before?"

Carissa raised her hand. "I have."

"Alright," I began. "What if you unscrew the tip from the spear and wedge the gun into the hull… or a seat or whatever for stability, then fire the spear toward the beach in an arc."

Carissa hesitated. "Are you sure that'll work? It seems dangerous."

"No. I'm not sure," I admitted, "but if you stand back and take cover, it should be safe. You'll just have to pull the trigger from as far as you can reach."

She nodded reluctantly, then set to work.

———

It was simple in theory: fire the spear, sending the line to shore. Once we had the end, the girls could lash the speargun to the thicker rope and send supplies across— keeping us out of the water and away from the croc.

———

Kavi and Logan joined me to watch as Carissa readied the gun.

"This feels extremely dangerous," Kavi said quietly, eyeing the setup.

"Yeah," Logan agreed. "I've never seen a speargun fired above water. It's not exactly like a bow and arrow, you know?"

"Worst case," I said, "it cartwheels and lands somewhere between us and them. I think they'll be fine."

"Okay, the tip's off. It's pointed at the beach—maybe a 45-degree angle?" she shouted, finalizing the setup.

The longboard was propped up as a shield between them and the speargun.

"That sounds good. Just make sure the reel tension is zeroed, and the line is completely free—no snags," I yelled back, nerves fraying at the thought of something binding up and causing the weapon to rebound.

"Okay! Tension's off, line is clear. We're set!" she confirmed.

"We're ready!" I shouted, gesturing for Logan and Kavi to back away with me.

The three girls got into position, shielding themselves with the big foam board at the back of the boat.

"Alright—three, two, one!" Carissa counted down, then reached around the board, releasing the spear.

The metal lance erupted from the boat with incredible force, soaring upward in an arc before it plateaued, and began an awkward descent. To call it clumsy would have been generous—the spear tumbled through the air like a gymnast mid-routine, vanishing into the sun's glare.

"Where is it?" Kavi asked, craning his neck.

"It's headed left." Logan shouted, pointing toward the oyster rock.

None of us were willing to take any chances. We stood still until a loud *clink* echoed across the rocks. The spear had landed.

"Everyone okay?" I yelled back toward the boat.

Carissa popped up, giving a triumphant thumbs-up.

"We're good! That was dramatic!"

I sprinted in a broad arc around Jack toward the landing site. I searched the rocks while Kavi and Logan distracted the croc with some well-aimed stones.

Meanwhile, Carissa created tension on the line, helping guide me toward the spear's resting place. Within moments, I spotted it—a glint of metal wedged between two boulders. I grabbed the spear and gave the line a firm tug, looking toward the boat. Kendal grinned as she held the reel.

"We've got you!" she shouted.

"No shit!" I replied, smiling wide. "Okay! Tie the thicker rope around the speargun—secure it tight!"

As I relayed the plan to Kendal, Jack began to close in, hissing and snapping as he advanced toward me.

"This fuckin' thing!" I cursed, backing away.

Logan stepped in, launching larger rocks at the predator.

"Piss off, you prick!" he yelled, frustration boiling over.

Back on the boat, Kendal and Carissa had finished assembling our makeshift care package. They'd lashed the speargun to the foam longboard and were lowering it into the water.

"Okay ready!" Kendal called.

We hauled the line, which pulled the gun, which dragged the longboard and the attached rope.

"Sending the board with the rope is next level!" Logan said, his face lit up.

He wasn't wrong. For a group of stranded survivors, it was a stroke of brilliance. We maneuvered around the croc, while Kavi kept it occupied with sticks and stones, giving Logan and I a clear window to reach a calmer patch of the bay. Within a minute, the longboard and its cargo were in our hands. The thicker rope remained with the girls on the boat, forming a lifeline between us. I tied our end of the rope to the raft, carefully assembling the speargun while Logan joined Kavi on croc duty.

I looked down at the weapon in my hands—now fully assembled, ready for whatever came next. We had the gear. We had a lifeline. But the island hadn't let go of us yet.

Not even close.

45

— Crocodile Conundrum —

We marched toward Fern as a unit, ready to attempt our escape.

Our exit strategy:

▸ Carry Fern down to the water and transfer him onto the longboard, which we'll have pre-tied to the rope.

▸ Elect one of us to distract the croc while the other two carry Fern and the board into the water.

▸ Pull Fern to safety with two of us swimming alongside the board, ensuring its stability.

▸ Once safely onboard, one of us would paddle back on the longboard to retrieve the last man standing.

▸ The remaining two would then paddle back to the boat in tandem, thus completing our task of boarding and otherwise (hopefully) cheating death, hightailing out of this godforsaken island and back to civilization.

—

Admittedly, it was less than perfect and much more complicated than simply swimming out and hopping aboard the boat. But considering the circumstances—and the massive crocodile between us and freedom—it was our best shot.

To determine roles, I gathered three palm leaves of varying lengths and organized them behind my back.

"Alright, here's how it works," I said. "Whoever draws the longest leaf wins and only has to help paddle Fern to the boat. The shortest leaf means you're the crocodile wrangler-slash-rodeo clown, risking life and limb to keep Jack off our backs. The medium leaf will help swim Fern to the boat—then double back for the clown. Easy."

The guys stared blankly.

"That's extremely confusing," Kavi said.

I shrugged and we each took our picks.

Kavi held up the longest leaf, Logan had the shortest, and I was left in the middle—for some reason, both looked relieved.

"Why do I feel like I just got bad news?" I asked.

"Your job sounds way worse than rodeo clown," Logan laughed.

"To be honest, rodeo clown might be the easiest job," Kavi added.

"Yeah, well… if anyone gets eaten, it's on the clown." I said. "Anyway, the leaves have spoken. Let's get to work."

———

We dragged Fern and the stretcher out from under the shelter. The bamboo brace squeaked and groaned as we moved, starting the slow, careful walk to the shoreline. The croc stared intently from near the water's edge—its patience only adding to the tension. Fern was barely responsive as we jostled him to and fro, his head flopping as we carried the stretcher closer to the surf. Finally, we set him down on the sand—just as Jack made his move—charging and jolting forward, kicking up sand as he closed the gap.

Logan sprang into action, playing his role brilliantly. He hurled rocks, yelled at the top of his lungs, and waved his arms in exaggerated movements, distracting Jack just long enough for Kavi and I to get to work.

"Okay Fern, we're going to transfer you to the longboard, then swim you out to the boat, you ready?"

Fern stuck his thumb up.

I looked to Kavi.

"What do you think? Count of three and we lift and slide?" I asked.

"As good a plan as any," Kavi replied, his face tight with concentration.

We positioned ourselves—me at Fern's thighs, Kavi at his shoulders—and counted down.

"Three, two, one!"

We heaved Fern off the bamboo stretcher and onto the foam longboard. He moaned in agony, his body writhing as his leg shifted, the motion torquing it out of alignment.

"Ahhh—Jesus, fuck!" he gasped, clenching his fists.

"Sorry, man," Kavi said, his voice heavy with regret. "This is gonna hurt, but we're getting you home."

I threaded the rope through the leash attachment point on the board, tying it off with several secure hitches. I yanked on the line to test the knots. It held firm.

"Please," Fern murmured, barely audible. "Don't drop me."

I nodded.

We were as ready as we'd ever be.

———

Logan had managed to lure the croc further up the beach, gaining us precious space to maneuver.

I glanced at Kavi, who was poised and ready for the next step.

"Ready?" I asked, gripping the longboard's tail.

"Ready," he replied with a determined nod.

With a deep breath, we braced ourselves and lifted the board and Fern, shuffling steadily into the water, while Logan and Jack remained locked in a tense standoff up the beach.

"Let's go!" I urged Kavi, glancing at the boat where the girls stood, watching for our cue.

Once we reached deep enough water, we gently set Fern and the board down. The foamy waves jostled the rig as we began pushing toward the boat. The saltwater stung as it lapped over my body, reigniting every nerve ending. Kavi moved beside me, stealing glances back at the croc and Logan.

"The croc's still on shore," he said, his voice calmer now.

For the moment, it seemed, we were safe. Now chest-deep, we signaled for the girls to start reeling in the rope.

"Okay, ready!" I called, giving them a thumbs-up.

The rope tightened, and Fern and the board began sliding smoothly through the water toward the boat. Our job was to keep everything stable, ensuring he didn't tip off either side. We pushed carefully, tripping clumsily over rocks hidden just beneath the surface.

"Faster!" I yelled as we reached the line of breaking waves.

The girls pulled harder, and we smashed through the first set without incident. The second, however, hit hard, sending loads of water down my throat. I coughed violently as saltwater poured from my nose, but pressed forward, jamming my feet and shins into coral heads and rocks as we pressed forward—until suddenly, we were in deeper water, and within reach of the boat.

The girls were lined up along the gunnel, smiling as they pulled the rope steadily, their voices syncing with each coordinated tug. The sound of the waves lapping gently against the boat—an elegant echo of civility—felt surreal.

"Hi," I said, bobbing in the water, Kendal only feet away.

"Hi," she replied softly.

Her face was streaked with tears, eyes full of relief. It was the look I'd seen in those soldier reunion videos—wives collapsing into sobs as their husbands stepped off planes. For a moment, I welled up, captured by gratitude and sheer emotional exhaustion. I took a deep breath,

"This is the part we didn't really plan," I admitted, glancing at Fern's fragile form.

"We have a ladder," Carissa offered.

Fern gave a slow thumbs up, then grimaced. "About time."

I let out an incredulous laugh and squeezed his shoulder.

"Carlos would be proud," I said, looking up at the girls.

Kendal's face darkened slightly. "He didn't make it?"

"I don't think so," I replied. "He disappeared right before the wave hit."

Carissa broke the silence, "Okay, let's get you in the boat," she said firmly, flinging the ladder over the side with determination.

I maneuvered around the board and grabbed the ladder.

"You know," I said with a faint smile, "You were dead right—this ladder is useful. Just give us a second to get organized."

Fern groaned, sticking up his thumb again.

As I reached the top rung, Kendal stepped forward and wrapped her arms around me.

"I can't believe you're alive!" she wept.

I held her for a quick second. We both knew there wasn't time to fall apart.

"Kavi, if you can climb aboard, I think all of us can lift him over the rail," I suggested.

Kavi climbed up, and we all took our positions along the port side—me at the nose of the board, Kavi at the tail, and Kendal and Carissa stationed on either side between us. Together, we prepared for the most delicate part of our mission: lifting Fern aboard without causing more harm.

"Let me get in the water—I can help stabilize him from below," Hunter offered as she slipped on two life jackets for extra buoyancy and jumped in.

"Alright," I said, looking around at the team. "I'll count us down from three."

I glanced at Hunter. "You ready?"

She gave a thumbs-up, treading water just behind Fern.

"Three… two… one…" I shouted.

With a collective effort, we strained against gravity, hoisting all 180 pounds of him over the gunnel. Every muscle screamed as we fought to get him high enough to clear the hull. With a final push, the board teetered, then settled across the railing and down onto the bench seats— Fern was securely aboard!

Kendal leapt toward me, throwing her arms around my battered frame. Pain shot through my raw back and chest as I hit the seat, but I barely noticed. A flood of emotions slammed into me, too fast to sort.

"Oh my god, your back!" she gasped, stepping back as her hand grazed one of the deeper wounds, her fingers coated in viscous blood.

She moved behind me to take a closer look.

"These are deep," she said, her voice trembling. "You poor thing!"

She turned to examine my chest and abdomen, eyes welling up with tears as she took in the scrapes, bruises, and open lesions.

"I'm fine," I assured her, though I'd never felt more broken physically.

She hugged me again, careful not to touch the worst of it.

"This must have been hell for you," she sobbed. "I didn't think I was ever going to see you again."

———

Carissa had turned her attention to Fern. She brought out water bottles, fruit, and makeshift provisions, offering him whatever she could.

"Oh my god," Hunter gasped as she climbed back onto the boat, getting her first clear look at his leg.

The seawater had rinsed away the charcoal and grime, fully exposing the infected compound fracture.

"We need to get him back immediately, or he's going to lose that leg," Carissa urged, squeezing mango pulp into his mouth.

"Not losing the leg," Fern muttered. "Not part of the plan."

I grinned, then drained an entire bottle of water in one swig. That's when the glaring flaw in our plan hit me: Fern was occupying the longboard, and he wasn't moving anytime soon.

"Fuck," I muttered, pointing at the board. "I knew we missed something."

"Looks like you're swimming back solo," Kavi said with a smirk.

"Lucky me," I quipped, already moving toward the ladder.

"Take this!" Hunter called, tossing me a PFD.

"I don't understand why you're going back if you can't take the board, what's the point?" Kendal asked. "At least let me come with you."

"I can't leave Logan to do this alone. If you come, it puts another person in harm's way. Plus, the more people on the boat pulling the rope, the faster we'll get to safety."

I tied one end of the rope securely to a cleat on the hull, grabbed the speargun, and lowered myself halfway down the ladder.

"Okay, here's the deal," I called to the girls. "I'll swim the rope back, we'll try to chase the croc off, and then make a run for it. Once we're in the water, you four pull the rope as hard as you can on my signal. Do whatever it takes to get us back on board."

Pain seared my wounds as I braced the gun against my abdomen, straining to load the rubber bands—preparing for the worst case.

—

The swim back was slow and deliberate. Logan's silhouette grew as I neared, stationed on the beach, keeping the croc occupied. The creature was right where I'd left it—an unblinking mass of muscle, planted firm and watching Logan with unnerving focus.

Reaching the breakers, I caught a small wave to speed my approach, body surfing briefly before my feet touched the rocky bottom. I trudged through the shallows toward Logan, who was in mid-swing with a palm frond, smacking it against the sand and occasionally landing blows on the croc's snout.

"Damn," he said as I arrived, "I guess Fern's commandeered the longboard, huh?"

"Yeah, so it's either swim or paddle the busted boards," I replied. "What's your take?"

Logan stopped and pointed at the croc. "You see this fucker? He's playing games. Watch this."

He turned his back and began walking toward the shore. Sure enough, Jack perked up immediately in pursuit. But the second Logan spun around and cracked the frond through the air, the creature froze again, settling back into stillness.

"Okay," I said, "that answers that. He's not letting us get away without a fight."

"Nope," Logan said grimly. "Tried making a break for it earlier—no shot."

"Well," I said, hefting the speargun and holding it out, "I've got this and the knife. Worst case, we might have to take him out."

Logan took the knife reluctantly, and together we devised a plan: drive the croc up the beach to buy enough time for a sprint to the water. If we could move it far enough, we might just pull this off.

"I'll try poking it," I said, gripping the speargun. "A little sharp encouragement should do the trick."

"Be my guest," Logan said, stepping back with the frond.

I advanced cautiously, the croc immediately hissing and bellowing in protest. Its massive jaws snapped once, a sound like dry timber cracking. I inched closer, jabbing the spear lightly at its snout. The beast lunged forward, teeth clamping down on the metal shaft with terrifying force, almost wrenching it from my grip.

"Shit!" I shouted, stepping back.

Gritting my teeth, I advanced again, this time jabbing the spear tip with more authority. The croc lunged once again, snapping its jaws inches from the spear tip, but I didn't relent. It felt less like a physical battle and more like a war of the will.

I jabbed again—

"Move back, you prick!" My voice boomed, deep and baritone.

Logan joined in, swinging the frond and yelling alongside me. The combined racket threw the croc off, its massive frame shuddering as it hissed and snapped in response.

After several dramatic minutes, it took its first tentative steps backward, moving ever so slightly away from the waterline.

"Maybe we get ready for the swim before pressing harder?" Logan suggested, sweat now pouring down his face.

He glanced at me and then at the waiting boat.

"Yeah," I said, nodding. "Let's not waste this window."

We inched away, preparing for the next critical phase of our escape.

I kept the croc distracted while Logan tied a loop in the rope large enough for us to hold and collected the surfboards we'd use for our escape. If we could push Jack far enough up the beach and time it perfectly, he wouldn't have a chance to catch us in the water. If we failed—well who knows what the result might be.

Logan rejoined me. "Boards are in place, rope is ready."

I nodded. "Okay, just give me a second."

I stepped away, walking the short distance to the battered raft that had carried us to this point. The sight of it brought a swell of emotion I hadn't anticipated. As much as I wanted to erase every second of this ordeal from my memory, I couldn't ignore the gratitude I felt for the things that had kept us alive.

I placed my hand on the perilous vessel, its surface rough beneath my fingertips.

"This nightmare could have been so much worse. Without this thing, we wouldn't even be here."

Logan stood a few feet away, watching me with an impatient but understanding look.

"Amen. But you can get sentimental later. Let's get the hell out of here."

I smiled faintly, kissed my hand, and pressed it against the raft. It felt like a quiet goodbye to something that had been both a lifeline and a symbol of everything we'd endured. Turning back to Logan, I squared my shoulders.

"Alright, let's finish this." My voice steadied. The end was close now.

46

—Tenacious Bastard!—

We maneuvered into position—Logan with the palm frond, me with the speargun.

"Ready?" I asked.

"Ready!" he shot back, eyes locked on the croc.

We charged forward together, yelling at the top of our lungs and swinging wildly, jabbing the air with our weapons like madmen. Logan lashed the croc's snout with the palm frond, each slap landing with a sharp *whap* against its armored hide. I jabbed at it with the spear, striking at its face, its snout—anywhere I could make contact. It hissed and snapped, teeth colliding with a dry *clack*.

At first, only a foot was afforded, but we kept up the pressure—yelling, flailing, kicking sand, relentless in our attack. Each lunge from us was met with another backstep from the croc. Foot by foot, it began to retreat, and soon it turned, its massive tail swaying as it lumbered toward the smoky remains of our fire pit.

"Go on, get the out of here!" Logan screamed. "Get the hell out of here, Jack!"

With every step it took, we took one too. In no time, our unrelenting tactics had pushed him back thirty feet toward base camp.

"We're going to make a run for it!" I called over my shoulder to the boat.

"Let's go!" Logan yelled, slapping my arm.

We spun on our heels and sprinted toward the water, scooping our boards before bolting into the surf with the coil of rope in hand.

"You ready?!" I yelled toward the boat as we splashed through knee-deep water.

"Ready!!" came the reply—a chorus of voices from the girls.

—

The water rose to our chests as we charged forward, sharp rocks slamming into our legs and scraping our feet. This was our chance.

"Let's go!" I shouted. "Pull!"

We threw ourselves forward onto our boards, chest-first, kicking hard to gain momentum. I jammed the speargun under my chest, wedging it against the foam of my life preserver to free up my hands. Logan was right beside me, gripping the rope as I did, paddling furiously with our free arms while the girls pulled from the boat.

Then I heard it—

"It's coming!!" Carissa's voice cracked

"Shit!" I muttered, panic shooting through me as I paddled furiously.

380

Logan twisted around, eyes locking on the threat.

"Oh fuck! We need to go!" he yelled, his voice an octave higher than usual.

I glanced over my shoulder just in time to see it barreling down the beach—mouth agape, tail carving a trench behind. Every instinct screamed to abandon the board and head back to shore—but it was too late. We were too far out, the water too deep.

"Paddle!!" I roared, digging forward with everything I had.

The surf pounded into us and foam burst up around our faces. The speargun dug into my ribs, and with every stroke, a fresh jolt of pain—but I clenched my teeth and held on, keeping it wedged beneath me. If I lost the gun, we'd have nothing left but two surfboards and our limbs to fend off the predator.

"Pull!!" Logan and I screamed in unison.

It was a tug-of-war with death itself—every pull from the boat yanked us closer to life, every slack in the line felt like the croc's window to strike. We were moving, but it wasn't fast enough.

I risked a glance back—the croc had hit the water with a splash, its massive body slicing through the shallows, head low, eyes locked on us.

"It's in the water!" I yelled.

Then it vanished—submerged completely.

The surface became an empty stage, Jack somewhere below.

The seconds stretched—

"Where is it?" I panted, scanning for any sign of movement—nothing but churned-up foam and sunlight.

"Faster!" Logan shouted.

We punched through the first breaker, then a second, each one threatening to destroy our momentum and throw us off course—right into Jack's jaws. A third wave slapped me hard, saltwater flooding my throat.

I choked, kicking harder.

Shouting from the boat grew louder. We were close now—maybe fifty feet. But I could hear the panic in their voices.

I looked back again—

Nothing.

Just surf.

No croc in sight.

I stared forward and kicked with everything I had—waiting for impact, certain it was just a second behind me.

"It's behind you! Hold on!" Kavi screamed.

I gripped the speargun, hands trembling uncontrollably, unable to speak.

Then the rope went slack—

"What the fuck?!" Logan yelled. "Keep pulling! What are you doing?!"

For a heart-stopping moment, we drifted—suspended in place. I pulled my legs toward my torso, buying myself a foot of space between my body and the impending crocodile.

Then—suddenly the engine roared, and the rope snapped taut, nearly yanking us from our boards. We shot forward, now dragging at high speed, skipping across the waves like flat stones.

I looked back—the croc breached, teeth flashing—just beyond where we'd been seconds earlier.

"YES!" I yelled, holstering the speargun beneath me.

The boat towed us far into the open ocean, leaving the predator shrinking in the distance. When we finally slowed, the shoreline was a blur.

Jack lingered for a moment near the breakers, then slipped beneath the water and vanished.

———

Kendal, Kavi, and Hunter hauled us in, hand over hand. We clung to the rope, dragged through the water like wreckage until we reached the hull and scrambled for the ladder.

As I climbed aboard, I glanced back. "You tenacious bastard," I muttered, shaking my head.

Jack had given us hell and nearly bested us. If not for the girls' quick thinking and the engine's burst of power, we might not have made it.

Once on deck, Logan and I collapsed in silence—soaked, shaking, and half-laughing from sheer relief.

We had made it—but not without one final fight.

47

— Rescued —

We were free. Free from the tyranny of the ocean, the croc, and that cursed island. The six of us huddled around Fern in silence, arms wrapped around each other. Just holding on. The group began to unravel—tears welled, shoulders shook, no one bothering to hold it in. I exhaled a deep, trembling breath. I felt like a balloon deflating, everything leaking out in slow, uneven bursts. Soon, we'd be back to Nias and our families would know we were alive.

"Thank you," I repeated, over and over. "Thank you for coming for us."

Kendal's voice cracked just slightly. "I'm just so glad we found you, I can't believe it."

She wiped tears from her face as the huddle finally loosened.

Carissa stepped back to the throttle. "Take a seat and hold on. Let's get you guys home," she said, cranking the engine to life.

I collapsed onto one of the few remaining bench seats, next to Fern. Kendal clung to me as the boat lurched forward. Her eyes traced my face, her fingers gently brushing against my raw skin.

"I'm so happy you're alive," she whispered.

My chapped lips stung, my face felt pan-fried, and my body ached all over, but none of it mattered.

"I don't understand," I said, words spilling out in a rush. "How did you do it? How did you get a boat? How did you find us? And... how bad is the resort?"

Her face darkened slightly.

"The resort is destroyed. Pretty much flattened. They evacuated us maybe ten minutes before the waves hit. We went back yesterday, but it was chaos. People said no one could've survived it. They told us not to go looking for you."

I nodded, the words slowly sinking in.

"Was it an earthquake that caused it?" I asked.

"We think so. The whole thing was so chaotic, though—they didn't explain much. Just told everyone to head for higher ground."

"Jesus," I murmured.

"When we got back, I tried to get Dani to take us out to look for you, but he refused. Said it was too dangerous." her voice broke, tears spilling again. "When we realized no one was going to help, we just... we found a boat. We got it running and grabbed anything useful we could find before heading toward Glaciers. We figured we'd start there."

"You girls are actual heroes," I said. "Bringing the board and the speargun... my god, Kendal, brilliant."

She smiled faintly, leaning in to hug me again.

"Is anyone else missing?" I asked, pulling back slightly.

She hesitated, her expression heavy. "We don't know. Dani's okay, and a few others—Maya, some bartenders—but a lot of people are missing."

I looked down and swallowed hard. My throat dry and constricted, as the news of the totality began to settle.

"I was worried no one would even think to look for us. And you three—I didn't want to let myself imagine..." My voice cracked. I leaned forward, elbows on my knees, trying to get a grip.

"I can't imagine," she rested a hand on my shoulder. "Were you surfing when it happened?"

"We were just finishing up," I said, wiping my face with trembling hands. "The ocean started acting weird, water started rushing out. We didn't know what was going on at first. Then Carlos and the boat just disappeared."

"Oh my god," she said, shaking her head.

I swallowed the lump in my throat, the image of Carlos's last moments playing over in my mind.

"Do you have a working phone?" I asked.

"We have our phones, but they're all dead. The resort's been without power since the wave hit."

"Okay," I said, exhaling. "We'll figure something out when we get back. I need to contact my family."

—

The world around us barely made sense. Islands we'd passed days earlier were twisted beyond recognition—shorelines gouged open, trees snapped like matchsticks, sand stripped away to reveal raw reef. Only the tallest

387

palms remained, clinging to whatever soil hadn't been dragged out to sea. The boat wove carefully through scattered wreckage—planks from shattered homes, broken hulls, splintered furniture—all drifting in the tide like ghosts of what had been.

"This is insane," I murmured.

My eyes drifted across the wreckage without really seeing it. Shapes blurred, colours ran together. I couldn't find the energy to focus. The adrenaline was gone and I was done—mentally and physically.

—

We reached the entrance to the resort's bay. The destruction was nearly total. The dock, once the heart of activity, was reduced to splinters, scattered along the shoreline like a broken spine. The speedboat lay marooned on the adjacent beach, its hull cracked and useless. The main building was barely standing, a skeletal frame of lumber swaying awkwardly in the breeze.

"Oh man," I said quietly. "This is brutal."

—

The closer we got, the worse it was. The casitas were still standing, but just barely. Windows were shattered, walls missing, and the once-charming, thatched roofs had been shredded into ribbons. The entire shoreline was choked with debris: fishing boats, surfboards, broken furniture—remnants of a place that, just days ago, had felt like the Garden of Eden.

"Is anyone still here?" I asked.

"Everyone's inland," Kendal said. "They're in the nearest village, waiting for evacuation to Sibolga. I think it's still being organized."

"We're going to have to get Fern out of here—like today," I said.

The medical chaos awaiting would be the next big hurdle. Fern needed help—real help—and time was running out.

48

—Paradise Lost—

We pulled up beside the only remaining section of the dock and tied off in silence. After everything we had endured, returning to this mess felt like another cruel twist. In my naïve mind, I'd pictured arriving to find Maya, Dani, and the resort staff ready to help. The reality, however, was far more bleak. Not a soul remained. The once-bustling haven had become an eerie graveyard of shattered memories. For us, it meant bootstrapping the recovery. Still, there was relief in being back to a semblance of civilization. At the very least, we might find a sat-phone or VHF radio to call for help. The hope was to get Fern airlifted to Sibolga for medical treatment while the rest of us waited to catch a boat back.

———

One by one, we disembarked onto the rickety dock to plan our next steps—chief among them, moving Fern somewhere safe.

"I think we lift him out of the boat and find some shade. Maybe some more water and food," I suggested.

Everyone agreed.

Logan, Kavi, and I climbed back aboard to carefully lift Fern and the longboard onto the dock.

"Ready Fern? Three, two, one," I counted, as we heaved together.

We placed the board down gently and slid it away from the precarious edge. The structure groaned under our weight as we shuffled forward, dodging missing beams and jagged debris like landmines. With slow, deliberate steps, the six of us carried him up the dock's broken runway and onto solid ground. We set him down in a shaded, level area where he could rest while we figured out our next move.

———

Logan and Carissa set off to scavenge for supplies—alcohol, disinfectant, towels, pain killers, anything that might ease Fern's suffering. Meanwhile, Kendal, Hunter, and I headed toward the remains of the resort to search for a way to contact the outside world.

We reached the main building. The entrance had collapsed into a tangled wreck of thatch, splintered wood, and broken glass.

"What a tragedy," I murmured, taking in the chaotic scene. "This place was a masterpiece."

Orange towels, splintered pieces of the teak check-in counter, a refrigerator, computer monitors, an AC unit, and smashed light fixtures were strewn across the salt-coated wooden floor. Glass shards flanked much of the ground, making it impossible to walk further without shoes.

"Power's for sure out, right?" I asked, watching Kendal and Hunter pick their way through the wreckage, dangerously close to some tangled electrical wires.

"Yeah, it's been off for a while. What are we looking for?" Kendal asked.

"I don't know exactly. Maybe there's a generator we can use to charge your phones? Or a handheld VHF radio? Maybe even a satellite phone?"

"Okay, what's a generator going to look like?" Kendal asked.

"Could be anything. Maybe a wheeled engine or a big metal box. Beige, gray—just flag anything that looks remotely useful."

"Got it," she replied.

I stepped back and surveyed the area. "I need shoes, I'm going to check our casita. Maybe some of my stuff is still there. I'll be back."

———

I had my sights set on the safe in my room, hoping it had survived the destruction. Carefully skirting the wreckage, I made my way to the path that once wound through the property. Now, it was little more than eroded earth and scattered garbage. Concrete footings and some framing remained, but the buildings had taken a catastrophic hit.

The first three casitas were flattened—nothing more than splintered piles of rubble. I passed what had been Kendal and the girls' place—it was no better. The roof had caved in and now lay across the patio, blocking the entrance entirely.

"This is so messed up," I muttered, the words falling flat against the enormity of the destruction.

I reached our front door, now barely recognizable. The roof sagged in defeat, partially collapsed, while the walls were shredded or missing entirely. Somewhere in the chaos, I hoped the safe was still intact. A steel box wouldn't have been carried away, but the real question was its contents.

Did I turn my phone off before heading out to surf that day, or would it be completely flat? Or maybe the thing had been waterlogged for two days.

Clearing debris from the patio, I moved toward the front door—or what was left of it. Inside, the concrete floor had done an excellent job of retaining a pool of filthy, stagnant water. The air hung heavy, humid and rancid. My bedroom was just across the living room, up a short flight of stairs, but the path was treacherous. The stairs looked intact, but I'd need to get creative to reach them.

I found a chunk of thatch that had broken free from the roof and pressed it into the murky, smelly water to check for hazards. Then, inch by inch, I shuffled forward, shielding my feet from hidden glass as I pushed through the knee-deep flood.

I reached the kitchen table—somehow still standing— and climbed onto it. The thatch mat had drifted a few feet away. I leaned out and dragged it back, then continued across the counter and took one final step through the dirty water to the wooden stairs.

Each board groaned beneath me but stayed firm. I stepped into my bedroom. The mattress leaned against a timber beam, the collapsed roof had left the ceiling fan dangling like a gnarled pendulum, and my teak dresser— the one housing the safe—lay flat on its back, half in the casita and half precariously cantilevered over the edge of the foundation. I approached it, pushing bits of broken wood and detritus aside, praying the safe was still there.

"Come on, please," I muttered, peeling back the debris piece by piece.

Finally, I saw it—a black box peeking out from the chaos. I crawled across the rubble to reach it, heart pounding as I inspected the code panel.

It looked intact.

I glanced at the sky. "Here goes."

I punched in the code. The buttons beeped. The lock clicked.

"No way…" I whispered.

I opened the door—and somehow, everything was dry. Just a small puddle lingered in the corner, right where my journal lay. My phone, passport, laptop, and wallet were untouched. Apparently, the resort hadn't skimped on the safe.

"Un-fucking-believable," I laughed, clutching the phone.

I pressed the power button, silently begging for another miracle. The screen lit up, and the phone powered on. I grinned at the black screen that showed 5% battery remaining. It searched futilely for a signal, confirming my assumption that the cell towers were out. I powered it down to save the remaining charge and turned my attention back to the room.

Sifting through the mud and debris, I found my small day bag buried next to the bed. Inside were my shoes, a pair of socks, and a few t-shirts—wet and sandy, but intact.

"Yes!" I breathed, pulling the damp socks and shoes onto my gnarled, callused feet.

The fabric was cool against my skin, soothing like a balm. I tugged a t-shirt over my sunburnt skin and sat for a moment, marveling at how something as simple as shoes and a cotton shirt could make such a difference. I packed the phone, passport, journal, and laptop into the bag, slung it over my shoulder, and carefully made my way back to the common area.

—

Now in shoes, I roamed the villa freely, gathering anything that might prove useful. First up was Kavi's room. Inside, I found a pair of sandals and some t-shirts—simple victories in a place where resources were limited. His safe lay in a puddle of seawater, buttons dead, reduced to a soggy brick. I tossed the gear into my pack and made my way back down into the waterlogged kitchen.

Then I heard it—

A sound so foreign, yet so familiar.

"That's an airplane!" I said aloud, my voice ricochetting through the empty villa.

I bolted for the door.

Outside, the unmistakable hum of a single-engine prop plane grew louder, vibrating through the humid air. I sprinted toward the dock and main resort building, where Kendal and the others stood at the far end, waving and shouting at the sky. Logan was ready with the flare gun, his expression tight and focused.

Just as I arrived, he fired the first flare. A brilliant red streak arced upward, briefly illuminating the hazy sky. Carissa handed him another round, and he fired again. The second flare shot higher, seeming to cross paths with the aircraft.

It was a six-seater floatplane, its pontoons gleaming in the light—exactly the kind of aircraft that could get Fern out of here.

"They have to have seen us!" I shouted, breathless.

"Where's he going?" Kendal asked.

"Is this dude out for a joy ride or what?" Logan growled.

"How many more flares are there?" I asked.

"Just one."

We stood in silence, watching the plane veer southeast, its engine fading until all that was left was the steady lap of waves

"That's really fucked up," Logan said, shaking his head. "The pilot definitely saw the flare, right?"

"Definitely," Carissa replied.

"I'm sure they called it in," I offered, trying to remain logical. "The plane might need to refuel, or they could already have passengers. Let's not lose hope."

"Maybe we should build another fire on the beach," Kavi suggested.

Logan kicked a crushed water bottle in frustration. "I'm tired of building fucking fires! I just want to get out of here."

His sentiment was valid. The sight of the plane had lifted us, only to drop us again.

"They'll come back," I said with a shrug. "We just have to be patient."

I paused, then added, hoping to shift the mood, "I found my phone. It's got a little battery, but there's no service. I also found some shoes and shirts—oh, and Kavi, I grabbed some of your stuff too."

I handed the pack to Kavi and tossed a t-shirt to Logan, who was still sulking

"Thank you," Kavi said.

"Would you mind if I borrowed the shoes to check our place? I want to see if I can find my phone and gather Fern's stuff." Logan asked.

A short-lived creature comfort—I slipped off the shoes and handed them to him. "Go for it."

Kavi pulled on the flip-flops and carefully tugged the t-shirt over his head. "Did you find anything else?"

"Your safe was there, but it wasn't working. The buttons didn't beep when I pressed them. Then I heard the plane and ran over here."

"Cool, I'll check when Logan gets back."

Carissa chimed in, "I don't mind starting a fire."

"Me neither," Hunter added.

They began gathering materials to burn on the small beach next to the dock, while Kendal offered to continue searching for a radio. The girls' optimism stood in stark contrast to our worn-out energy.

I sat down next to Kavi. The water beneath us shimmered faintly, the hazy sunlight catching on bits of floating debris.

"What do you think?" I asked him quietly. "The plane's coming back, right?"

He sighed. "I don't know, man. I hope so. But we should stick to the plan. There's got to be a radio or something we can use to communicate."

"Yeah, there has to be," I agreed, lying back against the warm wood. "I just want a break from this chaotic cycle of survival events. A real meal. A bed. To contact my family."

"The things we take for granted——" he murmured.

"Yeah," I said, staring up at the sky. "After this, it'll be hard to take anything for granted again."

"Don't worry, you'll find a way. Memories fade," he said with a half-smile. "You'll go back to a modern life, ordering food from an app and bitching about miracles in no time."

"Hey, now——was I really that bad before all this?" I shot back, though I paused to reflect.

Kavi smirked.

"Maybe I was," I admitted, shaking my head. "This whole experience has definitely shifted my perspective on my cozy little boring life."

"Let's just focus on getting through this last part," Kavi said. "We need to get Fern the hell out of here, and in a day or two, we'll be in air-conditioned rooms, heading home to our privileged existence."

We stood and got back to it.

"Let's get Fern over to the beach; we shouldn't leave him here alone," I said.

Together, we lifted him and his longboard stretcher and carefully made our way down onto the beach.

"Fern, you good?" I asked.

He shifted as we walked, briefly looking up at me.

"I'm great, why do you ask?" he groaned with a smirk.

"Smart ass," Kavi laughed.

We set him down a dozen feet from where the girls were working. Kavi peeled off to join Kendal in scouring the wreckage for a communication device. I turned to help the girls get the fire going.

By the time I reached them, they were already striking the flint. In no time, an ember caught, and a small flame took hold.

We waited for the flames to reach full heat before layering on damp wood and greenery to produce a thick, white plume of smoke. It rose steadily, clouding the beach and creating a signal visible from far beyond our little strip of coastline.

—

Logan returned, holding a pair of shoes, a few shirts, and a couple of towels. He also had his phone and a passport that appeared mostly intact.

"Phone's toast," he said with a resigned laugh, tossing it onto the dock. "Didn't lock the safe before we left. No sign of my laptop, and Fern's safe was wide open—filled with water. But hey, we're killing it in the footwear department," he smirked, handing my shoes back.

—

Kendal arrived, her expressions lit up with excitement.

"I found a radio—and it's got battery!" she exclaimed, holding up a sleek handheld device.

"Nice work!"

I recognized it as a waterproof ICOM VHF radio. I remembered spotting it behind the counter when we checked in days earlier.

"Have you called out yet?" I asked.

"Not yet. I wasn't sure how," she replied.

"Channel 16." I said, automatically.

Years ago, I'd begrudgingly taken a marine radio course when I first got into sailing—mostly just to tick a box. Now, it was suddenly proving useful. I tuned the radio and pressed the transmit button.

"Mayday, mayday, mayday. This is Nias Ohana Resort. Mayday, mayday, mayday. Nias Ohana Resort. We have seven stranded guests—one seriously injured, requesting immediate assistance and possible air evacuation. Do you copy?"

I released the button and waited, ears straining for a reply. Static crackled from the radio, but no response followed.

"I don't know if an Indonesian person's going to understand that," Logan said.

I shrugged, then keyed the mic again. "Mayday, mayday, mayday. This is Nias Ohana Resort. Mayday Nias Ohana Resort. We have seven, one seriously injured that needs assistance and air evac. Do you copy?"

Again, there was only static.

The smoke from the fire had thickened, now billowing heavily into the sky. Between the smoke and the radio calls, we were making our presence impossible to miss. I sat down low to avoid the smoke drifting over the beach, the radio still clutched in my hand.

"I'll keep trying," I said, more to myself than anyone else. "Someone will hear us."

I keyed the mic again. "Mayday, mayday, mayday…"

And I waited—

The group settled in, sipping water and waiting for a response. Kendal and I spread out one of the towels and laid down. Even this threadbare fabric felt like heaven in my battered state. Kendal reached into her pocket and pulled out a half-used tube of lip-balm, gently dabbing it onto my lips.

"This'll help," she whispered.

401

It stung for a second, then dulled the ache—cool, oily, medicinal. Exactly what I needed.

—

The past few hours had shifted my life so dramatically, it felt unreal. This morning, I was fighting a crocodile back on a cursed stretch of beach. Now, I was lying here—safe for the moment—with Kendal beside me, and a flicker of rescue on the horizon.

I glanced at my watch, just past noon—

Seven hours since I had woken up alone on that hellish shore, heart pounding and brain racing. I took a deep breath, letting my body sink into the sand, and keyed the radio again.

"Mayday, mayday, mayday…" My voice carried out into the ether, a plea I repeated every few minutes, hoping against hope that someone, somewhere, was listening.

49

—The Plane—

The distant buzzing of a plane echoed across the bay. I bolted upright.

"Do you hear that?"

Everyone froze, ears straining—

The sound grew louder—definitely a plane.

I grabbed the radio and frantically keyed the mic.

"Mayday, mayday, mayday. This is Nias Ohana Resort. Mayday, mayday, mayday! Nias Ohana Resort—requesting assistance. Do you copy?"

Static crackled, followed by a hiss.

I repeated the call.

A few tense seconds passed, the radio sputtering with faint sounds.

A long pause.

Then another hiss.

Still nothing.

Then—a voice broke through, scratchy but audible.

"Mayday, Nias Ohana, Nias Ohana, Nias Ohana. This is aircraft *The Flying Coconut,* mayday received. Sit tight, I'm comin' for ya… try not to burn the island down. Over."

The group erupted in celebration, the tension of the last few days finally breaking. I dropped to my knees, letting the radio fall into the sand. Kendal knelt beside me, gripping my shoulders, shaking me in disbelief.

"You should radio him back," she said, laughing through her tears as she picked the radio up and handed it to me.

I composed myself and keyed the mic again.

"Flying Coconut, this is Nias Ohana… we copy. Thank you! Thank you! Over."

—

The small amphibious plane appeared from the east, gently touching down about a kilometer from shore. It slowed as it approached the entrance of the bay, rotating to face west. Same plane as before—compact fuselage, twin pontoons for landing gear. Judging by its size, it could carry six, maybe eight—if we figured out how to accommodate Fern.

We waved and hollered, celebrating as our rescuer stepped out onto one of the pontoons in the distance. His calm, steady voice returned on the radio.

"Nias Ohana, I'm going to have to wait here. Entrance to the bay is too risky to pass. Over."

"Copy. We have a small boat here. How many can you take? We're seven total—one immobilized on a brace. Over."

"Copy that. Load 'em up, and we'll see what we can do. Over."

—

It was time to leave—

We scrambled to gather our things.

"Logan, take Fern with me?" I asked.

"Yeah, let's get the fuck out of here," he said.

Kavi and the girls extinguished the fire with sand, gathering the remaining supplies while Logan and I carried Fern to the boat. We were finally catching a break—and that made me nervous. After three days of chaos, my brain was primed for the next curve ball.

At the dock, we set Fern down.

"We're getting you out of here, buddy-boy! Back to civilization," I said, patting him on his shoulder.

Fern opened his eyes.

"Should we stay for happy hour?" he said with a dry smile.

"We'll take a vote," I laughed.

With coordinated effort, we lifted him aboard the watercraft. Carissa took her position at the motor, yanking the starter cord. The engine sputtered—then roared to life. We untied the lines and shoved off.

—

Ahead lay the gently bobbing plane, waiting in the swell just outside the breakers. Logan and I braced Fern and the longboard as we waited, timing the sets at the bay's narrow exit to the open ocean. When a lull came, Carissa cranked the throttle, and the boat surged forward. We navigated through the churning gap, breaking into calmer water. Within moments, we were next to the starboard pontoon of the plane.

Our faithful pilot hopped out of the cockpit. He was tall, fit and sun-weathered—his long brown hair tucked behind a sagging, beige Florida State ball cap. With a scruffy salt-and-pepper goatee and a laid-back Californian drawl, he looked like he'd been pulled straight from the kind of role Josh Brolin was born to play.

"What happened to you guys?" he asked, pulling his aviator glasses down to get a clearer look. "Thought everyone got out before it hit."

He reached out a hand to help Kendal aboard, then gestured toward Fern with a concerned glance. "Is he okay?"

"We were surfing out at Glaciers when it happened," I explained. "His leg's broken."

"Jesus Christ, surfing during a tsunami? You've got some stories to tell," he said, shaking his head. "Well, we can make it work. There's a luggage stow in back—I'll clear it out so we can lay him flat. If we're not overweight, I can take you all to Sibolga. We'll radio for evac support en-route."

"That's more than we could ask for. Thank you," I said.

"Alright," he nodded. "Take the boat around to the tail. There's a hatch back there—we'll slide him in. I'll meet ya there. Name's James, by the way."

He climbed back into the cockpit and slipped on his headset.

"Mary Jane, this is Flying Coconut," he said smoothly into the mic. "Currently in Nias Ohana bay. I've got seven, four need medical assistance, one critical. Loading now. Headed for Teluk Harbor. Request EMS support on arrival. Over."

I turned to Kavi and Logan, shaking my head in disbelief. "This is insane."

Kendal, already back in the boat, pulled me into a tight hug.

"Thank you for not giving up on us. You guys are heroes," I choked.

"We could never leave you out there." She swallowed hard. "I didn't care what it took—we had to try."

"Hunter, Carissa, thank you," I repeated, making deliberate eye contact with each of them.

Both smiled warmly as they pushed us along, maneuvering the boat to the plane's tail, where James was busy clearing the luggage stow. He pushed aside bags and cases, creating just enough space for Fern and the board. Then, with a quick twist, he opened a small hatch.

"Alright," he said, poking his head through. "It's a tight fit, but it'll work. If you can stabilize the boat, two of you lift the nose of the board, and two on the tail. We'll slide him through."

Logan and Carissa grabbed the tail of the board, while Kavi and I positioned ourselves at the front. Kendal and Hunter tightened the dock lines through the pontoon's D-rings, holding the boat steady against the swell.

"Ready?" James called out.

"Ready!" came the reply.

As we lifted the longboard toward the hatch, Fern cracked a faint smirk.

"Tell James I prefer a window seat," he muttered.

Kavi and I both grinned, maneuvering him carefully through the hatch as James guided Fern into position.

It wasn't graceful, but we got him in—finally safe.

I exhaled, arms shaking.

The boat lines were untied, and we repositioned at the starboard pontoon to board the plane.

"Come aboard one at a time," James instructed. "Watch your heads, and let me know your weight as you climb in. Need to keep us under limit."

The girls went first, followed by Kavi and Logan. I passed the last of our water bottles and gear to Logan before stepping onto the pontoon. My limbs felt like sandbags as I looked back at the boat—another lifeline through this chaos.

"I'm pushing this off. That okay?"

"Yep," James said with a wink. "No choice now. Let's send it back where it came from."

I gave the boat a final shove toward shore and climbed aboard the Flying Coconut.

"What's your weight, amigo?" James asked as I lingered by the hatch.

"About 165 pounds?"

"Bueno. Let's go. We're 50 pounds under," he grinned, closing the door behind.

He flipped a series of switches, and the turbine engine came to life—spooling up with a smooth, rising whir.

"Listen, we'll have you out of here and into Teluk Harbor in about an hour," he said over his shoulder. "Just relax. There's water and some granola bars in the back."

I slid into the seat next to Kendal, feeling the plane's vibrations in my bones. Behind us sat Kavi and Carissa, while Logan and Hunter tended to Fern in the rear. Bottles of water and granola bars made their way around the cabin as James maneuvered the plane into position for takeoff.

Kendal leaned closer, dabbing more balm onto my cracked lips with her fingertip. Her touch was tender and grounding, but my body felt disconnected—like a puppet with frayed strings. My vision blurred, my ears buzzing with a low-pitched hum.

"Cole, are you okay?" she whispered, a touch of concern sharpening her voice.

I didn't answer.

"Cole?" she nudged.

I blinked and refocused. "Yeah... yeah, I think I'm okay," I murmured. "Just tired."

It wasn't until I glanced out the window that I realized we were already airborne. The high-pitched drone of the turbines pressed against my skull—the endless sky stretched out beyond the glass. I had no recollection of takeoff.

—

The cabin was hushed, except for Hunter's soft murmurs as she coaxed Fern to drink more water. I caught glimpses of devastation below: swaths of flooded land, flattened trees, and heaps of debris scattered across beaches. Fishing boats and docks lay ruined. Entire islands bore the scars of relentless assault. It looked like the aftermath of a war—destruction drawn across the earth in broad, merciless strokes.

My mind couldn't keep up. The view blurred, the devastation below blending into abstraction. All I could register were fragments—the drone of the engine, the distant murmur of James's radio, and the high, constant ring in my ears.

—

I woke to the cool touch of water on my face. As I blinked my eyes open, Kendal's kind smile greeted me.

"You felt hot, just wanted to cool you off," she said softly, her empathetic eyes searching mine. "I can't

409

imagine what you've been through. I've been thinking about it a lot. I'm so sorry this happened."

"It's been a lot, but I'm okay," I replied, my voice rasping and unsteady.

I sat up, taking a deep breath to reorient myself.

—

The plane descended—

Out the window, the west coastline of Sumatra stretched into view, with the hillsides of Sibolga visible in the distance.

I almost smiled. Soon Fern would be in the care of professionals, and I'd have a chance to tend to my own wounds.

The engine slowed significantly as we descended the last few hundred feet. James landed the plane with impressive finesse, the transition from air to water so smooth it was barely noticeable. We coasted to a halt a few hundred feet from the dock and caught our first real glimpse of the mainland. Sibolga appeared largely intact; the city's coastal areas had escaped the devastation that had ravaged the islands.

"Not much of the wave energy made it here," James explained as he guided the plane toward the slip. "Just a bit of flooding along the coastline."

He glanced back at me. "Mind stepping out onto the pontoon to tie us off when we get there?"

"You bet," I answered, closest to the starboard door.

A wave of dizziness nearly buckled my legs as I stood. I gripped the seat waiting for it to pass. I opened the latched door and stepped out onto the pontoon, Kendal trailing close behind. The wind hit me, whipping my hair back as the noise of the engine grew louder. I braced myself against the wing strut while James maneuvered us alongside the dock.

Once in reach, we jumped off and tied the pontoon securely to the cleats. James powered down the engine, the turbine fading into silence.

—

Onshore, a small group of uniformed men and women approached, carrying a stretcher and basic medical equipment. I waved widely and made my way to the back of the plane to help retrieve Fern.

"Hey, brother," James called out, stepping down onto the dock with his signature calm demeanor. "Take a load off. Let these folks handle it."

I stopped and turned. It was time to let someone else take over.

"James, thank you," I said, walking toward him. "You'll never know what you did for us today. I'll never forget it."

I pulled him into a hug, my battered arms wrapping tightly around him.

"You'd do the same for me. Tell you what—buy me a tequila someday."

"You got it," I replied, swallowing the lump in my throat.

We stepped aside as the EMS crew reached the plane. They moved with efficiency, speaking rapid-fire Indonesian as they assessed the situation.

James called out instructions in Indonesian, directing the medics and gesturing toward Fern. The crew split up, three men heading to retrieve Fern while a woman approached the rest of us, her sharp eyes scanning our injuries. We stood back, watching as the they took over. We were no longer alone.

—

I felt faint again and stumbled toward a bench seat in the parking lot. Kendal followed, and we sat together, watching intently to ensure Fern made it safely off the plane. The nurse stood ahead of me, shining a flashlight in my eyes and inspecting my battered face and arms.

"Sir, tell me what your name is?"

"I'm Cole."

"Cole, can you tell me what happened?"

"We were surfing when the tsunami hit. I got dragged under, hit the reef," I managed to say, my voice thin. "I'm sorry, I... He's much worse than me," I added quickly, pointing toward Kavi to deflect attention.

"It's okay," she said softly. "We'll take you to the hospital now. Everything will be okay."

She moved on to Kavi, giving me a moment to breathe.

My gaze drifted back to the plane, where three men stood around Fern, now secured in a stretcher. They hooked him up to an IV and a heart rate monitor, which beeped steadily as they wheeled him up the ramp toward the waiting ambulance.

James approached again. "Hey, they've got transport ready for you guys," he said, pointing toward a white passenger van. "They'll take you to the hospital to get you all patched up. Go on, get yourselves looked at. Hopefully, your friend'll be okay."

Kendal and I rose slowly.

The others—Kavi, Logan, Hunter, and Carissa—fell in behind us as we climbed into the mercifully air-conditioned van.

The doors slid shut, and in no time, we were speeding toward the hospital.

—

Halfway there, a sudden realization hit me. "Oh, shit—my phone!"

I dug through my bag, pulled it out, and powered it on, praying it still held enough charge to make contact. I held my breath as it began searching for a signal.

Please let it work.

A moment later, the signal bars filled, connecting to a local service.

"It's connected!" I exclaimed, frantically opening my messages.

I typed quickly, fingers shaking:

Mom, Dad—I'm alive and okay! I've been stuck on an island without a phone. We just got to the mainland; we're going to be fine. I'm sorry! I love you!

I hit send, watching as the message delivered.

A flood of incoming texts began lighting up my phone from days of inactivity, draining what little battery remained.

Quickly, I typed another:

My phone's almost dead. Please tell everyone else we're alive, but don't call me. I'll reach out when I can. Kavi, Logan, and Fern are with me.

The message delivered just as the screen dimmed and the device powered off. My phone was dead, but the most important message had made it through.

I slouched back in my seat and let out a huge breath. It was probably 2 a.m. back home. I pictured my parents waking up to that miracle and smiled faintly through the sting of tears.

"I got through to my parents," I said, struggling to hold it together. "I told them to let everyone know we're okay."

Kendal slid closer, wrapping her arms around me and squeezing my hand. She pressed her body gently against mine, a comforting anchor in the swirl of motion.

"You did good," she whispered.

50

—Home—

We arrived at a hospital in the center of Sibolga, where chaos reigned. Ambulances clogged the parking lot, their sirens cutting through the humid air, while stretchers lined the entrance, carrying victims in various states of distress. EMS workers darted in every direction; their faces etched with exhaustion and urgency.

A triage worker approached us as we stepped out of the van, quickly assessing our condition before offering us more context for what had happened. A sudden slip of the Sunda plate against the Indo-Australian plate had unleashed a chain reaction—two earthquakes in succession, landslides, and finally, tsunamis that devoured coastlines with brutal efficiency.

Waves had slammed into Sumatra, the Mentawai Islands, and even as far as India and Thailand, leaving thousands dead, missing, or displaced. Her words felt like a grim postscript to everything we'd endured.

—

Images and sounds flashed: the ocean draining beneath my board as the first wave rose on the horizon, the helpless panic on Kavi's bloodied face as he clung to debris, Fern's agonized cries as we moved him to the board. I could still see the rippling reflections of the stars on the water as sharks began circling our raft and hear the distant bellow of the crocodile as I sat by the campfire. That we had survived all of it felt both miraculous and incomprehensible.

—

Inside, the hospital was no less chaotic. We were guided through the maze of overcrowded hallways into a small, air-conditioned recovery room. The flickering fluorescent lights cast a sickly-green glow on the cold linoleum floors, making the hospital feel more like a set piece—eerily generic and void of any warmth. For the first time in days, we were granted a moment of stillness—fragile, fleeting, and tinged with exhaustion and pain.

Nurses meticulously cleaned the sand and coral embedded in our wounds. They tweezed out stubborn bits of debris and rubbed ointment that stung like fire but promised healing. We were given antibiotics to fight systemic infections and IVs to rehydrate. Our sunburned faces and blistered shoulders were slathered with soothing balm, and our battered bodies were wrapped in fresh bandages. It felt like we were truly on the road to recovery.

—

Over the next few days, we slipped in and out of consciousness, our bodies forced to process the trauma they'd endured. Kavi underwent revision surgery to repair his head wound and minimize scarring. Fern's condition remained critical. Surgeons spent hours aligning the shattered pieces of his tibia with titanium plates and screws, while aggressively flushing the infection that had begun to take hold. The wound was necrotic in places, and at first, they weren't sure if the leg could be saved.

One of the doctors later told us that something had stopped the wound from going septic. When we explained the seawater rinse, the charcoal packing, and the makeshift tourniquet, he said it might've saved him—that without it, things could've gotten much worse.

That stuck with me. None of us were doctors. We didn't have antibiotics or sterile tools. But we'd kept our friend alive—despite the odds.

—

When Fern finally rejoined us, he was quiet at first—then the emotion rose up and broke through. He tried to thank us, but his voice caught, and tears slid down his face as he shook his head, overwhelmed. We didn't need the words. We all understood.

—

Kendal and the girls remained our lifelines throughout it all, renting a nearby hostel where they slept, showered, and returned each day with snacks, smoothies, and support. Their presence reminded me that even in the worst circumstances, people could rise to extraordinary levels of kindness and resilience. James dropped by to check on us. Just seeing him walk in the room lifted everyone's spirits. We exchanged contact info with promises to keep in touch, each of us taking a moment to thank him properly—for showing up when it mattered most.

—

After four days, Kavi, Logan, and I were discharged. We moved to the hostel, where we waited another week for Fern to be released. On April 6th, we finally boarded a flight home.

When we landed in New York, dozens of family members, friends, and colleagues greeted us at the airport, their faces a blur of relief and joy. The disaster began to take on a new meaning. It became something larger than us. News outlets, blogs, and social media had picked up our story. Photos of our rescue were circulating, and strangers called us survivors, even heroes. That attention made the memories feel even more like a dream. The trauma wasn't over—it had just entered a new phase, one where the world was watching.

———

Kendal, Hunter, and Carissa flew back to Australia, promising to visit us in a few months. We'd only known each other for a short time, but the bond forged in survival had made it feel much longer. There was a quiet understanding between us—a reverence for what we'd shared, and an unspoken promise not to let it fade. As they disappeared through security, it felt less like goodbye and more like the quiet turning of a page—one story ending, another just beginning.

———

The tsunamis in Sumatra were a turning point in my life, a harsh and unrelenting teacher. They stripped away every veneer of complacency and left behind a raw, unshakable gratitude. Simple comforts now felt like gifts. Boredom became a luxury I would never underestimate again. I still think back to that night in the ocean—floating in an indifferent expanse of stars, unsure if I'd ever see the faces of those I loved again. The isolation and the hostility of that moment reshaped me. It taught me to honor every breath, every sunrise, every moment of comfort or joy in my life.

—

The experience burned away the illusion that something was missing from my life. The feeling that I needed more—or that life owed me something—seemed laughable in hindsight. In its place is a quiet, steady sense of enough-ness—a deep awareness of the immeasurable value of the present moment.

—

If you're reading this, take it as a call to action. Savour what you have. Be deliberate with your time. Show the people in your life how much they mean to you. Because without warning, it can all be carried away—and the simplest things—the ones you've overlooked—are the things you'll fight hardest to keep.